Trade In Vengeance

The Rogues

Ruby Vincent

Published by Ruby Vincent, 2023.

Prologue

Saylor slowed down, fixing on Rafael. The man was standing there like a tall hot cocoa cooled with mocha sex ice cubes. She was looking where everyone else was, but Rafael was looking at her.

Crooking a finger, he tossed her a smirk that melted every panty in a ten-mile radius. Saylor promptly ditched her friends and slinked up to him.

I turned away, leaving them behind. That was my cue.

Outside, the pillow fights were in full swing, and I was surrounded by enough naked people to prove it.

Katie's backyard was a sprawling aquatic paradise. Between the Olympic-sized pool fed by six fountains, the water slide, two hot tubs, the pool house, cabanas, and the separate indoor pool, this was all the water park you needed.

Pillows claimed the lounger and partiers claimed everything else. They whooped, roared, and catcalled as two topless Royal girls battled it out for the victory of keeping their bottoms. The best thing about my ideas for the party: everyone was too distracted by boobs, wangs, and sex to give a crap about me.

No one glanced in my direction as I weaved through the crowd, coming out where concrete gave way to lawn, and clambered down the small dip to the path. My feet were soundless on the tickling grass. My breaths hot pants drying my lips. Anticipation swelled as I ducked into the indoor pool.

The space was as spectacular as the rest of the mansion. Molded after a Roman bathhouse, columns held up the second floor, and the pool's fountains were topped with resting lions. I scurried past the fellas to the back door. Cracking it open, I waited.

And waited.

And waited.

Goodness. How long does it take to—?

Giggles interrupted my train of thought.

"Shh. Over here." Rafael and Saylor stumbled into my line of sight—her hands all over him like she grew two other pairs. He stopped her within feet of the entrance, turning her back to me.

I slipped my phone out of my pocket. At least, it looked like a phone. The stun gun fit so easily in the palm of my hand. Why didn't everyone have one of these?

"Finally." Saylor draped her arms around my boyfriend's shoulders. "You played hard to get too long, Dumont. You almost missed your chance."

"I was waiting for the right time, darling. It's all about"—he flicked over her shoulder—"timing."

Straightening, my finger poised over the button. *You're about to wake up in your worst nightmare, Burkhardt.*

A hand clapped over my mouth.

Yanked back, the stun phone clattered on the welcome mat—replacing my shoes as they slid across the tile.

"Shh. Don't scream. I need to—"

I jabbed my elbow into hard flesh, ripping a grunt into my ear. His hold loosened and I broke free, racing for the stun gun.

"Sinclair, wait! You have to listen to me."

That voice stopped me dead in my tracks. Spinning around, I faced Giovanni Natale.

He hunched over clutching his stomach. Glassy eyes peered at me through wincing lids.

"What are you doing here? You weren't invited." Even as the words left my mouth, one look at him said he wasn't here for a party.

His *pajamas* were a ratty, oversized, paint-splattered t-shirt and pair of sweatpants. His hair, his most proud feature, pulled back in a greasy, haphazard ponytail. A shadow's dusting covered his normally clean-shaven jaw. The guy was a mess.

"Why did you grab me like that?" I snapped, widening the distance. "If you followed me in here for a fight, I promise you, Natale, you won't win this one."

"I'm not here to fight you. Will you just listen!" he burst out. "There are things you need to know."

I stopped backing toward the stun gun. "What are you talking about?"

"I didn't sign up for this." Giovanni clutched his head, pacing back and forth. "It was an easy dare. A simple one. Date some girl and dump her."

I froze. *Winter.*

"But I didn't sign up for this," he cried, thumping his chest. "No, not bombs. Not murder! Ashton fucking died for this shit and I will not be next. All I did was dump her. I didn't do any of the shit the others did."

I frowned following his rushed, agitated speech. "Giovanni... are you high?"

He laughed out loud, reeling me back. "Of course I'm high. My lawyers called this afternoon. I'm on tape starting the fight with Ashton, days after leaving my girlfriend at the bottom of the Bluffs and walking away from an explosion. The police want to talk to me first thing in the morning," he said, laughing louder. "I'm their number one suspect. Can you believe that? Me."

"Yes." I plumbed those glassy, darting depths. "I can believe it."

His smile wiped away. "That's because you don't know the truth. But I do now. Ashton's death?" Giovanni shook his head roughly. "That was what they wanted.

"All because of T.O.D. Club."

"T.O.D.?" I repeated. "What is that?"

Giovanni threw up his hands. "It's the reason all of this started. T.O.D. Truth or dare."

"What about it?"

"It was a dare, okay? Someone dared me to date your sister, string her along for a while, then brutally dump her."

"A dare?" Bile rose in my throat. "A dare club? Is that what sick fucks like you do? Make a children's game out of people's lives! Dared you to break my sister's heart? Why didn't you say no!"

"Because the penalties for saying no are worse than anything I could've done to her," he shouted. "People get dumped every fucking day, Sinclair. How was I supposed to know what was going on?"

"Is that how you justify what you've done?" My nails pierced my palms. "Lots of people get dumped, so I can lie and manipulate my way into the pants of a sweet, innocent person."

"I didn't say I deserve a medal for it," he said, jabbing a finger at me. "I only did it because the reward was insane. More than has ever been offered for a dare in the history of the club. I had a feeling something wasn't right, but it was too much to turn down."

Closing the distance, I punched him in the face. "Argh!" Howling, Giovanni hit the floor, covering his eye.

"If you justify what you did to Winter one more time, I swear. You're a monster, Natale!"

"That's what I'm trying to tell you! I didn't mean to be!" He staggered to his feet, nearly tripping into the pool. "This is the kind of shit you do in T.O.D., Sinclair. You fuck with people—play pranks. It's not a club for pussies.

"I took the dare, but it wasn't until after..." Giovanni squeezed his eyes shut. "After I did what I did that I noticed Winter was getting it too hard. Too many dares were about her. Someone was in her face every day. When that video of her attack in the dorm went viral, I realized she wasn't just another Dreg who became the club's favorite that month. Someone wanted to teach her a lesson. I figured out what that lesson was—"

"—after she killed herself." I stumbled back, feet tangling and nearly sending me to the floor. "Someone in your little... *club*... dared you all to bully Winter till you drove her over the edge."

"I didn't know Winter's death was the goal, but *they* did." Giovanni spat the sentence. "They came to me after she died. Owen, Levi, Wesley, and Ashton. Said they all got specific dares like me, telling them to do something horrible to Winter for a huge prize.

"They had an idea who was behind it, but they needed me to get the proof. If we were right, we could demand so much more."

My lips peeled back from my teeth.

"Yeah, I went along with it, but it's not what you think," he cried. "I just wanted to know the truth. Someone made me a part of driving a girl to kill herself! Winter never did anything to me. I didn't want her dead."

"What does that matter now?" Wetness soaked my face. "Tell me you found out who started this. Give me their name!"

"No, no." He resumed his pacing—rubbing his eyes and tossing his head. "Who did it isn't nearly as important as why, Sinclair. It's about the secret Winter discovered."

I jerked. "Secret? You know what it is?"

"It's big," he breathed. "She found out and they used the club as their own personal hit squad. Now it's happening to us. Winter was bullied until she lost it. Now everyone who knows why is getting fucked up. Bomb in my car. Money stolen. Humiliated. On the edge of being expelled. I lost Gabby and Annika. It's happening to me, just like it happened to Winter.

"They got in his ear." Giovanni slapped himself, smacking his ears. The man was unraveling before my eyes. "Convinced Ashton to get rid of us and claim it all for himself. Now he's dead too, and they're not even sorry! That's just one less person who knows. But you."

I stepped back as he flew at me, finger in my face. "You can end all of this. Once you go public, it's over. There's nothing they can do."

"Giovanni." I held his face still, forcing his darting orbs to lock on mine. "Focus. You're all over the place. Give me a name, then tell the secret. Name and secret—the only words that you need to say."

He licked dry, chapped lips. "If I tell you, will you protect me?"

"Yes." I didn't have to think about it. "After you tell me, the attacks on you stop. No one will mess with you again. You'll be safe."

"Okay." Shutting his eyes, he took a deep breath. "The name is... Sinclair."

"Wha—?"

"Sinclair, look out!"

I heard the footfalls behind me much too late. Electricity surged through my muscles, trapping them rigid. I crumpled, collapsing at the edge of the pool.

Black crept into my vision as two figures ran from me.

***

"—clair? Sinclair!"

My eyes fluttered open, pain flooding in ahead of consciousness.

"Luna!"

I pushed myself up. A resting marble lion came into blurred focus. It came back to me—Giovanni following me, our conversation, and...

Reaching to massage my temple, I struck my cheek with a hard object. Looking down, I found the stun gun clutched in my hand. *How...?*

"Luna, holy shit."

Katie ran in. Rafael right behind her. Over their heads, half the wet and naked partiers crept inside, gasping and clapping their hands over their mouth.

"What's... going on?" I rasped.

"That's my fucking question," Katie cried. "Luna, what did you do?"

I had no idea what she was talking about until Rafael picked me up, and turned toward the pool.

Floating facedown in the water was Giovanni Natale.

Chapter One

Rafael pulled the blanket tighter around me, drawing me closer. I buried my face in his chest, but didn't block my sight. The stretcher wheeled Giovanni past—a sheet covering his face.

"They were right there," I whispered. "I was so close."

"That's the problem." His grave voice curdled my insides. "You were that close."

"Miss Sinclair." I turned, facing the officer... and the crowd of people on Katie's steps watching us. "Please come with me. We need to talk."

"Okay."

I made to go and Rafael held me tighter. "She's not speaking to anyone without her lawyer present. I've spoken to her stepfather. She's on her way. But the decent thing to do is let Luna get checked out by the paramedics, and speak to her after. She was attacked, electrocuted, and has a head injury."

Rafael smiled a smile I had only seen one time. We weren't dealing with my handsome, fun-loving boyfriend. This was the Rogue. "I'm sure you wouldn't want it to come out that you denied her basic right to medical treatment in a rush to judgement. Something like that doesn't play well at trial."

"Whoa, slow down," the officer gruffed. "No one said anything about trials or denying medical treatment. We'll wait for your lawyer. In the meantime..." He flagged down his partner. "Officer Yang stays with you the whole time."

All I could do was nod. My head was spinning. When did Rafael talk to my stepdad? Was it while Katie was talking at me, pelting rapid-fire questions that I couldn't keep up with let alone answer? Was it while I walked through the deadly silent party, feeling the weight of condemning eyes like needles through the skin?

Or was it while I played and replayed everything Giovanni told me in my head... before someone shut him up for good.

It was them. The person who prompted Giovanni to chase me down in the middle of the night—high, paranoid, and frightened. The person he wanted me to protect him from—

—but we were both too late.

I was in a daze as Rafael led me to the paramedics. Everything she said went in one ear and out the other.

T.O.D. Club. Truth or dare. Some club where bored rich kids got off on cheap thrills and dirty secrets. I understood that just from the name, but everything else he said didn't make any sense. He got a dare for Winter with a suspiciously high price attached, but he didn't know at the time from who. Do the members of this disgusting club not know each other? Is it anonymous and that's why those bastards banded together afterward to find out who was behind it?

But not to do the right thing. Anger pierced the fog, shaking my limbs. *It was to find out this big secret and blackmail them for more.*

Why, Winter? What did you know? What could drive someone to do these horrible things? More money? More status? If that's the reason, I swear on my life... I will burn this whole town down.

"—Miss Sinclair? Miss Sinclair? What's wrong with her?"

The snap brought me back to reality. My vision cleared on a tall, middle-aged woman in a sharp suit with long dreads piled in a bun.

"Did you check her for concussion?" she asked the medic. "The poor girl is in shock."

"Hi, I'm sorry," I said, shaking my head. "Did Jack send you?"

"He did and you're not answering any questions until your parents are here, and I have the full story."

"Okay." I'd never been so agreeable in my life. I was attacked, Giovanni was murdered, and the stun gun placed in my hand left no doubt who the killer wanted to take the fall.

My gaze drifted over her head to the whispering, watching crowd. I helped Katie plan this party. I've stayed at her place many times, and I knew her security. She didn't have cameras in her home, but she did have them set up around the property and monitored. A random person didn't hop the fence and come for Giovanni. They had to be let in. They had to see the moment he followed me into the pool house.

And they had to still be there.

One of you killed him, and my sister.

The rest of the night was a blur of arguing, tears, and threats. None of them from me. If I was in a better frame of mind, I would've noted that the lawyer, Maliyah Stanton, said my *parents* were coming. That didn't register until Jack and Mom clambered out of the car. Mom was a mess.

"Oh, my baby. Are you okay?" She strangled me in a hug. "What happened—? Who did this to you?" she shrieked, seeing the knot on my forehead.

"I got it when I fell—"

"What's this?" She shoved my head against her chest, straining to see the bandage on my neck. The paramedic told her it was a burn from the stun gun and she lost it.

It'd been so long since Mom left the house. It didn't occur to me that she would come. Alternating between trying to downplay what happened for her sake, and telling the police and my lawyer the bare version of the truth, sapped all my energy.

By the time I trudged into my old room at three a.m. that morning, I was dish-rag wrung out. I didn't have the energy to do more than crawl fully clothed into bed. And I didn't say a word to Mom when she climbed in next to me.

We both drifted off that night, sensing the third presence in my bed. I swear Winter's warmth lay over our clasped hands, telling us something we didn't believe.

That everything would be okay.

***

"Is there any chance of her letting you return to school after this?"

"I haven't even tried to bring that up," I said. "I know the answer, but everything's changed now, Lucien. Giovanni didn't tell me everything, though he told me enough. Truth or Dare Club. Have you ever heard of it?"

"Not a word, Luna." I heard noises—arguing—on his end of the phone. "That is what's got us confused over here. Rafael came back last night saying something about a dare club, and that all the guys that came after Winter were in it. Wilder's spent hours looking through all their profiles, accounts, messages, and he can't find anything. What else did Giovanni say to you?"

"Not enough."

I sat on the deck the next morning, picking at my breakfast. Jack wasn't the warmest or cuddliest stepdad, but when things were tense in the house, he'd make my and my mom's favorite breakfast. Even though he was a terrible cook and managed to both burn and undercook the chocolate chip pancakes every time, he still did it to show what wasn't easy for him to say.

Gazing at those pancakes, my thoughts drifted to Winter and all the things she didn't say directly, but possibly told me in a different way.

What did I miss, sis? What is this horrible secret that has now destroyed two families?

"Everything happened so fast, then the cops wouldn't let Rafael come with us to the station. I didn't get a chance to tell him everything Giovanni said."

I relayed everything Natale said during our short, and final, conversation.

"He didn't know the person who gave him the dare," Lucien repeated. "Not until they got together and tracked them down later."

I sat up straight. "That means something, doesn't it? The members must be anonymous."

"Not entirely anonymous. The person picked the handsome and charming Giovanni specifically to seduce Winter. Same for the vicious, sadistic bastards who arranged for her to be beaten, attacked her in her dorm, and..." He didn't need to finish.

"That is true," I replied. "But if they were trying to keep their identity a secret, a dare club wouldn't make sense. Giovanni would've given himself away as the doer by seducing and dumping Winter." I tossed my head, working to get everything straight.

"Okay, okay. The members know each other, but they don't have to know who is behind a dare. No wonder the monster behind all this used the club. It let them sit back and do nothing while their buddies publicly attacked Winter and took all the blame."

"But what penalty could be so bad that they'd go along with it? You said Giovanni made it sound like he didn't have a choice."

"That's how he made it sound," I said, fist balling. "But he had a choice, Lucien. There's always a choice."

"We're going to figure this out, Luna." His voice was soft—gentle. "We know more than we did twelve hours ago."

"But we don't know everything. I was so close." My burnt pancakes blurred. "He was going to tell me everything. If only I made him focus!"

"It wasn't your fault. He was high and tripping bad by the sound of it. At least now we know this goes higher than Thasher, Thompkins, and the others. If Natale didn't find you last night, we would've punished only the henchmen instead of going after the mastermind."

I nodded, wiping my eyes. I needed him right then—telling me that all wasn't lost. That I hadn't failed Winter again.

Something he said finally penetrated. "Wait, hold on. Wilder checked all of their accounts and didn't find a thing on the club?"

"So far nothing," he said.

"How can that be? Winter was bullied by practically the entire class. If they were all doing it because of the club, how does that stay a secret? Someone would've slipped up, blurted the wrong thing while drunk, or just flat-out bragged like the nasty pieces of shit that they are."

"I don't get it either, and we've been arguing about it for half the night." From the noises on his end, the arguing was still going on. "Wilder can dig up the life-ruining secrets we put on those truth lists, but he can't find a single mention of this club. If the Royals can cover their tracks this well, why the fuck haven't they been doing it?"

A very good question. We can find out Wesley tortured innocent animals, but not that he's in some child's game club?

"Maybe because it's not online. They don't text about it. They don't send emails. These people have been going to school with Wilder long enough to know what he can do. It's possible they got smart and learned to play their games in person."

"If that's true, we'll have to play our game differently too. If we can't rely on Wilder's hacking skills, then it's up to my interrogation skills. We need Owen, Levi, or Wesley to crack, and that won't be easy."

"Why not?"

"Because they found out last night what happens to those who talk."

I fell silent, swallowing hard. We all learned that lesson. A killer stood over me, helpless and unconscious, they could've ended my threat to them right there. They more than proved they were capable with Giovanni.

I was certain the only reason I wasn't found floating in that pool is because they needed someone to take the fall for Giovanni's death. If two bodies were found stunned and drowned, the cops would've closed down the party and interrogated everyone. As it was, they accepted I didn't take a stun gun to myself, but they only did that *after* they let everyone at the party go home. If there was something to be found on the killer—pool water, Giovanni's DNA, any evidence—they've had hours to get rid of it.

"Am I safe, Lucien? Is my mom or my stepdad?" I rasped. "It was horrible enough when I thought this was bullying that got out of control, but now there's a fucking mastermind. Winter was *murdered*. Giovanni was murdered. I was almost framed. A real, actual killer targeted my family and what if they don't plan to stop until this secret is buried for good?"

"I've never lied to you, Lady Luna, and I won't start now. I don't know what all this means or what this person plans to do next but... no. You're not safe." My chest squeezed. "Someone who has gone as far as they have isn't going back now. But this is what I do know," he said, making me lift my head.

"No one is going to lay a fucking finger on you. That's a promise, Luna. We will protect you."

"Thank you, Lucien." My voice was small. "I want to give some speech about being tough and strong and able to take care of myself... but I only feel any of those things because you guys are with me. I couldn't imagine doing this alone."

"But you were going to, and you would've for Winter. You were tough and strong before you ever met us—"

"Luna?"

"—don't let that monster make you think otherwise."

"Luna, baby? Where are you?"

I glanced over my shoulder, seeing Mom turn the corner and head for me fast.

"I have to go, Lucien, but thank you. I miss you guys. I promise we'll see each other soon."

"Very soon in Cato's case. I hear he's going to sleep with you tonight no matter what bed you're in."

A tiny smile played on my lips. "When you don't care about a little grand larceny, breaking and entering is nothing."

We said goodbye and hung up as Mom stepped out onto the deck.

"Who were you talking to? That boy who was with you last night?"

I shook my head. "I was talking to Lucien. My roommate and... maybe more. He was just checking to see how I'm doing."

"How are you doing?" She kissed my temple, pulling up the seat next to me. "Oh, Luna, it must've been awful. Was that boy, Giovanni, a friend of yours?"

"No, we weren't friends. He's a class ahead of me, but it was a party and we started talking," I said, repeating the vague response I gave the cops. "I can't face what happened to him, Mom. I just wish I could've saved him." That I said honestly.

Mom held my hands. She was still dressed in the jeans and cream blouse she wore the night before. It was proof of how our life had been the last few months that it was odd seeing her out of pajamas. What was the same was the haggard lines around her mouth and tears filling her eyes. The only difference was this time it was for me.

"You never should've been in that position. This is my fault. You had no business in that awful place and I should've put a stop to it."

"Mom, please don't beat yourself up. If this isn't my fault, it's definitely not yours. Giovanni had a lot of stuff going on," I said. "We're not responsible for the enemies he made." *While he helped kill my sister and then covered it up instead of coming forward immediately.*

"But that enemy attacked you too," she cried. "Regalia has become such a nightmare. I don't know where I'm living anymore. Jack and I are thinking about selling the house and moving. I won't let this place take you too."

"Mom," I whispered. "It's just a town. And it's just a school. It's people who did this to us—destroyed our family. They bullied Winter until she couldn't see a way out and—and—doesn't that piss you the fuck off!"

She reeled back. "Luna?"

I shoved the pancakes away. "I'm sorry, but every time I think about it, I get so angry I can't breathe. *People* did this to her. They relentlessly attacked a kind and good person just because they could, and the thought of them getting away with what they did to her is so wrong, it just can't happen."

Her hands slipped out of mine, brows drawing together.

"No one paid for what happened, Mom. No one was expelled, or suspended, or even slapped on the wrist. Winter deserves justice and I'm not going anywhere until I get it for her," I cried, chest heaving. "Because she would've done that for me."

Mom stared at me for a long time—expression unreadable. "That's why you did this, isn't it? You enrolled in that school to find the people responsible."

"Yes."

"Why did you think you could do that, Luna?" The tears had stopped. "How did you plan to find them or get Winter justice?"

"I... I..."

I wasn't expecting that question. Mom never knew Winter's note to me said more than the one she sent to Mom. I knew exactly who was responsible, and my mother couldn't know how I planned to make them pay.

"It's a school, Mom. Students were there. They saw things. They gossiped about it, looked the other way, and even participated. Those cowards weren't going to tell the cops or the dean about how they did nothing to help her, but when I have the truth, I will."

She nodded slowly, face so blank unease settled in my stomach. "This meant so much to you, you agreed to marry Victor Wilson. Jack said you both came to an arrangement that secured your safety and his willingness to pay tuition. Marrying my child off at nineteen was the arrangement."

"Mom..." I curled around her hand. Cold and flat-voiced, she was starting to worry me. "Don't be mad at Jack. Now that I understand Regalia and the hierarchy around here, I see that he really was trying to keep me safe. People think twice about messing with me because I'm Victor's fiancée. They don't want his family as an enemy."

She didn't say anything.

"It was me who pushed him. I said I'd do whatever it took for the tuition. If he didn't step in, I would've done something desperate, and I wouldn't have had Victor's protection. Jack was trying to do the right thing."

"The right thing."

I hesitated, feeling like I was digging the hole for me and Jack deeper. I didn't want to cause any problems in their marriage. Jack was the one who stood by Mom's side every day when her and my grief got too big to deal with, and I went away to the beach house. It also turned out he didn't give up on seeking help for her. He loved my mother. I never doubted that, and most importantly, their love wasn't meant to be a casualty of my revenge. Those bastards didn't get to hurt my family any more than they already did.

"This was all me, Mom." My tone was pleading. "It really was. Don't be mad at Jack."

Her gaze refocused, as if she drew out of her thoughts and remembered I was there. "I'm not mad at Jack, baby. Jack may have thought he was protecting you, but he is not your mother. I am.

"I should've put a stop to this engagement a long time ago, but I didn't even ask questions about it. I abandoned you in every way that matters—"

"No, you didn't—"

She held up her hand, silencing me better than a scolding. "You're so young, my sweet girl. Losing your sister killed me, but you, you lost her and then you didn't have your mother by your side. Comforting and protecting you the way I was supposed to. Of course you felt alone in your anger and grief. You thought you had no choice but to enroll in that school and do what I should've done—get justice for your sister."

My grip on her was a stranglehold. "None of this is your fault."

"All of it is my fault, Luna. I was here. A twenty-minute drive away, but I didn't know what was going on with my own child, or that she needed me. For that to happen once is inexcusable, but twice..." She shook her head, getting to her feet. "My daughter shouldn't have to get arrested or marry a stranger for me to take notice. I'm sorry, Luna.

"I'm so sorry."

Mom walked off, leaving me speechless. Half of me screamed to run after her. The other half of me didn't know what I'd say if I did.

In a sudden, frustrated moment, I told her the truth of what brought me to Regalia, and made everything worse. Victor warned me we wouldn't like the consequences if we backed out of the engagement now. More than that, I couldn't face the consequences if Mom had Jack pull my tuition money, and I was forced to tell her I wasn't going anywhere.

The truth behind what happened to Winter was bigger than I realized. She was murdered. No matter what it cost me, her killer's fate was sealed.

Their days of laughing at me and basking in everyone's ignorance was over. Winter would have justice.

Her killer's headstone would look good next to Ashton Scott's.

Gazing down the empty hallway, I typed in his number. He was the last person I expected to call that day, and I was sure I was the last one he expected to hear from.

"What do you want?"

"Be nice, Victor." I walked to the deck railing, looking out over Regalia. Hell was such a beautiful place. "We're both about to get what we want."

***

"Are you sure you didn't kill him?"

I held on tight to my eye roll. "I'm pretty sure. Someone attacked both of us, Katie. And by the way, you running in screaming *what did you do*, wasn't very helpful."

"Eh," she said. "What was I supposed to think? I walked in, there was a dead guy in my pool and a stun gun in your hand. I know Giovanni treated Winter like shit and brutally dumped her. I wouldn't have put it past you if you did attack the guy. You didn't, did you—?"

"Katie!"

"Okay, okay." A gusty sigh crackled over the phone. "I had to be sure. Honestly, I kinda wish it was you."

My face screwed up. "Why would you wish I was a killer? Because you wouldn't care if I went to prison?"

"No," she drew out like that was a stupid question. "I wish it was you because then I would understand the motive. He was terrible to Winter, and probably a huge part of why she felt so depressed and alone."

No probably about it.

"Revenge for your sister is something I can understand, but this... If it wasn't you, what am I supposed to think, Luna? A killer was roaming around my party? Maybe even the same person who stabbed Ashton in a room full of people?" Her voice climbed the octaves. "All of this is really starting to freak me out, and I won't even tell you what I went through when Mom and Dad came home. I had to tell them everything. They don't think Regalia U is safe, Luna. They don't think the people I've known my *whole life* are safe."

"Katie, I hate to say this, but they're right. It wasn't me." I paced the length of my room—waiting. "Someone who was at your party did this. Someone you know."

"But we can't be sure, can we? It's not like we invited Giovanni, but he crashed. Whoever did this could've followed him to my place and cornered you guys in the pool house."

"Wouldn't the security cameras have picked them up?"

"I don't know. Dad has Kyson going over everything now. The cops made him turn over the footage, but we have backups."

"That's good. We might have answers sooner than we thought. Trust me, Katie, no one wants to know who did this more than me. No one."

"Ugh. Well, if you really didn't kill him...?"

I flopped on my bed, giving in to the eye roll. "You're not going to make me answer that again."

"If you didn't do it, then tell me when you're coming over. We need to go over every single thing that happened. It makes more sense for you to see the footage, and tell me if anyone looks familiar or suspicious. Damn it, I wish we had cameras pointed at the pool."

"You really want to do this? Look for the killer ourselves? I thought you were freaked."

"I *am* freaked. I'm even more freaked at the thought of sitting in class, sharing notes with a killer. I want all of this behind me so Mom can relax, and I can go back to not looking at my friends in suspicion."

"Okay. I'll do whatever, Katie. I'm actually glad you offered to let me see the footage, because I would've asked anyway."

A knock sounded at my door.

"I don't know when I can come, but I'll try to do it this week. I have to go," I said as my stepfather pushed inside. Mom trailed his heels.

Took them longer than I thought.

"Luna, we need to talk."

"What about?"

"We—"

"I've already spoken to the dean," Mom said, cutting off Jack. She perched on the edge of my bed and tugged him down with her. "He claimed you have to finish the semester before there can be talk of transfer, but I made it clear you're leaving that place and that's the end of it. You'll apply as a new, first-year student at another school."

"But this time I'll have a string of *incompletes* on my record because I dropped out in the middle of my semester." I goggled at her. "Mom, I'd be lucky if I get into a crappy community college, because none of the semi-decent ones would even look at me."

"We'll explain your circumstances." Jack squeezed Mom's shoulder. "Regalia U isn't safe, and that can't be denied after last night."

"I wasn't attacked on campus." Right then, I was very glad they didn't know about the time I was. "I was attacked at Katie's house. They can look these things up. They'll know it's just an excuse."

Mom lifted her chin. "So? Then they can look everything up, Luna, and see there's no denying our family has experienced nothing but tragedy in this town. Friday was your last day. Period." She leaned forward, gently rubbing my ankle. "I know you're worried about school. You worked so hard to turn things around in France, and that hard work paid off by getting you into one of the most prestigious universities in the country.

"Other schools will see that, baby. They'll know you're smart, determined, and responsible. I promise a crappy community college isn't your only option."

"I can swear to it." Jack stood, moving behind Mom. He rubbed her shoulders—the supportive, loving husband that backed her wishes one hundred percent. I recognized a man's attempt to save himself a move into the guest room. "Any colleges that have trouble recognizing their luck in having you as a student, will reconsider after receiving a hefty donation."

I was glad we could be straightforward and honest about privilege and bribery now.

"What about Victor? And the wedding?"

Mom's face tightened. "We've already discussed that. You're much too young to get married, and I'll gamble that Victor feels the same. Arranged, *strategic* marriages may be the norm around here where a son or daughter is another asset at the negotiation table, but that's not what my children are." Mom shook Jack off. He was definitely headed to the guest room.

"I recognize this as my fault for not paying attention to you, and seeing that you needed me. But it's not the Wilsons who are going to protect you, it's us. And it's n-not—" She inhaled a shuddering breath. "It's not your job to get justice for Winter. It's mine. No one will get away with the part they played in her death, but first, I have to protect the only child I have left."

I broke her gaze, then stopped myself. If I was doing this, I owed my mom and stepdad the respect of looking them in the eye. "Does anyone want to ask what I want?"

They frowned, sharing a look. "What do you mean?" Jack asked.

"I mean, that you came in here and told me my engagement was over, you're pulling me out of school, and I'm leaving behind my friends. Nowhere in there did anyone say, 'what do you want, Luna?'"

"Because I know what you want," Mom said, frown deepening. "You're my daughter. I carried you for nine months and raised you for eighteen years. You do not want to be a trophy wife and mother before you're twenty. You do *not* want to attend school alongside your sister's killers, and you don't want to steer the entire course of your future from the day it went horribly off-track."

I nodded. "Yes. If this all came out weeks ago, that would've been true. Victor and I were always sniping at each other. I was struggling in class. I had one sorta friend. And everywhere I looked, I saw the monsters that stood by and did nothing while Winter suffered. But it's different now.

"I like my classes and my p-professors." Visions of Adonis danced through my head, and brought traces of guilt with it. "Victor stopped being a smirky playboy for two minutes, and I got to see another side of him. My sorta friend stood up for me when no one else would. Also... I found out Winter wasn't alone."

Mom's lips curved down, eyes filling.

"She had friends who tried to be there for her. They were there when I wasn't." My throat clogged. "Now they're here for me. That school is a manure pile of dead-inside bullies who don't care about who they hurt. But there's also a lot of good people too. Kind people who are making sure the ones who hurt Winter don't get away with it. If they can do that much for my sister, how can you ask me to do nothing?"

Mom stared at me for a long time. "You want to stay."

"I do."

"And you want to marry Victor Wilson at nineteen years old."

I half-shrugged. "Honestly, I wouldn't mind the wedding part being put off until after graduation at least, but this is what I agreed to."

"Is it?" Mom snapped, rounding on Jack. "Because I'm still unclear on why anyone agreed to these terms. Why is this wedding even more rushed than the engagement? Why have I tried half a dozen times to speak to Martha Wilson, and her assistant keeps telling me she's unavailable? Is she unavailable to you too, Jack?"

"My love, this isn't some grand conspiracy," he said, dropping to one knee. "The Wilsons want to make a match for their son now. They disinherited their eldest and wish to secure Victor's future."

"How does my daughter do that? Our family has nothing to offer the likes of the Wilsons." She snapped between us. "What are you two not telling me!"

My chest panged. The same thing I feared the Wilsons and my stepfather weren't telling me. "Victor said it's because I'm the only one willing to marry him now. Most of these strategic marriages aren't even brought up until the couple is in their late twenties. Victor is afraid his father doesn't have that long, running at the speed he's been at all these years.

"His father won't hand the company over to a boy with no responsibilities, but to a man with a home, wife, and kids—"

Her eyes bugged. "Kids? You've discussed kids?"

"No," I blurted. "I mean, not seriously. Victor was just saying—"

"Victor brought up kids? The eighteen-year-old who was a kid himself less than twelve months ago, wants to use my daughter and her womb to take over a company?"

My mouth opened but nothing came out. That is exactly what it sounded like, wasn't it?

"N... No."

She spun on Jack. "And you agreed to this?!" Mom tossed her head. "What am I saying? *I* agreed to this when I sat by and let it happen. So, let me make this clear to *both* of you. The wedding is off. Victor Wilson can use someone else to prove his manhood to his father—"

"But—"

"There's no reason to keep up this farce because you no longer need his family's protection." She pinned me with a look. "You no longer attend Regalia University."

"Mom—"

"Enough, Luna." She got up, marching to the door. "The discussion is over."

"No, it's not!"

Mom froze, hand on the knob. She was almost as stiff as me—rigid at the shock that shout came from me. I never yelled at my mom.

Taking a deep breath, I tried again. "No, it's not. I wanted you to ask what I want, but the truth is, you don't need to. I'm not a child anymore, Mom. Where I go to school and who I marry became my choice six months ago. I love you but... I'm staying at Regalia U and marrying Victor."

"Luna," Jack said, warning lacing my name. "That's enough."

"It's not enough, Jack, and you know why. This is what you need to know about the engagement, Mom. Backing out of it isn't as easy as throwing the ring at his head. If we don't go through with the wedding, Martha threatened to disinherit Victor."

"What?" Mom cried. "That's nonsense. She wouldn't—"

"She already disinherited her first son, Adonis. The woman doesn't bluff. I don't know what she'll do to Jack if I refuse..." I flicked to my stepfather, who looked away—jaw tight. "But I won't risk that either. Our family and Victor's life would be ruined. I can't let that happen."

Tipping her head back, she made a harsh noise in her throat. "It amazes me all that you believe you must take on your shoulders. It is not your responsibility to save us from the consequences of a situation you were manipulated into. You only agreed to marry this boy for tuition money. I let my child be *sold*," she flung, and not at me. "I am putting this right, and I don't care what Martha Wilson does about it. As for disinheriting her son, that's her choice. No one is forcing her to banish her sons whenever they don't fall in line."

I swallowed hard. "I hope you remember you said that."

"Excuse me? What does that mean?"

I looked between them. "I know what refusing you means. I'm not leaving Regalia U, but because you want me to, Jack is going to stop paying my tuition. Aren't you?"

Hesitating, he looked to my mother. "I won't go against Eloise's wishes."

"That's what I thought. Well, since Martha is so determined to have this wedding that she's willing to lose another son, I figured tuition for two is a smaller price to pay." I held my mom's gaze steadily. "Martha is going to pay for me to attend the university. Since that payment stops if I don't marry her son next year, the wedding is going ahead. There's nothing to do now, Mom."

She rocked back like I slapped her.

"There's no one to call. There's no argument to have with Martha or Jack. The deal he had with her is now mine. I choose this, and nothing you say will change my mind."

Mom took a step. Then another. "You're doing all of this to stay at that school and see those that hurt Winter brought to justice."

"Yes."

"No," she replied. "You're doing it because you don't trust me to."

By the time I thought of something to say, I'd been sitting alone for a long while.

Chapter Two

The cabbie dropped me off at the gates.

Neither Mom nor Jack came down for breakfast the next morning. They didn't answer the door to their room when I knocked either.

I got the hint.

"You sure this is the place?"

"This is the place," I said, eyeing Wilson Manor. "But I'm not sure of anything." I left him with that and twenty-two bucks.

The gate guard waved me in. I made the long trek up the winding drive, trying not to think of what I'd just done to my mother. Trying and failing. "Betrayal," "deal with the devil," and "a thousand jellybeans" ran through my head on repeat. I'd broken our mother's heart over revenge Winter asked me not to take. That thought would mess me up for a long time.

The Wilsons' butler let me in. The dignified man didn't break form. He led me upstairs with a greeting, offered to get me something to drink or eat, then bowed and left me alone in front of the door.

I knocked twice.

"Come in."

Stepping inside, I met her cool smile with one of my own. "Good morning, Martha."

"Good morning." She swept out from behind the desk—a vision in a cream sheath dress and heels. She gestured to the leather couch between two rafter-high bookshelves. A passing thought made me wonder if Adonis got his love of literature from her. "Sit, dear. We have a lot to discuss."

The lock clicked shut behind me, ringing like the final gong.

***

My stomach growled loud and embarrassingly by the time we stood and shook hands.

"A floor up and three doors on the left," Martha said. "I'll have Reuben bring you something to nibble on."

"Thank you."

"No, thank you, Luna." She placed two barely there kisses on my cheeks. "I'm pleased we understand each other. I knew I made the right choice in a daughter-in-law."

"Of course you did." I looked her straight in the eyes. "I'm just as ruthless as you."

Her smile didn't slip. "Ruthless is simply another word for uncompromising. You're a woman, Luna. One that's about to take your place among one of the most important families in Regalia—nay, the country. You only need to back down from your position once—to compromise—for the world to see you're too weak to fight for what you want. You have the opportunity to become many things when you say *I do*." She tipped my chin. "Weak is not one of them."

Stepping back, I tipped my head to her and murmured goodbye. I don't know why it felt like I took my first breath when I left her office.

My feet followed her directions, carrying me up to the third floor and its third door on the left. It cracked open, filtering a thumping rap song that everyone who didn't spend four years in a French Catholic school likely knew.

I knocked once but didn't wait for him to let me in.

A low whistle escaped my lips. I knew Victor's room would be nice, but who the hell lived so large that they had an indoor hot tub next to the infamous minibar. I rounded the tub, peeking my head past the wall. A massive four-poster bed sat on a raised platform. Lying on the red silk sheets was my ex-but-not-fiancé in nothing but black silk boxers.

The only reason his parents didn't name him Adonis too is because it would've been too confusing to call his name and have them both turn around. But Victor Wilson was no less gorgeous than his painfully handsome brother.

The man was sculpted perfection stretched out on the sheets—the fabric sliding over his muscled calves and against his rock-hard chest like the opportunistic slut it was. He moved to the next page in his textbook, head turning to read, and his hair fell over his eyes—thick, wavy, and destined to stick around late into his nineties. I could tell just by looking at him. Victor would be handsome long after the other silver foxes slinked back into the forest.

"Knock, knock."

Victor snapped his head up. His eyes narrowed on sight. "What are you doing here?"

I shuffled closer, casually glancing around. Posters plastered his wall—bands, brands, and cars. They weren't nearly as interesting as the photos.

Victor and Adonis were all over the place, smiling and goofing off in almost every famous spot around the world. It was easy to tell the siblings that doubled as best friends and those that could barely stand each other. Winter's bedroom looked the same as this.

I assumed it did anyway. I hadn't gone inside in months.

"I came because I think we should talk."

He snorted, picking his book back up. "So you did it. Broke off from your folks and latched on to mine. Got Mom's check in that purse?"

"Course not. Who takes checks anymore? It's all done through direct deposit."

Victor's smile didn't reach his eyes. "Then there's nothing more you need from me, is there?"

I took another step, taking it as a good sign that he hadn't ordered me to leave yet. "Victor, let's get something straight. I never used or took advantage of you, or your family. I asked my stepfather for tuition money, and he introduced me to my new fiancé. None of this was my plan.

"But now that we're doing this, it was recently pointed out to me that *you* are using *me* and my baby-maker to prove yourself to your dad and take over his company. If I can be cool about that, you can be okay with me finishing my education."

He blinked lazily. "You done? Good." The textbook came back up. "Close the door on your way out."

I leaped over the bed, tearing it out of his hands. "You know what? I'm done with this!" Reddening cheeks reflected in wide eyes. "Do you have any idea what I went through this weekend? I was attacked. Giovanni Natale was murdered. And I'm pretty sure my mom is never going to speak to me again. So if you think I'm putting up with your petty shit for another second, you're in for a fucking surprise."

Victor pushed on my shoulder. "Luna, calm down—"

"No!" I shoved back, toppling us both over. Wrestling him down, I straddled Victor—pinning his wrists to the bed. "Listen to me, Victor. Nothing happened between me and Adonis. It was one stupid kiss when I was drunk and sad.

"It was over in a second, and Adonis didn't even kiss me back. He was as surprised it happened as I was that I did it. Afterward, I found out he was my professor, and I don't need to tell you that he hasn't let the stranger marrying his younger brother get in the way of the career he's worked so hard for. All we've done since that night is talk. Like we did the night I apologized for putting him in an awkward position. I did the right thing, Victor. You're the one who acted like a jackass!"

"Oh yeah?!" He reared up. "If it was all so harmless and innocent, why did you hide it?"

"Because it happened when we hated each other. Have you told me about everyone you've hooked up with before we agreed to give us a real shot?"

"You already caught me in the closet with Mara—"

"No," I said, staring hard at him. "Have you told me about *everyone*?"

A second passed.

Two.

Three—

Victor looked away.

"That's what I thought." I ignored the pang in my chest. "We've both messed up."

"But I didn't do it with your brother," he gritted, looking anywhere but at me.

"Neither did I. I messed up with a random guy I met at a party. He just turned out to be your brother." I tipped my head, making him meet my eyes. "This wedding is happening, Victor. There's no going back now. One thing you said that made a lot of sense is that we can either live in a home with the three of us—you, me, and our resentment. Or we can be friends and show the kids we might have many years in the future, an example of two people that respect each other. I don't know about you, but I still want the second one."

Victor's eyes glazed, looking through me. "How is it not too late, Luna? We've been terrible to each other. Said and done shit we can't take back."

"We do it by not looking back. Right here, right now, we have a fresh start."

"Fresh start?"

"Yes. With new ground rules and…" I worried my lip. "Complete honesty."

"New ground rules?" he drew out. "Because something's wrong with the ones we agreed to in the first place? Why do I feel like you're building up to something?"

Complete honesty. Complete honesty.

"Something is happening between me and the Rogues. Some things have already happened."

Victor wasn't fighting to get me off him before I said that, so it didn't make sense to say he'd gone even more still, but I sensed it anyway.

The silence stretched longer than was comfortable. So long, I blurted out more.

"Lucien and I hooked up, and it didn't feel like the last time. Wilder and I get closer every day. As for Cato, he pretty much claimed me as his the week he met me. It's pointless to argue that with him… especially because I don't want to. And Rafael," I whispered. "There's no wondering or *will-we, won't-we* with him. We're dating now, Victor. He's my boyfriend."

"Get out."

My heart fell out of my butt. "Victor, please."

"Out, Sinclair." He glared, dropping the temperature twenty degrees. "Get the fuck off me, and don't come back."

"Just listen to me. It's not what you think."

Victor bucked, trying to throw me off. "Out!"

"No!" I dropped, snaking my arms and legs around him.

"What the— Shit!" He flipped over on his hands and knees. Victor actually tried to shake me off.

I clung to his bare chest, legs hooked around his waist and sliding along his boxer band. Victor flung back and grabbed my thighs, trying to pry me off that way.

"Damn it, Sinclair! Let go."

"Not until you let me explain!"

The push-pull friction heated his lap, drawing his boxers down. Bunching my panties between my cheeks. We were skin on skin.

"If you don't let—"

"Heavens," a voice cried.

We snapped around, landing on a flustered butler. He hurriedly set down my lunch tray and rushed out without another word.

"Fuck's sake," Victor snapped. "You're more trouble than you're worth."

I locked my elbows just in case. My forehead pressed against his and I didn't care. I wasn't going anywhere until we worked this out. "You wouldn't be this mad if that was true."

"Are you serious? You came in here and actually tried to make me feel bad for hooking up with one—*one*—girl while we still hated each other, and here the fuck you were sleeping with all the Rogues. Now you're bragging about it while saying you want to start over—you, your fiancé, and your four boyfriends!"

"Rafael is my boyfriend. Wilder, Lucien, Cato, and I aren't there yet—"

"Do you think that's the point!?" He grabbed my hips but didn't pull. "How would you feel if I said I wanted a 'fresh start,' but by the way, I'll be fucking Everleigh on the side."

My teeth gritted. "Why do you keep bringing her up?"

Swirling amber eyes burned me. "Because you keep making that face when I do. You know how fucked up this is, Luna. I'd never expect you to be okay with being second best. Don't ask me to be okay with being fifth."

"Victor." My fingers tangled in his hair, stroking the nape of his neck. "That's not what I'm asking."

"Really? Because I doubt you were about to follow that speech by saying you're dumping all of them, moving out, and committing to starting over with me."

My voice was soft. "Is that what you want me to say?"

His jaw clamped shut. His ticcing vein beat as fast as my heart.

"You're not fifth best, Victor. I... I don't know what you are," I cried. "We haven't had a chance to figure that out yet. What I'm saying is I want us to have that chance. We get to know each other for real. See if there could be something between us, even if that something is just friendship. I believe that the Rogues could be okay with sharing me. Can you?"

"Why should I share my wife? What do I get out of that?"

Lips trembling, I cupped his cheek. "Me."

Something flashed in his eyes. Victor reached up, and for a moment, I thought he would cover my hand with his. "We're even now."

"What?"

He dropped his hand. "I tried to use you to take over the company. Now you're using the threat of my disinheritance to get all the power in our relationship. You'll marry me, as long as you get to fuck whoever you want, and I don't say a word about it."

My jaw dropped. "That's not it at all. I don't—"

"Save it."

Victor climbed off the bed. He didn't force or use his strength. Holding my gaze, he peeled my legs and arms off him. He set me on my feet, then walked away.

I don't know how long I stood there, staring at the door he disappeared through. It wasn't until the shower shut off that I finally picked up my feet and left. I didn't think he wanted to see my face when he came out, and I couldn't take round two.

I descended the stairs in a daze—his words playing over and over in my head. He thought I was turning the tables on him, trying to blackmail him into a relationship he didn't want. But what did it mean if he never accepted Rafael, or the growing feelings I had for Lucien, Wilder, and Cato?

Was I supposed to give up the men who accepted and protected me when no one else did? A paid security guard walked away when Katie called for help, but the Rogues didn't. They busted in and beat the shit out of Owen and the others. They've risked everything to help me avenge Winter. They held me while I cried in my sleep. Stayed up late talking to me. Made me laugh when I'd forgotten what that sounded like.

How could I walk away from them? People waited their whole lives for the support and loyalty my Rogues gave me from day one.

But what do you expect from Victor? Most fiancés aren't asked if their part-ner's four boyfriends can come on the honeymoon too.

I trudged onto the front porch, wincing at the sunlight. Why did I come out here like I had somewhere to go?

"Luna?"

Blinking, I glanced down. Adonis stood halfway in the driver's side—either climbing in or climbing out.

"Adonis? What are you doing here?"

I probably should've called him Professor, but he'd never looked less like one in his entire life. The clinging gray slacks, ties, and fitted vests were discarded for a button-up shirt he didn't button all the way up. It opened at his chest, revealing curling tufts of hair. Continuing down, I slid over his jeans and sandals—blushing for no reason at the sight of his foot tattoos. A soaring raven on one. An inkwell and dripping quill on the other.

"Mother summoned me. Had something she wanted to discuss." He drifted over my head. "I hoped to talk to Victor while I was here, but she said he was in the middle of a serious conversation and had to work things out with someone. Now I see that wasn't just an excuse." He hesitated. "Did you work things out?"

I laughed mirthlessly. "Believe it or not, I think he's fine with the whole kissing-his-brother thing. It's my love affair with four hot criminals that's holding him back."

"What?"

A sudden, frenzied energy gripped me. I ran down the stairs, falling against his chest. "Adonis, take me somewhere. Anywhere. Please."

"Luna, what are you saying?" He gently, but firmly grasped my shoulders—holding me at arm's length. "You know I can't do that. It's not appropriate."

"I didn't say take me somewhere and screw me in the back seat." My voice was louder than it needed to be. "Please, Adonis. I can't go home. I can't go back in there. And as much as the Gallery's been a sanctuary for me, getting there means walking through hell itself—remembering with each step through that campus how my life turned to festering, fly-covered shit.

"I just need to get away, and I'm afraid if I get in a cab, I'll tell him to drive and not stop until I've drained my bank account. Please," I repeated, eyes welling. "Please."

"All right, all right," he whispered. "Don't cry. I know you're going through the worst time, but there are lines we can't cross."

Can't. Not won't.

"Can you not be my professor today? Just be my—"

"Your what? Brother-in-law," he said, voice hard. "Because the lines he can't cross are even wider."

"I was going to say friend."

"We're not friends."

The reply didn't sting. "I'm your closest friend, Adonis. Because I'm the only one who knows what you're going through. No one else in this gold-paved town understands what it is to lose their future."

Sighing, he tipped his head back, curls falling over his eyes. "A couple weeks ago, you were convincing me I haven't lost my future. I'm just looking at a different one."

"Did you buy it?"

He didn't reply right away.

"Get in the car."

Holding my breath, I didn't chance saying anything that'd make him change his mind. I rounded the hood, hopping in the front seat. Adonis took off through the gates like someone was chasing us.

That energy was back. Sizzling my veins. Thrumming my pulse. Popping beads of sweat on the back of my neck. The closest I felt to this was the night I snuck out of the boarding school and caught two buses and a train to Paris for a concert. It's not every time you know exactly what the consequences will be, but you break all the rules anyway. But I knew then nothing good awaited me on the return journey if the nuns discovered we ditched.

And at the end of my journey with Adonis... I wouldn't feel as I did if deep down I believed there was something good in that future.

I chanced peeks at him during the drive. His folks dissolved his trust fund, removed him from the will, and kicked him out of the mansion, but it was clear they didn't take away all his toys. A man who sold tires knew a lot about the cars they went on. Years around Jack filled me with the useless knowledge of recognizing I was sitting in a teal, two-seater McLaren 720S. The only thing more impressive than its style and sleekness, was the cost.

Wind whipped through his curls, carrying the scent of sea salt and cedar. Adonis always smelled good—something I wasn't supposed to notice. He always looked like he stepped out of the pages of a magazine—something I shouldn't think about.

I forced myself to look straight ahead for the fifth time. I recognized the route we were taking as the same road Lucien and I drove down the day he took me to the vampire club. My face heated remembering the things we got up to in a room full of people. I bounced on his fingers like a wanton minx, dressed like a bloodsucker and surrounded by people way too committed to the life. That's not where we're going, was it?

Course it's not! My brain summoned an image of Adonis in a tailcoat, top hat, and cane. I'd fallen for Lucien too hard, because there was nothing about that fantasy that wasn't right in every way.

I shook myself, expelling a sharp breath. It was okay to have a crush, but it was even better to have a good relationship with my professor and fiancé's brother.

There can't be a me and Adonis. After today, I don't know if there can be a me and Victor while I'm with the Rogues. I feel like I'm losing all of my guys. I can't lose all my friends too.

It wasn't long before pavement gave way to dirt road. I sat up straight, raising my brows at the cozy-looking beach house. Blue paint and white shutters made it stand out from the white, white, white homes dotting the coast.

He pulled off the side of the road and parked. "Come on. We'll walk down."

"Okay."

Adonis waited for me on the path. Together, we climbed down the mound where grass turned into sand. The whole of the ocean heaved and rolled before us—calming that energy almost instantly.

Somewhere along the way I kicked off my shoes, leaving them where they fell. Adonis slowed down but I didn't. Sea-foam washed over my toes—cool, refreshing, and eager to take me back to its home. I glanced up and found Adonis beside me. Hands in his pockets, he gazed out over the water, feeling the same calm that I did. I knew it.

"Thank you."

He nodded. "This is where I come to when it gets too much. I passed out drunk in that very spot the night Catalina ended our engagement." Adonis winced. "Why do I tell you things like that?"

A smile tugged at my lips. "I told you. I'm easy to talk to. No one can help it." I peered over my shoulder. "How long can we stay? Will the owner of that house chase us off?"

"Not likely since I'm the owner of that house."

"You brought me to your place?" I couldn't keep the surprise out of my voice.

"I brought you to the beach," he corrected, a tad quickly. "I figured you wouldn't want to be surrounded by sunburnt, screeching tourists. This patch of beach is private and mine. We'll stay out here until you're ready to go."

"All right. Sounds perfect."

"We don't have to talk."

"You might let too much slip if we do."

He chuckled. "I might."

We lapsed into a comfortable silence as we walked along the shore, watching our toes turn to prunes. All the things I didn't want to think about—Mom, Victor, Giovanni, Truth or Dare Club—ran through my mind too fast for me to catch one problem and come up with a solution. Truth is I didn't try too hard. When you're dead last in the race, at some point you just stop running.

"I like your tattoos," I murmured, breaking into the lull of the ocean. "Edgar Allan Poe?"

"Sadly, I am that cliché."

I laughed. "It's not cliché if you truly love his work. Everyone thinks Van Gogh is my favorite artist because I'm too lazy to look up anyone else, but there's a story in his work. Through ridicule, poverty, and loneliness, he never gave up on painting. I can't imagine loving anything that much." A smile tugged my lips. "Yes, that's what Van Gogh paints. Love."

"Hmm. I never thought of it like that. You see the world in a unique way, Luna."

"I do?"

"Oh yes. I could tell that from your first paper."

I cocked a brow as we turned, heading back toward his place. "You hated that paper."

"I hated that you were hiding that unique perspective under tired metaphors and lazy comparisons. Where everyone else sees a mentally ill man who never saw success in his lifetime, you see a love story. Edgar Allan Poe is my favorite writer because he didn't fear the macabre and twisted tales that plagued his mind. He shared them. He *made* the world see what he saw, and as a result, he invented a new genre.

"The world needs the stories that only you can tell. Doesn't have to be through writing. Can be painting, music, film, photography, drama. It can be the way you know just the right thing to say to someone drowning in their sorrows."

I bit my lip—afraid I'd say the absolute wrong thing and stop what was happening.

"There is something you love that much. Don't hide from it because you're convinced the future ahead of you isn't worth a damn. Doing that would be a tragedy worse than if the world never got Van Gogh or Poe."

"Okay," I said, kicking my feet through clumpy sand and sea-foam. "I'll keep that in mind."

We lapsed into silence again. Without a word to each other, we drifted from shore at the same time, claiming a spot on the beach. Stretching out, heated sand cradled my back as the sun warmed my skin.

My eyes fluttered shut. "I wonder if this is what it's like in the womb."

"What? Where did that come from?"

I giggled. "You said you wanted more of my unique perspective. Feeling this warm, calm, and safe. This must be what babies feel. Then, one day, they're forced out into the cold and uncertainty of life, and have to figure it all out on their own. It's kind of cruel when you think about it," I mused. "We go from this time of complete peace to randomness, chaos, and violence, and we don't get to remember the first part."

"All we'd remember is the darkness."

I whispered so low, the wind may have snatched it before it reached him. "That's all I know now."

A beat passed, then my eyes snapped open. A pinkie curled around mine—so subtle and soft, my mind tried to trick me that it wasn't there.

But he was.

I held still—not breathing. Not looking at him. Just linked mine around his in turn under that warm sun on the tickling beach.

Adonis was right. We didn't need to speak.

We lay there for so long, I think I fell asleep. The next thing I knew, he was sitting up, clearing his throat.

"Come on," he said, hand sliding away from mine. "Your stomach's been growling since we got in the car. Let's get something to eat."

I stood, dusting myself off as he headed up the bank without me. "Wish we didn't have to go so soon," I said. "Could we get something and bring it back?"

"Easily. We'll grab something inside."

Then I understood why he was walking so fast and not looking at me. I bit real hard on my lip, not allowing even a grunt to slip out and make him change his mind.

The beach house was even cuter up close. I envied the wraparound porch and all the nights I imagined he sat on the chair swing, sipping a beer and listening to the crashing waves while he read.

We lived a simple life before Mom met Jack. Then I lived a utilitarian life in Catholic school. The stolen summers in between where I joined my folks on fancy vacations, yachts, and international hotels felt like what they were—vacations. None of it ever seemed like a life that could be mine. When I did picture my future, it always looked something like—

"This," I breathed.

I spun in the entryway, taking it all in at once. Adonis skipped the beach house standard blue-and-white décor. A freestanding fireplace claimed the middle of the living room. Black and gray squashy, warm couches and armchairs surrounded it—a home where a family sat around talking in front of the fire, instead of vegging in front of the television.

Nearly every wall was a bookcase, and nearly every book in the world was stuffed on their shelves. I padded over wood-paneled floors, leaving grains of sand like breadcrumbs. Adonis just followed me, watching me take it all in—a small grin riding his lips.

"Like it?"

"Love it." I twirled under a chandelier of twisted iron vines. "It's a book-lover's paradise." Something caught my eye. "And you don't just have stuffy books. I loved *Percy Jackson* when I was a kid— Oooh, you have *The Broken Earth* series too."

"I'm not one of those English professors who believe literature ended a hundred years ago. But I take exception to stuffy books. The classics are a classic for a reason."

I blew a raspberry. "The classics are a classic because a bunch of white privileged English-speaking men decided what other white privileged English-speaking men had to say about the world, was the only thing worth reading. Admit it, you didn't like *The Great Gatsby* either."

"Are you kidding me?" The man sounded ready to fight. "*The Great Gatsby* is a scathing and insightful look into class, greed, and the lie of the American Dream."

"*The Great Gatsby* is a scathing look into what the author truly thought of women. They were such flighty, self-absorbed, cardboard cutouts that one thought the only way out of a marriage she hated was with a married sugar daddy who broke her nose.

"And the other got the fun dilemma of choosing between a cheating, abusive bastard of a husband, and an old flame that saw her as a moth to attract with glitz, glam, and pretty things. Heaven forbid anyone see or treat her as an actual person rather than a trophy. Worse, she wished the same for her daughter." I flared out my dress like I was going to curtsy. "Lucky for women and minorities, we get to keep reading these sexist and racist stereotypes, and even better, are expected to like them because they're the *classics*."

Adonis reeled back, eyes blown. "I can't— That isn't— To reduce— I can't even speak to you right now," he said, turning away.

Giggling, I chased after him. "'Cause you know I'm right, *Professor*." I attacked his sides, ripping a yelp out of him. Darting off, Adonis was hot on my heels.

"Hey, come back!"

I zipped through a boxy, brown kitchen and burst into the den. Hands snagged me around the waist, lifting me off my feet.

"Ha!" I twisted, grabbed his shoulders, and kicked the back of his legs.

We went down.

"Shit!"

Adonis and I collapsed on a huge, furry beanbag chair. I scrambled free and pinned him down, grasping his shoulders. "Weren't expecting that, were you?"

He blinked at me. "I definitely was not."

"Lucien taught me a few moves." There wasn't a person alive more smug than me. "Perfect for getting a guy to admit I'm right. Do it. Go on. Let's hear it."

Adonis blew out a breath. "All right. I will admit—"

"Yeah, you will."

"—that you made a few valid points—"

"All valid."

"—about there being a Eurocentric, white-male slant to what's upheld as great literature—"

"Get it out," I sighed. "Get it all out."

Adonis fought not to crack up. "—but that's why we need this generation. We're challenging the meaning of great writing, and who writes it. A hundred years from now, they'll be discussing boy wizards and books narrated by Death in a class like ours."

"See?" Climbing off, I reached out a hand to help him up. "Doesn't that feel good to get off your chest? In the future, just skip to the part where you admit I'm right."

Adonis grasped my hand—rising to all five foot eleven of him. Our chests bumped, sharing heat and sprinkles of sand that brushed off him and escaped between the valley of my breasts. I looked down automatically, then up—catching the millisecond before he snapped his head up, jaw clenching tight as if he was lingering on my breasts... and knew I saw.

He quickly dropped my hand. "Let's grab some food and head back out. Actually, it's getting late. We should go. Where am I taking you?"

I stomped on my disappointment. I stomped even harder on the deluded thought that my English professor was checking me out—hard. It did both of us no good to read into his comforting me on the beach, or his goofing back when I tickled him. I'm a walking tragedy and Adonis was just being nice. The only thing I should take seriously is his constant and clear attempts to keep distance between us.

"Back to campus," I replied, following him into the kitchen. The quick glimpse as I ran by didn't do it justice. Charm leaked out of the wood paneling, gas stove, and little touches of him dotted around the space. A fifty-odd collection of mugs hanging on the wall. Espresso machine. And ravens painted beneath the crown molding. "My guys have been working on a problem for me, and it's past time I helped them figure it out."

Adonis crossed to the fridge. "Understood. We'll eat quickly."

That wasn't what I meant, went unsaid.

"What are you in the mood for?" he asked. "Chicken fettucine. Beef and broccoli bowl. Spinach and mushroom pizza. Orange chicken. Santa-Fe taco bowl."

I snuck around him, peeking past his shoulders. My brows shot up. "Adonis, these are all frozen meals."

He looked from me to the overstuffed freezer. Dammit, he was even sexy when he was bemused. "Yeah?"

"Is this what you eat every day?" I snorted holding back a laugh. "How do you drive a car like that and shop from the two-dollar dinner section?"

"Hey," he cried. "I was raised by nannies and private chefs. I never had to cook for myself. Besides, these are quick and easy."

"And taste terrible," I finished. "You were raised by fancy chefs and nannies. You hate everything in that fridge."

He shrugged. "Some of them aren't so bad."

"What else do you have? I'll cook for us."

"You don't have to."

"Sit," I said, steering him to a stool. "You're going to love this. At boarding school, we had kitchenettes in the common areas. Couldn't do much with it because it wasn't like the nuns let us skip out to the grocery store. But I'd still make little tasty meals from my mom's survival packages. A girl can only go so long without tater tots, grits, and Tex-Mex."

I zipped through his kitchen, opening up everything and grabbing ingredients until I had macaroni, spinach, pesto, and parmesan. I knew exactly what I was making.

"You really don't have to cook. We can grab something on the way." Adonis said that, but he was looking mighty fascinated by all the ingredients I laid out before him on the island.

"This will taste better. Trust me," I said. "Want to help? You can thaw the spinach while I get the water boiling."

For a while, the only sounds in the kitchen were boiling, chopping, whisking, and my instructions. Adonis stood over me while I did the final step—draining the pasta and mixing our sauce in.

"Voila." I placed our bowls on the countertop. "Pesto macaroni and cheese. I made extra so you can have leftovers."

"Looks good," he said, circling it. "Smells good."

I handed him a spoon.

"Wow." He moaned around his bite. "Tastes even better. Incredible. You did all that with some butter, spinach, and a box of pasta that's been in there for a year."

"Easy too, right? To quote an eccentric man, cooking is the only time in your life you can do everything right and it turns out exactly the way you expect. No surprises," I repeated. "Wasn't until he said that, I realized it's what I love about cooking. Follow a few instructions on a screen, and you've got something delicious in half an hour. If only life came with a recipe book."

"You wouldn't say the unpredictability gives it meaning?"

"What do you mean?"

Folding his arms, he leaned against the island. "We all think we want our lives to go according to this set plan, but it wasn't until the life I knew blew up, that I took a real look at where I was headed. Did I want it or was it what I thought I should want? You can also follow every step in a recipe... and hate what you end up with."

"Hmm. I thought I was the one being depressing today."

He flashed me the tiniest grin. "What I mean is, it's fortunate that we don't always get what we hope, because most of us hope too small. Your future has shrunk in your eyes, Luna. You don't think you deserve to be happy, so you're not dreaming of a future where you are. This hasn't been said before, but whatever it is you have planned for your future right now, I hope you don't get it."

If there was something to say in response to that, I didn't know it. Mostly because I couldn't deny a word. My current goal was to move ahead with a wedding to a man who hates me, so I could stay in a university I hated even more and avenge my sister. There was nothing but a black hole at the end of that goal.

I didn't know what would happen after I made all of Winter's killers pay. On my best day, I couldn't even summon the energy to care.

Breaking his gaze, I reached for my bowl but Adonis got there first. He picked both ours up and carried it into the living room. Pausing, I pushed away what he said and reclaimed the content mood we settled into while cooking.

I followed him out and snuggled on his couch, holding back a moan of my own as his cushions snuggled me back.

Don't get me wrong, Wilson Manor was beautiful inside and out. But so many pieces of furniture were chosen by how they'd look in a showroom, instead of comfort or function. Adonis's home by the beach was the opposite in every way.

I loved it.

Wonder if Victor would move into a place like this after we're married.

He won't, but he'll happily pack my bags and send me off to a place like this alone, another voice said. *At this rate, we'll have separate honeymoons, homes, and bank accounts to go with the separate lives.*

"Adonis, can I ask you something?"

He paused dipping his spoon in the bowl. "I feel like I should say no."

"Why?"

"People don't ask for permission to voice a harmless question."

My grip tightened on my bowl. "It's not harmless, but it's not inappropriate either. I need help to figure out how I got here, and at every step I hit a dead end. Please," I said, dropping my gaze. "It's for Winter."

He didn't hesitate. "Ask me."

"Have...?" I sucked in a breath and released it slow. My stolen afternoon reprieve was over. I couldn't be the girl eating creamy pasta with sand between my toes for long. "Have you ever heard of T.O.D. Club? Truth or dare?"

His face changed.

"Someone told me the reason the bullying against Winter got so out of control is because that club was egging on her tormentors. Giving—" I forced the rest out. "Prizes to the guys who hurt her worse."

"Fucking hell." He dropped back, scrubbing his face. "What the fuck is wrong with people?"

"I'll ask myself that for a long time." I stared into my bowl, remembering the first time I made creamy spinach macaroni for Winter. "I want to find this club, Adonis. All the members who participated in killing my sister. But I don't know where to start. I haven't heard a whisper about it on campus."

"You shouldn't have heard a whisper," he said, blowing out a breath. "T.O.D. Club is supposed to be dead."

My spine straightened. "Dead?"

"Long dead," he stressed. "It started back in the seventies when my father went to Regalia University. He told me about it— No, he warned me before I joined his old frat as a legacy. He said if this generation hadn't learned better and was still pulling the same shit, get out of there. He didn't raise a son to disrespect women that way."

I blinked. "He said that to you?" My surprise wasn't unjustified. So far all I knew about the man is that he pressured one son into marriage, and kicked the other one out of the family for not having kids. Didn't sound like the makings of Father of the Year. "What the hell were they doing back then that he had to?"

"At first, it was just a couple of idiots goofing off. You know, like every game of truth or dare. The truths were sexual. The dares were humiliating. But what happened in the frat, stayed in the frat. And anyone who didn't want to play along, went about their business," he said. "Then, a few of the older brothers started taking it too seriously. It wasn't a fun drinking game anymore. Dad said it morphed into a test of loyalty and courage. You had to prove yourself to get into the club, and do even worse to stay in it."

"What kind of things did they ask the brothers to do?"

Adonis fixed somewhere over my shoulder. "Dad told me the truths changed from revealing your own, to getting someone else's. *Find out if Tony took a little extra to help him win the last game.* Or *get proof Mandy is cheating on Phil*," he said. "Club members were tasked with snooping and deceiving people to gather secrets the T.O.D. could wield against the other Royals. And the dares—"

"—were about taking those Royals down," I rasped.

He nodded slow. "It got ugly, Luna. Guys were seducing and scheming girls into bed, dropping *I love yous* in their ears until they told their 'boyfriends' all their secrets. Disgusting in and of itself, then they started the Dirty Dozen."

"What was that?"

"The T.O.D. Club had twelve members. Every month, they each chose a girl, invited her to their monthly full-moon party, got her pass-out drunk, and took pictures of her in various *compromising* circumstances."

My food turned rancid in my throat.

"Leverage," he spat. "Against all the Royal girls, and their current and future boyfriends. 'Get the truth from Paisley that her father is planning a merger with Consolidated Oil. If she refuses, I dare you to show those photos of her in the back room with Nicky all over campus.'"

"Disgusting isn't the word."

"One of the rare times the English language fails me, because there isn't a word that conveys how soulless and foul those guys had become," Adonis said. "My dad left the club long before it got to that point. He didn't know what they were doing until they came for him. He's a Wilson. Blackmail against the man he'd become was the holy grail.

"One of the guys made the mistake of targeting his girlfriend at the time. He took one look at the pictures, and beat the shit out of him. A week later, he had the entire club booted from the frat—including the president and vice president. He severed business ties with all of their families, and dragged their social status so far down the ladder, leverage couldn't catapult them back up.

"That was supposed to be the end of the Truth or Dare Club."

"But someone brought it back," I rasped. "Could've been anyone in the fifty years since your father was at Regalia U."

"I was at Regalia U a few years ago. I'm not saying the club couldn't have been around then, but I didn't hear a word about it. If the guys in my frat started it up again, they did an extraordinary job of hiding it."

I bobbed my head. "I believe you. I haven't heard anything about it either. Neither have my friends, and they've been around these people a lot longer than me," I said. "They got smart. Made sure no one could shut them down this time."

"They got worse." Adonis took my hand. Not my pinkie. Not a subtle glance that conveyed more than I could comprehend. He slipped under mine—his palm warm and soft. "I'm so sorry, Luna. I promise you, I will root out the students in this club, and hold them responsible for what they've done. Playing with people's lives in their sickening games," he spat. "The club was stopped once. They'll be put down again."

The English language did not fail him. *Put down* was exactly the right word for what would become of the Truth or Dare Club.

I didn't have much to say after that. I was too lost in my head, thinking of an almost fifty-year-old club coming back to haunt Regalia once again.

Adonis drove me to campus and walked me to the Gallery. A few students passed us—catching a look at the casually dressed professor, and the freshman he shouldn't be seeing outside of office hours. He took his professionalism seriously. I knew that walk wasn't just a walk to him... and still he did it to be the gentleman to me that he'd always been.

"I don't want to make things harder for you," I whispered, bowed over the doorknob.

"You're not." His footsteps faded down the steps. "I'm making it harder for myself."

I wasn't sure if he said it, or if it was what I wished he said. I spun around but he was already far enough away, it was possible I misheard.

Tossing my head, I knocked the memory of my afternoon with him into the farthest corner of my mind and locked it away. Even if Victor could be okay with it. Even if Rafael and my Rogues didn't mind sharing me. There was no amount of acceptance from them that would make Adonis into anything other than my professor.

We couldn't have more than a friendship, and even that could risk his job. The man lost his family, his fiancée, and a future with biological children. I wouldn't be the reason he lost his last love.

"What are you doing?"

I jumped, almost falling off the step. "Wilder, don't do that. You scared the mess out of me."

"Come inside," came his voice through the intercom.

I went in and found Rafael, Lucien, and Wilder at the end of the hall, waiting for me. They looked like they'd been up all night— Scratch that, they looked like they hadn't slept all weekend. I trudged forward and fell into the first pair of arms that fell open for me.

Lucien held me close, breathing in the salty spray lingering in my hair. "How are you?"

"Not good," I said honestly. "Mom and I finally had it out. I told her I wasn't leaving Regalia U until Winter was avenged. She told me nothing from the closed door I walked past when I left this morning." My throat clogged. "I don't know if she'll ever speak to me again."

"Course she will." A warm hand stroked my back. I melted under Rafael's touch. "It's raw right now. She's scared and doesn't know how to protect you. But she's doing all of this because she doesn't want to lose you. She wouldn't cut you out of her life for good. That's just losing you in a different way."

"Please be right."

He kissed my cheek. "I'm always right, gorgeous."

"You should get some rest, Luna," Wilder said. "We can talk about Natale and that night later."

"No." I straightened, wiping my eyes. "No, we don't have time to waste. Lucien said the other guys just learned what happens to those who talk. We can guess what they did this weekend too. Made their plans. Got rid of anything connecting them to Giovanni. Thought up lies and cover stories. They've been ahead of us all this time. I'm not letting them get any farther."

"I don't have anything." Frustration laced Wilder's growl. "Thasher, Thompkins, Hill, Natale, and Scott. I've hacked into everything under their name, and there's nothing. No mention of T.O.D. Club anywhere."

"I might have a place to start."

I told them everything Professor Anthony said about the club and how it started. At some point, we ended up in the living room with three pairs of narrowed eyes on me.

"A frat house club started in the seventies," Rafael repeated. "Shut down by John Wilson. Or so he told his son."

"Why would he lie?" I asked. "John warned him to get the hell out if they were still playing these sick games."

Wilder, Rafael, and Lucien shared a look.

"What?" I flicked between them. "What is it?"

Rafael put up his hands. His hair was tousled and shirt wrinkled from a few long nights. Bloodshot eyes did nothing to lessen his handsomeness. "I credit the man with not being such a shit-covered cockroach that he'd be okay with the *Dirty Dozen*. Fair enough, the club got out of control and he kicked those bastards out.

"But John Wilson didn't get where he is today by being soft. The rivalry between his family and the Burkhardts is the foundation of this town. Every generation has tried to push the other down to bring themselves up," he said. "The Burkhardts aren't number one because they have more money—though fuck knows they've got a continent load. They're number one because of what you saw on that chart Saylor showed you."

Lucien nodded along. "Control. More families have ties to them than they do the Wilsons. Ties the Burkhardts turn into nooses whenever it suits them. If this club is all about secrets, control, and collecting more ties—"

"John Wilson would have every reason to want in," Rafael finished. "Luna, I'm not saying he would've been cool with those rapey pricks, or his son being involved with more of the same. I bet nearly every part of that story is true. I'm just asking myself if when young Johnny used his power to overthrow the guys in charge and make the others pay, if he shut down T.O.D. for good, or if he brought it under new leadership."

I swallowed three times trying to get the words out. "Are you saying... that my future father-in-law drove my sister to suicide?"

"We're not saying that," Lucien broke in. "We can't. We don't know enough yet. I just find it interesting that the club has been around this long. And a Wilson was close by when it started."

"But if he kept it alive for nearly fifty years, isn't it even more unbelievable that none of you guys have heard of it? Again, if the Royals are that good at keeping secrets, how does Saylor's chart exist?"

Rafael dropped his head back, sighing. "We keep coming back to that."

Wilder shoved off the couch. "Enough with these guessing games. There are three guys we know for sure are in the club. I say we take the questions straight to them," he said, pacing a tread in the carpet. Rafael may have looked rumpled, but Wilder was wrecked. He looked like he hadn't slept since Thursday night. "They're freaked by this phantom killer who manipulated them and who they blackmailed.

"No matter what deals were made, they must've been looking over their shoulders all this time—wondering if they'd be next." He jerked his chin at me. "That's why Natale was such a mess. He finally snapped. What if we pushed them all over the edge? We thought we were making Winter's bullies pay, but now we know they were *getting paid*. They were pawns in someone else's plan, and from the sounds of it, they know exactly who that someone is. If we can get them to think that someone is taking them all out one by one—"

"They'll run to me like Giovanni did!" I shot to my feet. "He was convinced I could protect him. Once I knew the secret, his puppet master friend would have no reason to come after him. But Giovanni's body was found floating in a pool next to me. Owen, Levi, and Wesley must've figured out that he tried to talk to me. Would they risk getting anywhere near me after that?"

"Giovanni was high," Rafael said. "A fucking mess. He tracked you down at a crowded party. Almost every damn Royal was there. Fact is they saw him go in after you and acted fast. When Wesley, Levi, or the other shit approaches you, they'll be a lot more careful."

"Lucien?" I noticed my martial arts teacher had yet to offer a word. "What do you think? If they're not leaving breadcrumbs for us to follow, let's bring the bastards to me."

"It makes sense," he offered, choosing his words carefully, "but it's risky. The Phantom is only a phantom to us. Those three know who he or she is. All they have to do is deny they've got anything to do with our attacks. Maybe even push the blame on someone else who has reason to hate them." Our gazes locked. "They've already tried to frame you once."

"We've got her back no matter what happens," Wilder said. "While they're panicking, trying to figure out what to believe, they'll get sloppy. Texts going back and forth. Secret meetups. More blackmail."

"We have to do this." Calm certainty settled in my bones. "I have everything to gain and nothing to lose. I do nothing, they all win. But it was still Owen who attacked her in the dorm. It was Wesley who fucked with her brakes. It was Levi who had her beaten. If I drive those bastards mad, hounding them day in and day out—maybe they give up the Phantom, maybe they don't. Either way, they will regret ever hearing the words truth or dare."

Silence followed my statement.

I sensed the guys exchanging looks, wordlessly communicating, and coming to a decision that was mine. Because there was nothing they could say to change my mind.

"We'll have to throw out the whole plan," Rafael spoke up. "We were going for slow mental torture—stripping them of everything they cared about. Now we need them to believe the Phantom is actively trying to kill them. Turning them into human pinatas and getting their girlfriends to dump them won't do it."

"Wesley is still deathly allergic to nuts." My voice was dead. "We poison him again."

Wilder shook his head. "He won't risk that again. He's got EpiPens strapped to the inside of his thighs by now. We can't risk it either. If he dies, that's one less person to spill the truth about the club and the Phantom. We need to think bigger but also subtler. They won't see the next hit coming, but it'll scare them so bad, they won't take a solid shit for the rest of their lives."

I bobbed my head, following him exactly. We had to make them believe their lives were in danger without going too far and actually killing them. Giovanni died before he could tell me the truth. That was not happening again.

"What if we—"

A low growl cut through the room, twisting my head around.

Cato stood in the entrance of the living room—muzzle nowhere in sight. His lips peeled all the way back as he snarled... at me.

"Cato?"

He launched at me.

"Cato!" I barely got those two syllables out before he was on me.

We dropped on the couch—a tangle of limbs, shrieks, and snarls. He was everywhere. Running his hands down my thighs, thumbing under my shirt, palming my chest as I tried to twist free of him. Cato snared my wrists and trapped them over my head.

"Guys," I cried, bucking against him. "Guys!"

Wilder, Lucien, and Rafael didn't move.

Grasping my neck, he tipped my head back, trapping the gasp in my throat as he bared his teeth and—

"Oh." I blushed hot. Goose bumps raced down my cheeks, alighting on each nerve ending.

Cato scraped his canines over my pulsing pain, then licked it in apology. I caught fire and crumbled to dust on the spot. He attacked my neck, nipping and sucking as his hand freely roamed my body. My middle clenched so hard, it hurt exquisitely.

"Cato wasn't fond of your weekend away," Rafael drawled, remarkedly unconcerned with the fact his brother was claiming his girlfriend like the last piece of sweet potato pie on Thanksgiving. "Hated that he couldn't check you were okay. He actually did try to break into your place, but the security around Bowden Manor is impressive."

My eyes popped. "You're not seri—"

The world spun. Blinking, I found myself on my stomach—nose buried in a black throw pillow. Cato drew my shirt up to my neck. He licked a stripe up my spine and I bolted. Falling off the couch, I ran upstairs, burst into my room, and slammed the door.

Chest heaving, I slid down against the wood, half-expecting Cato to come through it after me.

My whole body hummed like I stuck my finger in an electric socket. The guys just sat there looking like Cato pinning me down like an animal and having his way with me was another Tuesday, but it fucking was not.

Of all the nights he slipped in my bed, he was as perfect a gentleman as he could be considering he continually spooned me without needing my permission. Of course there was heat between us, and the engagement ring he put on my finger was a massive clue, but he hadn't acted on his declared possession of me and I didn't let myself think of if he would.

Why is nothing about that guy predictable!? I pressed my palm against my racing heart, my lower belly still clenched so tight, I didn't try to make it the rest of the way to my bed.

The wild thing is I'm pretty sure I just got my answer on if the guys would be okay with sharing me. If only the one holdout wasn't my fiancé. The guy with the power to take just as much away from me as I could take from him.

Chapter Three

Saylor Burkhardt

I wrote the last letter and stopped, staring at the name. Saylor and the Royal Wenches weren't on my list because Winter gave me five names, and they weren't one of them.

Visions of blue faces and dripping hair flashed before my eyes.

That all changed.

Saylor didn't get what was coming to her the night of the party. The germaphobe with the spotless, shining reputation would've woken up on a throne of garbage for the whole world to see. Yes, the whole world. We had the cameras and mics ready to go. This shit was going viral.

It was too late for all of that now. Katie was the only Royal willing to put me, Saylor, and the Rogues on the same party guest list, and I had a feeling as long as there was crime tape around the indoor pool, her parents weren't letting her throw another one anytime soon.

No, I had to think of something else for Saylor and all the beasts who heard her plan to dress as the final, traumatic vision of my older sister, and didn't say "fuck no, that's evil."

But what?

I flicked to the clock, reading eleven p.m. on the dot. I hadn't been thinking of Saylor all day, but I had spent the last several hours in my room, lost in thought. What the guys and I talked about earlier kept going around and around in my head. I assumed it did for them too, because all of their doors were closed when I came out to make dinner. Wilder searching for a trace of the T.O.D. Club. Rafael making a plan. Lucien sourcing what we needed to make it happen. Cato—

My cheeks heated. It was crazy that I still felt his touch all over my body—firm, insistent, and commanding. He was another one who plagued my thoughts, but for reasons so different than Wesley, Owen, Levi, or Saylor.

Well, maybe not too different reasons because the longer I sat there, the longer uncertainty had to work its way in. I wasn't sure what would happen next with Cato, and if I knew what to do about Saylor, I wouldn't be staring at a piece of paper with two words on it and nothing else.

Again I flicked to the clock, then down. I didn't think my temperature could rise any hotter, but it did as I stared at my robe, then at the two outfits I placed on my bed after my shower.

It didn't matter if I locked my door. It never stopped Cato from climbing into bed with me any other night and it wouldn't that night either. Soon, he would come to me. Wrap me in his arms. Tuck my head under his chin. Mold my body to his chest. Croon in my ear when my nightmares leaked whimpers through my lips.

He was coming, so what was I going to do?

I padded over to the bed, sizing up the regular baggy t-shirt and old pajama pants that I wore every night, and the sexy, satin tank and matching shorts that I bought during an outing from boarding school. At sixteen years old, the naughtiest thing my friends and I could think to do was buy lingerie from the little shop by the outdoor market. We took turns running in and out of there while the others kept a lookout for our eagle-eyed escort.

I'd never been more thankful for the giggly, guilty little secret I snuck into the bottom of my drawer and never wore. It was the only sexy nightclothes I owned, and as the man who'd seen all my others, Cato would know it.

What would he think when he lifted the covers and saw me wrapped in satin? What did I want him to think? What did I want him to do?

Pressure built between my legs. Scratch those stupid questions, I knew exactly what I wanted him to do. But would he do it? There was absolutely no predicting what Cato Dumont would do in any given moment. Lucien and Wilder still watched themselves around him—the guy was liable to attack whenever the mood struck him.

Letting out a slow breath, I picked up my ratty old shirt and baggy pants. My head was already wrecked. Signaling Cato to have his way with me wasn't the best idea when the number of enemies around me was growing. Yes, Ashton Scott was in a hole where he belonged. But I didn't anticipate that Saylor, Everleigh, Piper, and Gabriella would become the unrelenting problem that they were.

They had me jumped. Stole my ring. Taunted me with the secret that stole my sister. Threatened me to leave Regalia U. Then that day in the classroom...

It was clear that Saylor and her minions wouldn't stop until I was gone, and that was fine with me. If they wanted a war, they've got one. But I needed to focus if I was going to fight them, destroy the T.O.D. Club, squeeze Winter's killers of everything they know, and then execute them along with the Phantom who sicced them on her in the first place.

I got dressed and turned out the lights, burrowing beneath my covers. The last thing I should be doing is plotting how to seduce my muzzle-wearing neighbor.

The clock ticked the seconds, lulling my eyes closed. It amazed me how peacefully I drifted off into my nightmares. It should be a fight. I should toss, turn, and scream as they dragged me under. But no. My lids grew heavy. My body weightless. My skin cradled in warmth. And I surrendered, letting it take—

Footsteps sounded on the landing. I held my breath when the shadows stopped outside my door. It swung open, snapping my eyes shut.

Cato always appeared after I fell asleep. I figured it was because he wasn't interested in the part where I told him he couldn't sleep with me. He wasn't asking—a fact I accepted after waking up over and over again in his arms, flushed as I tried to convince him and myself that getting the best sleep I've had in months was a bad thing.

I didn't want him to see I was awake and leave.

Cato lifted the covers and slid in. He grasped my hips and stopped, the satin bunching under his fingers.

Maybe it was true that the last thing I should be doing is trying to seduce my muzzle-wearing roommate. But right then, Saylor, Everleigh, Gabriella, Piper, Owen, Wesley, Levi, and the Phantom were out of my reach, safe in their beds.

And Cato was in mine.

It took Lucien dressing me as a vampire mistress and giving me multiple public orgasms for me to accept it was okay to hang on to the tiniest thread of happiness. It wasn't a betrayal against Winter—my sweet, loving big sister who wanted me to be happy more than anything. The betrayal would be if I let those monsters take everything from me. Our story wouldn't end that way.

It was them who'd lose everything.

Cato had hold of me. Drawing me in, he fit my body to his like a puzzle piece—pressing his cheek against the curve of my throat. I knew for all that he was unpredictable, it would all stop here if I let it. Cato wouldn't wake me from a peaceful sleep or do anything more than hold me through the night. The one thing I never doubted since I met Cato Dumont... is that I was safe with him.

Whatever happened next was up to me.

Just flip over and do something sexy. Slip my strap off my shoulder or slide my hand over his shirt. Plant a kiss on the guy who bites anyone who touches him without permission.

I bit hard on my lip, penning in my panting breaths. Dear Thor, what did I know about seduction? I had sex a grand total of one time. Stripping naked and demanding it didn't go to plan the first time. What did that say about my one and only move?

Flipping over, I gazed in his eyes. Cato Dumont didn't say much, because he said everything with his eyes. Pine-green pools tempted me, drawing me closer still. I leaned in and noses bumped.

The breath from our lips mingled—minty sweet from toothpaste. Shaking, I held on to those steady orbs. In them was all I needed to do. All I needed to say...

"I'm yours."

Cato closed the distance, sealing his lips on mine. My cry swallowed in his hunger, then the rest of me went with it. Why should I have ideas of what kissing Cato Dumont was like? I didn't have ideas. I had fantasies of my snapping, snarling protector kissing me as gently as he held me through the night. He was soft and warm and everything people didn't know him to be.

But why should Cato fit my predictions any more than he did anyone else's?

He kissed me wild and reckless—devouring my moans like they were the last sustenance on earth.

Explosions burst in my mind, a million million fireworks going off at the same time—leaving me stunned and hypnotized. I could barely respond as his tongue battled mine. Clashing, sparking, boiling like fever.

Cato flipped me on my back, wrapping my legs around his waist. "Hmmpf!" I cried when he rose up on his knees, taking me with him.

He broke away. Both our chests heaved—rolling and bumping each other as his fists gripped the hem of my wonderfully sexy satin top.

"Mine," he growled.

I nodded so hard I knocked the last trace of breath out of me. "Yours."

Cato tore my shirt over my head, flinging it over his shoulder. Our hands fumbled and bumped into each other, ripping our clothes off. He yanked my bra down with his teeth. I scratched his thigh and tore his boxers yanking them down.

The clock hadn't passed the minute mark before we were both naked and ravishing each other, taking up where we left off on the couch.

The world spun and I was flat on my back. Cato nipped and growled a trail down my neck and between my breasts. Excitement built the further he went.

This is happening. My goodness, this is happening.

My legs flew up and landed on his shoulders. Grasping my chin, Cato tipped my neck and pinned me to the bed with a gaze of such heat, pinpricks of sweat beaded my skin.

"Watch."

My eyes widened realizing what he wanted me to do. What was with these guys and taking me from virgin beginner to expert seductive minx? What part of my red face and running away when he claimed me on the couch earlier, gave the impression I was ready to watch a guy go down on me?

I lowered my lids a little, blurring his handsome, perfect sight. A low, fierce growl spread through the room, making my pulse race. Why was that hot instead of threatening? When my Cato acted like a wild beast, everything in me ached to obey. Submit.

It made no sense, and all the sense in the world at the same time.

I opened my eyes as ordered, locking on to his. Without breaking contact, he lowered his head and swiped his tongue slow and languid past my slit.

I almost came on the spot.

He licked me slow at first, as if savoring me like a fine wine. I squirmed and moaned, wanting to look away but unable to even if I tried. Cato picked up the pace—his growl coming back as he nipped and bit my outer lips, punishing them for who knows what. They absolutely deserved and needed it all the same.

My moans filled the room—louder than I intended. I didn't want the others to overhear. Especially Rafael. He may be cool with sharing me. Even sharing me with his brother, but that didn't mean he should spend all night listening to his brother fuck me.

At least, that seemed the right thing to do. How did relationships like ours work? The only thing I knew about boyfriends was the summer flings I had when I was home from France. I was never serious with those guys, or dating more than one at once.

Cato's head bobbed quick and hard between my legs, tongue-fucking my eyes up in my head, and all the while not breaking eye contact. No one could silence themselves through that. I'd need a muzzle of my own.

"Uh, yes, Cato," I breathed. "Uh, that feels so good. Why did we wait so long to do this?"

He bit the soft skin of my inner thigh—not gently. "We had to talk about spoons."

It was strange how easy it had become to decipher him. *I had to accept I belonged to him.*

"Forgive me for being slow?"

"No."

"What? But—"

Cato dove for my clit.

"Ah!"

He sucked hard, flicking and tormenting the thing without mercy. Heat suffused my body, turning the pinpricks into a sheen that glistened in the low light from my lamp. The sheets were sticking to me—teasing my sensitive flesh, making me even more aware of my charged nerve endings.

People spend so much time talking about sex in the crudest, basic terms, they never tell you what's truly wonderful about it.

They don't let you know that your whole body lights up like a mad scientist flipping a switch and bringing you back to life. That's what I was before. Not living. Not feeling. Not experiencing the full measure of my body and what it could do for eighteen long years.

Now I felt everything.

I felt the ridges of his long, callused fingers gripping my thigh. I felt every individual hair brushing my inner legs, making my ticklish self squirm even harder. I felt his mouth on me like a force of nature, whipping the frenzied storm racing through my body to higher, more dangerous heights.

Cato slipped a finger past my folds and I was gone.

A wave of intense, bone-cracking pleasure bowled me over—arching my body off the bed. Cato slipped his hand behind my neck and drew me back, our eyes locked—our souls locked—as explosions went off in my core, rocketing from my pussy and up to my mind where everything went white.

I don't remember falling away from him. Euphoria blotted out my mind and then there he was—sculpted, chiseled beauty gazing down at me.

Cato propped on one hand, the other tracing lazy circles from my belly button and traveling up. My skin pimpled under his touch. It amazed me he could be so rough and gentle at the same time. The mess of contradictions that was falling for Cato Dumont.

His fingers reached my mouth and traced my lips. For a second, I wondered why they were wet... then I knew.

I lit on fire when he gently pressed, wanting me to open up and taste myself. Oh yes, these guys were definitely miles ahead of me in this game, and didn't care that I was tripping down the road trying to catch up. But that's another thing no one tells you...

Lips parting, my tongue snaked around his fingers, sucking him in deep. Cato released a long, sharp hiss—so turned on it hurt.

They don't say that this is the best thing about a guy who knows exactly what they're doing. The only one bumbling their way around my orgasm is me. My guys know how to hit the bull's-eye every time. And who is trying to leave the bedroom with anything less?

He dipped as I rose, lips connecting in a shower of sparks and attraction. Looking back, I tried to remember a time I didn't want Cato in every way. Nothing came to mind. I always wanted him.

Before I met him, I wanted him.

A guy who would do anything to protect me. Cared about me and my family. Didn't let anyone intimidate him. And was so hot, you couldn't stare too long at him without burning your eyes out.

I imagined that guy so many times in lonely years trapped in an all-girls boarding school. I just didn't realize it wasn't one guy I was looking for, and they were waiting for me within my worst nightmare... to make it into a dream.

We broke apart gasping. A sudden wild urge seized me, and I jumped on it before it could run away.

"Hold on," I whispered, guiding him onto his back. "I want to try something."

He flashed, fisting the hairs at the nape of my neck and tilting my neck back. I gasped when he licked up my chin. "On your knees." Again his growl was nothing less than a threat.

Again my lower belly contracted in exquisite pain.

"I want to try that too," I giggled. Snapping my arm up, I broke his hold and slammed his arm. Cato got no chance to recover. My hand was around his throat and shoving him onto the pillows while the other ensnared his wrist. Lucien said I was quickly becoming his star pupil. "First, I want you just like this, Cato Dumont. On your back and at my mercy." I winked. "If you disobey, you'll find out that I bite too."

His grin was positively feral. I knew right then that sweet, tender love-making was not in the cards for us. From then on, I'd be lucky if he let me leave my bed in the morning walking straight and sporting love bites I could cover with my clothes.

Releasing him, my hands splayed across his chest, keeping him where I wanted him. I tried to hold his gaze, licking my lips seductively as I ventured down. I wasn't at his belly button before I flicked away, cheeks heating, and filling with nerves at what I was about to do. *Baby steps.*

Rocking back on my legs, I came face to face with my new challenge. My grand total of two sexual experiences didn't include blow jobs. Lucien and Rafael were both completely focused on my pleasure, but I wasn't the kind of girl who wanted to lie back and let their man do all the work. I wanted to make them feel as good as they made me.

If only I knew how, I thought, reddening as Cato's smirk widened.

"Goes in your mouth," he offered helpfully, earning a swat on the thigh.

"Thank you. I'm getting to that." Taking a deep breath, I stared down my opponent.

They didn't look so formidable when being strangled by my pussy. I was quite fond of them then. But having one bobbing against my gag reflex was a whole other story. Trying it out, I licked the tip, receiving another sharp hiss in return.

Emboldened, I went for it. My lips wrapped around his head and moved lower—swallowing as much of him as I could. Cato tangled in my hair, but he didn't force or press. He also didn't insist on eye contact, which would have undone me like a frayed shoelace.

Moving slow, I bobbed my head—mouth suctioning like I knew what the hell I was doing.

"Uhh." Cato moaned low and deep, making me stupidly happy.

He didn't say much outside of bed, and I didn't expect that to change in bed either, but that didn't stop me from understanding him.

He did not want me to stop.

Picking up the pace, I grasped his thighs—enjoying the feel of him hard and strong beneath my hands... and in my mouth. Soon, I forgot what I was nervous about.

I dipped as he jerked. Sucked as he moved. Moaned as he moaned. My room was filled with the sounds of two bodies in sync, and suddenly, I wanted him inside me more than anything.

Cato tugged on my hair, pulling me up with a pop. I no sooner recovered than his mouth was on mine—hungrily drawing from the last of my strength. Weak and fevered, I melted into him, holding tight to his shoulders.

I didn't ask for what I wanted. I didn't have to. I knew his mind without speaking. I trusted that Cato knew mine.

The walls spun.

Blinking, I gazed up at the ceiling. Then he was there. Shielding me. Crowding me. Molding his body to mine.

"Cato," I rasped. "Please."

My legs fell open, needing and inviting all of him. Cato settled between me—the two of us fitting like both sides of a zipper. I held my breath waiting for the final thrust that would seal the next stage of our relationship.

I couldn't believe I ever thought of turning away my Rogues for revenge. Nothing would get in the way of making things right for Winter, but it was true. If I let the likes of Owen, Levi, Saylor, or the Phantom get in the way of what was happening between us, they would win and keep winning. Because they succeeded in destroying both of us. Winter may be gone, but they would succeed in neither.

"Luna."

I opened my eyes, meeting his deep, earnest pools. Cato truly had the most gorgeous, soulful eyes I would ever see. The truth, it wasn't the muzzles, the fires, or the growling that unsettled people about him. It was his eyes. One look, and he laid your soul bare.

"Yes?" I wrapped my legs around his waist. "It's okay. I'm ready. I want this."

"Your fiancé..."

The smile froze on my lips. "Look, I know things are weird with Victor, but right now, we're not exclusive. You don't have to worry—"

"Your fiancé," he said, "is me."

Cato pushed in with one hard thrust, catching my reply on my lips and tossing it back. There wasn't a chance to speak as he set a deep, mind-scrambling pace, and I tried for all of five seconds.

I dug my heels in the mattress, rising up and driving him deeper still. Cato moved like a beast—controlled but powerful. The glow from my lamp bathed one side of his body in light, and left the other in shadows. For the rest of my life, I'd try to mentally capture the flawless perfection that was his raven hair; sharp cheekbones; smoldering, intense eyes; and the dips and peaks down his muscled chest. I'd try but my mental imaginings would always fall short.

"Open your eyes," he whispered.

Forget my imaginings. The real thing was so much better, because it was all mine.

We both came hard—screaming and grunting and flopping on the sheets.

I sunk in a boneless heap, becoming one with my damp, limp covers. Oh yeah, I was ten kinds of stupid for not doing that the first time he slipped into my bed.

"But now," I said, draping his arms around me. "We get to make up for lost time."

His tongue caressed up my neck, drawing out a shiver all the way to my ears. I squeaked a giggle as he nipped the shell, then kissed it sweet. Cato really liked biting. The surprise was that I did not mind being bitten.

I reached up to touch him and the emerald glinted in the light. The emerald… from the ring… that he definitely stole… and placed on my finger in the middle of the night.

I guess now I finally know why.

"Cato, what did you mean when you said you're my fiancé?"

He nuzzled the back of my neck. Didn't stop me hearing him clearly. "There's only one thing to mean."

"True, but I don't want there to be any misunderstanding. Marrying Victor is the only way I can stay at Regalia U, and the only way to stop his parents from cutting him off. Our engagement isn't over. We—"

Cato dropped kisses down my shoulder blades. "Again."

"Yes, please. I'd love a round two, but first we should talk—"

"Can't talk. It goes in your mouth."

"Ca— Ahh!" I squealed as he pounced on me.

Talking could wait.

***

The guys were in the kitchen when I came down. None of them were dressed for classes, and neither was I. We got an official notice that morning classes were canceled on account of losing another student in the space of a week. The email also said they were holding a memorial for Giovanni Natale on Wednesday. I was going back and forth on if I should attend.

"Morning."

A chorus of greetings came back at me. I wandered over to the stove, busying myself with checking under pot lids and in the oven. I was partly delaying, and partly trying to get my hands on Rafael's breakfast creation as fast as possible.

It was a shame Lucien insisted on drinking that red smoothie and Wilder didn't touch anything made by other hands. This spinach eggs Benedict with a side of home fries couldn't get in my stomach fast enough.

"This smells amazing, Rafael." I carried my plate to the dining table—only blushing slightly when Cato claimed the seat next to me. Just his nearness did fuzzy things to my brain. "How do you have time to make these meals? When do you sleep?"

"I only need about six hours," he said, passing me the salt and pepper. "Cooking gives me something to do so I don't get up to mischief in the early hours."

"What kind of mischief?"

He shot me a grin that clenched my sore middle. "You can find out."

"I intend to," I purred. "But before we ride this flirting train off-track, there's something I need to talk to you guys about."

They paused in their chewing and drinking.

"What is it?" Wilder asked.

Straightening my spine, I cleared my throat. "I came to you guys for a reason. Your plan to make Ashton and the others pay was ten times better than mine, and it made sure I didn't get caught. I needed your methodical reasoning to balance my scorching rage."

Rafael set down his fork. "Why do I sense a but coming?"

"But," I stressed, "things are different now. There was too much I didn't know before we started this. I didn't know Winter was holding on to a secret that she refused to reveal even while her class made her miserable. I didn't know Ashton, Giovanni, Levi, Owen, and Wesley were chess pieces in someone else's game. I didn't know Saylor Burkhardt knew why all this was happening, but sat back in the name of protecting the stupid Royal caste system."

"But now we do know," Wilder said. "We know and we've got a plan."

"We've got the same plan. Keep pushing Winter's biggest tormentors until they crack. One of them gives up who rewarded them for torturing Winter, and then what? There're still three guys on my list of *who won't make it to graduation*, and that hasn't changed." I clenched around my fork. "Winter was just another Dreg to them. They didn't care about trading money, status, or whatever it was to beat, assault, or nearly kill her. They gave her rapist an alibi and got her thrown out of school like she wasn't even a person to them.

"They will die, but you know what? Even if they and the Phantom do, what will it change if the T.O.D. Club is still going? What will it matter if that network of secrets, deals, trades, lies, and marriages lets the Royals stay on top, free to continue pressing the boot on someone's throat to give themselves a leg up?"

"What are you saying?" Lucien asked.

"I'm saying there's a massive flaw in our plan. That flaw is going to cut us short of the finish line."

"What flaw?" Rafael spoke up.

I met their eyes in turn. "It relies on Owen, Levi, or Wesley doing the right thing."

Lucien started to say something... and stopped.

"And now you see." My voice was barely above a whisper. "Giovanni felt bad somewhere deep down. He didn't know the end goal was to drive Winter over the edge. In his mind, he was just dumping and humiliating a girl he wasn't into. Pretty boy like him did that plenty for free.

"He was the only one of them that actually got to know her. Spend time with her. He said he never wanted her dead. Looking into his eyes Friday night, I believed it," I said. "He found out after Winter was gone that he was used. When the others approached him. Giovanni said they needed *him* to get proof of who the Phantom is, so they could demand more, and I'm betting they didn't ask nicely.

"He went along with it because he wanted to find out the truth, but that secret and the person behind it scared him too much to do anything about it until he thought they were trying to destroy him."

I stabbed my egg, letting the yolky goodness soak the bread. "But think about the fact that he came to me at all, asking the person who hates him most to protect him. He didn't for a second think the others would back him up or do the right thing, so why should we?" I dropped the next sentence without inflection. "I mean, does anyone think someone other than Owen, Wesley, or Levi killed Ashton?"

One after the other they shook their heads—even Cato.

"They thought the Phantom turned Ashton against them, and they killed him. A plan Giovanni was not in on, or he wouldn't have been so freaked out. I don't think these guys are as afraid of the Phantom as we want to believe. They weren't afraid to blackmail them. One, or all three of them, weren't afraid to kill Ashton when they thought he was working for them.

They believe they have the upper hand as long as they know the secret, and they do," I admitted.

"The Phantom never turned on them. Our attacks and truth lists only made them think the Phantom did. If this mystery person convinces them they're innocent in these attacks and someone else is after them..." I shook my head. "They'll look to the only other person who'd want them to suffer for what happened between Winter and the Phantom. They'll remember that it was Rafael who gave them Ashton's name in the first place. They won't ignore that I live with you."

"Again, what are you saying?" Wilder broke in.

"I thought about this all night."

Cato ran a finger down my thigh under the table, popping goose bumps on the back of my neck.

"Most of the night," I corrected. "There's no way to do this that doesn't result in them figuring out I'm coming after them. Once they do, they're not coming to me to tell me shit. They're going to band together with their phantom friend to get rid of another Sinclair."

Lucien rose from his seat. "We'd never let that happen."

"I know you won't, but the fact remains that this is bigger than three sociopaths who have no reason to crack. Yeah, I could kill Owen, Wesley, and Levi, but there'd still be the Phantom. I could kill the Phantom, but there'd still be the T.O.D. Club—the murder weapon they set loose on my sister. I could expose the T.O.D. Club, but John Wilson shut it down once and it came right back like genital herpes.

"There's only one plan worth making and executing, and that's to bring the entire Royal caste system to its knees." I breathed slowly, then said the rest. "The one who has to do that is me. You guys are better at this than me. You have the resources and the skills, but Winter was my sister. I have the one thing you guys never had."

Lucien dipped his chin. "What's that?"

"Nothing to lose." I shrugged. "I don't care what happens to me. I don't even care if I get caught and thrown in jail after it's all over. Caution will hold you back." Reaching across, I brushed Rafael's fingertips. "Caring about me will hold you back. But I don't have those limits. I'll go farther, do worse, sacrifice everything to burn Regalia to the ground. Anything less, and it doesn't happen. Am I wrong?"

"Luna," Rafael began.

"Am. I. Wrong?"

"No," Wilder said. Rafael swung to him, glaring. Wilder returned his gaze calmly. "You're not wrong."

"Good." I pulled my breakfast to me, picked up my knife and fork, and started cutting. "I'll tell you guys what the plan is the minute I come up with it. I'll need your help to work out the kinks, but once I know what we're doing, that's what we're doing. I won't settle for anything else than imploding this entire town."

Rafael leaned over the table. "Luna, we want the same thing—"

Knock. Knock.

"—this any-means-necessary shit isn't—"

Knock.

He twisted around. "What the fuck? Is someone knocking on our door? Have they lost their mind?" He no sooner finished his sentence when there was another knock.

I was the first one up and out of my seat. "It must be Katie. I told her I'd meet up with her to check out the security footage. She's never been the patient type."

The guys relaxed, returning to their seats. I walked out into the hall, feeling lighter than when I entered the kitchen. The conversation wasn't over. Rafael and Lucien had plenty they wanted to say to me. It was written all over their face. Even so, they couldn't deny I was right.

My Rogues were brilliant. Their plan to drive those bastards insane with fear and paranoia was genius. Getting them to turn all that on Ashton—the worst among them—was so masterful, I'm pretty sure I fell half in love with them right then. It wasn't that I thought I could do this without them, or even better than them.

The simple truth was I couldn't take down every Royal from the very top of the kingdom to the bottom from the shadows. They'd figure out it was me... because I wanted them to know. They underestimated Winter, me, and every so-called Dreg. It was in the damn name for crying out loud. They walked around literally calling us worthless. So little did we matter that our lives were something to play with like a children's game.

Bringing Regalia to its knees would be my grandest accomplishment. I wanted the whole world to know.

Skipping into the hall, I threw open the door. My greeting died on my lips.

"About time." Victor tossed his duffel bag over the entryway, bugging my eyes open. "Which room is mine? I've got more stuff in the car."

***

I sat on the couch, legs jiggling and sweating like a criminal in an interrogation room with the prime piece of evidence in my pocket. Victor reclined next to me, sipping an ice-cold Malta of all things. I didn't give it to him. His butler/mover kept it chilled while he helped him get his stuff as far as the living room.

Lucien, Wilder, Cato, and Rafael towered over us. In Cato's case, he crouched on the chair arm, rumbling a low, steady growl that didn't concern Victor as much as it should.

"You're not moving in here, Wilson," Wilder gritted. "Tell your errand boy to pick up your shit and walk it out the way you came in."

Victor took a long pull and smacked his lips. "Correction: I am moving in here," he breezed. "Luna invited me."

I jerked as four pairs of eyes flew to me. "I did what? That never happened!"

He heaved a sigh. "You said you wanted us to start over, get to know each other, and do this right for the first time since we met. I already invited you to live in the mansion, and you said no. So obviously that leaves me moving in here." Victor tipped his head to the ceiling. "What's the bathroom situation like? I'll need my own."

Wilder advanced on him.

"Okay, wait," I cried. "There's been a misunderstanding. Victor, I meant it when I said I wanted us to start over. This..." I drifted to my Rogues. "This wedding is happening. It has to if I'm going to stay in Regalia U, but I truly believe we can have a relationship that works for both of us.

Getting there doesn't mean moving down the hall. I was more talking about—about—walking to class together and having dinner once a week."

"We tried that. Didn't work. This isn't about being boyfriend-girlfriend. It's about being husband and wife. I've got to get to know you for real, and I've got a feeling you're not your real self when you're on your best behavior for my parents, or hiding your contempt for everyone on campus." He swept out his hands. "You feel comfortable here, don't you?"

"I... yes."

He jerked a nod. "Then, this is where I should be. Getting to know the real you and..." I didn't like the smile on his lips when he turned to Cato, Rafael, Lucien, and Wilder. "The guys you want me to share you with."

"See, you almost talked me into it until that last sentence."

"Didn't talk me into shit," Rafael said. "This is our place. Luna lives here because we trust her—"

"She's ours," Cato sliced in.

"—but we don't trust you."

Victor shrugged. "I don't care if you trust me. You four are holed up in here, scamming on my fiancée and dragging her reputation to the bottom of the dumpster fire where all of yours are. Still, I'm willing to give this freak-ass situation a try."

"Are you?" I asked, rubbing my temple. "Because your word choice says differently."

He put his hands up in surrender. "Fresh start, Luna. We do this or not?"

I looked from him to the guys.

"No."

"You can't be serious."

"He's working you."

Cato jumped off the armchair, tackling and flipping me. I shrieked as I suddenly found myself three feet away from Victor and secured in his arms. The man didn't need to say much. He got his point across just fine.

Dusting himself off, Victor got to his feet. "I'm not here for a debate. The decision is yours, Luna. Either you were serious about that fresh start, or you weren't. If you are, I'm either moving in here or you're moving into the mansion. What's it going to be?"

I poked my head over Cato's arm. "Victor, you dropped this on me before I even had my breakfast. Just give me a minute to talk it over with the guys, okay?"

"Cool. I'll check out the room situation."

"The fuck you will," Wilder barked, stalking him out of the room.

It was just Rafael, Lucien, Cato, and me.

"He can't live here, Luna." Rafael didn't let his voice carry. "You know what I keep in my room. You know what Wilder keeps in *his*. A Royal tromping around the Gallery? We might as well get fitted for silver bracelets now."

"If he did that, it'd be over between me and him. I'd never forgive him. Victor knows that."

"But does he care?" Lucien crouched beside me, the glow from the neon lamps reflecting off his sharpened canines. "You said this wedding has to happen to keep you in Regalia U. You need him, but he doesn't need us."

My lips parted, but nothing came out. Lucien was right. Victor made his feelings about the Rogues clear. He saw them as a bunch of criminals, paranoid delusionals, and nuts that went around destroying people for money and conspiracy theories. What would he do if he popped his head in Rafael's bomb-making factory? Not to mention if he ever saw what Wilder kept in his second room.

"But I told him I wanted to make a real go of this," I said. "What do I tell him now? You can't live here because there are two hundred kinds of illegal activity going on?"

"You stop after he can't live here," Rafael stated. "He doesn't need more than that. No one invited him here in the first place."

"But..."

"But what, Luna? It wasn't twenty minutes ago that you were plotting to burn down Regalia and everyone in it. Think your Royal fiancé is going to sit by quietly and just watch? If we're going to do what we need to do, he can't be here."

"I know," I cried, trying to get up. Cato held me tighter, rubbing circles on the skin above my waistband for good measure. I forgot why I wanted up. "I know. Everything you're saying is true, but I can't help thinking that if by some miracle I survive this, don't end up in prison, and this wedding goes ahead, there will still be you."

I reached out, taking Lucien's and Rafael's hands. "If Victor can't accept you guys and your place in my life now, he never will. I want to be with you guys more than anything, but I gave my word that I'd marry him. Victor's right," I said, dropping my gaze. "I'd hate him if he forced me into a marriage where he fucked someone like Everleigh on the side, and I had to shut up and take it.

"I won't be a hypocrite. I asked him to try and accept that I have feelings for all of you, and... he came here, Rafael. He took the first step when he could've stayed holed up in his mansion—pissed and taking it out on me forever." I relaxed, resting my head on Cato's head. "I'm just afraid that if I turn him away now, he'll be done trying. Then, I really will be using and hurting him," I whispered. "Forcing him into an unhappy, loveless marriage—knowing he can't leave without losing everything.

"I'm not so far gone that I could be okay with stepping on his throat to get my revenge. If I'm honest, I feel differently toward the Wilsons now that I know John punished the first T.O.D. Club and warned his son from getting involved with them. I want to bring it all crashing down around the Royals, but not around the Wilsons. Not around Victor."

Rafael carded his fingers through his hair, frustration battling a dozen other emotions in his eyes. "I hear what you're saying. I really do. I hated seeing that ring on your finger before we were even together. If I was the one that put it there, I sure as hell wouldn't share you with Victor Wilson. He's trying to give you the relationship you want. I respect that.

"But there's about to be a war." Rafael's gaze pinned me through. "We'll have to choose sides. Us, the Royals, the Dregs, Katie, and Victor. All this has been his life for eighteen years, and he just met you."

I swallowed hard.

"What do we do when at the end of this experiment, he says no?"

"I—"

"What's your problem, man?" Victor blew back in with Wilder right behind him. "You and I never had beef. We were a year apart. Never even talked to you. Why are you so against a new roommate?"

Rafael and I shared a look. Silent words passed between us.

"We're not," Rafael said.

"Rafa," Lucien hissed. Cato's growl was no happier.

"You can stay," my boyfriend announced, turning on Victor. "But there are rules. We never hid what we do. We clean up the messes only you Royals can get into, and we're not nice about it. If you got a problem with that, carry your shit out now."

Victor stared him down. "No problem here. I think it's messed up but you wouldn't have a job if Royals weren't willing to pay. There are no angels in this town."

That was the truest thing Victor ever said.

Rafael grinned mockingly. "Your understanding warms my heart, but I'd like to make sure we're clear here. Everything that's said and done in the Gallery, stays in the Gallery. You don't talk about our business. You don't even tell your Royal buddies what color the walls are. If you break that rule, you won't only be evicted, we'll..." He flicked to Wilder. "My boy can explain better than I."

The veins popped in Wilder's jaw. He wanted no part of Victor moving in, and it didn't take a mind reader to know it. Wilder agreed to living with me and he still took my door off the hinges, treated me to daily pat-downs, and warned me off breathing too hard on the furniture. He wanted Victor out. Now.

Wilder moved from Rafael to me. His fists unclenched. "You share a word of what we say or do, and I'll freeze your bank accounts, burn your credit, and put you on the sex offender registry."

"What the fuck did you just say?"

"And that's just day one," Wilder said. "Day two, I'll dig up all the secrets you thought you buried and share it for the world to see."

Victor launched at him.

"Hey!" I shot up, untangling from Cato. "Okay, enough of this. Victor gets the idea and he's not going to say anything." I moved between them in case, grasping Victor's forearm. "He knows how to keep a secret."

"I know how to mind my own business. I'm not here for you or whatever crap you get up to. I'm here because I either marry this woman, or end up on the street." He smiled at me. "Haven't decided which option is worse yet."

"Charming." Rolling my eyes, I tugged him out of the room. "Come on. I'll show you where to put your stuff."

"Where's that?" Lucien spoke up. "All the rooms are taken."

"Don't worry about it." Victor snaked an arm around my waist. "I'll bunk with my fiancée. How big is your bed?"

Cato closed the distance between us—a look in his eyes that chilled my spine. Somehow, it was even scarier that he wasn't growling.

I quickly headed him off. "A second ago you were wondering if it'd be better to cuddle with an alley cat in a cardboard box," I said. "Now you're trying to hog my covers? You can just have my room, Victor. I'll sleep with—" I looked from Cato, to Rafael, to Lucien, to Wilder, breath picking up speed. "I'll sleep somewhere else."

Fixed on me, his eyes narrowed. "No, fuck that. I told you we were over and you hooked up with other guys. Fair enough, that was my fault. But the engagement's back on now, and I'm not lying there with a pillow over my ears while you're getting fucked down the hall."

"Who said anything about that!" I cried. "Ugh. We need to talk. Alone."

Grabbing his arm, I hauled him out of the living room and up the stairs. I didn't let go until we were behind my locked door.

"Victor, what is up with you? Why are you really here?"

He wandered around my room, picking up random things and putting them down. "What do you mean? You know why I'm here."

"I know why you should be here. To start over and see if we can make it work as a different kind of couple in a different kind of relationship. If that's the reason, I'm all for it. But is it?" I asked, eyes narrowing. "Or are you here to piss on my leg like a dog marking his territory?"

He laughed. "Chill. I'm housetrained."

"I'm serious. What's your endgame?"

Victor jumped, landing flat and comfortable on my bed. "After you left, I tried again to appeal to Mom. Told her our engagement stirred up interest in the other families, and a few were willing to discuss marriage deals. I could let you go on with your Rogue boyfriends and marry someone who knows what it takes to survive in our world."

I stiffened with every word. Victor didn't know what was at stake for me. Even so, I was not pleased to hear he tried again to take it from me.

"Since you're here, I can guess she turned you down again."

He nodded. "She won't approve another match, and she's not messing around. Dear old Mom showed me the papers the lawyers drew up. Dissolving my trust fund. Disinheriting me. All they need is a signature."

Perching on the edge of my mattress, I said, "I'm sorry."

"Are you?" He sounded like he was genuinely asking.

"Yes. I know what it is to lose my family, Victor. It's why I'd marry you even if Martha wasn't paying my tuition. I won't be the reason you lose yours."

Sighing, his eyes fluttered shut. "Why do you have to say things like that? Makes me feel like such an ass."

"You are an ass."

"That's better."

Our eyes met and we chuckled, piercing the heavy mood for a brief moment.

"Anyway," he said, looking away. "Mom won't budge. As much as I wanted to stay pissed at you, you kindly reminded me that I'd be an ass and a hypocrite if I did. I didn't pretend like I had any loyalty to you when we were just two strangers with rings on our fingers. Why would you act like you had any loyalty to me?"

I moved closer, reaching for him. "I'm so glad to hear you—"

"Just answer me something." Victor sat up and looked at me head-on. "Did you hook up with them *after* we agreed to be exclusive and make it work between us?"

"No." I grasped his chin, drawing him closer still. "No."

He searched my face, looking for the slightest hint of dishonesty. I guess he didn't find any because he nodded and leaned back.

"Then, if I can move past the whole 'kissing my brother' thing, I don't have a real reason to end our engagement. You're funny, hot, smart, and can hold your own like no one I've ever met." A lopsided smirk pricked the hairs on the nape of my neck. "I have a feeling our life together will be a lot of things, but never boring."

My mouth opened and closed for a beat, trying to form a response. "Wow," I breathed. "You really are here to give us a try. I don't know what to say."

"Have you seen my place? Of course I'm here to give us a try. I'm not moving into this dump for fun."

I rolled my eyes. "Sorry for your suffering, rich boy."

"It's all good. You and I will be out of here soon enough."

"Out of here?" I frowned. "What do you mean?"

That lopsided smirk widened. "Oh, did I leave that part out? I'm not only here to make up between us. I'm here to get between you and the Rogues."

What did he just say?

"But—"

"Don't worry. Two minutes in the same room with you guys, and how you feel about them was all over your face. If I force you to dump them, you'd only resent me. So I won't," he said, swinging his legs off the bed. "Date them—for now. You can even date them out in the open, and we'll tell everyone we're doing the standard Royal engagement where we get seeing other people out of our system before the *I dos.*

"You've only seen the asshole. You don't know the guy who got the reputation you keep throwing in my face."

Kneeling down, he took my hand and kissed my knuckles. "I'm going to seduce the shit out of you, Sinclair. I give it a month before you're saying *Rogues who*? I'll be the only guy you want."

I found my voice. "I won't forgive you if you try to hurt or sabotage them. They were the only people who were there for Winter. Who tried to protect her. That's bigger than us, Victor, and if you don't get that, we'll never work."

He put up his hands. "Whoa. Who said anything about sabotage? Whatever it is that y'all get up to in here that you're afraid of me seeing, no one is going to find out about it from me. I don't need to resort to underhanded tricks. You'll choose me all on your own."

I snorted. "It amazes me that anyone could be so full of themself. I'm willing to put aside your dozens of terrible first impressions and start over, but forgive doesn't mean forget. There's no way you—"

Victor closed the distance. Catching the insult on my lips, he sealed his on mine.

"Hmmpf!"

He cupped the back of my neck, tipping me back and off-center to a perfectly timed gasp that gave him entrance. The sun burst in the sky—exploding a wave of heat and light that bowled me over.

I was burning under him. Tongues clashing. Hands grasping. Lips battling. And all of it setting off sparks that ignited the flames again and again.

Victor trapped my bottom lip, scraping it slow and agonizing between his teeth. I moaned so wantonly, I teased a blush on my own cheeks. The kiss was amazingly, mind-blowingly, stomach-tighteningly *good*. Victor kissed me like he wanted to draw every ounce of pleasure from my body, and drown me in it.

He drew back and I followed him, whimpering softly as I slipped around his shoulders and held him still.

He tore away so abruptly, I nearly fell off the bed. Eyes huge, I shoved up and took in all the teeth flashing through that smirk.

"Full of myself, am I? Looks like I was being generous with that month." He winked. "Keep the room. I'm cool to bunk anywhere," Victor said, loping out. "Until you invite me to sleep with you all on your own."

"I... You..."

Who the hell knew who I was stuttering to? Victor was long gone—leaving nothing but his searing kiss on my lips, taunting me every time I told myself he had no effect on me.

***

"Are you going today?"

Katie swiped her lip gloss, then puckered at her reflection. Her black fit-and-flare dress looked better suited to the runway than the ethics class she was heading to, but administration only canceled classes in the afternoon. After morning classes, everyone was invited to attend the memorial for Giovanni Natale.

"No," I said. "I don't think I should. One day of classes yesterday, and it was a hell of whispers, stares, and two globs of spit on my shoes from people hissing that I'm a murderer." Katie and I moved up the breakfast line, collecting a few of those mentioned stares on the way. "It's clear some people think the cops got it wrong. If I show up at the memorial, it'll become about me and not Giovanni. I hated the guy, but there's no more revenge to take against him. The least I could do is not turn his send-off into a drama."

"Hate to say it, but I agree with you." Katie claimed two trays and passed one off to me. Seemingly sweet if not for her immediately loading my tray with the cinnamon doughnuts and chocolate muffins she wanted to eat, but instead would nibble off my plate, then leave for me to finish. "It'll pretty much all be Royals, and they're not a fan of you right now. You don't want to know what they're saying in the group chat."

"I do, actually. How bad is it?"

She winced.

That bad.

"They're saying it has to be you because it couldn't have been a Royal. You, Rafael Dumont, Dean, and, like, two other guys were the only non-Royals there. Dean wouldn't do this and Saylor said she was hooking up with Rafael when it all went down."

I bit back a sneer. She wishes she was hooking up with my boyfriend. That was another thing I loved about Rafael. He saw right through the Queen Bee, Saylor Burkhardt.

"Those other Dregs had no beef with Giovanni, while you..." She shrugged helplessly. "Gio dumped Winter brutally and in public. Everyone knows why you'd hate him. Almost everyone is convinced you did it." Her gaze drifted over my shoulder. "And they don't care what the cops say."

I resisted the urge to look. I snuck out early that morning and met up with Katie before the guys woke up. I didn't need a bodyguard that day, but I also didn't need to push my luck. You can sense in the air when people are spoiling for a fight.

"That's all it takes to pin murder on someone?" I asked. "Be a Dreg? It doesn't matter that he screwed more than a few Royals over too? The girlfriend he left to bleed out at the bottom of a cliff? The daughter of a rival he was secretly banging on the side who had a lot to lose if he ever admitted *she* threw his girlfriend off a cliff? Everyone is completely forgetting all those motives."

Katie gave me a serious look as she loaded my plate with bacon. "None of them were alone by the pool with him."

"That we know," I corrected. "I didn't tase myself."

"Look, I believe you." Katie strode off to the drinks section. "I'm just telling you what people are saying. More reason that you're coming to my place after the memorial, and looking through the footage with me. This is bigger than the Royal/Dreg shit. I need to know who came into my house and killed a guy I've known my whole life."

I squeezed her arm. "After the memorial is fine. Meet you by the fountain?"

"No, too crowded. I'll pick you up in the parking lot by your dorm."

That settled, I followed her to a table, set down her second tray, and went to get my own breakfast. I returned with pumpkin bread and a frittata. "How's your mom doing?"

"Still freaked," Katie replied. "She had security doubled and wants me to move back into the main house."

We turned the topic to other things, running down the clock. Katie's, not mine. She had an early meeting with her advisor. I had something to do before class too.

"I'll text you," she said, picking up her stuff to go.

I waved her off and waited.

Waited.

And waited.

The door flew open and in they came. I watched them get their food and leave through the same doors. Gathering my things, I followed.

I didn't have to keep my distance or trail them. I knew exactly where they were going.

Breaking away outside the doors, I took a shortcut to the music hall. It was early enough that there weren't many people on the terrace. I got nasty looks from them all the same when I plopped down at one of the tables.

Saylor got up and planted herself in front of me. "What do you think you're doing? This spot is Royals only."

"That includes me, doesn't it?" I flashed my ring finger—just that finger. "Marrying a Royal makes me a Royal."

"Actually, it doesn't. Especially if you don't make it down the aisle."

I spoke to her but watched the steps. "Is that a threat?"

"Course not." She moved into my line of sight. Saylor was impeccable as usual in a two-tone, black-and-white pleated dress. She wore her hair in a tight bun with little wisps hanging down, framing her face. How could someone be so pretty on the outside and so sour on the inside? It was like biting into a cinnamon bun and finding it filled with pickles. "I'm not stupid enough to threaten a murderer."

I slid off the stairs, focusing on her. "Are you stupid enough to protect one?"

"Excuse me?"

"Don't play innocent. Gabriella's been denying it, but you know your fellow fork-tongued harpy better than anyone. You know she's lying," I sang. "Gabriella pushed Annika off a cliff and left her to die. Natale was cracking under the pressure to come clean after the truth lists. The police were looking at them both as the main suspects, and if he cracked, the shining heiress was going down."

The smirk melted off Saylor's face.

"Have you asked yourself where Gabriella was when Natale was attacked?"

"She wasn't anywhere near him," Saylor snapped. I caught her quick glance at her table where Everleigh, Piper, and Gabriella were waiting. And watching us. "She was inside dancing with everyone else."

"Riigght," I drew out. "Inside that dark, packed, oversized fort with dozens of people too busy grinding up on their dates to keep eyes on her. There's no way she slipped away for a second."

"Slipped away to do what? Kill some guy she wouldn't touch on a dare? Gio and Gabby hated each other. Some sad, lonely Dreg made up all those lies on the truth lists, but if you really want people to believe they're real, *Pussy Muncher*, I'm sure the honor board would be happy to boot your ass for cheating on your SATs."

I hummed. "Are you sure they hated each other? Absolutely positively positive?"

"Yes."

"Then, what was she doing with Natale out at the Bluffs?"

"She wasn't out at the Bluffs. Never went near it that night."

"Then who messed up her face?"

"She took an elbow to the nose during a sale at Maxfield."

I laughed out loud. "And you bought that load of bullshit? Yikes, Saylor, I thought you were smart."

Her eyes narrowed to slits. "So this is your play? Throw suspicion on everyone else to cover up what you did to Gio? You can't possibly think that's going to work."

"This isn't a play or a game." Movement out of the corner of my eye drew me back to the stairs. Up they came, locked in heated conversation. "It's just a reminder of the lesson you taught me, Burkhardt. Royals will do anything to protect their money, reputation, and status. You guys came after my sister to protect a secret. If you heartless cockroaches could do that to her, why would Natale be any safer?"

I got up—our noses inches away as we stared each other down. "Giovanni told me something very interesting before I was knocked out and he was *murdered*."

Something flashed in Saylor's eyes.

"The only tie stronger than money is a secret," I whispered, repeating what she told me that day in her mansion. "And he knew a tasty one. You should ask your friends what they're hiding."

Pulling out my phone, I opened the pictures of Gabby bouncing on Giovanni's lap and shoved them right in her face. "I mean, what *else* they're hiding."

"Wha—? That's not—"

I blew past her.

"Come back here!"

Ignoring her, I marched straight for their table and pulled out a seat. Levi, Owen, and Wesley stopped chewing and stared at me like I was a corpse that fell out of the sky—with hostility and disgust.

"Are you lost, Sinclair?" Levi hissed. "Get your ass up and walk away."

"Oh, I will. Trust me, I don't want to be near you three. My skin crawls just looking at you. I'm here because there's something you need to know."

Wesley rose from his seat. I bet he thought he was intimidating towering over me. "There's nothing you've got to say that we need to hear, bitch. Get—"

Rolling my eyes, I flapped a hand in his face. "Sit down and shut up. The person who killed Ashton Scott will definitely want to hear this, and yes..." I grinned as Wesley paled. "I know it was one of you."

Levi's face wiped blank. "What are you talking about? If you came here to spin bullshit, we're not interested."

"Again," I snapped. "Shut up. I'm not finished."

I made a show of taking a deep breath and continued. "Anyway, one of you killed Ashton because you thought he turned against your little brotherhood. Welp, he didn't. He was framed." I beamed. "By me."

"What?" Owen hissed, face crumpling.

"Oh, yeah. That was all me. I hung you from the ceiling, Chicken Penis. I poisoned Wesley. I spread those truth lists. And I framed Ashton for all of it." The words dropped from my lips so easily, I could've been talking about my last English assignment. "I was hoping one, or all, of you would turn on that filthy rapist, and wow! You did big-time."

"You're lying," Levi said, his voice flat. "You wouldn't admit any of this if it was true. You're trying to manipulate us."

"No manipulation. No games. No tricks. I'm coming right out and telling you so that from now on, we understand each other." My smile wiped away. "You underestimated Winter and the people who loved her. It hasn't even been a month, and I've destroyed your reputations, your standing among the Royals, and had one of you put in the ground. I bet you didn't see this coming when you took those dares for the T.O.D. Club."

Wesley dropped hard in his seat. "How do you know about the c—?"

"Shut up, Wesley!" Levi barked.

I cocked a brow. "Why are you yelling at him? I know you disgusting, scuttling roaches took dares and big prizes to make Winter's life hell, then you found the person behind them and squeezed them for more."

Owen's and Wesley's expressions weren't nearly so cool. Their eyes darted around, faces cycling through a hundred emotions. But I looked at Levi.

Only at Levi.

"Here's how it's going to work," I said, laying out the first part of my new plan. The one I didn't tell the guys about because they would've tried to stop me. "You three have to pay for what you did to her. That's just how it has to be. The attacks will keep coming. I'll continue ruining your lives until you have nothing and no one left, then, I'll kill you."

Levi didn't blink.

"But—and here's where I show you mercy that you never showed Winter—whichever one of you comes to me first and tells me who turned you on Winter and why, you'll get to live. Your life," I forced through clenched teeth. "That's more than you left my sister."

I rose. "That special offer goes to only one of you, so be quick. If there's one thing you know about each other, it's that you three look out for your own self-interests."

Wesley got up. "Sinclair—"

His hand flashed. Gripping his shoulder, Levi slowly but firmly returned Wesley to his seat. "You're bluffing. Someone came after us. Maybe it wasn't Ashton, but it sure as hell wasn't you. You aren't strong enough to hang Owen from the ceiling. And you're not smart enough to plan all those attacks. But I will give you credit," he said, lips stretching across that horrible face. "There's a shred of cunning in you that has you sitting here, bold as shit, trying to turn someone's plot to your advantage. It's cute, but it's not going to work.

"Get up and walk away, Sinclair. The smell of Dreg so early in the morning is putting me off my breakfast."

"He knows I'm not lying." I gazed at Levi but spoke to the others. "He barely hid his flinch when I said T.O.D. Club. There's one reason he wants you to think I'm lying. If I'm willing to do what I say, then he won't risk either one of you getting to me first."

Owen forced a laugh. "Forget him. I know you're lying. What kind of idiot would admit all of this to our face? We'll just go to the cops."

"With what proof? There'll never be any evidence. I mean... I killed Ashton Scott without touching the knife." Laughing, I turned my back, striding away.

I felt no small amount of pleasure at seeing Saylor hissing at a wide-eyed, headshaking, hand-waving Gabriella.

My plan was still unfolding. Truthfully, I didn't know all that I was going to do, but I did know one thing. The Rogues and I were stronger together.

All of their talents combined with my ruthlessness made us a hard enemy to beat.

But the Royals. With their money and their ties and their nasty little club. They were stronger together too. The first step in bringing them down was snapping those ties.

I'd have Saylor and her crew arguing and suspicious of each other in a week. When all four of them were just as alone and isolated as my sister, then I'd strike.

As for Owen, Wesley, and Levi. I told them the plan without trick or guile. The attacks would never stop. I will ruin them, and by doing so, they'll turn on each other—afraid the other will rat them out to save their own skin. That's the thing about monsters banding together. They can never fully relax... because they're surrounded by monsters.

I rode my high all the way to English class. Yeah, the guys would flip when I told them. Plus, Wesley, Levi, or Owen was likely planning to do something stupid to get back at me, but I wasn't afraid.

This war was ultimately between me and the Phantom. I made my first move. Now it was their turn.

"Grab your seats. Settle down."

I pulled my head out of my thoughts, coming to when I stepped inside Professor Anthony's class. Our eyes met across the room and ping-ponged away. It's hard to believe I had time to obsess about our afternoon at his beach house in between hurting over my fight with Mom, plotting how to take down the Royals, thrumming on my first time with Cato, and processing the fact that my fiancé was set on seducing me. A lot was going on, but I made time.

"Luna." Victor waved me over. "Saved you a seat."

My eyes slitted even as my lips tingled. That ass had been smirking at me nonstop since that kiss. In the name of keeping Victor out of my bed, Rafael gave up his second bedroom which doubled as his music room and the home to his record collection. I knew what a big deal that was for him.

He had it soundproofed to keep life's jangling, painful noise out. No earplugs or hearing aids. In there, it was just him and his mother's favorite bands.

I felt so terrible, I tried again to give Victor my room and said I'd sleep on the couch. All the guys said no to that, including Victor. He said he'd sleep on the couch before forcing me on it—which was the kind of considerate bull-shit I didn't have time for. If Victor wanted to start acting like a decent human being, fine by me. It was the fact that he thought he could make me fall so in love with him that I forget about the Rogues that pissed me off. What had to happen to a guy for him to become so convinced he was God's gift to women?

When you've got muscles stacked on muscles, the face of a deity, and more money than one, I bet the cockiness comes easily.

Victor patted the seat beside him, smiling away.

"Behave," I warned.

"I'm totally behaved. What do you think I'm going to do? Kiss you and make you make that sound again in front of everyone?"

"I didn't make a sound!"

Chuckling, he draped his arm around the back of my seat, resting his hand on my shoulder. I started as he rubbed slow circles on my skin. "Do you want to lose that hand?"

"Not buying the hostility, sweetie pie. You're the one who mounted me and begged me to take you back."

"I'm going to stab you in your sleep."

Victor laughed out loud, but thankfully, he stopped caressing me. His touch was doing strange things to my body temperature. Took a second to notice he didn't move his hand.

I glanced up and found Adonis looking right at us. Did he see his brother laughing away while he touched me? Even if he didn't, he certainly saw his arm around me then.

"Ugh, is this still happening?"

I tensed up tighter than the muscled arm against my back.

"Victor, don't you know what happened this weekend?" Iris leaned over from her seat behind us and snatched Victor's hand off. "It's all over campus. Sinclair and Giovanni walked into an empty room, and only one of them walked out. She's a killer!"

I whirled around. "I'm not—"

"Miss Dalton," Professor Anthony barked. "That's enough. Normally, I wouldn't let rumors and nasty gossip take up a minute of class time, but I'm going to put an end to this right now.

"The police investigation into the tragic death of Giovanni Natale is ongoing, but the detectives on the case did release a statement to the dean that he passed on to the faculty. Miss Sinclair is *not* a suspect. Evidence proved she was attacked by the person who was responsible, and is a victim as well.

"Unless a single one of you has proof that contradicts the findings of seasoned detectives and an entire forensic team, there is no reason for you to spread the bald-face lie that Miss Sinclair is guilty. Understood, Miss Dalton?"

"I— But I didn't—"

"But if any of you do choose to repeat that allegation knowing it's a lie," Adonis said, sweeping a hard glare over the auditorium. "I will take that as your choice to violate the honor code, which has clear statements against bullying and slander. Any questions?"

"No, Professor Anthony," they muttered.

"Will we have this issue again?"

"No, Professor Anthony."

"Excellent. Then, let's begin."

I sunk back in my seat. The hot retort that bubbled up for Iris faded off my tongue, and tears rose in its place. Adonis said he had my back. That he would discover what he could about the T.O.D. Club and shut it down, but him saying it and then actually watching him shut down the whole class and put Iris in her place was another thing entirely.

I didn't want to think of Winter. My mind went there all the same. She didn't have any of this. There was no Professor Anthony threatening to invoke the honor code if they didn't shut up with their rumors and lies. There was no Victor wielding his power as a Wilson to deliver the only punishment these bastards understood—dragging her bullies' status lower than a Dreg's.

She didn't even have the Rogues. They could have done so much more for her. They wanted to, but Winter said no for reasons I might never know. It's been hard for me, and I'm not alone. Winter was, and I finally understood how much.

My sister was so very alone.

"—no writing assignment this week."

I wiped my eyes, trying to pull myself out of my thoughts.

"This is a difficult time for you all," Professor Anthony said. He leaned on his desk, legs crossed at the ankles. "A time that leads to reflection. I'd like us to do that today in a literary capacity. What is great literature? Is it stories that redefine or create a genre? Is it simply a tale that invokes connection? Something that we've felt or experienced put to words in a way we can't?

"I want you to think—truly think about what separates good writing and great writing?" He checked his watch. "I'll give you ten minutes. Choose your book, your series, your poem, your essay, and then tell us why."

Silence fell, broken only by the faint *scritch-scritch-scritch* of pens and pencils. I sat—unmoving and staring at a blank page.

"Time," Professor Anthony called. "All right. Who'd like to go first?"

Dozens of hands went up.

"Mr. Westbrook."

"I chose *The Inheritance Cycle* by Christopher Paolini," replied one of Victor's rugby buddies.

Snickers broke out.

"Enough," Adonis said, bringing it to an abrupt stop. For all that he had less than ten years on me, Professor Anthony was commanding. He stood there in his simple button-up shirt and khakis, radiating a confidence that most people never got in their lifetime.

Sexy.

I jerked in my seat, startled by the sudden, random thought. *No. No, no, no. Do not go there, Sinclair. I've got one confusing relationship with a Wilson brother. I don't need another.*

"Why that series?" he asked.

"I didn't read fantasy books. Too long. I didn't think any story could be interesting enough to read for five hundred pages, but then I picked up that first book and that was it," he said. "I've devoured dozens of fantasy books since then. It's my favorite genre.

"The last four years have been studying, tests, homework, and rugby practice. All to get in Regalia U. The pressure was intense, but kicking back with some *Game of Thrones*—that's when I turned my brain off and got to chill. That's great literature to me," he said, snapping his fingers. "It's when you're stressed as all hell and nothing else works to get you out of your head like that one great book or author."

"Interesting," Adonis said. He moved to the board and wrote *takes you out of your head/reality* on the board. "Anyone agree?"

Nearly every hand went up, including mine. We all knew what it was like to be stuck in hard or stressful times. Anything that could distract us from the pain for even a moment was amazing. No wonder drugs were so popular.

Professor Anthony went around the room, asking everyone what they thought made great literature. I expected he was coming to me after Victor spoke, though my hand wasn't up.

"Miss Sinclair," he said. "What's your pick?"

I flicked up from my still blank page. "*A Series of Unfortunate Events* by Daniel Handler."

He hummed. "I haven't read it but I know the series. What about it makes it great?"

"It's not," I said, voice flat. "Not in any of the ways we've talked about. But I chose it because it taught me my most valuable lesson at a young age.

"We don't all get a happy ending."

Chapter Four

Wilder waited for me outside my last class of the morning. My brows popped at the sight of him.

Wilder left his tight tees and jeans at home. In their place was a black suit—just as fitted and hugging him in all the right places. The guy would be more handsome than he had a right to be in a used trash bag with empty tissue boxes for shoes. Put him in a suit and the girl walking next to me literally walked into a wall—gaping at him.

"What did you do?"

I broke from the flow of traffic and grabbed his hand. "Yell at me out of earshot."

Wilder waited until we got as far as the front steps. "What did you *do*, Sinclair? You know I'm hacked into those bastards' accounts. Levi, Owen, *and* Wesley sent messages to their parents that they need increased security because Luna Sinclair threatened them."

"Wow. They ran to Mommy and Daddy? Bitch move."

Wilder tugged me down the steps and under a tree. "What happened?"

There was no hiding it and I wasn't going to anyway. I told him everything that went down that morning with *those bastards*.

Wilder goggled at me.

I goggled back. "Never seen you make that face before. I really have shocked you."

"Let me get this straight," he said slowly. "You told those three that you were behind all the attacks against them, that you framed Ashton Scott, and that you'd keep coming after them until they're all dead unless one of them tells you who the Phantom is."

"That sums it up, yes."

"Why?" he gritted.

"I told you that we needed a new plan. I also told you that they were going to find out I'm coming after them anyway. The only way to get to the Phantom is through them. Why pretend like I can do any of this from the shadows anymore?"

A hard, piercing glint lit his eyes. "That's not why you didn't tell us."

I tried to hold his gaze, and looked away. "No, it's not. I'm sorry, Wilder, but if you knew, you would've stopped me."

"Yeah, I would've stopped you." Wilder looked around, then snaked an arm around my waist. He carried me off, waiting to speak when there weren't people around us. "In general, it's wise not to tell the people you're going to kill, that you're going to kill them."

"I had to do something. Scare them into turning on the Phantom like with Giovanni."

"But what happens if one of them does talk?" he asked. "I assume you've given up on the endgame, because if those guys end up dead after telling their parents you threatened them, you're going down for it."

My jaw clenched. "The endgame will never change. I don't care if the Phantom paid them a trillion dollars. They claimed their fucking prize and drove my sister to kill herself. They gave her rapist an alibi! Their fate is sealed."

He blew out a breath, dropping his head toward the sun. "Okay, okay. I know what you're trying to do, Luna. Winter was your sister. Everything they've got coming to them they deserve but..." Wilder grasped my shoulder, turning me to face him. "You need to answer something for me right now."

"What?"

"Do you want to see the other side of this... or is this your final task before you join Winter?"

I jerked back like he struck me. My eyes filled. "Why would you ask me something like that?"

"Because," he said softly. Wilder moved up my arm, gently cupping my cheek. "I've been hacking emails for a long time. I've read a couple that forced me to anonymously contact the school counselor and tell them that person needed help. You're being the reckless I've only seen when the person doesn't think they have anything left to lose.

"I'll go as far as you ask me to go, Luna. I'll sit in that jail cell and not regret a damn thing. But I won't help you self-destruct. I'll never do that."

Sighing, my eyes fluttered shut. I couldn't resist leaning into his touch. "How could you think I want to leave you guys? You're the ones who made me see there is another side to this, and I'll be on it with you, toasting the end to the Royals and her killers." I threaded my fingers through his. "This isn't me being reckless, Wilder. Honestly, I've never felt more in control.

"While their tight little threesome is covering for each other and the Phantom, we'll never get anywhere. I have to make them doubt each other because when they did, Ashton Scott died. One of them did it," I said, "and the other two are looking at him close now, wondering what else he's willing to do to protect himself from the next wave of attacks. Because they're sure as fuck coming."

Wilder studied me for a long time. "All right. I'll spread suspicion in those ranks. Easily. But no more going off on your own. I know you took the blame for the paintballs, truth lists, and stealing the EpiPen to protect us, but I'm betting they didn't buy it."

"They didn't," I admitted.

"Levi is a violent piece of shit, but he's not an idiot. By now, he's figured out that we're helping you. Rafael is the one who told him Ashton Scott was behind the truth lists. We're in this together, Luna. I'll back up your plan and I'll make sure the guys do too, but no secrets. Promise me."

You know you're wrong when the conspiracy theorist who took your door off the hinges and checked you for a brain implant makes the most sense.

"No secrets."

He nodded, trusting me. Which made me fall a little harder for him. Wilder trusted no one. It was a huge deal for him to take me at my word. I wouldn't betray that.

"We'll talk later. Plan our next move." He checked his watch. "I've got to get to the memorial, but I'm not going anywhere until you're safe in the Gallery. Levi, Owen, and Wesley just became a lot more dangerous than they were twelve hours ago."

"Are you sure you should go?" I asked as we set off.

"You're going to look at the footage with Katie tonight, right?"

"Yeah."

"I haven't hacked her or the cops 'cause there's no reason to risk the heat when she offered to show it to you anyway. Get names for everyone her cameras pick up around the pool, and I'll get names for everyone who shows up at the memorial. I'm going because if I was the Phantom, that's where I'd be. Bawling and pretending to be another grieving friend."

I bobbed my head. "Good thinking. You know, I told Saylor Gabriella had a motive to kill Natale to mess with her, but while I was talking, I kind of convinced myself. I assumed his death had to do with the Phantom because he came to me in such a panic about them. But Gabriella was there that night too," I said.

"Giovanni told me the police were going to interview him first thing the next morning. He was the prime suspect in Ashton's death because he was the only one of them to leave his girlfriend to die at the bottom of a cliff. What if Gabriella was afraid he'd go in there and say it was her, not him? All her lies and lawyers couldn't help her if both Annika and Giovanni put the blame on her."

"Hmm. It is possible," he confessed. "We did assume it had to be the Phantom, but Giovanni knew things that could destroy other people. The guy he paid to do his assignments for one. Royal Giovanni could buy his way into academic probation, but Dreg Andy Elrod would be expelled."

"That's who cheated for him?" Wilder nodded. "Students kill themselves to get in Regalia U. Not to mention an expulsion for cheating on his record would ruin his life. That's motive for sure."

"The only other people I can think of are Wesley, Owen, and Levi," Wilder said. "Natale was the weak link, and that link was about to be interrogated by the cops. Levi in particular would've taken drastic steps to make sure he didn't talk, but I doubt it was one of them."

Surprisingly, I found myself agreeing. I knew all three of them were capable of shutting Giovanni up for good, and I'm sure Giovanni knew too.

"I doubt he told them he was going to confess to me," I said. "Which is the only reason they'd risk following him onto Katie's guarded property and crashing a party they weren't invited to, around dozens of witnesses, to get him."

"Not just that, but everything about Friday night screamed murder of opportunity." Wilder drifted closer avoiding a bike rider. His sweet, bergamot cologne wafted over me, tickling my brain. Wilder always smelled like something you could gulp down with honey. "The killer used your stun gun to attack both of you. If he or she knew in advance what Giovanni was going to do, they would've brought their own weapon instead of leaving it to chance."

I shook my head. "That just confirms it, doesn't it? The killer was definitely on the guest list. They were there, they saw Giovanni follow me to the pool, and they acted fast. The wild thing is the one person we know for sure didn't do it, is among the most vile Royals of them all. Saylor was with Rafael when it all happened.

"One cleared. Eighty suspects to go."

"We'll figure this out." The Gallery loomed up ahead. "We just said the killer didn't have a plan. They were desperate to stop Giovanni, so they acted fast. Which means they made a mistake. That mistake will get them caught—by us."

I paused before our door and kissed his cheek. Wilder raised a brow at me like I did something curious, teasing me to giggle. "I'll tell you what Katie and I find. Good luck at the memorial."

"Stay inside. Don't let anyone in but us. Decontaminate in the hallway."

"I'll miss you too," I called at his back.

Chuckling, I went inside. Things between me and Wilder were undefined, but that didn't worry me. At first it did after we kissed and then he found me in bed with Rafael. I'd thought there'd be jealousy, tension, or an awkward talk about having to choose between him and his friend.

None of the above.

I still wanted to have that talk with all of them. I couldn't go on sleeping and hooking up with these guys without defining what we mean to each other. Especially with my flipping fiancé living down the hall.

Wilder and I will talk. He has to know that even though our situation is complicated, my feelings for him aren't. That kiss knocked the wind clean out of me. I wanted to—

My thoughts stopped dead in their tracks. Frozen, I did little more than stare at him—lips parted to scream an alarm that no one else would hear.

The man calmly set his teacup down and cleared his throat. Lifting his chin, he gestured for me to take the seat across from him.

"Hello, Miss Sinclair-Bowden. Please, join me."

"Who are you?" I backed out of the kitchen. "How did you get in here?"

His brow crept up to his salt-and-pepper wings. "You don't know? I'm told the resemblance is uncanny."

He said it and I saw it. Wavy, raven locks. Enigmatic, flinty green eyes. An air of danger that clung to him like Wilder's spicy-sweet cologne.

"Leon Dumont."

Cato and Rafael's father raised his cup. "Pleasure. Now that introductions are out of the way, you can stop preparing to run."

I halted in my tracks, face warming. "Your sons aren't here."

"Of course they aren't. I'm here to see you."

"See me? Why w-would you be here to see me?" I tried to say that confidently and managed a stuttering rasp.

There was one stark difference between Leon Dumont and his sons. The cold, biting chill leaking from his eyes. He tracked me unblinkingly like one tracks a fly—waiting for the right moment to strike.

That such eyes could be within that handsome, lined face threw me further off-center. Even with the touch of silver in his thick hair and neatly trimmed beard, there was an ageless beauty about him that drew me like a moth to the flame. Who would think someone so beautiful would be dangerous? You don't fear a rose or a butterfly. You get in close—too close. Then the trap you didn't see coming strikes from behind.

"Miss Sinclair-Bowden," Mr. Dumont said, all trace of pleasantry gone. "Sit."

I took a breath and didn't release it. Slowly, I approached the table, pulled out a chair, and sat down. Mr. Dumont reached behind him, and got the kettle and extra teacup that was apparently waiting for me. I swallowed hard as he poured.

"So, this is it," I rasped. "Framing me didn't work, so they sent you."

"I beg your pardon?"

"You're here to kill me." It wasn't a question.

His expression gave nothing away. "Why would I want to kill you, young Luna?"

"Because they put that stun gun in my hand to get rid of two problems, but here I am. I was fooling myself thinking the killer wasn't the Phantom, but someone else who took their shot. They got rid of Natale, and now they've sent you here to get rid of me. The Sinclair-Bowden problem finally ended for good."

Leon Dumont listened without reaction or interruption. When I finished, he simply finished fixing my cup and slid it over.

"Funny," I spat, lip curling at the tea. "I thought your wife was the poisoner."

He chuckled. "Poison?" Leon dipped a spoon in my tea and brought it to his lips. He drank the harmless sip with open amusement in his eyes. "I don't know where you got such ideas about me, or my sweet Sasha, but I mean you no harm. Even if I were what you seem to think I am, I'd like to believe I'd have an age cutoff. Any number that ends in *teen* or under, for example."

My muscles didn't unwind. "Then why are you here?"

"I've come to meet you. Something wrong with the tea?"

I flicked down. Was this a test or proof of control? He wanted me to sit, I sat. He wanted me to drink, I would drink. What command was he working his way up to?

"Yes," I said. "I usually take it with honey."

"Ah, yes. Of course you do. Young people these days. You're so used to everything being altered or simplified for you, that it's almost an affront to consume naturally. You don't have to go to a record store for your music. You just tap on your phone." He swirled his finger around his rim. "You don't have to grow, tend, and harvest the leaves, so you think nothing of destroying the flavor of your store-bought bags with a microwave and bottle of honey."

"Wow. You feel very strongly about tea."

Mr. Dumont laughed. "I feel strongly about things being done the right way. My sons have been pestering me for information for you. If there's something you'd like to know, it's only right that you ask me yourself. Better yet, that we go through the trouble of introductions."

My ears pricked up. *Is he saying what I think he's saying?*

"Yes," I said, sitting up straighter. "I agree completely. Actually, I wanted to speak with you in person. But since you already know the question, let me ask straight out if you're going to answer it."

"I will not."

"Hmm." Getting up, I crossed to the cabinet over the sink and got the honey. "Now I see why the guys wanted to spare me you turning me down to my face. You didn't need to come here for that even if there's a right way to do things, so I'm guessing you're really here to check me out." I returned to my seat, feeling the weight of his gaze on me—though I tried not to make direct eye contact. Like the sun, you were meant to glance over them, not stare directly. "What do you want to know about me?"

Leon rested his elbow on the table, making me automatically lean back. His lips curved up. He caught that.

"What prompted you and my sons to ask me such a question?"

"Saylor Burkhardt." I wasn't going to lie. What would be the point? "She showed me the legacy of secrets, deals, and lies that binds all the Royals in Regalia going back to when it was first founded."

Leon sipped his tea. "Why would she do a thing like that?"

"I wasn't getting the hint. She wants me out of Regalia, so she told me why it killed my sister. Winter discovered a secret about one of the people on that chart. Threatening one of them can threaten half a dozen other families and their ties. Saylor wanted me to know I had more enemies than I could count. Or see coming."

"Where is this document now?"

"I burned it."

Rafael's spitting image paused with the cup halfway to his lips. "Excuse me?"

"I set the damn thing on fire while she screamed. It was deeply satisfying."

Mr. Dumont looked at me, and laughed out loud. It was harsh, sharp, and over as soon as it happened, but it was a laugh. "You burned it? Oh, Miss Luna. I'm starting to see why my boys are so taken with you. But I don't see why you thought I could help." His humor dried up instantly. "As you saw yourself, there's a web of secrets and lies connecting all the families of Regalia. Why would I know the specific one you need?"

"Because this one is somehow connected to Winter and our family. She was protecting us. That's the only reason I can think of for why she didn't out the truth when they started coming after her. Do you know anything about a secret involving Jack Bowden or Eloise Sinclair?"

"I did not know either name before news reached me of your poor sister's death. I certainly do not know of a secret she discovered."

I eyed him. "But you would say that even if you did."

Smiling, he raised his cup. "Touché."

"If you don't know, you could find out," I said, leaning in. "My family would pay any price you ask to know the truth. For Winter, we'd do anything."

"I'm sure you would. I am sympathetic to what your family has gone through. I do not keep up with the antics of college students, but news of her death rippled through the community." My throat constricted. "It's always a tragedy when a promising young person takes their life."

He sighed. "I say this so you do not think me unfeeling, because I must turn down your request. Your family cannot hire me at any price."

"Why not?" I snapped.

"Because if I was what you think I am, we'd run into that issue I mentioned earlier. I do not take jobs involving children, and no matter what the government has deemed, I consider everyone running around this campus a child in every way that counts."

"They weren't children when they tortured my sister to death! They made her feel like she had no way out, and it was all under the orders of some faceless bastard. I will find out who!"

"I sincerely hope you do," he said calmly, "but giving you a name so that you can do what I see in your eyes you want to do... is no different than me carrying out the sentence myself. If this person is my son's age, I will not give you that name. And seeing as I do not give refunds, I would most likely be setting up your family for disappointment as well as a huge financial loss. This is why my answer must be no."

I took hold of my tongue, biting back an unwise retort. What could I say that would make him change his mind? I didn't have the power or money to make this guy do anything. Crazy thing was that under normal circumstances, I'd agree with his rule. It was certainly good for me that the Phantom couldn't hire my boyfriends' dad to kill me.

But this wasn't normal circumstances, and no one could look in Levi's dead eyes and see a child. I wondered what I'd see the day I finally looked in the Phantom's eyes.

"Is there anything you can do to help me? I've been looking for something called the T.O.D. Club. Have you heard of it?"

Something flashed in his eyes. "Why ask me? If you know of the club's existence, a member must have told you about it. Ask them."

"That member died before they could give me any details, so I'll ask you." I peered at him through my lashes. "Because if you know of its existence, that makes you a member."

Leon shook his head. "Not quite. I know it exists because I know a lot of things about a lot of things. It's one of Regalia University's old secret societies. I also know the member list doesn't include graduates. Grown men don't play truth or dare."

I inclined my head, accepting this. Not even I could picture Saylor's, Everleigh's, or Piper's parents sitting around, taking payments to play vicious pranks and spread sex secrets. There was something very college about this stupid club. Make that high school.

"What can you tell me?" I asked.

"I can tell you that you've entered the arena, Miss Sinclair-Bowden. The lions have been unleashed, the audience is braying for your blood, and you have no weapons." He pinned me with a look. "But you do have my sons as a shield. I'd be very careful of your next moves from here on out. There'll be casualties if you self-destruct."

"That's why you wanted to see me." I finally poured honey in my cooling tea. "To warn me off Rafael and Cato. I wouldn't have expected that."

"It surprises you that I'm a concerned parent?"

"You cut them off and kicked them out of the house at eighteen."

"Naturally," he drawled. "A man cannot build an empire on his father's shoulders."

"Okay, but you raised them to build a specific kind of empire. The outside-the-law kind," I said. "You know a lot of things about a lot of things, so you know how they got the name Rogues. Between Rafael blowing things up and Cato being Cato, you haven't seen the need to play concerned parent." A slow smile spread across my face. "Begs the question, why are you here now? Checking me out, seeing what I know, and warning me that I'm starting a war that'll be dangerous for your sons. More dangerous than all the other wars they've started all on their own.

"You do know the secret," I dropped. "You know who came after Winter, and that *child* or not, they're dangerous. You can't have your sons in the middle of their war. Tell me who it is."

Mr. Dumont drained his cup in no kind of a hurry. "Oh yes," he said, matching my smile. "I see why my boys like you." He stood up. "I'm afraid I must get going."

"No, wait—" I jumped to my feet.

"It was lovely to meet you. I hope we do this again soon."

"No!" I seized his arm, heart rocking into my throat when he slowly turned and zeroed in on my grip. I held on tighter. "Please, Mr. Dumont. She was my sister. My *sister*. I will never give up on this. I won't stop until everyone who hurt her feels what she did before *they die*! If you care so much about your sons, you'll help me end this war quick and quiet."

I glared into his eyes. "Because my way is going to be messy."

"Compelling argument." Dumont peeled me off of him. "But I know nothing that can help you."

"You're lying." No wonder Wilder thought I had a death wish. Watching the hit man's face harden, I asked if I did too. "But what would I expect from someone who won't even help his sons find their mother's killer. Their own mother. You've sent them off to fight that war alone too. You're just like every other Royal in this hellmouth. Nothing matters more than your secrets."

Frost darkened his green pools. Closing the distance, Dumont shrunk me where I stood. Oh yes, I was trying to get myself killed.

"This, Miss Sinclair-Bowden, is why in my eyes you're no more than a child. You hear that I refused to give my sons the list of suspects in their mother's murder and think I'm a monster. It never occurred to you that I refuse to tell them the many ruthless, unstable enemies I collected in my youth because I know they would run straight at them with the same recklessness. I've already lost my wife," he hissed, getting in my face. "A true monster would risk the two most important gifts she ever gave me."

My lips parted and nothing came out. He was right. It didn't occur to me that... he was protecting them.

"It is not the job of adults to stop you from making a mess. It's our job to not put the bucket of mud in one hand, the gun in the other, and send you off. I will protect what's mine at any cost—even my life." Leon stared down his nose at me. "In the midst of your righteous indignation, you should ask yourself if your sister was trying to do the same."

"What?" I rasped.

"You said yourself that she wouldn't go through hell to protect some Royal's secret. She would do it for you. To protect *you*." He gestured to me. "Knowing that, how could this war of yours be what she wanted? How could putting yourself and my sons in danger be what she wanted?"

He backed away. "Perhaps this is another hard decision an adult needed to make for you. I will not help you, Luna. I will not invalidate that poor girl's sacrifice, and make her death in vain.

"Goodbye."

I could do nothing—say nothing as he walked out as silently as he came in. I reached for my seat and missed, collapsing hard on the tile floor.

How could this war of yours be what she wanted?

It wasn't what Winter wanted. Her note made that clear in no uncertain terms. She told me about Levi, Ashton, and the rest to save me a lifetime of wondering why. She also asked me to promise on a thousand jellybeans that I wouldn't do anything about it.

"This isn't what you wanted, but I'm doing this for you," I whispered. "Aren't I?"

***

"Hey, what's up with you?"

I shook myself, coming to. Leon Dumont played a broken record in my mind—filling me with doubt and shame. All I kept thinking is *Winter doesn't want this. I'm breaking my last promise to my sister.*

"This is kind of important." Katie gestured to her laptop. "Am I boring you?"

"No, I just didn't realize how hard it would be to make anyone out. The camera gives a great angle of all the half-naked guys battling it out over the pool, and the huge crowd watching them, but they're all blocking the entrance to the indoor pool. I can't see over them to who might've gone inside."

Katie groaned, slumping against her bed. We went over the footage three times from four different angles. On any other night, the coverage would be perfect and we'd have a life-sentence shot of someone walking from the house and into the indoor pool. But the night when dozens of people are running, dancing, and jumping all over the place...

"This is hopeless," she said. "I mean, I figured it wouldn't be easy since the cops haven't arrested anyone yet, but not one camera picked up a thing? Are you sure you don't remember anything about who attacked you?"

I shook my head. "They got me from behind. My vision was going out before I even hit the floor. At least we can eliminate people right off the start. That's Dean, isn't it?" I pointed to a handsome guy laughing over beers with his buddies. Time stamp said that was a minute before I went lights out. "Good news. You're not hooking up with a cold-blooded murderer."

She rolled her eyes. "Great," Katie drew out, then sobered. "No, that is great. All these deaths, attacks, and truth lists. I've been feeling like I can't trust anyone."

I gave her a sad smile. Never heard Katie talk like this before, but then I was pretty sure her life had been on the right side of perfect for a long time. Then, her mom gets cancer, we lose Winter, she starts seeing the Royal Wenches for who they really are, Ashton is murdered, Giovanni is murdered, and the bullying and viciousness on campus hasn't let up for a second. That would knock some sobering reality into anyone.

"Do you see anything that could help?" she asked.

"I don't see crashers, but I don't know everyone in your class. Do you see anyone that shouldn't be there?"

Squinting, she leaned in close. "Hard to make out, but no. No one that was disinvited except for Saylor, Gabby, Piper, and Everleigh. But we've been friends forever. I don't blame Nick for letting them in. He thought they didn't need an invitation."

"Would he have thought that for Giovanni? We still don't know how he crashed."

Katie was shaking her head before I finished the sentence. "The only time Gio was ever at my house was to party. Otherwise, we weren't really friends. There is absolutely no reason Nick would just wave him in."

He wouldn't, would he? Especially when the guy was high and dressed for a soup kitchen, not a party.

"We could be making it too complicated," I said. "Maybe he hopped in someone's trunk and let them ride him through the gates. He was desperate to talk to me. Figures he did something desperate to get in."

"Yeah." I felt her gaze on the side of my head. "Why was he desperate to talk to you? You never said."

"Guilty conscience. Between the truth lists, his car getting blown up, his money stolen, Gabriella, Annika, and expulsion hanging over his head, he realized karma was catching up to him. He came to admit what he did to Winter."

"That's it? That's what was so urgent he had to crash my party and end up dead in my pool? Seems like he could've called you."

"Maybe he wasn't such a complete shitbag because he knew this was a conversation to have in person. Although, he wasn't making any sense." I purposely didn't meet her eyes. "He said something about a dare club and a high prize. I think he was trying to tell me someone dared him to do it, but that doesn't make any sense, does it? He had *two* girlfriends at the time. Why would they sit quiet while he slept with my sister for some stupid dare?" Then, I looked at her—narrowing on her normal expression. "Do you know what he was talking about? Ever heard of a dare club on campus?"

Katie shook her head, lips pushed out. "No, nothing. But I wouldn't be surprised. The guys around here get up to all kinds of disgusting shit. We just found out thanks to those lists that they've been passing locker room nudes of the girls. Some nasty-ass club where they dare each other to treat women like trash?" she snorted. "Doesn't surprise me."

I analyzed every line of her speech. Nothing rang as false but still... I couldn't say that I knew Katie long enough to tell when she was lying or hiding something. "I just wish I got a chance to ask him about it. We were attacked before he could say more. You know Giovanni's friends. Think I could get one of them to talk to me?"

"Doubt it." Katie turned her back and slid off the bed. "They think you killed him, no matter what the cops say."

"What about Annika? Giovanni had to give her some kind of explanation for why she had to be cool with her boyfriend dating my sister. She must know about the club. Is she still in the hospital? If I could get in to see her—"

"We're overthinking this again," Katie said, picking her phone off the nightstand. "Everyone was bullying Winter and outdoing themselves with how horrible they could be. Annika said it was cool because she's just as sick and twisted as her boyfriend. Whether they started giving each other prizes for it doesn't make a difference."

I nodded slowly. "So you think the dare club is a dead end? Even though Giovanni rushed here to tell me about it?"

"I think he was high and looking for redemption, but he didn't deserve it, and don't try to give it to him now that he's dead. It's even fucking worse if he did those things to Winter because someone dared him to."

That we agreed on completely.

"I—"

"Hello," Katie said into the phone. "Luna is going to be staying the night, so bring two dinners. LuLu, what do you want?"

It was news to me that I was staying the night. *If I leave now, I leave with nothing. It wouldn't hurt to spend more time looking closely at the tapes. At the very least, it's showing me who definitely did not do it.*

"Your chef has never let me down. I'll eat whatever she puts on the plate."

"We'll have your pan-seared salmon with tomato pesto. Light on the oil," she said. "Send up caffeine too. Lots of it.

"What? What are you talking about? What other guests?"

I glanced up from the laptop, catching her frown.

"I didn't invite them. I—"

A knock sounded on the outside door. Katie looked toward the exit, then at me. *Oh no.*

"Yes," she said. "Send over six plates—"

"No."

"Thanks, Maria."

"No, no, no," I cried as she hung up. "Tell me that four plates are for Dean and the guys he brought for the orgy."

Katie laughed. "We're not that kinky, LuLu. Sorry but it's Saylor, Piper, Everleigh, and Gabby. I didn't know they were coming, but they know I'm here. If I don't answer, they'll think we're still fighting, and I'm over the drama for a lifetime."

"But if they see me here, drama is exactly what you're going to get."

"Not in my house," she said, gliding out to my internal screams. "If they cause problems, I'll throw them out. And you know what? This is a good thing. It's past time you and Saylor buried your beef."

My teeth clenched hard. Visions of Saylor painted blue and dripping wet battered my mind. We weren't burying anything. Saylor Burkhardt would suffer for what she did in that classroom. That was the last time she mocked my sister's memory.

"Hey, ladies," I overheard. "Heads up. Luna is here, so behave yourselves."

"Get rid of her." That snap could only be Saylor. "What is wrong with you, Katie? That bitch is bad news. When are you going to get that through your head? After she leaves you floating face-first in the pool?"

"Whoa. Ease down, Saylor. If she had anything to do with Giovanni, she wouldn't be here right now helping me go over the security footage. We're looking for who shouldn't be there."

"I can answer that question for you," Everleigh replied. "Luna Sinclair."

"What's it going to be?" Katie asked. "You guys staying or not, because we're about to have dinner?"

"Let her stay."

My brows shot up my forehead.

"I don't care if she's here," Gabriella continued, "and things have been shitty between the five of us lately. That's why we're here. To make it up to you with movies, wine, and mani-pedis. Come on, ladies. We're not going to let that Dreg trash get in the way of our night, right?"

I rolled my eyes. Nope, I didn't hit my head. That last sentence was for sure Gabriella.

"Ugh. Whatever." Footsteps barreled toward me, then the door flew open. Saylor curled her lip at me like I was a pile of dog droppings on the pillow. "We should be here," Saylor said loudly. "Sinclair's new tactic is casting suspicion on everyone else to protect herself. We're not going to let her infect you with lies, any more than we're going to let her hurt you."

I cheesed wide and crass. "Good to see you too, Saylor. You're looking lovely this evening."

"Shut your mouth. Dregs are seen, not heard."

The quartet filed in—all dressed in robes and pajamas, and carrying wine, movies, and nail gear as promised. They were ready for a sleepover, and I was looking at twelve hours confined in a small space with them. I didn't kill Giovanni, so why did it feel like the universe was punishing me?

Or giving me an opportunity. My cheesy smile melted into a real one. *Saylor Burkhardt will know the crushing, heartbreaking loneliness of my sister that she's mocked and disrespected since we met. Might as well start now.*

An idea popped into my head. I shot a text off to Wilder.

Gabriella slid in behind Piper, fixed on me. If that argument between her and Saylor that morning was about what I thought it was—

Gabriella flicked to my phone, brows twitching.

That's why she wants me to stay.

My phone buzzed. The others started setting up their party, but Gabriella watched me pick up and open the message.

Rafael: It's been too long since I've tasted that sweet, dripping pussy. What are you doing right now? Because I'm imagining you sliding up and down on my cock while those little lovelies bounce.

Face flaming, I dropped my phone. Where the heck did that come from? Was I supposed to be expecting this?

My phone went off again, shining the hot red spotlight brighter on my head. I practically hid my phone under the covers before I read the text. It was very much not Wilder.

Rafael: Come on, Cloud Girl. You wanted me to teach you dirty talk, but I believe you learn by doing. Or by telling. Me. What you want me to do to you. Tonight.

There was something I was supposed to do that night, but Thor help me if I remembered what.

Another message came through. It was a pair of bouncing clouds.

I giggled, body lighting with warmth even while my middle lit with something else. How could he always make me laugh?

"What's so funny?" Gabriella barked, tearing my attention away. I couldn't see her eyes anymore. They were narrowed to tight slits. "Share with the class, Sinclair."

"Nothing." I put my phone behind my back as they all stared at me. They were fast about ruining my happy mood. "Just a text from my—from Victor." I almost said my boyfriend. "He's got quite an imagination. So naughty."

Saylor snorted. "Oh, please. Like anyone believes Victor is really into you. Stop trying to show off. We all know that was a text from your carrier saying your phone bill is due."

Gabriella, Piper, and Everleigh laughed louder than that dig deserved.

I shrugged. "Whatever you say."

They all crowded the bed, piling on with their snacks and nail polish. I pulled my feet in, leaning against the headboard. I was surrounded.

"Enough of this." Saylor snapped Katie's laptop shut. "The police know what they're doing. They'll put the right person behind bars." She didn't even try to pretend she was speaking to anyone other than me.

My phone went off again. Two messages.

Wilder: I've got what you want. There's a lot of it though. Want the highlights?

I typed a reply to Wilder before daring to read Rafael's text.

Rafael: We'll do it in the car. Away from your fiancé. I'm going to bend you over the wheel and drill you from behind. The honking horn will bring everyone running, but no one will see us through the fogged windows.

I sunk low against the pillows, hiding my face behind my knees.

Me: I'm in the snake den and your mission to make me melt faster than my dripping pussy is not helping. Somehow, I ended up in the middle of a sleepover with Katie, Saylor, and her crew.

His reply came back immediately.

Rafael: Get out of there.

Me: Trust me, I want to, but I'm not done looking at the footage. Or fucking with Saylor. She didn't get what's coming to her Friday night. But she will.

I peered at her over my knees.

Me: That's a promise.

I burst out laughing. "Victor is so funny. You know, people look at him and see a playboy jock, but there's so much more to him. It makes all the difference when you're with someone who accepts you for who you are. That's why he's so comfortable with me."

Saylor rolled her eyes and I cringed.

"Oops, sorry," I said. "I forgot only Katie and I are in relationships. You'll find someone, Saylor." I patted the sheets beside her knee. Actually touching her wasn't going to happen. "Just remember to be vulnerable. You have to let someone in to find something real."

She reddened. "Shut up! No one asked for your dating advice."

"Yikes, so touchy. She was totally right about you," I muttered under my breath. "Emotionally unavailable for sure."

"What did you say? Who said that?"

I looked at Piper. Shaking my head, I grinned and rolled my eyes at Saylor like *can you believe her?*

Piper goggled at me like I was insane. Nothing compared to the look on Saylor's face. Flicking between us, her lips pressed into a thin line.

"What are we all sitting around for?" I clapped. "Bust out the wineglasses. That moscato looks good."

"Want some?" Everleigh asked, smiling sweet. "Then, you should've brought your own."

"Be cool," Katie warned. She got up and rescued six glasses from the minibar. She poured drinks for each of us herself.

My phone buzzed as I reached for mine. I smiled when I read Wilder's text. *Bingo.*

"How are things with you and Dean?" I spoke up. "Still just a hookup?"

"Hookups are all I have time for," Katie said. "But he's a particularly tasty one."

I looked at the others. "Oh, sorry, guys. You don't know. Dean is—"

"We know who he is," Everleigh sliced in. "Don't pretend like you know Katie better than us. We've been friends forever. She only hangs around you out of pity."

Her insults rolled off my back. "I thought you didn't know him because he's a *Dreg.* That's all. You're the one always going on about Dregs being beneath your notice. 'You shouldn't have to go to school with us,' and 'We're not fit to polish your Pradas.' Blah, blah, blah."

Everleigh's brows snapped together. "I didn't— How did you know—?"

"Right, Piper?" I tossed, giving her a wry look.

The pixie-haired girl looked around like I was talking to someone else. "What?"

"Piper," Saylor gritted. "When did you two have that conversation?"

"What conversation!"

I turned on Katie. "Anyway, Dean seems like a cool guy. There aren't many of those around here. You can put the man-child in Missoni, but you can't stop him belching the alphabet."

Saylor's eyes bugged as Katie cracked up. "That's good."

"Where did you hear that?" Saylor demanded. She grabbed my arm. "Who told you that!"

"Hey, watch it." I shook her off. "No one told me. I overheard it while I was in line for breakfast. I thought it was funny," I said, then I looked at Piper.

Saylor balled her fists. "Enough. Sinclair, shut the hell up. Piper," she barked. "Put on the movie."

I made a show of buttoning my lips. Reclining against the pillows, I picked up my phone and went back to some interesting reading.

Wilder said he monitored the communications of all the Royals. Thor knows why I didn't do something with that information sooner.

He wasn't hacked into their phones, reading their texts. He couldn't do that unless he got hold of them and implanted spyware on their cells. Since Royals upgraded phones every time a new one came out, Wilder would spend half his life stealing and putting spyware on the phone of every single Royal. That wasn't his way.

What he did was hack into accounts. Email accounts, bank accounts, Netflix accounts, and messaging accounts. All the ones where an email address and a password got you in. People tended to use the same password for everything, so once he had it, Wilder had access to it all.

"Security is only as good as the person," he had told me. *"Alarm system only protects you if you remember to turn it on. The vault is only protected if you remember to lock it. And you're only safe from me if you stop using your cat's name as a password and change the thing every day. Otherwise, you want me to get in."*

Gabriella unwisely logged into HapApp right next to him during a school game. HapApp was a messaging platform, and Gabby had several chats and group chats going with all the Royals—including ones with her friends. All of it was the usual stuff young rich heiresses talked about.

School, international vacations, parent drama, guys, girls, etc. The point of Wilder sending me screenshots of their conversations wasn't to get dirt. No, my plan was so much simpler than that.

I got bored halfway through *Amélie* and whispered for Katie to hand me her laptop. They were all laughing, watching the movie, and doing each other's nails. That left me free to do what Wilder asked me. I paid careful attention to who was around the pool before Giovanni found me, and paid better attention to who disappeared when the killer found us.

It wasn't enough to bring to the cops, but it was a start.

The food arrived while I was finishing up.

"Yum." Katie handed me a plate and I dug in. Letting Chef Maria work her magic was the right call. The woman did not make food people liked. She made food they *loved*.

"Who do you keep texting?" Gabriella asked when I took another peek at their screenshots. She swiped at my phone.

"Hey! Chill out. I already told you I'm texting Victor. His mom has some ideas for the wedding that he's running by me."

"That wedding is never happening." Saylor twirled her pasta between newly painted sparkly blue fingers. "Better, proper families have been sending Martha and John marriage proposals since the engagement party. It's only a matter of time before they get the right one."

"Now that is never going to happen," I replied. "Victor wants me and only me. He'd never leave me for the money-grubbers that slunk out from under their rocks the minute they heard he was looking for a wife." I looked pointedly at Everleigh, who flushed. "What we have is real."

"Then you wouldn't mind if we read lover boy's texts."

Gabriella lunged for my phone. I reacted quick, twisting away, and dumped salmon, pesto, and pasta all over my lap.

"Gabby," Katie cried. "What are you doing?"

"Oops, sorry, Katie." Gabriella seized my forearm. "I'll help her get cleaned up."

It wasn't a request. She hauled me up in a grip like iron, dragging me to the bathroom. I barely got out a shout before she shoved me inside and slammed the door.

One hundred and ten pounds of flowing locks, makeup, and impeccable genetics turned on me with a snarl that made me grimace. She wasn't looking too pretty right then.

"Give me your phone. Now."

"Uhh, no."

"Don't mess with me, bitch." She moved and I moved, maintaining as much distance as I could in the small space. "Saylor said you have pictures of me and Giovanni on your phone. Give it to me now. It's going in the toilet."

"Make that hell no." I squared my stance like Lucien taught me. "I'm not giving you anything."

"Yes, you are, because the only way you'd have those photos is if you were there. Someone blew up Gio's car. Someone texted Annika and sent her to the beach house." She smirked. "Now I know who. The police didn't have enough evidence to arrest your ass Friday night, but when they find out you were stalking and terrorizing him, you'll be some tatted-up thug's bitch girl by the weekend.

"Either give the phone to me, or give it to the cops. Your choice."

"The cops."

Her smirk twitched. "What?"

"I'll give it to the cops," I repeated. "Go ahead and call them. I'll wait."

Her mouth opened and closed for a minute—confusion all over her face. "You're bluffing. You think I won't do it."

"I think it doesn't matter if you do. Those photos don't prove anything. They were sent to me like I bet they were sent to a whole lot of other people."

She stiffened. "You're lying. No one has those photos."

"Of course they do." I rolled my eyes. "Why do you think no one believes your lies about not pushing Annika off the cliff? Everyone knows, Gabriella. They've been laughing behind your back. Or at least they were until Giovanni was killed. It's not so funny anymore."

"That was you!"

"It wasn't." My voice was calm. "I had no reason to kill him. He came to me that night to give me what I've been waiting a long time for—the truth."

"The truth about what?"

I didn't reply.

"The truth about what!" she cried, erasing the distance.

"The truth about why you and Annika were so cool about watching your boyfriend seduce my sister. I mean, he and Annika clearly weren't in an open relationship, or you wouldn't have a battered face or her a busted head." A vein popped in her forehead. "There had to be a reason neither of you did anything when he chased Winter down."

She laughed. I never heard anything more forced. "There was a reason. I knew he was playing that slut for a fool, and I had too much fun watching. It was freaking hilarious and Annika was laughing too."

I schooled my expression. "Was that it, or was it all"—I stuck my face in hers—"a dare?"

"Don't know what you're talking about."

"Save it. Like I said, Giovanni told me the truth." I lifted my shoulders. "When the police come, I'll tell them exactly what he said to me and they'll agree I had no reason to hurt the guy. They'll also laugh at the idea that I could blow up a car." I laughed. "Me? Where would I even get my hands on the stuff to do it?

"But you," I whispered, "with your millions and a pesky little attempted murder that you keep lying about. You've got reason to blow up a car to sell that someone else was out there. You've got motive to keep Giovanni quiet. You've got reason to threaten me with prison if I don't let you destroy evidence."

She jerked. "That's not what I'm—"

"That's exactly what you're doing, so call the police, Gabriella. I'm waiting."

Her whole body trembled. Backing away, she looked from me to her phone. Leon Dumont's words roared in my mind again.

"You said yourself that she wouldn't go through hell to protect some Royal's secret. She would do it for you. To protect you. How could this war of yours be what she wanted?"

This war isn't what Winter wanted. She suffered to protect me... but that isn't what I wanted either.

Standing there as the rancid monster who said my sister's torment was hilarious, was shaking like a puppy who peed on the rug. This is what I wanted.

Maybe it was selfish. Maybe it went against Winter's last wish. But if I let them get away with what they did to her, I'd regret it for the rest of my life. Just like Winter wouldn't have forgiven herself if something happened to our family.

Sometimes sisters do things for each other that they don't agree with, but that's loving each other.

That's being an adult.

Rafael and Cato may never forgive their father for not helping them find their mother's killer, but he was protecting his sons. Some things you have to do.

Knock. Knock.

Gabriella nearly dropped her phone.

"What are you guys doing in there?" Saylor called. "Get out."

"What's it going to be?" I asked. "You calling the cops or what?"

Saylor banged on the door.

"Delete them," Gabriella hissed. "Delete the photos."

"I could do that, but what's in it for me?"

Her eyes bugged. "In it for you? What do you want?"

"Open the door," Katie joined in.

"What I've always wanted. The truth."

"I don't know anything!"

I tsked. "Come now. Don't underestimate yourself. I'm sure you know plenty. Meet me tomorrow at Grover's bench. Lunchtime. You'll tell me everything you know, and I'll delete the photos in front of you."

She threw out her hand, stopping me leaving. "How do I know there aren't more? You said someone sent those to you."

"Someone sent out those truth lists, bombed Giovanni's car, stole his money, and nearly got him expelled. He had an enemy and no one is trying to incriminate themselves by flashing the attacker's creepshots. Anyone else who has them is pretending they don't. I, on the other hand, am happy to take my chances. The cops already know it wasn't me."

"Gabby! Luna! Open the door."

I shoved her hand away. "Grover's bench. Will you be there or not?"

"I..." She gritted her teeth. "I'll be there."

I threw open the door. Gabriella breezed past me.

"What's everyone shouting about?" she said. "I was just helping her clean up. We're good here. Right, Luna?"

I beamed. "Right."

Katie and Saylor looked us both up and down. Katie held concern for me. Saylor looked like I was the nastiest thing she'd ever seen with a side of suspicion.

"The movie is over," Katie said. She passed me a spare set of pajamas. "You pick the next one, Luna."

"Okay. I'll be right out."

I changed and returned to the sleepover. The ladies had moved on from their hands to their toes. They huddled on the bed, laughing and ignoring my pick of movie, *Pretty Woman*.

Gabriella pointedly ignored me when I retook my seat.

Rafael: What's going on over there? Are you okay?

Me: I'm fine. What do you think they're going to do to me?

Rafael: I'm more concerned about what you're going to do to them.

I eyed Saylor.

Me: So very much.

"Oh my goodness, Piper." I took her hand. "This color is so cute on you. It'll look great with your green dress."

She beamed. "I was just thinking the same— Wait. Get off me."

She snatched her hand back, but the damage was done. Saylor's face was red and pinched like a smacked bottom.

Me: Does your father really have an age cutoff for the jobs he takes?

Rafael: Yeah. Why?

Me: Makes me feel slightly better to know the Phantom can't hire him to get rid of me. But only slightly. We all know they're happy to let the TOD club do their dirty work.

Rafael: Who told you Pops has a cutoff?

I truly did not know how this news would go over, but I wasn't going to hide it.

Me: He told me when he came to see me this afternoon. We had a nice chat over tea.

One minute passed.

Two minutes.

Ten.

"This must be so boring for you, Luna."

I snapped up to Saylor.

"No wonder you're on your phone the whole time. Why don't we play a game?" Saylor moved the nail files and polish out of the way. "Never have I ever. Everyone in?"

"Sounds fun."

"Let's do it."

"Haven't played in so long."

They all turned to me.

"All right," I said.

"Perfect." Saylor slid over us. "First, the rules. When it's your turn, name something you haven't done. Anyone who has done it has to drink, and I don't mean a sip. Drain the glass." She fixed on me. "Got it?"

I saw where this was going, and it was not meant to be good for me. "Got it."

"Also, you have to explain what you did or didn't do. I want the full story."

Everyone nodded.

"Good. Katie, you first."

"Glasses out, ladies." We held out our glasses for Katie to fill each one to the brim. "Okay, how about this. Never have I ever played hooky."

"What?" I cried. "No way. I don't believe it."

Katie smirked with canary feathers practically stuck to her lips. "No one does, but I've got a perfect attendance record. The only time I ever missed was because I was sick." She flicked her hair over her shoulders. "You didn't think I got in Regalia U for my looks, did you?"

Blowing out a breath, I drained my glass with Saylor, Piper, Everleigh, and Gabriella.

"Spill," Saylor said.

Everleigh giggled. She had already drained half a bottle of wine before we started the game. "The time I skipped was with you guys. Bryant Rhodes got a new car for his birthday and drove us all up the coast. We totally hooked up in the back seat while everyone else was down at the beach."

"That was my first time too," Piper said. Saylor and Gabriella agreed.

They turned on me.

"My first time playing hooky, I caught a bus and train to Paris with some friends. We went to a Bruno Mars concert." Short, sweet, and to the point.

"And?" Saylor pressed.

"*And* it was a fun concert."

"Ugh, whatever. Who's next?"

"Me!" Everleigh raised her bottle. "Never have I ever... been arrested."

"Oooh, good one, Everleigh." All of them except Katie burst out laughing.

Nostrils flaring, I forced the alcohol through gritted teeth.

"Explain," Everleigh sang.

"I was arrested for taking my stepfather's yacht out. He thought it was stolen and reported it."

"Aww." Saylor brimmed with glee. "So you've always been a felon."

"And you've always been a bitch."

She laughed, not fazed in the least. "Yeah, I have. My turn. Let's see. What's a good one? Oh! Never have I ever lied to someone in this room."

The smiles evaporated quick. Looking around, no one drank.

"Come on, guys," Saylor said. "Not even a little white lie."

I raised a finger. "Uh, am I misunderstanding the game? I thought you were supposed to say something you haven't done."

"Excuse me?"

"I mean, you lied to Piper about her cheating scum of a boyfriend, Ahmed."

"True," Piper muttered under her breath.

Saylor swung to her, glaring. "*He* lied, not me. And how does she even know about that? I didn't know you two were so friendly."

"I know because you told me, and everyone else, at Toussaint's that night. Did you forget?"

She gave me a withering look, but didn't correct me. She couldn't. "Fine, I'll do another one. Never have I ever been shipped off to boarding school."

I bit back a grimace. "If I didn't know any better, I'd think you were trying to get me drunk, Burkhardt. You're not planning on taking advantage of me, are you?"

"Nope. I can do much better than you." She flapped a hand. "Drink."

Hesitating, I stared in the depths of my glass. The moscato was already starting to make me feel warm and fuzzy. The last time I got drunk was in my boarding school dorm with my friends. I woke up the next day and discovered I tossed half my clothes out the window and wrote *Luna Was Here* in lipstick all over the dormitory walls. I was gearing up to make another fool of myself in front of the worst possible person.

No. It's Saylor's turn to be fucked with. I downed my glass. *And the cracks are already showing.*

"Explain."

"Already did," I said. "The police picked me off that boat, so my folks sent me to boarding school to get me away from bad influences. Gotta be careful with Royals."

Saylor smiled back. "Very careful."

"My turn. Never have I ever... created a fake account to catfish a guy who didn't know I existed."

Saylor froze, gazing at me. I winked.

"Oh my fuck!" she shrieked, whirling on Piper. "You told her about that! What the hell!"

"I— I didn't tell her anything!" Piper whipped her head around, looking at her friends for help. "I don't talk to her, Saylor. You know that!"

"I know you're the only one I told about Rhys!"

She is the only one you told. In a HapApp message.

"I can't believe you. You're spreading shit behind my back to get back at me for Ahmed."

"No, I'm not, but if I was, you'd deserve it," she exploded, blowing me back. "What kind of friend doesn't tell you your boyfriend cheated on you!"

Saylor flung a hand at Katie. "What kind of friend fucks your boyfriend in a toolshed? How are you mad at me and not Katie?"

Katie slammed her glass down. "I told you I was wasted and he lied and said they broke up. I also apologized a hundred times."

"Like sorry makes up for it," Everleigh scoffed. "You said *sorry* after hooking up with Ivan at Graham's Christmas party."

"You never told me you liked him!"

"Like that would've stopped you," Everleigh flung, spilling her wine. "Besides, it was obvious I liked him. Even Ivan knew it. He only hooked up with you to make me jealous, but all is good for Katie. She plays innocent and we're all the assholes for not taking her side."

"What else have you told her?" Saylor asked. "Huh? You and Sinclair are such buddies now. I'm betting she also knows you went skinny-dipping with your sister's husband."

My eyes popped. That was not in any of the chats.

I edged back, letting the cross-fighting play on. Far be it from me to interrupt them when they were burying their friendship all on their own.

Let's see how you like having nothing and no one, Saylor Burkhardt.

"I can't believe you, Saylor," Piper screeched. "You swore you'd never tell anyone!"

"You swore you wouldn't tell anyone about Rhys!"

"I didn't!"

"Guys!" Gabriella shoved in the middle of the group, holding up her hands. "Stop it. We came here to make up after all the stupid fighting and drama. We've been best friends forever."

Best friends Piper, Saylor, Everleigh, and Katie glared at each other like they wished they could telepathically explode heads.

"We're not throwing that away for Ahmed—" She swung to Piper. "Who always lied and treated you like shit. The best thing you ever did was leave that asshole.

"We're not throwing it away for Ivan, who did know you liked him, Everleigh, but still hooked up with Katie to play mind games with you," she said. "And we're sure as hell not throwing it away for a cheating skag of a husband, or a guy who refused to date Saylor because it turned out he was gay. So can we all just chill out and go back to having fun?"

"Sure we can," Saylor said, folding her arms. "As soon as someone answers the question you all dodged. Have you lied to anyone in this room?"

A long, pressing silence spread through the room—smothering every victim she got her claws on. No one moved. No one breathed.

My phone buzzed.

Moving slow, I peeked at the screen.

Rafael: I'm outside.

I blinked, reading it again. Then again through blurry vision.

Rafael: Where are you, Cloud Girl? Security is about to call the cops 'cause I'm not leaving without you.

"Gotta go, guys." I got off—fell off the bed. Righting myself, I gathered my things as quickly as I could. "My ride is here. See you tomorrow, Katie."

She didn't answer. None of them did. I left them locked in their stare down.

Rafael was waiting outside the gates as promised.

"Sir, you need to leave. You can't—"

"It's okay, Marc." I waved through the gate. "Let me out and we'll go."

Pissed, the guard marched off and opened the gate. I slid in the passenger seat, turned my head to say hi, and swung it too fast. My forehead bounced off the headrest, sending me into a giggle fit.

"Are you drunk?"

"No, but I was on my way. Good thing you got me out of there. Saylor did not have good intentions with that game." I grinned. "But neither did I."

Rafael backed out of the drive. My eyes traced his face, following the curve of his strong jaw, and the pink tinge to lips that were as soft as they looked. Rafael was his father's son for sure, but looking close, there were signs of someone else in the warm eyes and mischievous smile.

"Your mom was beautiful, wasn't she?"

His brows crumpled, not expecting that question. "Yeah, she was. Why?"

"You look so much like your father, but I can tell the parts of you that aren't him are all her."

"When did you talk to my father, Luna?" He spoke to me, though he faced the road. His whitening knuckles on the steering wheel stirred concern under my tipsiness.

"When everyone was at the memorial. I walked inside and he was just sitting at the kitchen table."

"What did he do?"

"He... made me tea," I confessed. "He told me he wasn't going to help me against the Phantom or discovering what the secret is, which gave away that he knew it, or knew how to find out. He also knows about the T.O.D. Club. Not that he admitted that or anything else."

"Why didn't you call me?" Tension leaked into his voice. "Why did you wait until now to tell me he was in our house?"

I looked away. My bubbly mood was fading fast. "I wasn't sure if I would ever tell anyone about the conversation we had. Your father... he doesn't need poison or weapons to destroy someone."

"No," he said softly. "He doesn't."

We didn't speak for a long time.

"Do you want to talk about it?" he asked.

"No." I rested my hand over his. "Do you want to talk about it?"

Jaw tight, Rafael shook his head.

"No."

Chapter Five

"I always knew a beautiful woman would be the death of me one day." Rafael draped the blankets around my shoulder, squeezed, and hauled me up. He kissed me slow and deep until a soft, moaning noise escaped my lips for the *first time*. Not the second no matter what Victor imagined he heard. "At least you're worth it, Cloud Girl."

Rafael was back to his grinning, devil-may-care self by the time we returned to the Gallery. That was until Wilder outed me to Lucien, Rafael, and Cato at the dinner table. In less than two minutes, we were holed up in his room behind half a dozen locks and soundproofing. Victor wasn't home yet, but Wilder wasn't taking chances.

"Let me get this straight," Lucien began. He propped himself against Wilder's door, twirling his cane. "You accused them of murder, confessed you were behind the attacks, and said they wouldn't stop until one of them gave up the Phantom. And *that* guy would live while you killed the others."

"Sums it up," I said.

"Then, yes," Lucien said calmly. "We're all going to die."

"What's with the negativity?" Dropping back, I curled up on Wilder's bed. The man kept it way too cold in his room. Gave me the perfect excuse to curl up under his covers. The sweet, spicy smell of him enveloped me. "Who says we're going to die?"

"At least one of them is going to try to kill you," Rafael said. "The one that killed Ashton Scott for sure. Since no one is getting to you except through us, we're going to meet with our own accidents. They're coming for us. Have your bags packed and by the door, gorgeous. Levi's getting his boys together for another burning."

"I'm not worried."

"Why is that?" Wilder spun around in his desk chair, narrowing on me. "Did you get something off those security tapes that we can use?"

I shook my head. "Dead end. I know dozens of drunk, naked college students who did not attack and try to frame me for murder, but I have no clue who did. The only thing I got out of that slumber party from hell was our first step toward finding the T.O.D. Club."

The four of them moved on the cage. Cato kept coming and slipped under the covers with me. I squeaked when his hand found itself between my legs.

"What do you mean?" Wilder demanded.

"I... uh— I— Oh!"

Cato snuck past my flimsy, cotton defenses. I flushed hotter than a house fire as he caressed my lower lips, circling my opening. I was getting better at understanding Cato's unique way of communicating.

He was daring me to stop him.

"What I—I mean is...?" I shivered as he bit my neck, then licked it in apology. Apparently this was happening right there, right then, and the guys were just going to watch.

Wetness dampened his teasing fingers. *Why does that turn me on?*

"What I mean is Gabriella is meeting me at the bench where all this started for us. I told her I'd delete the photos of her and Giovanni if she tells me everything she knows. I'm going to get her to spill about the club."

I scooted a bit away from Cato and he growled low and deep in my ear. My nipples hardened to pebbles.

Yep. There was definitely something wrong with me.

"How can you be sure she knows about the club?" Lucien asked.

"Mr. Dumont said—"

"Mr. Dumont?" Lucien and Wilder sliced in.

Cato stopped nibbling on me in an instant—hand disappearing from between my legs. "Papa?"

"Ah, right. I didn't get a chance to tell you everything that happened today." I glanced at Rafael. He nodded, gesturing for me to go on. I spilled my entire conversation with Leon Dumont. Well, I spilled most of it. I left out what he said about me going against Winter's wishes. I also didn't share what he said about keeping his secrets to protect his sons. That was something he needed to say to his boys to their face.

An *I love you* should always come from the person who said it.

"Gabriella has to know," I said. "Annika and Giovanni were not in an open relationship, or she wouldn't have gotten her face punched in. Giovanni had to give his girlfriend an explanation for why she should look the other way while he seduced and slept with my sister. Don't you think his side chick wanted an explanation too?"

Rafael inclined his head. "Any reason he came up with for why he had to sleep with her, instead of just dating her, would've made him sound like a cheating pig. Annika would've straight dumped him. But," he drew out. "If he told her about this grand prize of money or moving their status higher in the Royal hierarchy, I could see him selling her that it was all for their future.

"I'm doing this for us, baby. Sleep with one Dreg and we're the new king and queen of Regalia, not Victor Wilson or Saylor Burkhardt." Rafael cursed. "Yeah, I could see it going like that. And if he spilled the truth to Annika, he spilled the truth to Gabriella. He really did love them both."

"Gabriella knows more. I can feel it." I snuggled into Cato's arms. He wrapped around me, but didn't head south. Seems I killed the mood by bringing up his dad in the middle of foreplay. To be fair, that would kill it for anybody. "I'm squeezing her of every bit of information. We also need to talk about how we're going to get Wesley, Levi, and Owen before they get us."

"You threw out the plan," Rafael reminded.

"Because now we need them scared. Piss-their-pants, trembling-in-a-puddle-of-vomit scared of me and what I'll do to them. That's the only way they'll turn on the Phantom."

"You've thought about this for a long time. Tell us."

A slow smile spread across his face. He was right. I've thought about what I'd do to those five every day since I got Winter's letter.

"This is what I had in mind..."

***

I tossed and turned on the sheets. Sweat dampened the back of my neck, untouched by the spinning fan or wheezing air vent. Giving up, I slid out from Cato's arm and padded downstairs.

Light crept up the staircase. I slowed down, listening to someone's shuffling footsteps. Who else was up at three in the morning?

"Wilder? Lucien?" I came down a little more. "Rafael?"

"Keep going," said a dry voice. "You'll get to my name eventually."

"Victor." I stepped off as he turned off the stove.

"Hey," he said, waving me over. "Join me."

I inhaled deep. "What's that smell?"

"That, Luna Sinclair, is the best damn hot chocolate you'll ever drink in your life." I blinked when he took my hand, leading me inside. Victor grasped my waist and picked me up, getting an "ooh" out of me. Gently, he placed me on the countertop.

"Milk, chocolate, cacao powder, and maple syrup. The maple syrup makes all the difference."

I watched in fascination as he got out more ingredients and started making mine. His movements were sure and precise chopping the bar of chocolate and whisking it into the bubbly, milky, syrupy goodness.

"I didn't know we had organic cacao powder."

"You didn't," he said. "I brought some things from home."

"Didn't need to bring the chef." I breathed deep, tension leeching away. "Who taught you how to make this?"

"Learned a few things from running around the kitchen when I was young. It became a late-night treat when I couldn't sleep. I wasn't allowed to use the stove, so I'd wake up Adonis to make it for me." He smiled—the same kind of smile I made when thinking of good memories with Winter. "He never got mad or chased me off. He'd make our cocoa and we'd drink it on pillows in the living room. I'd almost always pass out and wake up in my bed the next morning."

"That's really sweet," I whispered. "Sounds like a great big brother."

"The best." Victor turned his back and went to the pantry—Wilder's pantry. I opened my mouth to warn him, and stopped. That wasn't late-night cocoa talk. Let the things that could be said in the morning, wait till the morning. There were so many other things Victor and I had to say to each other.

"Want anything with it?" he asked. "Cinnamon stick? Marshmallows?"

"Marshmallows, please."

Victor poured out our drinks, topping them both with marshmallows. He stepped between my legs, handing me mine. I held my breath as he rested on my knees, blowing on the hot treat.

Taking a sip, a moan escaped unbidden.

"Yep, that was the sound."

My eyes popped open. "I didn't make a sound."

Laughing, Victor made himself comfortable on my lap. "Why can't you sleep?"

The back of my neck was ten times as hot then. His nearness was doing worse for my internal temperature than my racing mind. I was not into Victor Wilson. My body just didn't know that.

"It's been kind of a weird day." I laughed mirthlessly. "It's been a weird week. I don't know where I go from here, or what's going to happen."

"No one does."

"True, but the unknown is more frightening when you have as many enemies as I do." My mug grew out of focus. "Every time I step outside, I see pretty, poised masks. Which one hides a monster?"

"Dark. That would keep me up too."

"What is keeping you up?"

He looked around. "I don't sleep well in any other bed but mine."

"Must be tough. You spend a lot of time in beds that aren't yours."

We looked at each other, and laughed.

"I respect that you didn't let that opening slide," he said, grinning. "I set it up and you spiked it."

"Too hard to resist, but I was kidding. I had insomnia for an entire month when I first moved to France. I couldn't get comfortable in a bed that wasn't mine either. I know what it's like to be homesick," I said, tracing my rim.

"I wish it was homesickness. Makes me sound all soft and cinnamon-rolly. No," he said, rising up. "I haven't been able to get a good night's sleep outside of my house since I was eleven years old. The summer I went to camp."

My last remnants of humor disappeared. "What happened?"

"Mom sent me to an exclusive, fancy camp with a bunch of kids from school. She thought I'd have a great time with all my friends but..." He paused to sip, using the chance to break my gaze. "I didn't know how much my *friends* wanted to take a Wilson down a notch. From day one, they hit me with prank after prank.

"Harmless stuff at first. Putting makeup on me while I was sleeping. Shaving cream in the suitcase," he said. "I gave as good as I got, pretending like we were all just goofing around even while the pranks got bigger and harsher. It kept going until one night they carried me—mattress and all—out onto the lake. I couldn't swim."

I clapped my hand over my mouth. "Did they know...?"

He raised his head, and nodded. "I woke up drowning, Luna. Water filling my lungs, choking me out before I could scream. It was only by chance one of the counselors was out for an early jog and saw me. Otherwise, I wouldn't be here to make you the best damn hot chocolate there is."

I didn't give in to his attempt to lighten the mood. "Victor, I'm so sorry. I can't imagine how terrified you were. An eleven-year-old should never experience that terrible moment when they believe they're going to die."

"Yeah, well." He cleared his throat. "It was one bad day in an otherwise charmed life. I should be over it by now."

"You don't have to do that," I said, cupping his cheek. "Not with me."

"Yes, I do." The words scraped out of him. "Every time I look at you... the pain in your eyes..." He let out a slow breath. "I don't have the right to complain to you."

"Opening up to me about how you feel isn't complaining, Victor. I'd never be such a horrible ass to make someone feel their trauma is smaller than mine. Because it's not small to you. That little boy's fear matters. The stress you still feel matters. Which makes it even more incredible to me that you moved in here. I haven't said it yet, but I really appreciate that you're trying. Right now, this ring is my lifeline." My pinkie stroked his. "I don't want it to be your noose."

"Is it weird to say it's not?" He straightened, smiling into my eyes. "I'm eighteen. I should be pissed at being tied down. Freaked at becoming a father before I'm twenty-one."

"You've got to stop talking about our children so casually."

He laughed. "But that's it. None of that scares me. I've always known a strategic marriage was in my future. Just like I've always known my father underestimated me. I've been waiting to prove him wrong my whole life. Now's my chance."

"You've always known you wouldn't get to pick your wife?" I was still stroking his ring. "That didn't bother you. You didn't want love. Love like your parents have."

"Love breaks people, Sinclair. It broke my mom when she lost Adonis's father. It broke my brother when his fiancée left him. It breaks my parents because they're the two most incompatible people you'd ever meet, but love each other so much they can't be without the other—even if they'd be happier."

"I didn't know that about your parents. Seeing them together, I wouldn't have guessed."

Victor grinned without humor. "Don't get me wrong. I mean it when I say they're crazy for each other. They still flirt and giggle and make out, and it's completely disgusting."

I giggled.

"But Mom is the 'day at the beach' type, while Dad is the 'day in the boardroom' type. She's champagne and he's scotch. She's big parties with guests she's only met once. He's a couple of beers on the porch with his buddies. They love each other, but my whole life I didn't feel they understood each other."

He lifted his shoulders. "I thought it wouldn't be that way for me and my wife. I'd pick someone who was a true match for me without lovesickness blinding me. We'd have things in common. We'd do stuff together and actually have a good time. Instead of one of us standing in a corner with a fake smile, pretending we're having fun. I thought we'd stay up all night talking about our favorite books and movies. I guess I believed I would... marry the woman who'd become my best friend."

"Instead you got me."

Victor chuckled. "Could still be you. Quick. Don't think, just answer. Iron Man or Captain America?"

"Iron Man."

"Singing or dancing?"

"Dancing," I shot back. "My voice makes children cry."

He cracked up. "An island or the city?"

"Oooh, an island for sure. Private island would be even better."

"Agreed," he said. "Share your food or defend your plate?"

"Defend my plate! I can't stand creeping forks coming for my food. Get your own."

Victor threw up his hands. "Tell me about it. What is it with dates that order the boring, tasteless, polite meal only to sweet-talk me into giving them mine? Get the chili onion steak burrito," he cried. "Because I'm not giving you mine."

I laughed so hard, I wheezed. "Well, if not sharing food is the basis for a good marriage, we're set."

He smiled. "Lucky us."

We gazed at each other... for too long. I quickly looked away, taking a deep gulp of my hot chocolate. *You are not into a guy who is so full of himself, he thinks a wink and kiss will make you forget the four men you're falling for.*

I'll prove that to both of us.

"Do I get some questions?" I asked.

"Sure. What do you got?"

"Hmm. Breakfast or dinner?"

"Breakfast," he replied without skipping a beat. "Ever notice how all your best days start off with pancakes?"

I started, surprised. Chocolate chip pancakes were my favorite food—period. Did he know that? He couldn't know that.

"Big family or small family?"

"Big family. Lots of kids," he said. "Growing up, I never knew who my real friends were, but I always had Don."

"I always had Winter." It was out of my mouth before I could stop it. "My best friend."

Victor turned his palm up, lacing his fingers through mine. I didn't look down. If I pretended it wasn't happening, I couldn't stop myself from tracing the lines on the palm of his hand.

"Luna?"

Heat collecting between my breasts, I found my tongue again. "Oh, um." I fell into his gaze. "Me... or a best friend?"

Victor smiled. "I'll let you know."

I didn't need to see my cheeks to know they were tinged pink. "We're getting dangerously close to a sweet moment." I dropped his hand. "Since we're both up, let's watch a movie. Wilder's collection is insane."

He swept out a hand for me to go ahead. "After you."

I relaxed as we watched *Sherlock Holmes*, and then struck up a game of playing detective. I made assumptions about people based on the things I observed, and since Victor actually knew them, he told me if I was right or wrong.

A harmless game without an ounce of sexual tension, but I'd never been so highly aware of a person. Of his knee two inches from mine. Of the arm not touching me but draped behind me on the couch.

I studied him while he guessed things about the Rogues. I never denied Victor was handsome, but I did deny loudly and often that he was my type. What would happen between us since there was every chance this wedding would go ahead? Would he accept that I didn't want to let go of the Rogues? Would he ask me to be okay with him sleeping with other women?

Irritation flared hot and acrid at the thought. I could already see Everleigh wrapping herself around him like a boa constrictor.

I'd cut that fork-tongue bitch in two.

I audibly sighed, dropping my head back. I could tell right off that my double standards were going to cause problems.

"What's up? You okay?"

"I'm fine. It's just... I know we need to have a serious conversation about us, but I'm not up for it tonight."

He shrugged. "No one said we had to have it tonight. You know, I've actually been thinking that what you said before was right." He lifted his leg onto the couch, turning to face me. Our knees brushed and I jerked, shocked by the stinging electricity that zipped up my thigh.

What the hell is going on? You're allowed to think he's attractive, but you're not allowed to react like a swooning maiden from an accidental touch. His arrogant ass would sniff that out in a second, and there can't *be an us unless there's a we.*

"We should start at the beginning and date like we would've if we were a normal couple." He gestured with his chin. "I don't want that ring to become your noose either. We should figure out now if we can have something friendly, or if we'll be splitting Wilson Manor down the middle."

"I can tell you right now if you answer one question."

"Yeah? What?"

"Will your parents be living with us?"

Victor cracked a smile. "My father's going to be carried out of Wilson Manor—his words. So yes, if we live there, we'll have roommates."

"No, you'll have roommates," I replied, "on your side of the manor."

"They're looking forward to being one big happy family. Grandkids running around. Vacations in St. Croix. Filling the main dining table with loads of people. Despite how everything's gone down, they're excited about the wedding."

I dropped my head on the couch. His arm brushed my temple, but I didn't move.

Neither did he.

"Can I ask you something that might piss you off?"

He copied me, resting his head against the cushion. We were so close we shared the same breath.

"It's the first time you've asked for permission. I'm curious enough to say yes."

"Why did your parents kick Adonis out of the family?"

His grin dimmed.

"Would it have been so bad if Adonis didn't marry Catalina? Would it be so bad if you married someone else? If family is what your folks want so desperately, why are they treating the one they got the way they do?"

Sighing, he turned away—looking up at the ceiling. "I know all this is hard to understand," he began. "I won't pretend I understand either, or that I even want to defend it. He's my brother. Their son. Nothing else should've mattered."

"But," I gently pressed.

"But..." A faraway look glazed his eyes. "There's been a rivalry between the Wilsons and the Burkhardts going back to the founding of Regalia."

I didn't mention that I knew this, or what his ancestor had done to innocent people just to get his hands on some money.

"It's like an obsession. A sickness, my grandfather called it. Infecting each generation with a need to one-up each other. If a Burkhardt acquires a town, a Wilson has to acquire a city. If a Wilson makes it onto *The New York Times* Best Seller list, a Burkhardt has to win a Pulitzer. It's gone on and on until Adonis and Catalina."

I frowned. "Catalina?"

"Don't get me wrong. Adonis truly loved her. Their engagement wasn't arranged or strategic. They did it all the old-fashioned way. Met in college. Started dating. Moved in together. Planned a future," he said. "Then, things got complicated and they split."

"I know about the diagnosis," I admitted. "It's more than complicated. It's a tragedy the decision he had to make."

Victor gaped at me. "He told you about that?"

"He didn't mean to. He was drunk."

"Drunk? My brother doesn't get drunk."

Clearly, Victor had yet to give Adonis a chance to explain the story behind our kiss. Did that mean they were fighting? I hoped not. The last thing I wanted was to get between brothers as close as they were.

I gave him a sad smile. "I think he does when the woman he loves dumps him because he made a difficult choice."

"Yeah," Victor said, blowing out a breath. "Fair enough. I'd swallow a keg whole if it was me. So if you know, then I can tell you the whole story. Even though it's not why they got together, my parents supported the marriage because the Wilsons have never been real competition in the markets that the Burkhardts dominate, but Catalina's family is.

"Her father, Mungo Dobson, completed a huge merger a few years ago that's brought nearly as many private hospitals and clinics under his company umbrella as the Burkhardts have. If Adonis married her and brought them under Wilson Industries, we'd not only outstrip the Burkhardts, but we'd lead the country in private healthcare.

"I don't have to tell you that my parents supported the match like they arranged it themselves. I'm pretty sure Catalina is the only person on the planet who never received a *compliment* from my mother, then realized it was actually an insult after she walked away."

"I know what that's like," I muttered. "Are you telling me that's the real reason they cut Adonis off? It wasn't about grandchildren or carrying on the Wilson name? It's all about besting the Burkhardts?"

He stroked my cheek, startling me into shooting up. "You don't have to say it. It's all over your face. What a stupid, shallow reason to abandon your son."

"Of course it's a stupid, shallow reason. Especially since Adonis was never interested in all that nonsense. He fell in love with someone and wanted to spend the rest of his life with them. And because his parents forced their own expectations on their relationship, he lost them on the same day he lost her. That's awful!"

Inexplicably, he smiled. "No wonder Adonis spilled all this to you. You look ready to pull your cape on and take on all of Regalia to make this right for him. Anyone else around here would've sided with my parents."

"He said the same thing to me, but how can that be true? You didn't side with your parents, did you? You told them it was wrong."

"Till I lost my voice, and my car, and my bank account. I let them hear it until my folks started leaving the room when I walked in. But it didn't do any good," he said, voice hard. "They were so close to finally crushing the Burkhardts underfoot. Making them second best. I told you it's a sickness, Luna, and we're not the only family who has it." He waved a hand. "Everyone around here is so obsessed with moving up the ladder."

I sunk down, resting my head on the cushion again, and his arm. "Why aren't you?"

"Don't know. I mean, I like my life and all the privileges that come with it. But it was always enough for me. I didn't need more, more, more like everyone around me, though there's privilege in feeling that way too. It's easy for the guy on top to roll his eyes at everyone scrambling at the bottom. If I wasn't a Wilson, it wouldn't be so easy for me to survive in this town. It wouldn't be so easy for me not to care."

Rising up, I scooted closer. "I get what you're saying, but I won't let the Royals off the hook. Yes, it's a brutal game of secrets, lies, and favors, but they don't have to play. There are neighborhoods all across this country where people just live. They wake up, go to school, go to work, come home, be with their family, and do it again the next day.

"They don't plot to benefit from their son's marriage and kick him out when it falls apart. They don't drive innocent young women to suicide."

Victor looked away.

"The Royals are like this because they want to be. Because deep down, they enjoy playing with people's lives and crushing someone's head to get to the top. You're not like them, Victor. That should make you feel proud, not out of touch."

A smile stretched his lips. "You wouldn't have said that a week ago. That I'm not like them."

"A week ago you were acting like a jackass."

He barked a laugh. "Need I remind you, you made out with my brother while engaged to me. I was entitled."

"Do you want to hear the truth of what happened that night, or not? Because if you do, I want you to make up with Adonis afterward. Don't punish him for something I did when I was drunk."

"Now you were drunk too?"

"There was a lot of alcohol involved."

Heaving off the seat, Victor cuffed my chin. "Maybe another night. I want to hold on to my anger at you both for keeping it a secret for a little longer. Can't do that if it really was harmless."

"Why would you want to be angry?"

Victor gazed at me for so long, the silence crept beneath my skin. "Because we're not best friends yet," he said, voice soft.

He walked away, leaving me to wonder what that meant.

And fear that I already knew.

***

I was first to arrive at Grover's bench. I chose it for a reason. It was the spot Owen was sitting while basking in his after-blow-job cruelty to his date. This was the bench where I planned to kill him, but the Rogues stopped me.

That night started the journey to where we are now. It was only right that this was the place I finally came full circle.

A shadowy figure hurried down the lane, decked out in oversized sunglasses and a long, black designer coat.

It was only right this is where I find out the truth.

"Hello, Gabby. Thank you for coming."

Gabriella joined me on the bench, glaring hard through her shades. I didn't need to see her eyes to know. I felt the heat from her hatred clear as day. "Pictures. Delete them. Now."

I smiled. "Come on. You know that's not how this works. First, you tell me what I need to know, and then *poof*, the photos proving you were at the Bluffs with a sweaty, naked motive to push Annika to her death go bye-bye."

"Stop saying it like that," she snapped. "It was self-defense. She kept coming at me."

"Was it self-defense that made you leave her broken and bleeding on the sand without calling an ambulance?"

She said nothing.

I shook my phone at her. "Might want to come up with an answer to that question, because the cops will surely be asking that. Your lawyers may have scared Annika into silence, but she'll find her voice the second these hit her inbox."

"Okay! I'm here. I'll tell you what you want to know. Enough already."

Satisfied, I leaned back, crossing my legs at the ankles. "Good, then let's not waste time. What's the T.O.D. Club?"

Shock bled through her grimace. "How do you know that name?"

"Giovanni told me about it before he was attacked. I got quite a few details, so think carefully before you lie to me. If you say anything that contradicts him, our deal is off."

Her jaw tightened. I bet the thought did cross her mind to lie, but since she couldn't be sure what Giovanni told me, it'd be too big a risk to test me. "Fine. What do you want to know?"

"Everything."

She turned away, directing her glare into the trees. "The T.O.D. Club is what it stands for. Truth or dare."

I didn't say anything, and she continued.

"It was started years ago by the Greeks. Some frat thing. They shut it down, and then Royals picked it up when my mom was in school. About six years ago, new players took over and changed everything. Made it secure, and opened it up to Dregs."

"Dregs?" It was out of my mouth before I could stop it. I couldn't have her figure out that I actually knew next to nothing about the club. I needed her to spill all out of fear.

But Gabriella didn't seem to notice. "I didn't want to join because of it. We've got to deal with Dregs all over our campus. Now what was once a Royal-only club was taken over by them too? I wasn't into it but Giovanni said to trust him. Join and find out why we needed the Dregs.

"Piper and I did, and it became obvious real fast why the club was opened to Dregs. They're the entertainment."

My brows furrowed but I otherwise didn't react. I already hated where this was going.

"The club is hardcore," she said. "No rules. No limits. But going after each other is a quick way to make powerful enemies. Instead, we save the messed-up dares for the Dregs. It's laughable what they'll do for money. From shit that gets them expelled to..." She smirked at me. "Drenching your ass in mocha vanilla."

I kept my face blank. "The day everyone came after me with lattes is due to your little club? You'd think you guys would have better things to do."

"We do. That's why I sent the Dregs after you. You ruined one of my favorite tops."

"Send me the dry-cleaning bill, so I can crumple it and toss it in your face. Do I look like I give a shit about shirts and lattes!" Gabriella jumped. "Tell me about Winter!"

"There— There's nothing to tell! Giovanni got a private, anonymous dare. I didn't know anything about it until he told me I had to be cool with him hooking up with her. The reward was seven figures and a deal that would move the Natale name three places up the Royal ladder. That would put him right below me. He... he said..." Wetness dabbed the corner of her lids. "He said he was doing it for us. One day, my folks could get over their hatred of the Natales, but they'd never get over it if I married far below me.

"If he moved up, we could be together for real. Out in the open. Just us," she whispered.

I searched my heart for sympathy and found none. She could shove those tears back in her ducts. The future she and Giovanni wanted to build was on the back of my sister's torment and torture.

"Who gave him the dare?"

She shook herself, wiping her eyes. "I told you. I don't know."

"Bullshit. I assume very few people have the power to move a family that high up the ladder. You must know."

"There are twenty-seven families on the third rung. Twenty-two of them have heirs that are enrolled at Regalia U. How am I supposed to know which one of them offered a shadow deal to move Giovanni as high as their family?"

My eyes narrowed to slits. "I warned you about lying to me. Giovanni knew exactly who it was. He was about to tell me before I was knocked out, and he was killed. I don't buy that he didn't tell you."

"He didn't," she cried, swinging around. "If you're saying what I think you are, you believe this guy killed Giovanni. Why would I protect them? I loved him."

My gaze was steady. "You'd protect them if you know they killed Giovanni, and you don't want to be next."

Her face hardened. Tight lines wrinkled the corner of her eyes, casting the first emotion other than superior haughtiness she'd ever given me. "If I knew who killed him, it's them who'd be afraid of me."

I quieted. I couldn't say why, but I believed her.

"Fine," I said when the silence got uncomfortable. "But the fact remains that Giovanni found out. More than that, he was approached by the other guys who got dares for Winter because they knew he could find the person behind it. Why would that be?"

"Giovanni could?" She frowned. "Maybe, because... He recruits for the club. I mean... he did. Giovanni knew the members, or at least more than any one of us. Everyone only knows the person who got them in. Giovanni got me in. I invited Piper, and she invited Everleigh. We each get one, but Giovanni recruited whoever he wanted. As long as they could keep a secret," she said. "Before you ask, I don't know who he recruited besides me. He was serious about following the club rules. Didn't want to risk the penalties. He said the people in charge would know. Don't know how, but he swore they'd know."

My mind spun with the information she was throwing at me. Every word out of her mouth made it clear the T.O.D. Club evolved. This was more than a bunch of drunk frat boys getting off on sex secrets.

"He recruited for the club," I repeated, getting it straight in my mind. "So, those twenty-two Royal heirs with the power to help the Natales, and the other guys' families. He was in the perfect position to narrow the pool. He'd know if those guys were even in the club or not."

She nodded.

"And he did find them," I continued. "He figured out who it was and came to tell me. He wrecked himself to get up the courage. Got high and tracked me down at the party. Someone that scared and trying to be cautious, wouldn't keep a list of member names taped inside his notebook. How am I supposed to find out what Giovanni knew?"

"You don't. It's impossible. If I don't know the club members outside of my friends, then you sure as hell aren't going to find out."

I ignored this. Naturally, I wasn't taking her word for it. "You said Giovanni got an anonymous dare, but it sounds like you're all anonymous. What's the difference?"

"You'd have to see how the site is set up."

Website? So it is all online. How in the hell have they been staying off of Wilder's radar, then?

"We sign on with usernames. KitKat57 and stuff like that. When enough people have logged on, the computer randomly chooses us. Like spin the bottle," she explained. "Then it chooses the person who'll give the truth or dare.

"But there's also a message function. You can click on a name and message them privately."

"Giving them a private dare," I finished. *Wouldn't want everyone in the club to freak out when KitKat dares one of the members to rape someone.*

"But what the Dregs don't know is that their handles come up as a different color," she went on. "The Royals all know when we're daring one of them, or one of our own."

I sat up straight. "Which means it doesn't matter that they reveal themselves when they go around completing the dare, lobbing lattes at me. You're not protecting their privacy anyway."

Gabriella shrugged. "Like I said, they're the entertainment. A Royal isn't going to risk everything by leaking their own nudes, but I dared a Dreg to do it last month for five hundred dollars." She rolled her eyes. "That was all it took.

"Not to say the Royals don't put their asses up too. The club isn't for pussies. If you get a dare, you do it. I was dared to steal the answers to Mrs. Maruka's midterm and share it with the club."

My brows shot up. "And you did it?"

"The penalties for refusing are more brutal than you can imagine." She dropped her gaze. "Even worse than expulsion."

I thought of Giovanni floating facedown in the pool. It was hard to argue with that.

"What's the website?"

"Why even ask? You must know you can't access it."

I smiled sweet and wide. "Then, there's no harm in telling me."

"It's a long string of numbers and letters. Not something anyone can memorize. Plus, you get on it through your student account," she said. "Once you accept the invite to join, an extra tab just shows up in your account one day. You click the link, get rerouted like a dozen times, then you're in T.O.D.

"You'd have to come back to my place and see after I logged in, because I'm not giving you the password to my account. My grades, medical records, permanent record, and everything is on there."

Layers and layers of protection. Can only be accessed on a desktop and behind private information that no one has a reason to share. It's also a subtle threat.

The fact that they were able to put a link to the site in their student accounts proves they have access to their student accounts, and someone can do a lot of damage with that.

Gabriella scoffed. "Now you're going to say you want to go to my place and see it."

"Nope," I replied smoothly. "Nothing so obvious as that. Giovanni was too afraid to tell you anything, and you guys were regularly screwing in secret. If he didn't trust that what he told you wouldn't get back to the guys in charge, then how would it look if it got back to them that the two of us went traipsing to your place? I've got my own ways of getting on that site. I'm good."

"Good for you." She got to her feet. "That means we're done here. Give me your phone. I'm deleting those photos myself."

My hands didn't twitch. "There's something else I want to know. You said you invited Piper and she invited Everleigh. What about Saylor?"

Gabriella huffed, folding her arms. She was way past tired of talking to me. "Obviously, I told Saylor all about it, but she wouldn't join. Said it was a childish waste of time." Her face changed. "Although…"

"Although what?"

"She's Saylor Burkhardt. She's not about to be a member of anything. She's going to be in charge. I think that's the real reason she turned it down." She cocked her head, brows screwing up. "Either that, or she already is."

It proved how well I understood that loathsome bitch that I had to agree with Gabriella. Saylor Burkhardt wouldn't sign up to be a pawn in someone else's game. If anyone's going to pull the puppet strings, it's her.

Saying nothing, I handed over my phone and let her delete the photos. Gabriella tossed it back on my lap.

"Perfect. Now that's done, I can say you're a sad, bitter whore that should've done the world a favor and stayed in that French brothel you crawled out of." She slapped me across the face. It came so quick and sudden, I couldn't stop it. "Stay away from me and my friends. Especially Katie."

Jumping up, I lunged at her. Gabriella raised her arm to block me. I twisted her wrist, wrenching it away from her face, and punched her dead on the nose.

We went down in a tangle of limbs.

"Your sister got what she deserved!" Gabriella tangled in my hair and yanked. My scream ripped my throat. "She started all of this! Giovanni would still be alive if it wasn't for the two of you!"

"Take that back!" Rage welled over hot and acrid. "My sister was beaten, humiliated, raped, falsely accused, and expelled! Don't you dare say she deserved it. Take it back." I flipped and pinned her. My hands wrapped around her throat. "Take it back!"

Eyes bulging, Gabriella gasped—clawing at my fingers.

My grip tightened.

She blurred around the edges, falling out of focus as black crept into my vision. It was all too much. After everything she told me, I didn't feel any closer to the Phantom. Owen, Levi, and Wesley were still walking around free, clear, and rich. My calls to my mother were going to voicemail. I somehow had two fiancés and wasn't sure about my future with either of them.

And Winter was still dead.

No matter what happened. No matter what I did. No matter who I destroyed. I would wake up every day for the rest of my life knowing I had to live another one without her.

"You picked the wrong day to mess with me," I hissed. "Take it back, or you and Giovanni will finally get your wish. You'll spend the next eternity together in hell!"

Blue-tinged lips began to foam. She rasped something—terror bleeding into her eyes, and weakness leaving her limbs.

"I— I—" Her blows against my hands began to slow. "P-p-please..."

"Luna!"

Arms seized me, dragging me off Gabriella. The Royal didn't waste any time. Gasping deep lungfuls, she half ran, half crawled away—falling on her face a dozen times as her sobs echoed behind me.

"You're next, Montana. You're next!"

"Luna!" He whirled me around, shaking me. "What are you doing! Are you trying to end up in jail?"

My chest heaved, rolling against the one pressed tightly to mine. Adonis crushed me against him, using his whole body to stop me... doing what? Not even I knew. My whole body trembled with rage, and the only thing on my mind was that I wasn't finished with Gabriella yet.

Gasping, choking, and running away wasn't a sorry.

I twisted around, straining in his hold. "Which way did she go?"

"The opposite direction you're going in." Adonis hooked me around the waist, and before I could think, lifted me off my feet. He carried me quick through the trees—staying away from the path.

"What happened?"

"Put me down."

"I've never seen you go off like that, and I'm fairly certain students have been giving you reason to since the day you set foot on campus. What did she do that made you lose control?"

I shoved against his chest. "I said put me down!"

Adonis skirted a stream, and the sound of voices floating over our heads. He looked like he just arrived to campus, fresh from a shower. The tips of his hair darkened with water. A minty sage smell filled my nose. The weather was turning cool which traded in his thin, long-sleeved dress shirts for an argyle sweater.

It clung tightly to him—providing no barrier to my fingers pushing back on his pecs. I felt each muscle against my palm—as immovable as the arm around my waist.

"If I put you down, I'll have to go to the dean and report that I stopped you from strangling a girl that you threatened as she ran away crying, so ask me to again."

I bared my teeth, but I didn't ask again. He had to put me down anyway when we broke from the trees. Students milled around, not paying us, or the hand firmly against my back, any mind. It was a silent trek to the administration building. I didn't speak until we were inside his office.

"You didn't see what you thought you saw," I said, tone dead. "She attacked me first. The girl pushes women off cliffs. I had to defend myself."

"Keep working on that excuse." Professor Anthony disappeared through a door to the left of his desk. "You might get someone to believe it."

"She did attack me first," I snapped. "Unprovoked."

"I'm sure she did." Adonis came out carrying a first aid kit. He motioned for me to sit. "But you didn't respond the way you did unprovoked. What did she do?"

I arched a brow, and winced. Gabriella clawed up my face pretty good. "Do you really want to know, Professor Anthony? You made it clear you don't want to speak about anything other than this week's writing prompt."

Adonis gently towed me to the seat I was refusing to sit in. Ignoring my glare, he poured antiseptic on a cotton ball and started dabbing my cuts. "I'll make an exception to the conversation ban on the day I find you strangling a student on the way to lunch. What did she do to you, Luna?" His face was so close to mine—intense eyes tracing me as he worked.

"Doesn't matter," I said, looking away. "You're still going to tell the dean because Gabriella will. She'll go running to him with a sob story of minding her own business when the Dreg went psycho. She'll tell him you saw the whole thing, and you'll have to say that the only part of the fight you saw was the bit where she was pleading and gasping for air. What do the details matter?"

"I don't have to do shit."

He dropped that so bluntly, I started.

"I especially don't have to back up a one-sided tale by someone who's sore because they started a fight they didn't win." Adonis paused, his fingers lingering on my cheek. "Now tell me."

"She... She said..." Tears prickled the back of my eyes. "She said Winter deserved what she got. That it was all her fault for coming in and upsetting her perfect little world."

Adonis slowly leaned back. "Luna, I can't— I'm sorry."

"I know all about the new T.O.D. Club now." I spat the name. "Someone started it back up six years ago, but with a lot more planning and security so it couldn't get found out and shut down. It's exactly what it sounds like—rich kids getting their adrenaline junkie thrills from stealing, cheating, sex, and lies. But they had to take it a step farther and include the Dregs as entertainment."

"Entertainment?"

My lips twisted. "They're getting off on it, Adonis. On making Dregs do terrible things for money. On sending us after each other. It's like fucking cock fighting. They throw lattes at me, harass me on the quad, destroy my clothes, and lure me into traps. Meanwhile, people like Gabriella get to sit back and laugh while keeping their hands clean.

"It's what they did to Winter," I cried. "She said it was like everyone just turned against her, but they didn't. Why would they? No one knew the secret she discovered that set all this off. The real person after her paid Dregs to bully her, and then when she wouldn't give in, they unleashed the worst of the Royal hounds.

"And while all this is happening, no one—*no one*—is doing a thing to stop it. No one warns her. No one refuses the dares and money. No one finds a shred of decency in their soul. What do the Royals care about the life of one Dreg? Dregs are their playthings."

"Stop calling yourself that." Adonis dropped to his knees at my feet. "You're no Dreg, Luna."

"No, what I am is an idiot." Salty wetness dripped onto my tongue. I realized then that I was crying. "We're all idiots. Here we are, wasting our lives trying to be a good person. Following the rules and doing right. And what did that get me? What did it get Winter?"

"But the Royals don't even try. They're cruel, selfish, and self-absorbed. They take what they want, when they want it. They treat everyone like garbage. Literally call people garbage! And what do they have? Everything.

"They have wealth, privilege, and standing. They're all a few years away from taking control of the country."

"Luna—"

"It's a lie, Adonis. It's the great lie that good people—kind people will be recognized for what they do, and one day that good fortune will come back to them. While they're sitting around waiting, people like Gabriella, Saylor, and Levi are snatching it away and laughing all the way to the top."

Adonis cupped my cheek. "Luna, slow down—"

Lurching forward, I grasped his face with both hands. "Aren't you fucking sick of it? You did everything you were supposed to do. You were a good son. A good brother. You worked hard and earned everything you have. You met a woman, fell in love, committed to a future with her, and where are you now, Adonis?

"Single. Cut off from your family. Looked down on by the uptight pieces of crap around here who should applaud you for standing up for yourself. But right or wrong, it doesn't matter, because you'll still have no family, no inheritance, and no children. And Winter will still be dead!" The scream tore from my lips. "So why be good and follow the rules? All it gets you is a fatal inheritable disease and a dead sister."

Adonis just looked at me.

The words drew from deep in the ruined crater of my soul. "Aren't you tired?"

"Yes," he whispered. "Yes, I am."

"I don't want to be good anymore. I want to lie, and steal, and cheat." *And kill.* "I want to take everything from the ones who have it all."

Adonis gazed at me for a long time. "So do it."

It wasn't a conscious thought. One minute there was distance between us, and the next I erased it, shooting forward and crushing my lips against his.

"Luna!" Adonis tore away, knocking over the first aid kit. Antiseptic spilled and spread a hospital-like scent through the cozy space. "What are you doing?"

"What you told me to do." I fell off my seat and landed on top of him—grabbing his shoulders and pinning him to the floor. "I'm being bad."

"That's not what I meant!" He seized my hips with no real strength. "This will not happen."

The guy had fifty pounds and a foot on me. If he wanted me off him, I'd be flying.

"Here's how it is, *Professor Anthony*." I purred the title. "You can be good, follow all the little school rules, and get absolutely nothing for it. *Or* you can fuck me on this desk."

His eyes darkened. By Thor, he was perfect in that tight sweater pulled taut over his rigid muscles. Soft locks fell over his lined brow, drawing me to his eyes—which burned me where I sat.

"What's it going to be?"

Adonis's grip on me tightened. "I'm not one of these little boys getting weak-kneed for a coed."

"Thank goodness." I reached behind me, palming his impressive and ridiculously hard length. "I don't want a little boy. I want a man." I rubbed harder. "I want a teacher."

He growled, snatching my wayward wrist and pulling. The momentum tossed me off-balance, and our noses conked—lips brushed. "Luna, stop."

The demand ghosted over my mouth. My tongue darted out, tasting it and him. "Say it again and I just might." I met his gaze, daring him to with every breath in my body. "Say it."

Rough pants heaved his chest. He was still holding my wrist. He was still so close to me I could practically taste the spearmint toothpaste on his tongue.

"Either make me leave..." I pressed the tiniest kiss on the corner of his mouth. "Or make me come."

I squealed—pulled up so fast and hard, my forehead conked his shoulder. I didn't have a chance to recover before he snapped my head back and slammed his lips on mine.

It was in the deepest, most secret part of my mind that I could admit I never let go of my crush on Professor Anthony. Guilt at hurting Victor tried to bury it. Fear that my engagement would end and my stepfather would pull me from school, fought to convince me to let it go.

But it never went anywhere. Nearly every day I thought of the wild, perfect moment when my heart ruled my head, and I kissed the handsome man who comforted me and shared in my pain. I imagined so many times what it would be like to kiss him again... and I hadn't even come close.

Sunbursts exploded behind my eyes, blanketing my mind in warm, white light. It was as if I was transported to a safe, warm place where nothing existed but his hands on my body, and his mouth on mine.

Adonis devoured me like a starving man—tongues battling, mouths clashing, moans pouring down our throats.

Crash!

I shrieked again, giggling. Adonis shoved everything on his desk to the floor, laying me flat out. I reached for his belt but he was already there—tearing the obstacle free. I shivered under his gaze. The way he looked at me...

I gave up trying to undress him and ripped off my clothes, eager for the promise in those orbs to be fulfilled.

"What the fuck am I doing?" he said, snapping my hips to him. I grinned as he made short work of my thong—tossing it somewhere over his shoulder.

"Hope I don't have to explain it to you," I teased. "This isn't your first time, right?"

A firm swat landed on my backside, blowing my brows up my forehead. My core lit up so hot and fast, it melted the juices leaking from my pussy. *Did he just spank me?*

"Stop talking."

I caressed my toes down his chest, marveling at the body hidden under those dress shirts and sweaters. How could a man this gorgeous exist? "Will you punish me if I don't, Professor?"

"Oh," I cried when he spanked me again, painting the left cheek red to match the right. It was insane how turned on I was. I was learning a lot about myself that day.

Fingers scrambling, I unhooked the last stitch of clothing on me—losing my bra. Adonis took one look at me, naked and spread out like a buffet, and groaned deep in his chest.

"Fuck, Luna." He climbed on top of me. "You're incredible."

If I thought the spanking was hot. Those words burned me to a crisp.

Adonis made like he was going to kiss me and missed, nipping my chin instead. My head fell back as he burned a trail down my chin to my breast. My nipple disappeared in his mouth.

"Fuck's sake," I moaned, arching off the wood.

Adonis flicked and tortured the helpless nub, sucking harder to the tune of my cries. It occurred to me that I should be quiet so we don't get caught, but that thought fled as soon as it arrived—chased away by two fingers pushed past my folds.

I'm glad I can say Professor Anthony did not take it easy on me. Once they were in, his fingers set off like the races, plunging in and out of my pussy at a punishing speed. I told the man to fuck me. He was completing his assignment for an A plus.

"Yes. Ugh, yes, Professor. Right there. Ri— Hmpf!"

A hand clamped over my mouth, wisely muffling my increasingly loud moans. It thoroughly impressed me how he managed to finger-fuck me, muzzle me, and worship my breast at the same time. We were past expert level to a level not meant for newly non-virgins like me.

My body warmed fast. Electricity zipped through my muscles, twisting and contorting them—telling me to run from the pain but bend to the pleasure.

Adonis crooked his finger, striking a spot inside me that made me slam my heel on the desk. Once undid me. Twice—

Eyes rolling up in my head, I came hard—screaming my orgasm into his palm.

"Uhh," I huffed, flopping boneless on the desk. "Holy shit, Professor Anthony. How bad do I have to be... to make you do that again? Please, sir—"

"I thought I told you"—he fisted my hair—"to stop talking."

Adonis slid me off the desk onto my knees. I gazed up at him with fevered eyes and parted lips.

He shoved his boxers down, and I swallowed hard.

I felt him through his pants and even that didn't prepare me for the flagpole I just begged to stake me. *It won't fit*, I thought, raking his thick, uncut cock. *There's no way this fits.*

"Open."

I obeyed, swallowing him happily.

"Don't let me hurt you," he said. "Pinch my thigh if it's too much."

I smacked his thigh, shouting "*get on with it,*" around his cock. By his smirk, he got the message loud and clear.

Adonis started pumping, sliding in and out past my swelling lips. He held me firm—making it clear he wasn't here for a blow job. He was here to fuck the shit out of my mouth.

Gripping his thighs, I gagged trying to take all of him in. He filled my throat to bursting—warm and pulsing in my cavern. I just relaxed—ordering him with my eyes not to stop. I wanted him to hurt me, gag me, fuck me. I wanted to forget there was a world outside this office. A world determined to bring me lower than a person can go.

"Holy shit," Professor Anthony groaned. "Why am I not surprised this tasty little mouth is as hot as it's sharp?" He pumped faster still, plowing the back of my throat.

If someone walked in right then, I'd either be expelled and him fired, or they'd use that to blackmail us into a threesome. No doubt there was no hotter sight than this man plunging in my mouth while I moaned and begged on my knees. If someone told me that morning that this was how my day would go, I'd have flipped them off for talking impossible nonsense.

Adonis's thighs tightened under my grip. Even my limited sexual experience told me what was coming.

I ordered my body to relax. Take all that he had to give me. I wanted this. I wanted him—

Professor Anthony pulled out and exploded on my face. I cried out as hot ropes of cum covered me. I accepted right then that sex with him would not be predictable. I knew nothing of what it was like to be with a grown man with his kind of experience.

"That's one way to stop me talking." My grin was wicked. "Didn't quite work though." I bent over the desk, wiggling my ass. "I should be punished until the lesson sinks in."

"Yes, you should." Adonis palmed my breasts from behind, rolling my nipples over his writer's callouses. "Beg for it."

"Fuck me, Professor Anthony. Split me with that yummy, fat cock." Dirty talk was coming easier to me. "I'm going to be a very, *very* bad girl from now on. Better teach me to obey while you still have the chance."

He pinched my hardened pebbles. "More."

"Ah." I ground back on his hardness. "I want you inside me. Please, sir. I'll do whatever you ask." I felt his tip tease my entrance, drawing it out to torture me. "Teach me how to be your favorite kind of dirty little slut."

Adonis thrust inside, catching a cry on my tongue. The last coherent thought through my head was, *"finally!"*

We rutted like animals. He jackhammered between my legs, competing against my muffled screams. It was me who clamped his hand over my mouth. I couldn't tone it down and I didn't plan to. He was so strong and powerful behind me. I felt safe at his mercy—that he would both take everything from me but not more than I could give.

The dam broke, flooding my electrified nerve endings and making them short-circuit—the only explanation for the very unsexy way I flopped and flailed on the desk, rocked by such an intense orgasm, my eyes rolled up in my head and I saw only black. I came to as he tensed.

His hoarse grunt sounded in my ear. Adonis spilled hot, messy, and bare inside me.

His weight suddenly bore down on me, and we both dropped—collapsing in a heap on the floor.

"Wow," I breathed. I twisted over and curled up against his side. "Just... wow."

"Fuck..."

"Yes, please." My fingers traced lines through the beaded sweat on his chest. "You don't have class, do you? Let's do that again."

Adonis tensed beneath me. "What the hell did I just do?"

"What?" I craned my neck to look at him. "No. Please, no, Adonis. Don't come to your senses yet."

Gently, but firmly, Adonis lifted me up and leaned me against the desk. Whatever spell I cast to shed my no-nonsense professor for the sexy, demanding beast who bent me over a desk, was broken.

"I can't believe I did that," he rasped, snatching up his clothes. "Had unprotected sex in my office with a student *who's covered in my cum*!"

I shrugged. "The last part was a surprise, but I was into it. What's the big deal? We're not in high school. The 'having sex with a student' thing is a lot less scandalous when everyone involved is an adult..." Climbing onto his desk, I let my legs fall open, and my hand travel down. "And very willing."

Adonis stopped hopping into his pants and fell on me, and my wayward fingers. His breath hitched as I spread my pussy, and let him watch my middle finger disappear inside it. "Now, do you have class or not, *Professor*? Because once was not nearly enough for me."

Eyes darkening, he took a step toward me. His gaze flicked up and he stopped. "I'm sorry, Luna, but no. Please, get dressed."

I turned to see what he was looking at. My smile dimmed.

Staring back at me was a beaming picture of Victor. My fiancé. His brother. The guy who left his home to make things work with me. Who was willing to give us a try while I slept with other guys... who now included his brother.

"Oh no..." The haze lifted, freeing me from the vengeful, immoral spirit that seized me when I strangled Gabriella. How crazy was it to say that I hadn't thought of him until that second? "I'm the worst piece of shit there ever was."

"No, you're not." Adonis cupped my cheek, turning me to face him. "You and Victor are still strangers, and it's an unspoken agreement around here that there's no need to be faithful to a fiancé your parents forced on you. But me, on the other hand..." He blew out a breath. "*I* am the worst piece of shit there ever was. And the worst brother."

"That's not true. This might not be so bad," I tried. "Victor and I agreed to start over from zero. More than that, I'm in a relationship with other guys and he—"

"What?" Adonis dropped his hand. "You have a boyfriend? *Boyfriends*?"

My jaw worked. "I— What I meant is—"

Everything was perfect five minutes ago. How did we get here?!

"It's not like that," I blurted. "We're not cheating." *I don't think.* "They know about each other. Victor knows about them. They're okay with sharing, so it's okay. I mean it's not like Victor expects me to be faithful, like you said. I'll explain to him—"

"No." His sharp retort ceased my babbling. "No," he repeated in a softer tone. "Don't say anything to him. If he doesn't expect anything from you, then he doesn't expect an apology. It's me who needs to tell him. Let me do that."

"I will, of course." I reached for him and caught air. Adonis used picking up his shirt to dodge my touch. "Whatever you're thinking," I whispered, "I promise it's not that. I don't just go around collecting guys like trophies. The Rogues are everything to me. They were there for me when no one else was, and our connection is real. As real as the one I have with you."

The muscles rippled on his back as he pulled up and buttoned his pants. Adonis spoke to the bookcase. "We don't have a connection, Luna. We're professor and student. Nothing more."

My chest squeezed. "So that's it. Nine minutes. That's how long it took for you to call what we did a mistake."

He stopped, sighing. "It... wasn't a mistake." Sounded like the words wrenched from his chest. "We shouldn't have done it, but it wasn't a mistake."

"How is saying we shouldn't have done it not calling it a mistake?"

"I haven't done a good enough job teaching you about the English language"—he twisted and kissed me so quick and fierce, it knocked me off-balance—"if you don't know the difference."

Adonis released me dizzy and confused. I tried to say something but my swollen lips weren't forming the words.

"I'll leave first," he said, picking up that sweater I loved so much. He made for the door. "Don't tell anyone about this until I have a chance to talk to Victor, and even then. I love this job, Luna. I can't lose it."

"I won't be the reason you do. But I also won't give up on us."

Adonis halted with his hand on the knob.

"Now that I know you want me as much as I want you, I'm not holding back. I'm going to shamelessly and ruthlessly take up all the free space in your head until it drives you mad, and the only cure is me in your bed." I shrugged.

"Or on your desk. I'm not picky. All I know is this won't be our last time to-gether."

He threw open the door, walking out. I'd never know for sure, but it sounded like he said, "I hope you're right."

Chapter Six

It was a long, silent trek to the Gallery—longer still for my slowing steps the closer and closer I got. I wasn't a Royal. I was not the person who could do, say, and take whatever they wanted and damned who I hurt.

I forgot that in the midst of strangling that vile monster who dared to say my sister deserved to be driven to suicide. But the fact remained that I didn't want to become her. I didn't want to be like someone who, for all that she claimed to love Giovanni, dumped him the minute things got difficult and her shining reputation was on the line.

I would bring down the Royal ladder and all the people clinging to it. To do that, I had to become someone else. Someone stronger. Someone who didn't hesitate. And yes, someone who could sink as low as the Royals, because I'd never win if I wasn't willing to go as far.

But what I wouldn't do is risk my guys. And maybe, just maybe... I wouldn't risk Victor.

I entered the Gallery and got smacked in the face with a wave of noise.

"—it's not possible."

"Well, he got in and was sipping tea with Luna, so it is possible. You said this security system was impenetrable."

"I said it because it is. No one gets in here without the code."

I rounded the corner. Wilder and Rafael faced down across the kitchen. In between them, sitting at the kitchen table was Lucien and Cato. Victor was in the class that I skipped. I couldn't sit next to him with his brother's dried cum in my hair. That'd be a new level of messed up.

Speaking of...

I ducked the other way, going upstairs through the living room. I needed a shower and an internal pep talk before I faced the guys. Adonis asked me not to tell anyone we had sex, and keeping that secret filled me with guilt the second I agreed to it. It was past time the Rogues and I had a talk about what we were to each other, and what our relationship was supposed to be.

I showered and washed my hair quickly, savoring the last lingering memories of his touch on my skin. The person I was in that office with him, was nothing like who I was curled up under Cato, or rolling around in bed with Rafael.

Everything with Adonis felt illicit, naughty, and dangerous, and before I knew it, I took on that role. *And Adonis loved it.*

I shivered picturing that long, hard cock. There was something deeply satisfying about knowing I had that kind of effect on a grown, worldly man. I made him lose control. I made him risk everything just for the chance to hold me—be inside me.

That day could not be the last time we were together. Rafael and Cato were clearly cool with sharing me. It was possible Victor and Adonis could be too.

Wake up, Luna. What kind of relationship could you have with your English professor? There's so much more in your way than your marriage to his brother.

I pushed the thoughts away, along with the uneasy churn they kicked off in my stomach. Complete trash bags masquerading as people got to have everything they wanted. I could have the men who made my face heat and heart flutter. Please, just let me have them.

After I dressed and showered, I returned downstairs.

"—fuck does any of that matter!" I'd never seen Rafael so agitated. "The point is that he can get in, so we're junking the system and getting a new one."

"There isn't one better." Wilder propped his fists on the table. "Seriously think I'd install second best? Besides, I looked at the security tape. He didn't break in. He typed in the code and walked in, after waving to the damn camera. Cato must've told your dad the code."

The Cato in question ate his lunch while ignoring the pile of pills beside him, and all the people talking.

"I'll change it," Wilder said. "Done."

Rafael slammed the countertop. "I'm telling you—!"

"Guys?" I broke in. "Maybe this should be obvious, but why is it such a big deal that your dad was here? Are you on bad terms? You never said."

Jaw tight, Rafael threw open a cabinet and started taking bowls and seasonings out. "I told you he kicked us out of the house and has refused for years to help us find our mother's killer. Being estranged is implied, gorgeous."

"Fair enough," I muttered. "But you're so estranged he's not allowed to step foot in here?"

"It's not him being here, it's how he got in," Rafael replied. By the ingredients, he was about to make his famous beef curry. I sat my butt down for the first bowl. "*Neither* of us gave him the code, but somehow he got his hands on it. There's how he got it. There's why he went through the trouble just to speak to you here, when he could've done it anywhere. And then there's why he doesn't care that we now know he found a way past our security."

"No one gets past my security," Wilder corrected. "I'll change the code and make some upgrades. This won't happen again."

"There's something else we should talk about," I spoke up. "It's about the T.O.D. Club. Gabriella spilled everything..."

I told them what she told me, kicking off another argument.

"If it's hosted online, I would've found it by now," Wilder said. "Forget hacking, we would've found out because no way that many people kept the secret. Half the freshman class went after Winter. We're supposed to believe they all did it because they were paid by the T.O.D. to bully her? Dozens of people and not one slipup?"

I shook my head. "Gabriella said there are scary penalties for snitching. Giovanni said the same thing now that I think of it. They were both serious about it, and scared. Whoever is in charge must be holding something over each member. That's the most effective way to keep someone quiet—make it hurt if they talk."

The guys shared a look.

"We need access to that site," Lucien said. "Now that we know it's linked to their student accounts, you can get in, yes, Wilder?"

"No," he replied. "I hacked the student accounts of Montana, Starling, and Natale only last week. There was nothing there that shouldn't be."

"Gabriella told me that too." Rafael broke away to go to the stove. He came back with two bowls of curry for the both of us. We'd been talking for a long time. "She said she could only show me on her computer at home, even though she can get on her student account through her phone. Whoever runs the club must have some way to control that."

"There is a way," Wilder admitted, "but I don't know anyone around here who could do it. That kind of computer programming is on my level. Whoever started this must've hired out, but why go through that much trouble and expense for some stupid dare club?"

"We're a step closer to getting the answers," I said, "and I know how. Giovanni's dorm room… They haven't cleaned it out yet, have they?"

Rafael's brows shot up his head. "Are you suggesting we steal from a dead man, Cloud Girl?"

I raised my chin. "Don't make it sound like that. Giovanni wanted to tell me the truth, and he'll definitely want me to avenge his death. All of this is to find the person who started this nightmare. If one desktop computer can do that, then we steal it."

"Then *I* steal it," Lucien amended. "Now. Don't know when they'll clean out his dorm. Shouldn't leave it to chance."

"Before you do," I said quickly, stopping him in his tracks. "There's something we should talk about. Honestly, we should've talked about it a long time ago."

Wilder heaved a sigh. "Yes, those cannisters really hold radioactive material, but it's perfectly safe in the containers, and I know how to handle them."

"Wha— That's not—" I held up a finger. "We're coming back to that topic and discussing it at length, but that's not what I'm talking about. We need to talk about us."

"Us?" Rafael repeated.

"Yes, us. What we are to each other. What's our relationship." I tried to speak confidently, but I was doing it at the table. I couldn't bring myself to look any of them in the eyes. It was easy to flit between them, exploring our connections, and doing whatever in the moment we felt like doing when there weren't any rules or expectations.

After Adonis, we needed them. Didn't make me any less afraid of what they'd say. What would I do if Wilder said he wasn't a fan of sharing and wanted me to himself? What did I do if Rafael told me no relationship between us would last past my "I dos" to Victor?

"I've done stuff with all of you," I said, staring hard at my bowl of curry. "Is that… okay?"

My goodness, I sounded like an idiot.

A finger tickled my chin, lifting me up. "Is this about Wilson?" Rafael asked.

"No. Well... maybe a little bit. I told him that I won't give you guys up, but I was getting ahead of myself. We haven't talked long-term about us, or what happens when I get married in less than a year. I promised Victor I wouldn't force him into a relationship he doesn't want, but I haven't asked what kind of relationship you guys want either."

Sighing, I sat up straight, finally meeting their eyes. "This is me asking. What do you want? A relationship? A hookup? A friend? A no-strings relationship that ends when I walk down the aisle? Tell me."

No one spoke for long enough that the silence grated on my ears. I was two seconds away from taking my bowl and running upstairs.

"These questions are for the three of us since Cato's been clear about what he wants." Rafael jerked a thumb at his brother. "I don't have to tell you he wasn't joking."

I smiled at Cato. "Never had two men want to marry me before. Actually, make that one and a half."

"That's the thing, Luna. Do you want to marry him?"

"If I don't, I'll have to leave Regalia U and Victor—"

"No," Rafael sliced in, taking my hand. "Do you want to marry Cato?"

I blinked at him. "What?"

"Do you want to marry Cato? Do you want to date me long-term? Do you want to hook up with Lucien? What do you want, Luna?" His gaze bore into me. "We haven't talked relationships because we didn't want to pressure you, or give you ultimatums. You're engaged to another guy, and you're engaged to that guy so that you can be here for Winter.

"How fucked up would it be if we let our dicks get in the way? Cloud Girl, we haven't told you what we are... because we've been waiting for you to tell us."

My lips parted but nothing came out. Not for a second did it occur to me that we didn't have this conversation because they were waiting for me to be ready for it.

"Oh."

"What do you want, Lady Luna?" Lucien claimed my other hand and pressed a soft kiss on my knuckles. "Because I need there to be no confusion. I want you."

"I... I..." I flicked between them. My intense, strong, unyielding Wilder. My smooth, sweet, dark Lucien. My wild, dizzying Cato. And my sexy, confident Rafael. What did I want from them... other than everything? "I can't say." I squeezed my eyes shut, shamed at the thoughts going through my head. "It's too terrible. Too selfish."

"Tell us," Wilder said. A gentle hand through my hair turned my head to him. "It can't be terrible or selfish. It's you."

My stomach twisted thinking of what happened in Adonis's office. I wasn't ashamed of what we did—which was the problem.

"I'm not as wonderful as you guys think I am. The Luna that I'm still pretending to be died the day she lost her sister."

"Look at who you're talking to," Rafael said. "We've sat at this very table night after night, planning blackmail, revenge, and murder. We've only ever seen the person you are now. And she's hot as fuck."

I cracked a smile. Of course Rafael would slip that in. Of course he'd make me smile. It's what he did. He never judged me or made me feel anything less than amazing. Lucien never told me anything but the truth. Wilder always made me feel safe. Cato made me feel like the darkest, most twisted parts of me were beautiful. If I could tell anyone what I wanted, it was them.

"I want to be with you. All of you. In every way you can be with a person, but..." I took a deep breath. "I want you to only be with me."

Wilder twisted my strands around his fingers. "We share you, but you don't share us."

I slumped over. "I told you it was awful and selfish. Victor called me out on the same crap, but I can't help it. I have feelings for all of you. I can't choose. Though when I think of you being with anyone else, I want to claw that girl's eyes out and toss her body in the grave next to yours."

"There won't be any girl." Lucien rubbed slow, mind-scrambling circles on my palm. "I accepted a while ago that there's only you."

Rafael cocked his head, grinning. "You don't need to ask what this brother wants either. You know everything, Cloud Girl. Everything about what I do and what I've done, and none of that scares you. I've found my match. Why would I waste my time with anyone else?"

I was so happy, I thought I'd cry. I dared to glance at Wilder. "Wilder?"

"You've yet to pass all the background checks, and there's still your Royal spy of a fiancé to consider, but I ended it with all of my hookups two days after meeting you."

"Who are these women!"

He chuckled. "They're women I stopped thinking about when my head was taken over by you. I'm down to share"—he walked off—"once you win me over, that is."

"Meaning I haven't won you yet?" I called after him.

"Send me a few of your videos. That should seal the deal."

My face lit up. "I told you to stop teasing me with stuff you made up." I rose out of my seat. "And where are you going?"

"We need that computer. We're not losing it because we sat around telling you what you should already know." With that, he walked out the door—abrupt and no-nonsense as ever, but leaving me practically vibrating in my seat. He thought it was a given that he wanted me and the relationship I wanted. Wilder said a lot of things that didn't make sense to me, but he always said the right thing.

"I wasn't done," I muttered. "Though we do need that computer."

"Not done?" Lucien repeated. "What else do you need to tell us?"

I took a breath, choosing my words carefully. "I'm the only one for you guys... What if it's not just you guys for me?"

Rafael scoffed. "You mean Victor? We know why you have to go through with this wedding, Luna. We've accepted it. It's up to Victor to accept you, and the boyfriends you come with."

"I know he does, but it's not Victor I'm talking about." I swept over them, and landed on the fridge. I couldn't look at them while I asked this. "Could you guys be okay with me being with someone outside of our group? Someone other than Victor?"

Cato pressed his cheek against mine. A gesture so sweet shouldn't come with a snarl so menacing. "Who?"

I can't say who. I promised I wouldn't risk the last good thing Adonis has.

I didn't for a second think the guys would rat us out, but it wasn't me risking everything and Adonis didn't know the Rogues. He should decide if they discovered he had unprotected sex in his office with a student. Plus, it wouldn't be right for anyone to know before Victor did.

Soon, he will know them. I won't have to keep us secret forever.

"I can't say. He's not ready for people to know about us." I pulled a face. "He's not ready for there to be an us."

"Then no."

"No."

"Fuck no."

"What?" I cried. "Why?"

"This guy is an ass," Rafael said. "Where the hell does he get off treating you like some secret? And he's not sure he wants to be with you? I'd give my left nut to be with you. You bring this guy around, I'm going to kick his ass."

"After I do," Lucien said smoothly.

Cato dropped a lighter on the table. "He will burn."

My jaw worked. "Guys, you're so sweet, but—but it's not like that. It's... We..."

Rafael's phone went off. He glanced at the screen and his expression hardened. "It's him. Cato, let's go."

Rafael was up and out of the kitchen before he finished the bark. Cato trailed him out.

"Wilder's not known for subtlety," Lucien tossed over his shoulder, leaving as well. "I'll help him retrieve the laptop."

I was on my own in the space of fifteen seconds. Sighing, I dropped my head on the table. Explaining Adonis to the guys went about as well as trying to explain the guys to Adonis. There wasn't much I could do about it then though. Everything depended on the outcome of Adonis's conversation with Victor.

My phone buzzed. I fished it out of my pocket without lifting my head. "Hello?"

"Luna, what the hell!"

"Good evening to you too, Katie," I said calmly. "To what do I owe the pleasure?"

"What did you do to Gabby? She's a mess, Luna! She said you attacked and tried to kill her!"

I shot up straight. "That's a sweet little fantasy she's spinning! Montana will be the next J. R. R. Tolkien. What actually happened is she started a fight she couldn't finish. She threw the first hit."

"She's got bruises on her neck."

"You should see what she did to my face."

There was quiet on the other end of the line. I waited her out.

"So you didn't say you were going to kill her next?"

I snorted. "What am I? A villain in a children's book? Why would I tell her I'm going to kill her, let alone that she's *next*? There isn't a first." I was getting really good at spinning bullshit. "But you should know that while I was beating her ass for slapping me, ripping out my hair, clawing my face, and saying my sister deserved to be driven to suicide—while all that was happening, she threatened me and said to stay away from you. She's lying to your face to drive a wedge between us."

"Did she really say Winter deserved it?"

"Y-yes," I replied, voice cracking. "She did."

Shuffling sounded on the other end. I heard muffled shouting like Katie was covering the phone. A keening whine came through. That would be Gabriella.

"I'll call you later."

Click.

I shook my head, making my way upstairs. I wasn't even mad that Gabriella used the fight to spin herself as a victim to Katie. With everything that happened that day and my new resolution to stop playing by the rules, I finally accepted the punishment for those four that had been in the deepest, blackest part of my heart but that I had said no to.

Those punishments I had promised to the five men in Winter's note—giving myself permission to go that far because they had taken a life. The standard rules didn't apply. Society's morals could no longer hold me. Even a country that condemns murder allows the death penalty to punish those who commit it.

Levi, Owen, Ashton, Wesley, and Giovanni were murderers. They earned what was coming to them.

But Queen Saylor and her Royal Handmaidens didn't kill Winter. The other Royals didn't kill Winter. I couldn't unleash my fury on them. I had to stay within the rules.

Not anymore.

That morning as I wrapped my hands around Gabriella's throat, I realized how wrong I was. The evil callousness that made her blame my sister for her death was the same callousness that Winter faced every day while the Truth or Dare Club made her life hell, and they all stood by and did nothing about it.

Everyone that could've stopped her and didn't was just as guilty of her death as those five. And everyone who didn't have the fucking decency to feel guilty about it, and instead taunted me and mocked her death—they were begging to finally be put in their place.

I wasn't holding back anymore. I wasn't clinging to the final remains of the good girl I used to be. Murderers met one of two fates: death or life in a cage.

T.O.D. Club chose their path. Now I'll choose their future.

Sitting down at my desk, I pulled that piece of paper with only Saylor's name written on it. My hand whipped back and forth across the sheet as I planned her revenge, and her friends, and the club, and the Royals.

I was done being the only one holding myself back. The Royals were used to being the biggest bully on the playground. They would find out what happens when the smallest, quietest kid brings a surprise to the fight.

***

"Luna."

I snapped my head up, squinting at the door. Wilder leaned against the frame, glancing at the mess of papers in front of me.

"You need to see this."

"The club," I rasped. How long had I been sitting there that my voice had gone rough from disuse? "You got on to the site."

"I did." He ducked out. "Come and see."

I pushed away from my desk without hesitation, hurrying after him.

Wilder's room was as cold as ever. The cage around his bed was open. I tugged a warm fleece throw and wrapped myself in it. "Where are the guys?"

"Cato and Rafael are in Rafael's room, talking to their father. Lucien went out to handle some business for me." There was an odd note in his voice. "For us."

"Okay," I said, accepting that easily as I narrowed on the reason all this began. "Finally."

"Don't say that yet." He wheeled a chair beside his.

"Why not?" I sat down before the computer. **Truth or Dare** flashed bold and large across the screen. "We have them now."

"Luna, all we have is what we're looking at."

Looking at Wilder, I frowned. I'd never seen this expression on his face before. He almost looked...

"I can't hack this site."

...defeated.

I flicked from him to the laptop. "What do you mean you can't hack this site? You hack government websites like their password is one, two, three, four. You can hack anything."

His fists balled. "I never said I could hack anything, and I can't hack this."

"Why?"

But Wilder wasn't looking at me. His eyes glazed staring at the screen. "Because he's too good."

"He?"

He blinked, shaking himself. "Yeah, he. Whoever the club hired to code and protect the site. Considering who we're dealing with, it's not a surprise that they can afford the best that money can buy. They'd have to. Take a look at the truths and dares they're doling out," Wilder said. "If the dean ever saw this, he'd close Regalia U, burn it down, and scorch the earth. The web of cheating, corruption, and lies here goes too deep for anyone to get rid of."

I pulled the laptop toward me, scrolling and scanning down.

It was interesting that the site itself was rather simple. The front page was set up kind of like a text screen. On one side there were truths and dares, and on the other side were screen names. I put together right away that the screen name was who had taken on the dare or truth. Like Gabriella said, some of the names were in purple—a Dreg.

"Otaku56, RosesAndThorns, RichBitch124," I read. "This is really how they do things. No one knows for sure who they're daring to—"

A window popped on the screen, making me jump.

"It's done that five times in the last hour," Wilder said. "This is what Montana was talking about. When enough people are logged in, the system automatically starts up a game. It picks two people randomly."

My head bobbed. "One to give the truth or dare, and one to accept it. Want to be in the club, then you have to play. No one sits on the sidelines."

"Check out what people are asked to do," he said. "No one knows who they're talking to, so for truth they have to find out a truth instead. *'Find out if it's true Harlow Peters is sleeping with her Chem T.A. for better grades.' 'Find out if it's true Cortland Holmes went to rehab last summer.'*

"I went back through the history and found truths based on our lists. *'Find out if it's true Wesley took locker room shots of the girls in high school.' 'Find out if it's true Owen Thasher assaulted the caterer's assistant.'*" Wilder tapped the screen. "You click on these and there're photos, PDFs, videos, links, whatever it takes to show proof of the truth. Whoever got Wesley's truth, showed his laptop and the file he has with all the pictures. This is prime blackmail material, Luna."

"It's like the first club too," I whispered. "They went after people's truths instead of giving their own too. Whoever restarted this must've known about the original club. Heard it from their father," I said, leaning back in my seat. "The private dares. How do you do it?"

"It's as simple as clicking on a name and sending them a message."

Wilder chose RosesAndThorns. A message box immediately popped up. At the bottom, next to *send*, was the option to be anonymous. RosesAndThorns didn't have to know my username if I didn't want them to. I flicked to the bag-of-money emoji.

"The reward I'll give if they accept my dare. You're right, Wilder. It's all so simple. Ruining someone's life is as easy as typing a few sentences." A thought occurred to me. "But what about the penalties? All these usernames are people, and all these people have done an impressive job keeping this a secret. How do they know to be so scared? Does it say anywhere what happens if they snitch or refuse a dare?"

Wilder's voice was grave. "Take a look for yourself." That time, Wilder clicked on Giovanni's username and brought up his profile.

My eyes widened.

"The hell..." I breathed. "What is this?"

"It's everything I said. I warned there was something off about this town and the people who live here. Even more so than the average uber-rich village of out-of-touch trust-fund babies and moguls." He smacked the screen. "The kind of surveillance operation it would take to get this information is off the scale. I mean, we're talking parabolic microphones, hidden cameras, human plants, spies, trackers!" he shouted, shooting to his feet.

There was no stopping my Wilder when he was on a roll, so I didn't try.

He paced the length of the carpet. "I've been going back and forth on this for the last thirty minutes. At first thought, you'd believe the government is collecting this information. Regalia is home to the majority of the country's most influential families. The majority of our titans of industry. But again, the government can't get their hands on the kind of protections that are on this site.

"Someone else wants this info, but why and for what purpose? A foreign government? Possibly. Foreign business leaders? Likely. A well-funded anarchist group? I'd have to go through the list." Wilder was mostly talking to himself at that point. "One of the Royals? Keeping tabs on everyone for leverage their family can use for three lifetimes. Like Saylor Burkhardt and her scroll."

"Before it ended up a pile of ash on the carpet," I reminded. "I'd wonder if Saylor is behind this, but that scroll was old. Much older than six years. Her family has been keeping the Royals under their thumb for a long time. They don't need this club for blackmail."

I drifted back to the screen. "But whoever does is doing a scary good job at it."

Looking back at me wasn't a list of rules, threats, or penalties. It was a list of Giovanni Natale. Everything he'd never want someone to know about him from birth to death.

The extra toe he was born with that his parents had removed.

His preoccupation with touching himself during his childhood that made not one, but two teachers in two separate grades recommend homeschooling.

The test he was caught cheating on in the ninth grade that resulted in his parents paying off the teacher.

The name of the tutor he hired in the tenth grade to do all his homework assignments.

The guy Giovanni hired to take the SATs in his place.

The severe dyslexia diagnosis he was hiding that explained the history of cheating.

His secret relationship with Gabriella. His coke addiction. His Asian porn addiction. His continued love of public masturbation, and the many places around town he's taken his penis out for the thrill. And that was just a fraction of the list.

It was all there written out, and just like the completed dares, it came with photos, videos, documents, and whatever was needed to provide proof. A photo of him kissing Gabriella against a tree with his hand up her skirt was taken shortly before he died. I recognized the outfit Montana was wearing, and the latte stains Cato got on it.

"That's why he swore they'd know if he ever said something he shouldn't," I said. "That's why he was so freaked the night he tracked me down at the party. Someone's been watching him, digging into his life, unearthing his secrets. Fuck's sake, the owners of this club don't need to make threats or list penalties. One look at this list when you join up, and you'll keep your mouth shut."

"This goes beyond hacking," Wilder said, reclaiming his seat. "It's like someone implanted a camera in his forehead and a recorder up his ass. They know things they shouldn't know. They have access to information they shouldn't have access to. And of all things, they use it to run a dare club."

"But look at what this dare club has been able to do." Pain choked me. "Look at how it's been weaponized to control Royals, put Dregs on puppet strings, and destroy a member's enemies. This club was the Phantom's murder weapon and we never would've known if it wasn't for Giovanni. How many other people have been hurt, tormented, raped, or killed because of this club, and no one ever knew?"

"*We* might never know. The page only shows recent truths and dares, and they don't show private ones at all. I can't hack this site, Luna. The Phantom sent a private message to the very fucking account we're on, and I can't tell you who." His expression shredded my heart. "I'm so sorry."

"Hey," I said, dropping everything and taking his hands. "You have nothing to apologize for. I wouldn't even have gotten this far without you. You, Rafael, Cato, and Lucien. We're getting closer to him, Wilder. I know it. It's only a matter of time."

I chewed my lip. "There is one thing I don't understand though."

"What is it?"

"Why in the hell would a member see all their dirty, dark secrets listed out like this, and then turn around and invite their friends? Gabriella said Giovanni got her into the club. Why would he do that when the people in charge freaked him out so much?"

He scrubbed his face, sighing. "I don't know, but there has to be a reason. It only benefits the leaders to have dozens of flies spinning in their web. They'd make sure their recruiter was effective. But that's the good news."

"Good news? What do you mean?"

"Natale is gone. It's only a matter of time before we lose access to his account. Fortunately, he was a recruiter..." Wilder scrolled down and clicked a link that read *share*. "He would send the link for people to join and create profiles, Luna. He also sent the instructions to prevent hackers like me from finding the link if I ended up in the wrong student account." The first smile stretched his lips. "I don't have to tell you where I'm going with this, do I?"

My smirk matched his. "No, you don't. But is it that simple? Won't whoever is behind this club know I've joined? I have to sign up through my student account."

His smile didn't go anywhere. "Not a problem. I can't hack this site, but I can hack a student account hogtied and blindfolded in my sleep. Just pick one."

Squealing, I jumped on his lap and planted a searing kiss smack on his mouth. Wilder was never sexier than when he was helping me plot Royal destruction.

"Speaking of," I drew out, giggling as his hands found their way beneath my shirt. "There's something else we have to do tonight, and someone else we have to torment in the morning."

"Just tell me who."

Chapter Seven

I craned my neck, straining to reach the zipper on my new dress. It was tight, short, Katie-approved, and lethal. It was also the single most frustrating piece of fabric on the planet.

First, there was forcing it over my hips. The chains up and down the sides had no give, and they scratched me for the trouble. Then, there was doing up the lace over my cleavage. Super cute and sexy. Super intricate and irritating to do up. But the last and final step, reaching the damn zipper down my back, was proving the most difficult.

"Rafael."

My boyfriend stretched out naked on his sheets, watching the show. The guy looked like a Roman god, reclined on the mess we made of his bed.

"You could help me, you know."

Stretching, he slinked off the bed. "If you insist."

Rafael got behind me, tore the zipper down, and slid the dress off my shoulders over my squawking.

"Rafael— Ah!"

He tossed me on the bed, then tossed himself after me. I laughed when he peppered my throat with kisses, wrapping my legs around his waist.

"Sorry, Cloud Girl. I help you out of clothes, not into them."

"A very clear and specific rule." Goose bumps popped along my flesh, following Rafael's kiss trail to my breasts. "But we can't," I whispered for no reason. "I have to get to class."

"Skip."

"I skipped yesterday. Besides, today is going to be a very good day. I can feel it."

"Is that why you're dressed to have everyone who sees you cream their pants?"

Grinning, I shrugged. "I just felt like dressing up today."

He slipped my nipple free. Holding my gaze, he languidly encircled the tip with his tongue. Maybe I would skip classes that morning.

"You're a terrible influence on me."

"They don't call me a Rogue to flatter me, darling." He rolled off, groaning like the act physically pained him. "But today is going to be a good day. I won't be the reason you miss the look on her face."

I kissed him. "Another thing. We didn't get to finish our conversation yesterday, and I want to make sure we're on the same page. I won't do anything to betray you guys because what we have means everything to me, but the truth is a relationship like ours is new to me. I don't know what the rules are."

"This about that joker that wants to hide you?"

"Yes," I confessed. "But he has a good reason. His being with me is forbidden in more ways than one. As long as he respects and isn't treating me like a secret, are you okay with me being with him?"

Rafael tangled in my hair. His touch was soothing tracing circles on my temple. "You have to tell us who *him* is eventually."

"I'd tell you right now if I could, but it won't be long. There's someone who has to know first. When they do, everything will be out in the open."

"All right, then it's cool with me."

"Really?" I asked, cupping his cheek.

"Yeah, Luna. After you and Lucien came back from the vamp club, he came to me kicking himself for hooking up with you when he knew I was into you, but he was still ready to kick my ass to keep you." He grinned lopsidedly. "I did get in the free shot he offered me 'cause who wouldn't?"

"Rafael!"

"But then we got into it with Wilder and Cato, and laid it all out. We really meant what we said about letting you decide what our relationship is. We don't care who you're with, as long as we're with you."

I bit my lip, penning in my smile. It seemed strange to be happy my boyfriend was okay with me fucking my English professor. Didn't stop me being happy as hell. How did I get so lucky finding four guys who supported and accepted me through everything?

Life shat on me for years. Dealing me the worst hands and putting my sister through hell, and now it decides I deserve some good luck?

It didn't decide anything. I made my own luck. I'm the one who said no more, came to Regalia U, took charge of my fate, and found the men who were meant for me. That bitch karma doesn't get any credit.

I kissed him. "Want to join me today?"

His smile twitched. It was so fast, I could've imagined it. "Can't. I'm meeting up with my old man this morning."

"Is this about how he got into the Gallery?"

"It's about his chat with you." Rafael stood and started getting dressed. The atmosphere had shifted. We definitely weren't sneaking in a quickie that morning. "The whole thing doesn't make sense. He didn't need to come here just to tell you to your face that he won't tell you anything."

"I got the impression he was checking me out." I went to work doing up my dress again. "And warning me not to bring you and Cato down with me."

"We can take care of ourselves," he said to the wall. His back was to me while he pulled up his jeans. "Something else he didn't need to come here and say."

"I brought up the same point. You're paid to get into all kinds of danger-ous situations. You make enemies that try to burn you alive. Why the fatherly concern now?" Coming up behind him, I slid my arms around his waist. "I said it was because he knows the enemy that we're facing. An enemy that's more dangerous than Levi ever could be."

"Your body is delicious, but I fell in love with your brains too, Cloud Girl."

I heated up at the casual mention of "love."

"I guessed the same thing," Rafael continued. "We're going to get him to tell us who. If we can cut the bullshit and end this today, we have to try."

"I agree, but can you get your father to tell you?"

He turned and beamed at me. "I've never gotten my father to do a single thing he didn't feel like doing in nineteen years. But there's a first time for everything."

I cupped his cheek and kissed him slow and deep, pouring waves of sup-port and comfort into him. "Good luck."

"Good luck to you." Rafael lightly pecked my nose. "Make them cry, ba-by. Make them fucking cry."

"Oh, I will."

A few more kisses and some light fooling around later, I finally made it downstairs. Voices floated up the steps, deflating my happy balloon.

"—know that's not blood. Admit it."

"What else would it be?"

"Fruit juice. Water and dye. An over-commitment to the act."

I stepped off as Victor set his breakfast of jam and toast on the table. Life with a nanny, chef, and butler didn't prepare him for making his own meals.

"Are you faking it because I'm here, or do you really put on this show twenty-four seven?"

Lucien raised a perfect brow. They faced off across the dining table. "Show? Act?"

"Yeah. Everyone knows you pretend you're a vampire, so you can't be called as a credible witness against your family and the family business. Gotta really commit to go for the insanity defense—"

I stifled a sigh. Victor made friends everywhere he went.

"—so respect for keeping it up all these years. But you've got to take a day off, man."

Lucien took a slow, measured sip of that red drink. "I'm sure I don't know what you're talking about. I'm not putting on an act, and if I was, it wouldn't be for any legal reason. My descendants run a perfectly legal and upstanding business."

"And I'm a fairy princess."

"What you get up to is your business."

Time to step in. "Whoa, okay," I said, entering the kitchen. "This is a fun conversation, but how about another one?" I sidled up to Victor, tentatively laying a hand on his shoulder. "Victor, are—are you okay?"

He pulled a face. "Yeah, I'm fine. Why?"

I scanned him. Victor lost it when he found out about the kiss. If he had talked to Adonis, his poker face wouldn't be this flawless. He didn't know.

"Just asking. I hope you're sleeping better."

"Actually, I couldn't sleep last night. I got up and made cocoa, then I went to see if you were awake and wanted some." He pinned me with his gaze. "But you weren't in your room."

Because I was in Rafael's.

"No, I wasn't." My hand was still on his shoulder. I squeezed. "Do you want to talk about it?"

Looking away, he pushed back from the table. "What's there to say? I need real food. I'm grabbing something from the café. See you in class."

He was gone before I could get another word in. I slumped on the stool, eyes fluttering shut. If he was like this about Rafael, what chance did I have that he'd be okay with me and Adonis? Adonis was barely okay with me and Adonis. Everything became so complicated, so fast.

"Everything all right, Lady Luna?"

I opened my eyes and tried for a smile. "Everything is fine. I'm heading out early today. Want to join me?"

He offered me his arm. "It'd be my pleasure."

Lucien and I headed out arm in arm like the old-timey couple we would be if I'd worn a Victorian outfit to match his. Thinking of that reminded me of the one time I did, and what we got up to in that vampire club.

"Lucien, how come we haven't gone back to the club?"

Heavy clouds blotted out the sun, spreading an ominous warning like the lightning ripping through the atmosphere. Damp clung to my skin and hair, frizzing my ends, and beading on the back of my neck.

It was the perfect morning. Like me, Zeus knew what was coming. He sent the right greeting to darken this day. It marked the beginning of the end for *them*.

"I don't go that often. It used to be smaller. Intimate. Just me and a dozen friends and acquaintances from the old days. Now it's overrun by new blood and their dates, or their lunch. There won't be such an audience the next time I have you."

"Next time?" I bumped his shoulder and lingered. "When is next time?"

"The excitement is in not knowing," he said, "but screw that. How does tonight sound?"

I laughed.

"We'll get out of the Gallery and grab dinner. Then, we'll see where we end up."

"Sounds perfect. What do you think of Toussaint's?" I dropped my chin on his shoulder, breathing the sweet, bergamot scent that was him. "It's infested with Royals, but they've got the best stuffed salmon I've ever tasted. I swear I didn't even like seafood before that place."

"We can go wherever you wish."

We talked about the date while we weaved through campus, picking up looks. Everywhere Lucien went he got stares. Whether it was because of how he dressed, or that he was one of the most gorgeous men anyone would see in real life. Or both. I couldn't stand next to him without being in the spotlight of a dozen pairs of eyes. And jealousy was in every one of them.

Soon the music hall came into view. There weren't that many people loitering around the Royal-only eating spot, but those that were there were already preoccupied with some interesting reading.

I couldn't hold back my smile as we slinked up to the tree. It was perfectly planted to block us from view while allowing us to overhear and see everything on the raised balcony.

Lucien leaned against the bark—one foot bent and resting on the tree. He wore all black that morning. Black tailcoat, black pants, and a black stud through his ear—adding an air of bad-boy sexiness that he couldn't shake for all that he called me lady, kissed my knuckles, and was more polite and kind to me than anyone had been in my life.

There was a devil under the gentleman. He couldn't be hidden.

My legs moved toward him on their own power. Lucien raised a brow as I molded myself to him, running my hands down his chest, his abs, his thighs... and spreading his legs to interlace mine with his.

As naturally as breathing, I closed the distance, pressing my lips to his.

Lucien groaned like the act hurt him. Burned him. As though I was the sun come to steal all those years spent without me, and return him to where he belonged. In this afterlife with me.

The briefest pause, then he snapped me around, throwing me against the tree. I moaned loud and wanton as his mouth devoured me. Lips bruising. Tongues tangling. Breaths mingling. Kissing Lucien was like sticking my finger in an electric socket. I knew I'd never survive him, but for the time he'd overtook my senses, I never felt more alive.

I broke away gasping. Lucien didn't stop.

Nipping and kissing his way down, a soft "oh" escaped me when his canines lightly scraped my throat.

My fingers curled on the nape of his neck. "Have you ever bit anyone with those fangs?"

"Naturally."

"Bite me." It was out of my mouth before I thought about it. "Go ahead, Lucien. I want you to."

"Luna, I..." He fixed on my neck, licking his lips. Lucien gazed at me like I was a shiny red apple, begging for a bite.

Breathing me in, Lucien licked the vein pulsing beneath my skin.

"I can't," he said, shaking himself. "I get... carried away. Trust me, this isn't the time or place to do this."

"Tonight is the time." I traced the line of his jaw, leading up to his lips, and those sharpened canines. "You pick the place."

"Don't ask for this unless you truly want it." His eyes darkened. "Because I won't hold back."

"I've never asked you to."

Lucien untangled from me. It brought me no small amount of pleasure to see the bulge in his pants.

"They should be here soon," I said, rising on tiptoe to hawk-watch the door. "They come every morning because heaven forfend they eat in the café with the serfs— Look," I hissed. "There they are."

Piper, Everleigh, Saylor, and Katie blew onto the balcony with a crowd of sophomore girls trailing them.

I clicked my tongue. "I guessed that Gabriella would stay home to get pampered and babied rather than let anyone see she got her ass kicked again, but I'm still pissed she's missing this."

"What exactly is she missing?"

"Patience, my Lucien." Saylor and the others slowed when they saw the stacks of paper weighted down on their favorite table. "Won't be long now. Seconds, in fact."

"What's this?" Piper asked.

The students milling about watched the group and suddenly dropped their conversations to whispers.

Katie pushed through them and picked one up. "What the hell? It's a truth list. But I thought those were over since Ashton..."

Since Ashton was murdered. The guy everyone thought was behind the lists. It didn't affect my plans that they'd all figure out he wasn't. That's just more blame and pressure brought against Wesley, Levi, and Owen. They sent an angry mob after the wrong guy and now he was dead. Most likely killed by one of them.

"Who is it about this time?" Everleigh asked, gliding to her chair.

I wished I could use another word. The fact of life was that Everleigh Starling moved like a model and a dancer's love child. She was the most glamorous person I'd laid eyes on. Some would say more glamorous than Saylor—if not for Saylor's unrelenting confidence. Your eyes just kept going back to the woman who owned the world and knew it.

"It's about..." Katie cringed. "It says the truth about Piper Alvar."

"What? Me? Let me see that!" Piper snatched it from her.

My grin stretched across my lips. I knew the exact moment she reached the best part when—

"Ahh!"

I sighed. "This is my favorite day since I started at this school."

<u>The Truth About Piper Alvar</u>

Number One: Piper used to fool around with her cousin. They broke it off a year ago.

Number Two: Piper didn't spend the summer in Spain. She was in rehab.

Number Three: Piper sneaks her sister's ADHD meds and other pills to get through school and competitions. Hence, the rehab.

Number Four: Piper is in love with Everleigh Starling.

Number Five: And Everleigh feels the same way about her.

Piper stopped her shrieking once she reached the end. She just stood there—eyes huge staring at the paper.

"What is it?" her friends carried on. "What does it say?"

Everleigh read through the list. I knew exactly when *she* got to the right part because—

"Wait, what?!"

"Everleigh..."

Both Everleigh's and my attention snapped to Piper.

"Is it true?" A soft, tender smile broke through. "You feel the same way?"

"Do I—?" Everleigh whipped around at the rapt, silent audience. "No! Of course not—"

Piper reeled back, tears springing to her eyes.

"No, I mean— Not of course not," she said quickly. "I just meant— Piper, I'm sorry, but I don't have those kinds of feelings for you. I have no idea why this says I do. You and I are just friends."

I'd give Everleigh credit. She dropped the haughty, better-than-you tone for five seconds. Gentleness entered her words. She took a step toward Piper, reaching for her. "We are friends, right?"

Piper flung herself away and tripped over a chair. Both went down with a crash that made me and Lucien hiss.

Katie ran to her.

"Get off!" Shoving up, Piper stumbled over her feet—sobbing. Flat-out, crimson-eyes, snot-running-down-her-face, open-mouthed sobbing.

"Piper, it's okay," Katie said, getting her arms around her. "Whoever made that list is a sick, twisted shit who copied Ashton for attention. No one believes it— Piper, please don't cry."

"It w-w-was a sick, twisted piece of sh-shit," she howled. It was hard to make her out through the tears. "But they didn't... do it to copy Ashton."

Piper broke free of Katie and turned on her as she approached to pile on the hug. She punched her in the mouth, popping Saylor off her feet.

Eyes bugging, I choked on a cry.

"How could you!?"

"Piper!" Everleigh and Katie screamed.

Everyone else just screamed—hollering their shock at the Queen Bee herself laid flat out on the concrete.

Did that just happen? That didn't just happen!

"I trusted you," Piper shrieked. "You did this just because you thought I was spilling secrets to that Dreg bitch, Sinclair? I told you it wasn't me!"

The groaning heap that was Saylor Burkhardt tried to get up and lolled. She tipped onto her front and choked, spitting blood. "What. The. Fuck!" Saylor's voice reached new decibels. "You hit me! I can't believe you hit me!"

"I can't believe you wrote this!" Piper flung the stack at her.

The wind caught it, carrying sheets over the balcony to shower around us. Lucien and I ducked out of sight. Drawing me in, Lucien encircled my waist—his arm warm and solid around me. I didn't see a reason to move. So I didn't.

"I didnth't thrite it." Saylor's mouth was swelling fast. "It wasn't me, you thucking idiot!"

"Oh," I crooned. "Saylor is not striking the right tone right about now."

Lucien chuckled in my ear, then nibbled on it. Heat pooled in my middle. What was happening right then was the only possible thing I could want more than seeing Saylor Burkhardt as a bleeding mess on the ground.

"I know it was you," Piper flung. "You're the only person I told. If it wasn't you, who was it?"

Saylor didn't get a chance to answer. Piper grabbed Katie's hand and dragged her away, marching them both off the balcony and away from Saylor. Piper's sobs echoed back long after I lost sight of her.

No one on the balcony was speaking. Two girls rushed to help Saylor up, but they didn't say anything. They were looking where everyone else was. At Everleigh who gazed after Piper but stood beside Saylor—not making a move in either direction.

"Saylor, you did this?" Everleigh asked so softly, the wind tried to snatch the question away before it reached me. "All because you thought she told Sinclair about Rhys?"

"It wasn't me!"

Everleigh shook her head. "This is fucked up even for you. Even if Piper spilled to the Dreg, she didn't tell the whole damn school. She didn't do *this*."

"Shut up and thisten to me." Saylor shoved her helpers off her. Blood soaked her mouth and chin. Flailing around on the ground knocked her hair loose from her bun and dirtied her expensive, cashmere sweater. Between the wild eyes, the shock still on her face, and her staggered walk, she looked like she just escaped the Hunger Games. "I had thothing to do with that list—"

Everleigh walked away.

"I didn't— Everleigh! Everleigh, get back here!"

A low whistle brought me back to Lucien. "I didn't appreciate until now what a lethal combination you and Wilder make."

I smirked. "One little hacked messaging account and that's one Royal Highness knocked off her throne. I swear, Wilder could rule the world if he wanted to."

"Don't put the idea in his head." Lucien jerked his chin toward the balcony. "Was she covering? Did Everleigh admit to having feelings for Piper in one of the messages?"

"Nope," I breezed. "I made up number five so that Piper would do exactly what she did and get her hopes up. Once she proved one truth was real, no one would believe the other three were false. Now everyone knows she messed around with her cousin, is addicted to pills, and is in love with Everleigh... and they know it because one of her best friends since diapers cruelly spilled it to the entire campus."

"Lethal."

I shrugged. "I try."

"Was this punishment for Piper or Saylor?"

I looked up as Saylor stormed away. "I never could've predicted she'd punch the girl out," I said, laughing. "But it's for both of them. It's for all of them. Gabriella, Everleigh, and Piper joined in on Saylor's sick revenge, and dressed as my dead sister. They're all going to pay, but I'm happy to let them fight Saylor for the life vest on the way down."

Lucien and I snuck away, leaving the Royals overhead to gush about what happened, and spread it to everybody.

"I can't tell you what's going to happen," Lucien said. "In the years I've been going to school with them, Saylor and her friends have gotten into fights, but it was only ever Katie who was willing to really tell her off. The others quickly backed down from any true confrontation. And none of them— Scratch that, no one in Saylor's whole life has hit her other than you.

"Don't know what she's going to do next, but Saylor can't sit back and take that kind of thing. Even so, everyone thinks she kicked this off by making that list, so anything she does to Piper now—"

"—will still make her look bad," I finished. I wished I could stop smirking. It'd been so long since I used my smile muscles, my face was starting to ache. "No doubt my first plan against Owen, Wesley, Levi, and the others wasn't good, but I've been learning from the best since then. No amount of money, privilege, or status will save Saylor Burkhardt from what I've got planned for her.

"The destruction started at the top and spreads all the way down. I promised her she wouldn't need that scroll anymore because I was bringing every Royal to their knees. I keep my promises."

***

I said bye to Lucien at the door. I was a little early, but that was the point. I knew he'd be there.

Professor Anthony didn't look up from his laptop. "Good morning."

"Morning."

He flicked up and landed on me, and my outfit. Adonis quickly schooled his face, though not quick enough to stop me catching the quick widening of his eyes, and the lust burning inside them.

"Miss Sinclair."

I came toward him, internally chuckling at the stiffening of his shoulders. This man couldn't be afraid of little old me. *More like afraid of what he'd do to me. On this desk.*

I glanced behind at the half a dozen students who came to class early too. *Not likely.*

"You can take your seat, Miss Sinclair."

"If I did that, how would I give you this?" I fished that week's writing assignment out of my backpack—the picture of innocence.

His hand brushed mine taking it from me and I bit hard on my lip. I was real excited that morning to put on the sexiest dress I'd ever seen, and come in there and tease him, but I underestimated the effect he'd have on me.

Adonis chose a simple button-up and tie that morning, but that was all the man needed. His shirt hung tight on his frame, outlining the muscles that rippled up his biceps as he moved. Tousled locks hung over piercing eyes that focused so firmly on my face, I knew what he really wanted to look at—and was fighting not to—was my cleavage.

He leaned forward to place my paper with the rest and a wave of citrus and sage washed over me. In a blink I was in that office with him, moaning into his palm while he pounded me from behind. If you had told me, the fresh-from-Catholic-school girl, that I'd hold the memory of a professor coming on my face, I would've cursed you out for being crude and creepy. Wild how quickly life and people can change.

"Is that all, Miss Sinclair?"

"When will you talk to him?" I dropped, blunt as a truck. "Are you doing it today?"

Adonis flicked over my shoulder. "Now isn't the time for this conversation," he gritted.

"Doesn't have to be a conversation. Tell me yes or no."

"No. And to save us both some time." He blew out a breath. "I'm not going to."

"What does that mean? You're not going to what?"

Sighing, he looked away, then met my gaze. "I'm not going to tell him."

"Are you saying you want me to do it?"

"I'm saying I was wrong," Adonis replied. "My job isn't all I have. I also have Victor. I'm sorry, Luna, but as far as I'm concerned... yesterday didn't happen."

I went still. "So that's it? You won't give him a chance to surprise you? To forgive you?"

"I'm not willing to risk that he won't." Adonis straightened and schooled his face with a finality that chilled me. "Now, unless you've got questions about the assignment or the reading, we have no more to discuss."

I gave him my back and claimed a seat in the front row without a word.

The class slowly filled up with yawning zombies and chipper morning people.

What I wouldn't give to be a sophomore sitting in on Saylor and the Handmaidens' general classes. I couldn't watch the fallout from that morning's glorious sucker punch, but the guys promised to keep me updated.

Me: What am I missing?

Lucien: Not a thing unfortunately. Or fortunately? None of them have showed up for class.

Me: Not a surprise. Saylor wouldn't want everyone seeing her with a busted lip. Piper will want to avoid Everleigh, and Katie will want to be there for Piper. Is everyone talking about what happened?

Lucien: They're talking about nothing but. You were right, Lady Luna. Public opinion is not on Saylor's side.

My fingers flew across the screen.

Me: What are they saying?

Lucien: Some are saying it's sick that she copied Ashton after these lists got him murdered. A few are laughing at all of them. Saylor and her friends aren't liked among the Dregs, and they're pleased to watch them tear each other apart. But the rest are on Piper's side. To sum it up, no one is on Saylor's.

"Phones away."

Adonis's order tripped me up mid-reply.

I left the text unsent and tossed my phone in my bag. Lucien and I would pick up the conversation later. That night. On our date. I loved all those words together and on their own. I loved even more picturing what we'd do on our date that night.

The Rogues weren't the dinner-and-a-movie type. The first time Lucien took me out, we went to a vampire club where he finger-fucked me on the dance floor to multiple orgasms. The first time Rafael and I went out alone, we sat car-side eating empanadas and fried plantains while blowing up cars and ratting out affairs. The only thing I expected of that night was that it'd blow my expectations out of the water.

Taking out my things, I glanced around looking for Victor.

Not here.

Worry trickled into my good mood. Victor said he was grabbing food in the café, then meeting me in class. Why would he ditch? Was he avoiding me because he was more upset about me and Rafael than he let on?

"All right, everyone." Adonis clapped, bringing the class's attention to the front. "Today, we're starting a new section. After weeks of enduring me analyzing and critiquing your work, it's now your turn."

I reached in my bag and pulled something out. I unwrapped it—the crinkling making Adonis glance at me and quickly look away.

"You have a list of twenty books that I attached to your syllabus. Choose whichever interests you and, here's where it gets interesting, you'll also analyze it in whichever way interests you," he said. "You choose the lens through which you'll critique this work."

I twirled the lollipop stick through my fingers. It was a huge jawbreaker of a thing. Swirls of pink, green, red, and white coated a caramel center, promising a treat inside as tasty as the one outside.

Adonis glanced at me again, then looked away again. "Yes, Mr. Marks?"

"This isn't one of your tricks, is it, Professor? You say we can choose the research topic, and we think it's going to be an easy paper, then we're all crying the day you hand them back. Because our weekly papers are pass-fail, and I've never worked harder on anything in my life."

The class cracked up. It was funny... because it was true.

Adonis chuckled along with everyone else. "No tricks here, Mr. Marks."

I pressed the lollipop to my lips and licked—slow, sweet, and thorough. Rainbowy sweetness coated my tongue.

"You can choose the topic, but I said nothing about e-easy."

I caught his slip of the tongue as quick as his eyes ping-ponging me again.

Adonis cleared his throat. "I've read all twenty of these books cover to cover, at least four times each, and analyzed them through every angle. Your challenge is to bring something new to the discussion."

Slowly, I slid the pop in, out, in, out of my mouth—lips forming an "o" around the candy ball.

"Not necessarily a new... topic," he said, "but... a point of view that is uniquely yours." Adonis shook himself. I could practically hear the phrase *get a hold of yourself!* go through his head. "It said on some website that inhumanity is one of the main themes of *The Grapes of Wrath*, so you hand in five pages based on what someone else told you the book was about.

"Do you agree the main characters were treated unfairly and without compassion? Maybe you don't," he said, shrugging. "Life's hard, man. You fall into the gutter, it's up to you to get yourself out. No one owes you a hand up."

I slid the pop further in and softly gagged. Adonis flung around the desk and gave his back to the class. I giggled as he continued speaking to the whiteboard.

"If that's your take, then write it. As long as you back up your thesis with the text and other supporting literary works, I'm intrigued to discover what the *classics* are to you. To some, *The Great Gatsby* is a masterpiece. To others, it's overhyped, sexist drivel. Tell me why."

"Uh, Professor Anthony?"

His back stiffened harder than stacked bricks. "Yes, Miss Sinclair?"

"Are we limited to only these twenty? Can we make a case for another book?"

He took a beat to reply. "What did you have in mind?"

"*Frankenstein*."

"Hmm. There are certainly a lot of themes to mine there and—"

"Sorry, Professor." A smirk danced on my lips. "I didn't get that."

Slowly, he stopped pretending he needed to write on the board and faced me. "*Frankenstein* would be a great story to explore, and it almost made this list."

My hand traveled down, finger skating down my throat to the network of silk ribbons holding my flimsy split dress over my breasts.

"Though, to keep it fair and simple for everyone," Adonis forced through gritted teeth. "We're sticking to the approved list."

Tongue swirling around the lollipop, I loosened the ribbons.

"But you're free to reference *Frankenstein* or another work to support your analysis." The man sounded like he was in physical pain.

"Professor."

Adonis seized the chance to look away from me and focused on Eva. It didn't stop me for a second.

I wasn't worried about anyone seeing me. No one but me was sitting in the front row. I strategically placed my notebook, binder, and bag to block everyone's view but his. Only his.

"What about doing a modern take?" Eva asked. "Like analyzing how the characters, or how society would respond differently if the story was set today. So many of these *classics* feature misogyny and non-consent like it's a given. I'd like to write how the same story of a middle-aged man and his predatory relationship with a teenage girl would end with him in prison, not living his one-sided happy ever after."

"That is exactly the kind of thing I'm looking for, Eva. Well done. I can't wait to read it."

She preened like she never received a compliment before.

My ribbons dangled on the desk, no longer attempting to do their job of scantily covering my cleavage.

Professor Anthony was fighting so hard not to look at me, veins shown stark on his forehead. It wasn't working though, because another part of him was straining just as hard.

"Really, Professor? Anything goes?" Alice asked. "Because Eva gave me an idea to do a gender swap. Like how *Cinderella* is a classic fairy tale, but if you take all that and turn Cinderella into a guy, all of a sudden the story is ridiculous and you're wondering why this guy doesn't stick up for himself. He needs rats and a fairy to grow him a backbone."

Skimming the hem of my top, I slipped it off my breast, freeing the rock-hard pebble that used to be my nipple. My sweet candy treat teased the poor thing stiffer.

"—I was thinking I could—"

"Enough!"

I jumped—smothering a laugh as I quickly covered up and innocently popped the candy in my mouth.

"Professor?" Alice cried.

Adonis scrambled. "Enough— Enough talking, everyone. Miss Warner is speaking. Let's have some respect," he said, claiming his seat. "Go on, Miss Warner."

For the first time since we entered his class, Professor Anthony delivered his entire lecture seated and behind his desk. When he dismissed class, I fixed myself and packed to leave. Yes, I spent the whole lesson teasing myself and getting pornographic with the lollipop until it was nothing but a plastic stick.

"Miss Sinclair, hang back for a minute, please. I'd like to discuss your last paper."

I let everyone stream past me, then stepped up to the desk as the last person closed the door behind them.

"I know what you're going to say," I breezed. "I didn't go deep enough on this week's paper. But I didn't connect with this prompt, Professor."

Adonis rose from his seat.

"Tell me of a time your fundamental beliefs were questioned. How did you react and what did you learn?"

He stepped around the desk.

"I don't know that I have any beliefs so firm that it'd be some big story if one was questioned. I'm pretty open to learning all that I can from everyone and— Ah!"

The classroom spun in a kaleidoscope of beige, white, and more beige. I gasped as I landed on my back, spread out on Professor Anthony's desk. He planted his hands on either side of my head—trapping me, pinning me, covering me, protecting me.

My heaving chest pressed against his as he leaned over, furious eyes swirling with so much more.

"What are you trying to do to me?"

I smiled. "Pretty sure it's about what I'm trying to get you to do to me."

"Luna!"

"Damn, Professor Anthony," I whispered, arching my body and pressing up against a prize. "You're still so hard."

His growl so reminded me of Cato, wetness pooled in my middle.

"I'm sorry, but you left me no choice," I said. "I knew you'd be difficult about this, and I already told you that I'm not giving up on us. So from now on, I'm going to give you *incentives* to change your mind."

"You can't do things like this in my classroom for everyone to see." He grabbed my wrists and pinned them over my head. Couldn't blame them, they were inching toward my ribbons again. "Are you trying to get us caught?"

"Course not. I'll be careful. Although..." My legs were very free. My thigh brushed what my hands couldn't reach. "You wouldn't be so hard right now if me doing it in the middle of your class where anyone could see didn't turn you on. Don't pretend to be this good, upstanding guy, *Professor Anthony*." His cock twitched. "We're both past that now."

"Argh!" He dove down, lips seeking mine, and halted. His heat washed over me—lips brushing so close but not close enough. The battle raged in his eyes, but need spread through his body. He rocked back on my thigh, grinding his cock on me.

Groans escaped our lips.

"No. No!" Adonis flung away, releasing me. "We can't do this. Luna, you have to go." He dug the heel of his palm into his crotch and looked to the clock. "Shit! Go now. You can't be here."

I realized immediately why he was trying to get rid of me. "No, I don't have to go. Let me help you take care of that." I got on my hands and knees, stalking toward him. "We don't have to touch each other."

"Are you kidding me?" he hissed, shooting a look at the door. "I have another class in fifteen minutes."

I hung off the edge of his desk, letting my legs fall open. His breath hitched when I tugged my thong aside. "Then, we'd better be quick."

His eyes darted back and forth from me to the entrance. The battle raged on his face for a millennium, then the winner finally kicked the other's ass. He freed himself with impressive quickness. "Take them out and lean back."

I didn't have to ask what he meant. My boobs sprang free of their ribbonless pen. Stretching out before him, I slid two fingers inside me and set a furious pace—palm *slap, slap, slapping* against my clit. No foreplay. No messing around. We didn't have time before the classroom filled with students, and if any one of them wandered in early, we were screwed.

Ripples went up my spine at the thought of someone walking in on us. It both terrified and thrilled me. The danger laced through our relationship was a drug pushing me to do things I wouldn't have dreamed in a million years.

I understood my mother and father—whoever he may be—a lot more all of a sudden. Of course they couldn't resist the forbidden relationship that created me and Winter. There was something about a man you couldn't be with that made you want him more than air.

Adonis leaned over me, cock strangled in his fist. He started pumping fast and furious, his meat missile aimed and loaded at my entrance. All he had to do was take two steps and he'd be pumping where he belonged instead of in his hand.

Imagining that quickened my pace. I could almost feel him inside me—stretching my walls. Pounding that spot. Slapping the back of my legs with his hard and muscled thighs.

"Ahh," I cried, back arching off the desk.

"Three fingers," Adonis grunted. "Spread that pussy."

"Yes, Professor Anthony."

"Dammit, Luna," he growled.

I grinned unashamedly. I knew it made him feel dirty when I called him Professor when his pants were down. I also knew he hadn't told me to stop.

Filling my newly de-virginized hole with three fingers, I whimpered from the heady mix of pain and pleasure. I cupped my breast and brought it to my lips. Holding his gaze, I licked my nipple. It still tasted sweet from the candy.

Adonis's leg buckled. He slammed his hip against the desk, expression pained but not from the hit. Every ounce of willpower he possessed was keeping him from touching me. If possible, he pumped harder and faster, his tip turning purple from the pressure. Sweat beaded on his brow, sticking to silky strands.

It amazed me that Martha knew to call the wrinkled pink potato she gave birth to Adonis. Twenty-six years later, the god of beauty himself stepped down from his throne and bowed before his namesake. He was beauty, sex, power, and intelligence in one tightly built package, and he wanted me.

I crooked my fingers, seeking that spot he found for me. Our muffled moans increased in urgency and intensity. Five more minutes till the start of his next class.

"Fuck's sake, Luna. You could turn this country into a matriarchy without lifting your finger. All men bow before you."

Goodness, his compliments made a girl feel good. Was that the perk of sleeping with a writer? Their way with words.

Adonis tensed—body bending and bowing over me. He came hard, shooting hot, thick spurts of cum all over my opening. The act careened me over the edge like a dropkick to the clit. I screamed like a banshee, my hand clamped over my mouth as my orgasm ripped through me.

I flopped boneless on the desk. One of the best orgasms of my life, and we didn't even touch each other.

"Fuck," Adonis breathed. "Why? Why you?"

The question was said so softly, I almost didn't hear it. Rising up, I reached for him. "Adonis—"

"—test was so hard. Half of the questions weren't in the book."

We sprang apart.

I tipped off the desk and fell flat on my face. Biting back a pained grunt, I let Adonis help me up and we rushed to stuff our bits back in our clothes.

The voices faded, becoming nothing but muffled mumbles beneath our ragged pants.

"Holy crap," I wheezed. "That was close—"

The door flew open and two students walked in.

"Good work on that paper, Miss Sinclair." Adonis was suddenly on the other side of the desk, busying himself with his laptop. "That'll be all. Have a good day."

Gathering my things, I walked out, letting one word float to his ear.

"Incentive."

I left the classroom smiling from ear to ear.

"Luna."

It froze on my face. "Victor?"

I took in the guy leaning against the opposite wall, gazing at me expressionlessly. My mind spun out of control.

What was he doing here? He knew he was way late to his brother's class. Did he come here to talk to Adonis?

Did he stick his head inside... and see us?

I swallowed hard, not moving an inch. I was ready to have this conversation with Victor, but Adonis wasn't. He was right that his brother was the only family he had left. It wasn't my intention to get between them. I just couldn't let Adonis go when things were still up in the air between me and Victor.

Not wanting to lose his family, home, company, and inheritance wasn't the same as wanting to be with me.

"Victor," I croaked, finding my voice. "You're here. Did you...?"

He cocked his head. His face was impossible to read. "Did I what?"

"Did you come to walk me to class?"

Victor peeled off the wall. "I came for you, but not to take you to class. I want you to go somewhere with me. You down to skip?"

"I really shouldn't skip class two days in a row." *Or go out with you when I'm once again covered in your brother's cum.*

"I'll text Branlon to give us the notes." With that, he walked off—expecting me to follow.

I hesitated only a beat before trailing him. If he did see what happened in that classroom, going off to talk was exactly what we should do. There were a lot of talks Victor and I needed to have. We were supposed to get married in less than a year. Even though everything was riding on this for both of us, I never felt further from the altar since we met.

I caught up with him on the steps outside. "Where are we going?"

"You'll see."

I didn't ask any more questions while we trekked across campus to the student parking lot. Victor's impressive ride glinted in the sun, inviting me to cuddle with its leather seats and tease all its special features. I slid in on the passenger side and watched Victor.

He was cool and impassive starting the car, pulling out of the lot, and taking off in the opposite direction of his house.

"Want to listen to music?"

"No, that's okay," I replied. "I just want to talk about whatever it is that you want to talk about."

He mouth-shrugged. "Who says I do? Maybe I just want to take you for a drive."

I stopped pressing. Whatever Victor wanted to say to me, he'd do it in his own time.

What if he did see me and Adonis in the classroom? What would be going through his head right now?

I didn't mean to strum myself off with my professor between class breaks. Adonis was looking at me like I was both the biggest mistake of his life and its greatest gift. A look like that was made to drive you crazy with its contradiction.

Leaning back, I rested my head on the window—watching mansions whip by. Cherry blossom trees lined the pavement, sharing their soft, beautiful petals with the rest of the world like little treats meant to brighten our day.

I thought back to the first day I met Victor. My stepfather had finally told me the conditions for him to pay my tuition. That morning, I stood in the entrance to their bedroom while he told Mom he was taking me to a marriage interview, and did she want to join us? She stared at a spot on the wall and didn't acknowledge that she heard a word he said.

I wish I could say I felt some kind of outrage. The guy shipped me off to boarding school. Now he was marrying me off to a complete stranger in exchange for paying for my education. It was like stepping back into an eighteenth-century nightmare. I should've been mad then. I should be mad now. But I lived in a nightmare waking and sleeping. What difference did a brooding fiancé make?

That's what I thought. Then, I met him... and discovered he was a complete asshole.

I chuckled.

"What's so funny?"

"I was thinking of the first day we met. It's weird that I've never really minded being engaged. I just hated being engaged to you."

A ghost of a smile crossed his lips. "Well, shit. It was love at first sight for me."

"Were you really into my Coke-stained sweatpants and overall sucking void of misery? I heard that's a turn-on."

"Like you wouldn't believe. I nearly married you on the spot."

We cracked up, though it ended quickly. He returned to his silence.

Victor drove farther and farther out of town. I didn't get a hint of where we were going until he turned left down a familiar road.

I cringed. This place did not hold good memories for me. "What are we doing here?"

"Don't get impatient now." Victor pulled into a parking spot in front of the marina. "You're thirty feet away from finding out."

"Yeah, but you're giving off a weird vibe right now," I said, eyeing him. "If you've brought me here to kill me, you'd better say, because I have the right to fight for my life."

He snorted. "I'm definitely not putting out the right vibe if you're getting serial killer. Just get out of the car, weirdo. You're ruining the surprise."

Victor came around and helped me out. I turned my head to the sun, eyes fluttering shut as I breathed in the salty sea breeze. Regalia Marina was a watery maze of sun-bleached mega yachts. On a good day, vendors came from all around town, parking their food trunks, setting up tarot readings, drizzling out caramel popcorn and other sweet treats to cute couples walking by.

On that day, the marina was a quiet place for just us. Waves lapped beneath the wooden slats of the dock, chiming a soft, steady rhythm that brought back memories.

The seas were calm that night too. The perfect opportunity for me to showcase my one lesson and take my stepfather's yacht out for a spin. Especially because Richard Cooperson, son of Roger Cooperson—the man who used to employ my mother as a housekeeper—kept running his mouth about the help, and how I wasn't fit to lick the decks of my stepfather's yacht, let alone step foot on it.

I shot back that he was mad that fortune changed for my mother, but not even divine intervention would cure him of being a dick. Then somehow the two of us and his smirking friends ended up on the boat, and I ended up spending the night in a police station. The cops wouldn't tell me who made the late-night anonymous call to my stepfather, reporting a theft from the marina, but I wasn't really asking. Like I said, Richard Cooperson was a fucking dick.

"Do you remember a Richard Cooperson?" I asked. I accepted Victor's hand, letting him lead me to the farthest section of the marina, and the biggest boat. "Did you go to school with him?"

"Yeah, I remember your half brother. He was kind of a dick."

I rolled my eyes. "I don't know who my father is, but he's definitely not a Cooperson. Mom was clear about that. The dick doesn't fall far from the scrotum. Roger Cooperson wasn't a nice man either. Mom would never be with a guy who disrespected her."

He turned a beaming grin on me. "Please tell me at least some things on that truth list were real."

"You can kill your fantasies of the Pussy Muncher right now. She never existed."

"Shame, but I'm holding on to my fantasies. There's one where you've covered your conquest in whipped cream and you're eating her up like a sundae. It's the highlight of the spunk reel. I cue it up almost every night."

The water held my wavering, red-faced reflection. "You're taking a real risk for someone who can't swim."

Victor howled. "Why are you asking about Richard, then?"

"It's natural to be curious about the rotted asshole who got you shipped off to boarding school."

"Damn, that was him?" Victor gestured up ahead, pointing to—I guessed it right—the four-story mega beauty at the end. "Then you'll be glad to know he applied to Regalia U, and only Regalia U, even though he was a C and D student. He thought Daddy's connections would get him in... and it didn't.

"To knock some sense into his cocky ass, Dad made him take the lowest-level job in the Cooperson company. Last I heard, he's still fetching bagels and running around the mail room."

"That does bring me joy," I said, grinning.

Together we climbed onto the boat. I stifled a whistle, but my widening eyes wouldn't be held back. I kept saying that one day I'd get used to the wealth surrounding me. When would that day come?

The whole thing was a sleek piston forged to slice through the seas. We came up next to the glass hot tub, equipped with a dozen jets and an in-floor wine chiller. Victor led me past it and through the lounge area with its comfy couches and firepit.

Visions of relaxing on that couch, roasting marshmallows while the sun set, floated through my mind. It struck me that if I married Victor, that life wouldn't be a wistful dream. It would be my reality. The future I didn't let myself think about.

It's not a bad future by anyone's definition. I just wonder who will be sharing these sunsets with me.

"You okay?" A gentle touch caressed my back. "I'm not going to kill you, I swear."

I laughed. "I'm okay. I was just picturing us on this boat in thirty years—roasting marshmallows and watching the sunset. Think we could ever get there, Victor? Get to... happy?"

"I'm glad you asked that"—Victor guided me inside—"because that's why we're here."

"Oh, Victor..." Words failed me. They too stopped to take in the sight.

A ring of candles surrounded the table, casting a soft, warm glow. I stepped lightly through the sea of rose petals—tiptoeing where they led me.

In the middle of the room, a tiny, two-person table held my surprise. Champagne, strawberries, and my favorite meal: chocolate chip pancakes.

"Oh my gosh, you did all this?" I cried. "Why?"

"Because this is what we wanted, right?" Victor held out my chair. "To start over. Get to know each other like a normal couple. Past time I took you out on a date, Sinclair."

Guilt and joy battled for dominance in my chest. Here he was planning sweet, thoughtful first dates for us. And there I was, fucking his brother.

"This is perfect, Victor," I said, meaning every word. All of Regalia stretched out before us. The mansions and the university, sure, but also rolling hills. Mighty oak trees. Colorful cottages. And the feeling I was in the most beautiful place there was. If only it wasn't surface deep. "I love it."

"I give good date, Sinclair. You should know this about me." His smirk did funny things to me. "Just wait till our second."

I cocked a brow. "Just wait till the end of our first to find out if you get a second."

That smirk went nowhere. "I'm not worried."

"Too bad we're faced toward the town instead of the ocean," I said, changing the subject fast. "What's better than eating homemade pancakes while watching the sun glinting off the water?"

"Actually, we could move to the other side, but I wanted you to see Regalia like this." He gazed out over the deck. "I know you hate this place, and you have every reason to, but when we get married, I'll make this town your home."

Lacing his fingers through mine, Victor brought them to his lips. My heart slingshotted into my throat.

"We'll have moments like this where it's just us—so far from the Royals and their games that we forget what it is to play."

"I think I'd like that," I whispered, lightly tracing his lips. "I'd like that very much."

We sat there for a long time, gazing at each other—eyes holding traces of all the things we wanted to say.

Clearing his throat, Victor shook himself and released my hand. I didn't let my disappointment show on my face.

We settled in—keeping to light topics while we ate the second-best pancakes I ever had. Number one would always be Mom's.

"What happened?" Victor asked. "Where'd you just go?"

"Oh, I—" I straightened, surprised he caught that brief flicker when my smile dimmed. "I was just thinking of my mom. Wondering what she's doing right now. I'm worried about her," I blurted. "I need her to know I'm here and that she hasn't lost me."

"I'm sure she knows, Luna." Victor looked away. "But if she does feel like she lost you, it's because of me. She wanted to end the engagement and I told you to scare her straight." His jaw clenched. "I guess I'm not that different from my parents after all."

"Don't say that. It was my choice in the end. I think even the coolest of parents struggle when their kid starts making their own choices. Especially when it's the opposite choice they want them to make."

Victor picked up the bottle to pour us more champagne. "Is staying in Regalia U worth all this? Worth marrying me?"

"It is one of the best schools in the country."

He held my gaze steadily. "Not to you."

It was my turn to look away. "I won't be chased out of my home or school. Someone has to teach the Royals that they don't always win. They will some of the time, maybe even most of the time. But when it comes to me, they already lost."

"That's why you're with the Rogues." An odd note entered his voice. "They have no love or loyalty to the Royals. They'll take anyone out for the right price. And now that they have you—"

"You have me too," I sliced in. I couldn't have him follow that thought somewhere dangerous. I didn't know what Victor would think of my vendetta against the Royals, the T.O.D. Club, and everything this town was built on. But I did know I wouldn't let him stand in my way. Better not to put him in that position in the first place. "Or you could. You just have to tell me what you want, Victor."

I took a small sip of champagne to delay the question.

"Can you accept sharing me with the Rogues?" Adonis floated through my mind, and left pressure in my core on his way out. "Or with other guys?"

"I'm thinking about it, Luna." He gazed somewhere off over the horizon. "They're your boyfriends, but I'll be your husband. You'll move into my home. You'll take your place beside me as industry leaders in the country. You'll carry the children that carry on the Wilson legacy. We'll sit on top of an empire together. Asking me to scoot down a little to squeeze in four guys with reputations black as sin, isn't an easy decision."

"But it's a decision you already made, and we both know it." I got up and stood in front of him, making him look me in the eye. "No guy on the planet needs to sit around and mull over if he wants to share his wife's pussy."

He looked at me through hooded eyes.

"You made up your mind the minute I asked you, but you're not telling me your answer because it'll change things between us. Good or bad—something will change." I dropped to my knees, placing my hands on his thighs. "Don't you think it's time you told me? It's better to move on knowing where we stand."

"I don't know what you think I have to tell you, but I haven't decided anything yet." He tipped my chin. "And even if I did, I wouldn't say it now. It could end us before we start. Or it could seal us in a promise we don't know if we want to make to each other. Right now we're not friends or lovers. We should figure out if we're one, the other, or both before I give you an answer that might change."

I nodded slowly, accepting this. Victor had a point. If in the end we decided we were just friends, then an open relationship wasn't a problem. But if he had feelings for me and decided he couldn't share...

I shouldn't force him to give me an answer I may not want to hear. I traced his face. *Even though I know he's made up his mind.*

"How do we figure it out?" I asked. "Friends or lovers. We've known each other for months. That's not a question people take this long to answer either."

"Well, we haven't been friends because you're the most stubborn, sarcastic person on the planet who holds a grudge like no one's business."

"Yes, and you're an ass."

He barked a laugh. "And we haven't become lovers because..." Victor trailed off, smiling knowingly. "That gives me an idea actually. Wow. Why didn't I think of this before?"

"Think of what?"

"We should have sex," he dropped. "Today. Right here. Right now."

I blinked at him, waiting for the words I imagined I heard to become what he really said. "Excuse me?"

"We should have sex."

He said it again, so I didn't imagine it.

"It makes sense," he continued. "Like you said, no one needs this much time to decide if they're into each other. So much shit has gotten in our way that it's messing everything up. You're hot. I'm hot. You're into my body, and I want to crawl inside that dress and die there. Fuck knows it's gotta be the happiest place on earth."

I choked. "Victor! What are you saying? We can't have sex."

"Why not?"

"I don't know! We just can't."

"Oh, well, when you put it like that." He stood, bringing me up with him. "We're about to get married. Don't you want to know if we click in that way?"

"I..." I chewed my lip. Why was I taking this long to say no? "I can't believe you're trying to get some on the first date."

He winked. "This is what no one wants to admit. Sex on the first date tells you everything you want to know. One night with a guy who smacks his own ass and calls you by his mom's name, and you're blocking his number."

"But what if it makes things more complicated?"

"More complicated than the two engagement rings you've got on your finger."

I stilled.

"Yeah, your muzzled boyfriend was kind enough to fill me in on that one. Told me you would inevitably marry him because I was going to die in a fire. Nice guy," he said sarcastically.

"Cato is not going to kill you."

"Weird that needs to be said."

"He's just trying to protect me. The guys think I'm marrying you because I have to, and that's true," I whispered. "If it was my choice, I wouldn't be planning a wedding at eighteen. Right now the only thing holding us together is our lack of choices, so... let's do it. Let's have sex."

His brows popped. "I can't believe I'm questioning a yes, but I gotta ask how you got there."

"The only thing that connects us is all that we'll lose if we call it off. Anything built on that is going to feel forced and awkward. I want us to share something else," I admitted. "Whether it's staying up late talking and drinking hot cocoa. Or crazy chemistry in bed."

Smiling, Victor brushed his fingers down my arm, and laced through mine. "Come with me."

Victor led me out of the dining room and up a spiral staircase. Excitement and nerves built in equal measure. Me and Victor? For the longest time I swore I wouldn't let him near me with a Hefty bag condom. We were shaking hands at the altar, and maybe not even that.

It was different now. I meant what I said to him. I wanted something that was just ours that would bond us through the engagement and my relationship with the Rogues. I connected with each of my guys in different ways. Even Adonis and I shared a secret pain. It was time Victor and I shared something too.

We stepped into a room at the end of a short, golden-wallpapered hallway. It was a small space, but cozy. A king-sized sleigh bed took up the middle of the room, weighted down with a plush cream comforter and satin pillows. I padded to the bed and sat on the edge, waiting for him to join me.

Victor came in close, leaning me back onto the bed without touching me. He was built so big and sturdy—the body of an athlete. But as he lay on me, wrapping my legs around his waist, all I felt was safe and secure. Like he was shielding me from the ugliness of the world. Here on this boat with him, nothing else mattered.

Victor dipped as I rose.

"Ow!" I pulled back, rubbing my nose. It bonked on his and not gently.

"Sorry, I wasn't expecting—"

"I should've let you—"

We laughed.

"Let's try that again," Victor said, lightly kissing my nose.

I lay back, riding the goose bumps down my body as his lips pressed to mine. He kissed me firm and sweet. No hesitation or nervousness. But no rush. Victor Wilson kissed me like he had all the time in the world.

Moaning, I melted into the sheets. Shudders climbed my spine and tightened my grip on his shoulders. I had to give Victor credit. The man had brilliant ideas when the mood struck him.

I felt tugging on my side, bringing me out of my haze. "Oh, that's not a real zipper," I said, seeing what he was pulling on.

"What the hell's the point of that?"

I giggled. "Women's clothing is about style, not function. But this zipper..." I reached behind me. "Is *very* functional."

"That's a zipper I can work with. Flip over."

Flat on my front, I kicked my legs in the air—playfully patting his bum. Victor confidently said that I was into his body... because I had a working pair of eyes. Every inch of him was sculpted perfection. The kind of perfect that made you want to pump Martha Wilson for the truth of which lab she grew this guy in.

I am marrying the guy. It's about time I got to see what every woman age eighteen to twenty in Regalia keeps in their clit reel—

Pain spiked through my scalp. "Ah!"

"Oh, shit, I'm sorry! Your hair got caught in the zipper. Fuck, are you okay?"

"I'm fine," I said with just a bit of a snap. "Just help me get it out."

"All right. Hold still."

"No, don't pull like that."

"I have to. The zipper closed on it."

"Just let me do it," I cried, craning and twisting to see.

"Don't. You're making it worse—"

"You made it worse!"

After ten minutes of pain, bickering, and flailing around, our clothes finally made it to the floor.

Victor gave me a soft smile as he caressed my sore scalp. "I'm sorry. Should we try that again?"

"Yes, please."

I rose as he dipped. That time, our lips met perfectly.

An hour later, I gazed up at the ceiling—sweat cooling on my skin. Victor stretched out next to me, studying the same spot next to the light fixture.

I cleared my throat. "That was nice. We should do it—"

"That sucked," Victor dropped. "Worst sex I've ever had."

The breath whooshed out of me. "Oh, thank goodness you said it. That was freaking terrible. I thought you were good at this?"

"Me?!" Victor shot up. "You stabbed me in the eye with your toe while we were kissing. How in the hell does that happen?" He pointed at the angry red orb. "I think you scratched my cornea."

"Oh yeah? Want to talk about how someone elbows a girl in the tit while giving her head? I have a bruise."

"That wasn't my fault. You were never where you're supposed to be. And you're so stiff." He slid out from under the sheets and snatched up his pants. "Push down your legs and your top half pops up like a seesaw."

"That's not true!" There was no one alive more outraged than me. I shoved out of bed and grabbed my clothes. "If anyone is stiff, it's you. I heard the gears grinding in your hips while you were pumping."

"Gears. Nice comeback as always, Sinclair. Why did I think this was a good idea?"

I lobbed my pillow through the air. It snapped off his head, taking his shout with it. "You don't get to be the one who regrets it. *I* regret saying yes to this. I'll never unsee the sight of you sneezing out your own cum."

"Why did you point my dick at my face! Have you never given a hand job before?" Victor half tore his shirt yanking it on. "What do you and Dumont do in his room all night? Knit?"

"No, he fucks me—thank you very much. And he does it well."

Victor muttered under his breath. "...ass..."

"What was that?"

"I said you're an asshole!"

"You're the asshole!"

Getting my dress on was even more frustrating in the middle of a fight. I yanked on the zipper and heard an unwelcome sound. The damn thing broke.

"There goes the idea of us being lovers," I snapped. "And since you think I'm such an asshole, I doubt we're going to be friends either."

Scoffing, Victor finally got his pants on. He turned on me as he zipped up and buckled. "Oh, sure, give up at the first chance. I bet you messed this up on purpose, so I'd accept there was no sexual chemistry between us and jump at an open marriage."

My eyes bugged. "What kind of manipulative jerk do you think I am? Even if I wanted that, no one could have sex that bad on purpose. I think you put me off it for good."

"That's my line. I used to love a tight pussy. Now I'm wondering if I'll ever have a full erection again. You strangled the thing half dead."

I flashed him a tight smile. "Damn, I was so close."

He cursed. "See? There you go again. We can't get through one day without you picking a fight or finding an excuse to get pissed off. When you said you wanted to start over, I actually thought you meant it. But you can't help yourself," he said, flapping his hands at me. "You have to self-sabotage. It's what you do."

"Excuse me? What I do?" I planted my hands on my hips—facing him down with a ruined dress and sore boob. "Don't act like you know me."

Victor glared. "No one knows you better than me."

"What?" I shrieked. "Where the hell did you—?"

"You're loyal," he sliced in. "When you care about someone, no one will fight harder to protect them than you. You're not afraid of what you don't know. Life is for learning, experiencing, and taking chances. Most people will live their life in the box they were born in, but not you. You want more and you always have."

I quieted, sinking back on my heels.

"You don't need attention, or money, or fame, but you do need purpose. A reason to get up in the morning," he said, closing the distance between us. "Despite what a massive pain in the ass you are, you have trouble fighting for yourself. You spend so much time making sure that everyone else is okay, that what you need becomes an afterthought.

"You hate olives, reality TV, and people who adopt dogs only to leave them chained up in the backyard all day and night. You love rainy days, sleeping in, and anything purple."

I drifted down to my purple heels.

"I know all about you, Sinclair." His voice was hard. "You're rare. No one like you has ever lived in Regalia, and I can't help holding on to everything you say and do. The stupid fucking fact of the matter is that we do belong together."

I blew back. *What did he say?*

"My mother was right to choose you, and I realized that too late to stop myself sticking my dick in another girl's mouth and getting caught. I messed it up the first time, but refusing to forgive me, constantly picking fights, ignoring my calls, standing me up when I asked you out, moving in with the Rogues, hooking up with them the second we split, and kissing my brother..." He shook his head. "That was all you."

"Victor..."

He let out a small bark of a laugh. "The funny thing is that I know you so well, I also know why I'm the one you won't let yourself be with." Victor met my gaze. "You look at me and you see a Royal. My family, my home, the wedding. Marrying me is stepping into the world that destroyed your sister."

I swallowed hard, lips trembling.

"Why should it accept you when it rejected her? How can you go where she couldn't, or be happy where she wasn't?" He stopped just short of my reach, and backed away. "One day you're going to realize that the sweet, kind girl I used to pass in the halls doesn't want your unhappiness. But by the time you figure that out, who knows if there'll be anything left between us to save."

Victor slammed out the door, leaving me shell-shocked and frozen on the carpet.

"Wait," I croaked softly. "Victor, wait!" My legs came alive. Taking off, I ran through the hall after him. "Please, stop. You can't just leave me here."

"I'm not." Victor slammed his keys down next to our forgotten pancakes. "Take the car back. I need to think."

"Think about what?" *Leaving me?*

He didn't answer.

Victor climbed off the boat, heading down the marina. I waited against hope that he'd come back, but he never did.

***

"Everything all right, Lady Luna?"

I shook myself, coming to and finding Lucien leaning against my door-frame. He was sex dipped in chocolate—wearing a tight black-and-red waist-coat, and even tighter pants.

I tried for a smile. "I'm okay. I just had a weird date with Victor. I'm not sure what to think about how we left things."

"Did he give you an answer on if he can handle this?" He gestured between us.

"He told me a lot of things," I said softly, "but not that."

"Are you up for this tonight?"

"Yes," I replied before he finished the question. "There is literally nothing else I'd rather do tonight than go to Toussaint's with you. I even dressed for the occasion."

I twirled in the lace, black-and-blue embroidered Victorian gown I bought online. I was starting to understand why Lucien wore these clothes every day. It was one hundred percent a choice because vampire or not, there was nothing stopping him from slipping on jeans and a t-shirt.

Still, he didn't because there's something about this era's clothes. Both modest and sexy. Elegant and understated. Creative but simple. Prudish and fun to get out of.

"What do you think?"

"Luna, you look so incredible, I'm tempted to slam this door and do very ungentlemanlike things to you for the rest of the night."

"Good," I teased. "That's what I was going for."

Lucien held out his arm. "Shall we?"

We left for the restaurant, heading out in his rarely used car. I put Victor out of my mind—for the moment.

Toussaint's was packed that night as it was most nights. The Royals loved it because most Dregs couldn't afford to eat there, and everyone else loved it because the food was ambrosia fallen from the buffet of the gods.

"Table for two. Calais."

I peeked through the busy restaurant to the back.

Toussaint's molded their space in the French bistro style. A blue sky of painted, wispy clouds covered us, and green vines covered the columns reaching to meet them. Dotted around the space were small, intimate tables covered in white linen and candles. It was all open floor plan except for the space in the back which was slightly blocked off by columns and a well-placed tapestry of the French countryside.

It was obvious that tapestry was added after the restaurant was built, because the Royals wanted separation from the regular patrons.

"Here you are, sir," said the hostess. She cut a striking figure in an elegant black dress and a charming smile. "Right this way."

"I requested a table in back."

"We were able to accommodate, sir." She winked. "Along with your special request."

"Special request?" I repeated. "What special request?"

Lucien brought my fingertips to his lips. "You'll see."

Together we weaved through the tables and stepped past the tapestry. Dozens of pairs of eyes snapped on us. Whether it was because a Dreg was on the arm of a Rogue, or because we were both dressed like we left a costume party, or both—I couldn't guess.

The hostess led us to our table.

"Uh, excuse me?" Iris spoke up from her seat two tables down and too close to mine. She sat across a handsome guy who was still cute with disdain written all over his face. "Are you lost, Sinclair? Hometown Country Fried is on the other side of town."

"What is this restaurant and why does everyone think it's meant for me?" I muttered. Louder, I said, "Iris, shut the hell up. I'm on a date."

"Excuse—? Who do you think you're talking to, bitch!"

I turned my back on her and claimed the seat Lucien held out for me. Her squawking faded in the background when I looked down at my plate.

"What's this?" I picked up a sweet, baked treat. "Toussaint's doesn't serve fortune cookies. Lucien, did you do this?"

"I did." He winked back at the hostess. "Open it. Discover your future."

Trying not to cheese too wide, I cracked the cookie.

Ding.

"Oh, Lucien." I stroked the tiny necklace that fell on my plate. A beautiful white gold band with a diamond charm. Looking closer, I saw it was a switchblade.

"For the night I became a Rogue." My hand found his across the table. "Thank you, Lucien. I love it."

"There's more."

I almost forgot about the fortune. Finding the paper, I unfurled it and read—

Tonight, you will get fucked hot and dirty, but respectfully, by a vampire.

"Hmm." Lucien innocently poured water in my glass. "What's it say? What does the future have in store for you?"

"A very fun night," I said, smile tugging on my lips. "But I don't know about respectfully."

"Well, those things are never fully accurate."

I laughed. This is what I loved about my Rogues. I was surrounded by a bunch of uptight trust-fund babies, so obsessed with their reputation and status. While Lucien and I were flirting with each other over fortune cookies and nineteenth-century dress. There was my insanely mind-boggling attraction to them, but more than that, I had fun with my guys. I didn't doubt for a second that when we were old and wrinkly, we'd still sit around laughing over fortune cookies.

"The funny thing is that I know you so well, I also know why I'm the one you won't let yourself be with."

His words crashed through my mind, stealing my smile. Why was Victor the only one I wouldn't let myself have fun with? Yes, he made a terrible first impression, but we were strangers then. Deep down, I had let that go a long time ago. Was he right about why I sabotage every attempt he made to make it up and get closer to me? Did I—?

I tossed my head, shaking thoughts of him loose. *I can't think about him right now. I'm here with Lucien. Victor and I will talk when he comes back.*

If he comes back.

"Good evening." Our waiter arrived with two menus and a lighter. I relaxed into our evening as he lit the candle. "Can I tempt you with our house red? Its subtle, smoky flavor is a favorite among our patrons."

It boggled my mind how casually they served alcohol in here without even pretending to card anyone.

"Just apple cider for me, thank you."

"I'll have the same," Lucien said.

"Really? You're going to drink cider?" I asked after our waiter left. "Are you going to order off the menu too?"

"Of course. Didn't think I'd let you eat alone, did you?"

"I did. Can't have these mortals seeing you do something so utterly human as chowing down on a plate of fries."

Lucien traced designs on my palm. "Is there anyone else here? All I see is you."

I didn't need to see my face to know I was blushing. Guys didn't talk like that anymore. In my limited experience before I went to college, all the compliments I got from silly little boys were backhanded. As if someone told them the way to get into a girl's pants was by wearing down her self-esteem.

It was the complete opposite with Lucien Calais. He told me nothing but the truth. And his truth was that I was amazing in every way.

Our waiter returned to take our order. I asked for steak frites while Lucien helped himself to the steak tartare.

"Where are we going after this?" I asked, leaning in. I wanted to be as close to him as possible. Damn the table for getting in the way. "I've got a fortune I'd like to come true."

"There's a spot I go to for peace and quiet. It's private. Secluded. Under the moonlight." Lucien traced my lips. "The perfect place for me to get... carried away."

"I can't w—"

"Fuck, this place has gone downhill."

Hairs rose on the back of my neck.

"Once they start letting the freaks in, it's time to eat somewhere else."

Stiffly, I turned my neck, landing on Owen, Levi, and Wesley passing by the tapestry. These guys had become quite the trio since Ashton's and Giovanni's deaths.

As if they think there's safety in numbers.

"We should eat somewhere else," Iris chimed in. Owen did not speak quietly. "Dregs have left their ooze all over our town. If they're invading this place too, I'm out."

"Why should we leave?" asked someone I didn't even know. "Those two can get the fuck out and catch up with the cosplay tour that left them behind."

"Good idea, Devin," Levi said, smirking away. I tensed as he loped over to us. "You heard him. Take your shit and get—"

Lucien palmed his cane. Without a change in expression or a pause between breaths, he flipped and stabbed the walking stick in Levi's stomach.

"Argh!" Levi dropped, wheezing and clutching his abdomen.

"Hey!"

"What did you do?!"

Wesley and Owen rushed their fallen friend. I could only gape at all of them.

"Am I one of these oozing Dregs?" Lucien rose from his seat. Silence fell so fast and quick, I thought my ears popped. "Are one of you going to make me leave?" he asked Owen, Wesley, and the shuddering heap on the floor. He twirled his cane over his fingers. "I would truly love to see you try."

Neither one of them moved.

Lucien grinned—flashing unnaturally long, glittering canines. "Every few months, you all need a reminder of who you challenge and who you don't. If anyone would like to be an enemy of the Rogues, drop the show and just say so."

Eyes ping-ponged off of him, suddenly focused on their food, phones, or dates.

A Rogue was not a Royal, but they were also not a Dreg. There were some enemies you just didn't make... and the martial arts master of a mob family who really liked the sight of blood was one of them.

Lucien's smile shifted. "Now, you," he snarled, glaring down at the three. "You'll have some manners when you're addressing Luna, or I'll teach them to you. Apologize to her for disturbing our date."

"Fuck you," Wesley bit out. "I'm not going to—"

Lucien whipped the cane across his face, snapping his head around. Wesley crashed to the floor, his skull bouncing off the hardwood.

"S-sorry. I'm sorry."

"Better," Lucien said. He leveled the cane between Owen's eyes. "Who's next?"

"Whoa. Easy, man." I knew the last time Lucien and the Rogues beat his ass was going through his head. "We were just messing around. Sorry, okay." He picked up Wesley and half-dragged him to the table furthest from us.

Levi slowly got his knees under him and stood up. Glare hard, he looked in Lucien's eyes, and spat at his feet.

"You think because you beat me once, you're untouchable." Levi's voice carried only to our ears. I bared my teeth when I realized he was talking about the night he tried to burn the Rogues alive. "But you're going to get what's coming to you, Calais. People who piss me off always do. It's only a matter of time."

Of all things, Lucien smirked. "I like to move around in the dark too, Thompkins. But the difference between me and you? My victims don't get away."

"Just wait."

"Not too long," I said, nibbling on my cookie. I flashed Levi a sweet smile that went nowhere near my eyes. "You don't have much time. Unless I find out what I want to know, you're lucky to make it to the end of this... sentence."

Levi backed away. For a lifetime, I'd never unsee the swirling depths of those eyes, and the emptiness within them. "Just wait."

Levi joined his table in time for our waiter to return. I felt their eyes on us throughout the meal. Wesley nursed his swollen cheek while talking to the others in low tones.

I knew they didn't take me or my threats seriously. Lucien's—yes. But mine? I was all talk until I proved myself an enemy worth taking seriously, instead of one trying to look tough by sleeping with the enemies that are.

That's perfectly fair. I contentedly cut my steak into smaller bites. *If they wanted me to step up and prove Sinclairs aren't to be messed with, I'm more than happy to. Those three will sit in hell, regretting the day they ever heard the words truth or dare.*

Sliding off them, I focused on a much more handsome and appealing sight. "Lucien, can I ask you something?"

"Anything."

"Why don't you guys ever talk about your families? Sure, Rafael told me what happened to his mom and a little about his dad's history, but otherwise, I don't know anything about your family, and Wilder still won't give a straight answer on if he was birthed by man or grown in a laboratory."

He laughed. "Wilder wants to keep that a mystery, but he's got a belly button the same as the rest of the mortals and former mortals. Proves an umbilical cord attached him to his estranged mother."

"So they are estranged?"

Lucien lightly lifted his shoulders, reaching for his glass. He swirled the liquid like he did the strange drink that normally left his lips. "I couldn't say. I've never met her. He's never spoken of her. But if she is alive, that says a lot, doesn't it?"

I tipped my chin, agreeing. Lucien has known Wilder since he was a high schooler and a minor. If his mother wasn't around then, that did say a lot. *Was my paranoid lover an orphan? Maybe that's why he didn't trust the world. There was never anyone around to show him how.*

"What about you?" I asked.

"What about me? I told you my story. I abandoned my wife and son after I was turned. They passed a long time ago."

I smiled at him with infinite patience. Lucien clearly had no interest in dropping the act—even with me. Still, Victor was right that it wouldn't hurt him to take one day off.

Don't do that, a voice warned. *Don't open the door on Victor. Not yet. He needs time to think, and so do I.*

"Tell me about your descendants."

"Sam and Nina are a sweet enough couple. They met in middle school and the rest was history. There was never anyone else for them after that."

"That is sweet." I skated my fingers over his knuckles. "It's so rare to meet someone and just know."

The look he gave me made my lower belly contract in exquisite agony. "Not that rare."

"Did they have children?" I asked, changing the subject. I'd been surprising myself with the depths of my sexual curiosity. If Lucien kept looking at me like that, I'd find out what it's like to be screwed in the middle of a crowded restaurant.

"They do," he replied. "A little girl."

My eyes popped. Lucien has a younger sister?

"Really? What's her name? How old is she?"

"She's six. They've struggled for a long time to have a child. Two years ago, they adopted Antoinette."

"Can I meet them?"

"They live in Boston, but yes," he said. "Say the word and we'll go. My descendants keep a plane in the private airstrip just outside Regalia."

Of course Lucien just casually drops that he has a private plane on standby. I really lived in a different world now.

"I'd like that." Glancing down, I checked the time. "I want to hear more about you, your family, everything. And I want to do it away from the hostile glares they keep shooting us. How about we get dessert to go?"

I flagged down the waiter and ordered a chocolate tart covered in chocolate sauce and hazelnuts to go. Lucien didn't order anything because he said he'd be eating my dessert off me. Why were we still there?

We were up and out of our seats the moment he returned with our food and receipt. The wrong number of shadows detached themselves and trailed us out the door.

"You see them, don't you?" I whispered.

"I do." Lucien held open the door for me. His hand was firm on my back as we stepped up to the valet. "I suspect they're going to wait until this guy leaves and then corner us."

"Smart. Toussaint's doesn't have cameras pointed this way. Wouldn't want video of all the underaged students stumbling drunk out the door."

The valet took off to get our car.

"You think you're such a badass, Calais." Owen slunk out—right on cue. "But what are you without your little stick and your three freak friends to back you up?"

"Without them I'm a master of five styles of martial arts. Think carefully about what you do next."

Levi fell in on Owen's other side, flanked by Wesley. "It was you, wasn't it? You and the freaks," Levi said. "You hung Owen from the ceiling. You poisoned Wesley and stole his EpiPen. You spread around those truth lists, and of course, it was Rafael who lied and said Ashton was behind it all."

Our faces were impassive. Didn't stop the mirthless grin stretching Levi's mouth.

"Sinclair here wasn't smart or strong enough to pull all that off, but she was clever enough to fuck the four of you into doing it for her. Well done." He clapped. "I'm impressed. That was what you meant when you said you killed Ashton without touching the knife."

I blinked lazily. "Wesley, why are you standing behind Levi like that? Trying to hide that swollen face, or do you not want me to see that you're recording this on your phone?"

He started, eyes widening over Levi's shoulder. I couldn't see the phone, but the look on his face—and the irritation on Levi's—proved I was right.

"If you want to record something, record your confession," I continued. "Tell the world how you took bribes to torture an innocent girl." Iris and her date chose that moment to leave the restaurant. I raised my voice. "Tell everyone how you protected her rapist. You gave him an alibi, told the dean she was a liar and a blackmailer, then got her expelled. What do you think about that, Iris?"

She jumped. "What?"

"Who is the real trash? Because if you ask me, it's your Royal friends here. For the right price, they'll throw in with a rapist—"

"Shut up!" Levi barked. "Don't listen to her, Iris. She's lying."

More Royals filtered out, just in time to catch a show after dinner.

"Am I?" I asked, cocking my head. "Am I lying about one of you killing Ashton Scott—said rapist—so that he couldn't put the worst of what you guys have done in those truth lists?"

"Wait, what?"

"Ashton Scott?"

"Rape?"

"Yes!" Levi cut through the spreading whispers. "You are lying! None of that happened."

"Oh, but they all know it did because they know you better than me. They know you like to force yourself on women—Owen. They know you get off on your sick games and traps—Wesley. And they know you're a sadist who sets fires and carves up women—Levi. It's what you did to your girlfriends and tried to do to me.

"Iris," I called without looking away from Levi. "Did Sadie ever tell you why she transferred schools out of nowhere? Did you hear from her at all the summer after she dated this"—I gestured at Levi—"thing."

"I... No," Iris said slowly. "I kept calling and texting but... she never got me back. Oh my—" She clapped her hands over her mouth. "Levi, what did you do!?"

"Nothing!" He whirled on her. "You're going to believe some worthless Dreg over me? I didn't do anything to Sadie, and I have no idea what shit she's spouting about Ashton."

"Tell the truth, Thompkins." My gaze slid over him, Wesley, and Owen. "One of you better tell the truth or..."

"Or what?" Owen snapped. "You're not going to do anything. You'll get one of your pet freaks to do it for you. Too bad we know to look out for them now. It's over, Sinclair. You lost. It's all a fucking failure like you can do. Must run in the family."

He brushed past me. "Let's go, guys. We're not putting up with this crap anymore." Owen stepped off the sidewalk, back to the street. "And all you Royals who are letting her lies get to your head—wake up. That Dreg didn't know Sadie or Ashton. She never spoke to them. Sinclair is making up lies to—"

Screeeeeeccch!

Owen turned white in the glow of headlights. He spun around in time for the front bumper to careen into him, throwing him off his feet. Owen crashed to the pavement—his crunching bones echoing in our ears.

The barest weak groan rattled in his chest, then he was silent.

Then he was still.

"Hey!" Levi bellowed. "Stop! Come back!" He took off running after the black sports car.

Swerving around Owen, the car tore out of the parking lot.

Screams, shouts, and wails went up around us. The Royals rushed Owen—all of them clamoring at once to call an ambulance, get the police, remember the license plate. All of them except Wesley, who stood frozen to the spot. It was only polite since I was whispering in his ear.

"I guess Owen didn't know to look out for that," I purred. "Tsk. Such a shame. He should've paid attention to his surroundings. You never know what's coming for you."

Wesley shook.

"I'm sure you'll be smarter." I playfully flicked his nose. "Call me whenever you're ready to have that chat." Lucien looped his arm around my waist, holding me close. I wiggled my fingers at Wesley as we strode off. "But don't wait too long. You never know what'll happen."

Lucien and I shared a smile on the way to the car, and a kiss. "As first dates go, where does ours rank?"

"Ten out of ten, baby." Laughing, I glanced back at the chaos. "I especially loved the part at the end."

"Oh, this isn't the end. I believe we said something about private spots and chocolate tarts?"

"I hope this spot is close."

Chapter Eight

Lucien's private spot was close by, but we never made it.

"Walk me through the events of the night once more."

I sat on the sidewalk, bemoaning my ruined dress. Lucien and I no sooner pulled out of the parking spot than Levi jumped in our way—shouting and carrying on not to let us get away, because we killed Owen.

In the rush of people that flooded the parking lot, we couldn't get through without mowing them down. Too soon the police came and we were still trapped. We had no choice but to get out when Levi repeated his accusations to them, and they approached the car—hands on their guns.

"It's like I said, officer," I repeated for the fifth time. "We were on a date, minding our business. We left, Owen followed us out, he said horrible things, and then he walked out into the street without paying attention. How could I be responsible? I wasn't driving the car."

"Mr. Thompkins claims that you threatened him." Officer Philips was a young, attractive woman with short black hair and a beauty mark smack on the tip of her nose. "Threatened all three of them. Said you were going to kill them."

I snorted. "That's a load of crap. Levi Thompkins is a pathological liar and a sociopath. He's putting me through this because I rejected him. He does that, you know. A girl says no to him and he makes them regret it. Just ask his last girlfriend, Sadie Knowles."

"Lying bitch!"

I twisted my neck. I hadn't noticed Levi sidling up behind us. One of the other officers barked at him to come back.

"What is she telling you?" he demanded. "She said she was going to kill us! We didn't take her seriously, so she got one of her boyfriends to mow him down like trash. Arrest her!"

"Who the hell knows what that guy is talking about," I breezed. "I didn't kill him or get anyone to do it. I didn't even know he was going to be here tonight."

"She's a liar. Rafael Dumont, Cato Dumont, or Wilder O'Rourke. Those are the guys you want. One of them was driving the car."

Turning my back, I dismissed him. "Check my phone. I didn't know the three of them would be here, and I didn't call anyone to hurt him after they showed up. I have nothing to do with this, officer. Please, I just want to get back to my date. That sad, pathetic little man-boy shouldn't get to ruin my night just because I'm here with someone else."

Philips looked from me to Levi. She was too new to stop me seeing the doubt creeping into her eyes.

"Let me see the phone."

I handed it over. Twenty minutes and a warning not to leave town later, Lucien and I were finally free to go.

We got in the car and turned right instead of left. The mood was definitely gone, and my chocolate tart was an unappetizing melted lump. No secret spot for us that night. We headed straight back to the Gallery.

I flopped on the couch, melting my weary bones into the cushion.

"I've seen what this club can do and I still can't believe it." Lucien freed my aching feet from their heels and placed them on his lap. I sighed under his foot rub. "One private message and one of the members got in a car and ran a guy over. Just like that."

"Not quite just like that," I said, grin coming back. "I had to offer him or her almost all the money Wilder siphoned out of those bastards' bank account. I basically took out a hit and called it a dare."

"Who's next? Wesley or Levi?"

"Both. I'm not going to have them killed yet, but I will keep up the pressure." It was hard to believe that a year before at the same time, I was sitting in Catholic school discussing the meaning of ethics and morality. "You saw Wesley standing there off to the side, not moving or responding to anyone. He was always the weakest of the group," I said. "He's about to crack. I'll give him a chance to do the right thing while I deal with some other people who deserve my attention."

I fished my phone out of my bag and searched for a number I didn't save. Finally, I found it and sent them a message.

"Done."

Lucien tugged on my foot, sliding me closer. "Our night doesn't have to end with sirens and car searches. Come upstairs. I'll give you a real massage... with that bottle of chocolate sauce in the fridge."

My tiredness evaporated in a blink. "Let's go."

Swooping down, Lucien lifted me giggling into his arms.

"Luna?" a voice called from the kitchen. "Hey, did you see this?"

"See what?"

Lucien changed course and carried me into the kitchen. Rafael stood at the stove, prepping to make something delicious. He jerked his chin at the table, and the note lying on top of it.

Happiness dimming, I climbed out of his arms. Resting next to the paper was a key to the Gallery. Victor's handwriting looked back at me, spelling out two simple words:

You win.

***

I Dare You To Hit Owen Thasher With A Car.
Dare: Accepted

"—can't believe—"

What does that even mean, I win? Win what?

"—they're saying about you—"

And not responding to my calls or texts? My fists balled. *How childish is that? If Victor has something to say to me, the least he could do is say it to my face. Discuss it with me and give us a chance to work it out. I won't spend our whole marriage dealing with this passive-aggressive crap. Because we were still getting married.*

"Hello?"

We had to be.

"Hello," Katie cried. She knocked on my forehead. "Are you listening to me?"

"What? Oh, sorry. I was out of it."

She clicked her tongue. "I'll say. But I can't blame you. They're getting real out of control around here, blaming you for everything that goes wrong. Some drunk idiot hits Owen and runs, and Levi tries to blame you. I never liked that guy." She said the last part mostly to herself. "He's got a mean streak. Meaner than the average Royal."

"That he does," I muttered. "But I'm okay, Katie. They're not going to pin this on me."

We climbed the steps to the café. I was already dreaming of banana hazelnut pancakes and a steamy mug of oolong tea. What I was not worried about was that rotting corpse in the morgue. Owen Thasher harassed my sister day and night, and got his buddies to do it too. It got to the point that she shut herself away in her dorm... so Owen attacked her there.

Snapping pictures of his friends violating and assaulting my sister, and then posting it all over his website like she signed up for the world's worst gang bang.

He had that car and more coming to him. My only regret is that he died quickly.

"But you did have beef with him, didn't you?" I saw her study me out of the corner of my eye. "Melanie told me you were saying something before he died. About Ashton Scott, Levi, and Owen? Something about rape and assault?"

I replied without hesitation. "Ashton Scott raped my sister. Levi, Wesley, and Owen helped him get away with it. They swore to the dean that Ashton was with them all night, and that Winter was lying to get money out of him."

Katie stopped dead in the café entrance, jaw hanging open. "What! Are you serious?"

"Never been more serious about anything in my life," I said flatly.

I tugged Katie on. I was hungry and didn't need the people streaming past us to overhear our conversation.

"But... But how do you know this?" she asked. "Why didn't you say anything before?"

"I know because Winter told me." My throat tightened. "Besides, what was there to say? The dean already decided it was a lie and let that monster get away with it. I'm the one who would've gotten in trouble for slander or something if I told everyone what they did."

"Luna, still. I would've believed you and Winter. Hey." She grabbed my shoulder, making me look in her eyes. "I would have."

My tension eased just the slightest bit. No mocking. No haughtiness. Only sincerity... and compassion.

I just wish it came sooner to make a difference for you, big sister.

"I know you would have, Katie, because you're not blind. You see those guys for what they are. That mean streak in Levi goes deep," I gritted. "Just look at what he's trying to do to me now that I told the truth about what he did to Winter. He got my sister expelled and ruined her life. Now he's trying to throw me in jail for murder."

Katie bared her teeth. "The fuck he is. The filthy shit isn't getting away with it. None of it. I'll catch you up after."

"After? After what?" I called at Katie's retreating back. She was gone and out the door too fast for me to get out anything else.

I rejoined the line and grabbed a tray. I told the guys they didn't need to trail me that morning since I was going to breakfast with Katie. She wasn't anybody's bodyguard, but I noticed that no one messed with me when she was by my side. Katie didn't talk about it. She didn't have to. I saw for myself that being the only one not chained to the Royal system of lies, bribes, and secrets had its benefits.

I sat down to eat alone for the first time in a while. *The time with my thoughts is actually nice. I can finally process the fact that I'm close. We're close, Winter. Three of your five killers are dead. The final two will be soon but not before one of them tells me everything I need to know about the Phantom.*

You will rest in peace soon, Winter. I promise.

I picked up my knife and fork, slicing into my pancakes. Yes, a morning to myself was perfect.

I brought my fork to my lips, then dropped it. Shoving my plate away, I took off across the cafeteria.

"You!"

Victor looked up from the tray station, eyes raised at my rapid approach. "Me."

"So you are alive."

He glanced down at himself. "Last I checked."

The asshat was casual as ever in his skintight, stain-defying, green-and-white rugby uniform. He was fresh from a shower—*that wasn't my shower.* And well-rested from a good night's sleep—*that wasn't in my bed.*

"I called and texted you all last night and this morning," I snapped. "After the eightieth text, I accepted I was going to find your body in a ditch today."

Victor flicked over my shoulder. "So you celebrated by having pancakes. Nice one, Sinclair."

"Don't put this on me!" My voice was three octaves louder than it needed to be. I was drawing attention. "What happened? What was that note supposed to mean?"

"Thought it was self-explanatory." With that, he turned his back and joined the line for bacon.

I slapped the tray out of his hand, snatched his collar, and dragged him over to the soda machines. He let me because if Victor really wanted to get away from me, the six-foot-tall rugby player could do so easily.

"You thought wrong," I hissed, shoving him against the wall. "Why did you take off and leave your key?"

He shrugged. "Because you win."

"What does that mean? What did I win?"

"I'm moving back into my house. You've got the place just you and your Rogues again." He sidestepped me. "We done here? I need to calorie up before practice."

I shot in front of him, shoving him back. "Why did you move out? I didn't ask you to. I didn't want you to."

He shrugged again, making me almost lose it. Victor was so relaxed and nonchalant; you'd have thought we were talking about what I liked on my pancakes instead of our messed-up relationship. "Wasn't about what you wanted. We've been doing this back-and-forth for months. I'm done."

I flinched, breath trapping in my chest. "You're done? So that's it," I rasped. "Are you serious! We get into one fight because you're crap in bed, and you're ready to end it."

The calm mask broke. "I'm not crap in bed! And it wasn't one fight. It's dozens of fights we've had every other damn day. The only civil conversation we've had since we met was that night in the kitchen."

"So what, Victor? We fight. That's what happens when your fiancé is an arrogant, insensitive jerk who says you belong together one minute, and then dumps you in a note!" Tears stung my eyes. "You could've at least ended things to my face."

"I'm not ending anything, Luna. That wasn't a breakup note."

"It—it wasn't?"

He rolled his eyes—almost fondly. "Course it wasn't. Think I put up with you for months, just to give up when you finally start putting out?"

"I will kill you."

Victor barked a laugh. "I'm not breaking up with you, but I am done with this thing we've been doing. I can deal with marrying a woman who doesn't love me. I can't deal with marrying one who refuses to."

I quieted.

"Our folks picked us, now you need to pick me. Propose to me," he announced. "Ask me to marry you for the right reasons. Because you want me as much as I want you. Do that and we can elope tomorrow. Don't... and consider us over, Luna. My inheritance can go fuck itself."

"Propose to you." I repeated it and it still didn't make sense.

"Woo me, baby. It's your turn to do the chasing."

I gaped at him. Victor swooped in and kissed me open-mouthed, ignoring my squawk. "Decide what you want, Luna, then stop feeling guilty about it."

My voice didn't return until he was out the door with a bacon-and-egg sandwich, heading out to practice.

I wanted to sit my butt in that booth and enjoy my morning in my thoughts—basking in the victory of killing Owen and walking away from the cops before the enraged Levi. If only I'd done that, I wouldn't be standing in the middle of the café, more confused than ever.

I had to propose to a man I was already engaged to? Convince someone who already wanted to be with me... to be with me? How was I supposed to do that?

Do I want to be with him? The question bowled me over. *Do I want to be with Victor Wilson? If I didn't have a deal with Martha. If I didn't have a promise to Winter. If we were just two people who met and started talking about forever, is that something I'd want with the rude, brash, hot jock who sees right through me?*

My shoulders slumped. Can I even answer those questions while I'm falling for his brother?

"—go. We're going to be late."

I roused myself, checking the time. I was going to be late too.

Hurrying, I scarfed down my pancakes, ditched the tray, and rushed out of the cafeteria.

It was early. Early enough for practices and sweet breakfasts. Too early for students who scheduled late classes so they could sleep in. There weren't many people milling about as I crossed the quad, making for the natural sciences building. But the few students that were around had one topic on their lips: Owen Thasher.

"—hit and run. The guy just ran him over and kept driving. Kimberly said they didn't even slow down."

"I can't believe it. First Ashton, then Giovanni, and now Owen? It's awful."

"Wait. Did you hear what they're saying about Ashton?"

I slowed down on the steps to the building. Two girls propped on the railing, not bothering to lower their voice.

"No, why?"

She made a disgusted noise. "Don't shed any tears for him. Turns out he was a rapist. I bet the girl he attacked saw her chance and stabbed him while everyone was rushing him. She went easy on him if you asked me." The girls set off inside. "If it was me, I would have..."

I smirked. *Good. That shithead doesn't deserve an ounce of sympathy.*

Word spread fast about Ashton, and the wild thing was, no one had trouble believing it. Despite Levi shouting me down, saying I was lying. If they didn't believe I was lying about Ashton, what were the chances they believed me about Levi too? I'd bet anything that Iris spent last night trying again to contact Sadie.

I made it to the third floor of the building, and snagged a seat on the bench outside the chemistry class. I didn't have class for another hour. Let's just hope I had her as figured out as I thought I did.

Five minutes passed.

Then ten.

Then seven.

Then five more minutes.

I checked my phone again, worrying my lip. If I missed it, the guys could tell me what happened, but I really wanted to see for myself—

"This way, officers."

I shot up straight.

"Although, I'm sure there's been a misunderstanding. What you're saying just isn't possible. She's one of our best students and a credit to the community."

"There's no misunderstanding."

Shit! I ducked into a corner, concealed by an oversized potted plant. Officer Philips and her partner walked past inches from me. I waited until the dean let them into the classroom, then snuck into the auditorium. I would not miss this.

"Excuse me?" Professor Keen stopped mid-lecture. "Can I help you?"

"Pardon the interruption. We're here for Gabriella Montana."

Gabriella's head snapped up from the third row, eyes comically round. Sharing the seat next to her was Everleigh. Five rows away sat Piper and Katie. And sitting toward the front in a row all her own, was Saylor.

Rafael winked at me from the very back. I scurried over, plopping low on the seat between him and Wilder.

"Just in time, gorgeous."

"Me?" Gabriella cried. "Why?"

"You know why, bitch." Annika marched beside the cops—a riot of healing bruises, a new haircut from her head getting shaved for surgery, and her arm in a sling. Despite her banged-up state, I'd never seen anyone readier for war.

She flashed her phone like a badge of honor. "It's all right here. She was at the beach house that night with Giovanni, not me. I showed up, caught her fucking my boyfriend, and she threw me off the Bluffs!"

Gabriella jumped up. "Wait, that's not—!"

"I was barely out of surgery before she sent a bunch of guys to threaten me. They said if I ever told the truth of that night and got Gabriella in trouble, she'd come after me! The night he died, Giovanni called me and apologized. He said he loved me and didn't want to lie anymore. Then he was gone!" Annika snatched a random guy's binder and threw it at Gabriella's head. "You killed him!"

"That's a lie!"

"Whoa, let's calm down." Philips physically got between Gabriella and Annika. "Miss Montana, get your things and come with us. We need to ask you a few questions."

"I'm not going anywhere with you," she shrieked. "Everything she said is bullshit, including that he loved her. Giovanni was only playing with you, bitch. He used you to hide our relationship. Why would he want you? He said being with you was like fucking a dead fish."

Annika launched at her. The girl just got out of the hospital and was not letting that slow her down. Philips locked around her waist, retraining her.

"Saylor getting punched in the face is still my favorite day, but this is a close second."

The guys chuckled.

"Want to know what he said about you?" Annika replied. "That you were a mistake! He said he wasted his time chasing after a stuck-up princess who was never going to publicly choose him. All the while he had someone who loved and wasn't ashamed of him—me." The words were bullets shooting from her mouth. "He said he wished he never met you!"

The final bullet struck, knocking Gabriella back. Her face crumpled. "Th-that's not true. He knew I—"

"He knew you were insane," Annika flung. "And when he threatened to tell the truth about you, you killed him and tried to frame some Dreg."

"I would never hurt him!"

"Just like you *never* hurt me. But whose flabby ass is that bouncing on my boyfriend's lap the night you attacked me?" She shoved her phone in the face of the guy nearest her.

He took one look and bugged out. "Oh, damn! Get it, Montana." He passed it off to his friends too quick for Philips to swipe it off him.

"Hey! That's evidence!"

Her partner was forced to stumble through the row, chasing down and retrieving the phone. By then, they both had enough.

"Miss Montana, you will come with us now—either voluntarily or in cuffs," Philips snapped. "What's it going to be?"

Swallowing visibly, Gabriella stepped out in the aisle... and bolted.

She tore up the walkway, screeching to the exit over my hanging jaw. Philips's partner tackled her like a linebacker. They went in a crunch of bones that made me hiss.

"Get off me! Get off me!" Gabriella wailed. "It wasn't me. I loved him. Gio! Gio!"

She shouted his name down the hall before switching to obscenities. If she came away with any charges that day, resisting arrest and abusing an officer were high on the list.

"Guys," I breathed. "Don't take this the wrong way, but that was better than sex."

"You called it," Wilder said. "Annika wasn't going to waste a second once she had proof Gabriella was there that night. Glad you got to see that in person."

"It didn't have to go down like this. If she hadn't said what she did about Winter, I might've been tempted to go easy on her. Gabriella's the reason I'm not holding back against the Royals anymore. Their friends, their status, their reputations. I'm going to laugh over the burning flames of everything they care about."

"Fuck's sake, you're so hot right now," Rafael said. "Let's find a storage room after this."

"I'm being serious," I replied, "and also yes."

I rose up in my seat—satisfaction pumping my heart better than blood. *Two down, two to go.* Twisting around, I chanced a look at Saylor… and found her looking back at me.

***

Find Out If It's True Levi Thompkins Mutilated His Ex-Girlfriend.
Truth: Accepted

"You sick, twisted son of a bitch!"

Iris's smoothie exploded on Levi's jacket, showering everyone in his immediate vicinity.

My weekend was incredibly fruitful. I spent it planning Everleigh's fall from grace, sending out private truths and dares for Wesley and Levi, and working on a little side project.

I also spent it obsessing about Victor and wondering if it would all even matter after he found out about me and Adonis.

I went back and forth for two days on if I should just tell him myself. That line of thought always ended with me accepting that I needed to respect Adonis's wishes. I would lose a frustratingly, mind-boggling fiancé, but he would lose a brother. As someone who lost a sister, I couldn't take that lightly.

All that aside, what did it mean that I had to propose to him, or decide if I was ready to stop self-sabotaging us? The guy acted like I was secretly head over heels in love with him but refused to admit it because he was a Royal.

Arrogant ass! I stabbed my spinach quiche. The guys and I were all in the café grabbing breakfast. Campus was never more fun than it was right then. I wasn't missing anything.

I bet he thinks everyone is secretly in love with him. And who goes around saying they're willing to give up their billion-dollar inheritance if it means giving me the choice to marry someone I truly love? Am I supposed to swoon? Is my heart supposed to flutter over how selfless he is?

As if! My quiche was getting utterly destroyed. *I won't fall for his tricks. Victor Wilson will not get me to admit or do anything.*

"You did assault Sadie." Iris brandished the photo of her old friend before she had the cosmetic surgery to remove Levi's brand.

How the T.O.D. Club member got their hands on that, I'd never know. But the photos of his initials clear as day on her forehead, spread faster than the truth lists. Who was the lying bitch now?

I dragged my thoughts out of Victor drama and focused. This is what he was doing to me. The most important thing I had to do was take down these bastards, but he kept invading my mind.

"That's the worst photoshop job I've ever seen." Levi shook off his jacket, casually shaking off its new whipped banana accessory. "I didn't touch her, and that fake pic isn't proof otherwise."

"Save it. Sadie finally got back to me after I sent her the photo and asked if it was real." Iris turned on the gathering crowd. "It is! Levi saw she was texting her ex, so he held her down and carved his initials on her face. He's an evil, twisted sociopath who scared her so badly, she moved away and changed her name because she thought he would kill her!"

I'd never seen anyone so calm. "Bullshit," Levi said. "You and your friend are making it up because Sadie finally has a chance to get back at me for sleeping around and then dumping her." He shrugged. "Yeah, I cheat, but you're not pinning anything else on me."

"Levi Thompkins calling a survivor a liar."

The crowd parted. Katie came through, taking her place next to Iris. "Why am I not surprised? You did the same thing when you told the dean Ashton was with you the night he raped a girl."

"What? That was true?"

"Ugh, man. What's wrong with you?"

"How could you do that?"

Levi's jaw clenched—his composure cracking under the rising tide of disgust. "Shut the fuck up, Katie. That never happened!"

"Aww." She pulled a sad face. "So all these women are lying and being mean to you because you're such a nice guy." Katie looked around. "Ladies, can you back me up here? Is Levi a nice, safe guy who respects women?"

"He's a monster."

"A bully."

"He's abusive!"

Katie tipped her head, a cold smile on her lips. "I thought so. That kind of behavior isn't fitting of a Royal, Thompkins. You're out."

"Out? Out of what?"

"You're not one of us," Katie said, folding her arms. "I'd say you're a Dreg now, but even Dregs deserve better than to be lumped in with a mutilating rapist-lover. You're less than a Dreg. You're... well, you.

"Get out of our café. You can get your breakfast from a McDonald's drive-through."

"I'm not going anywhere." Levi shoved her, throwing her into a group of girls.

I knocked my chair over jumping up. I made it two steps, and so did Dean.

He punched Levi so hard and fast, I blinked, and one minute Levi was on his feet, the next he was bellowing on the floor with a gushing nose.

"You heard the lady," Dean said. "You're not allowed in here anymore. Guys, help him out."

Half the rugby team seized Levi and dragged him across the floor—including Victor.

"Let go of me! Do you have any idea who I am? I'll ruin your whole family, Dreg! Your great-grandchildren will be born with my boot on their necks! Let go—"

The guys lifted him in the air and literally threw him out the door. "Oooh," I hissed, watching him tumble down the stairs—smacking a body part on each step on the way down. "I hope that hurt."

Righting my chair, I sat and burrowed into Cato's side—dropping a kiss on his muzzle. "Don't take this the wrong way either, but I'm in love with Katie."

"I don't blame you," Lucien said. He was back to his regular diet of that strange red drink. The students sitting around kept tossing him looks. "What she just did, Luna, that's big. There's no punishment worse for a Royal."

"There isn't?"

Rafael shook his head. "Imagine that scroll Burkhardt showed you. Then imagine all the lines and connections around the Thompkins name going up in smoke. It doesn't stop at a bunch of coeds icing him out. No one in Regalia will have anything to do with him or his family now."

"His entire family? Katie has the power to do that?"

"When you're ranked as high as her, you can tell a Royal to sit, stay, and bark, and they will," Wilder said. "No one wants to piss off someone with more money, power, and connections than them. Still, that power truly lies with Saylor. Normally, her crew wouldn't do anything like that without her permission, and her handing down the sentence herself, but"—he grinned—"they're not talking these days."

"Oooh, such a pity," I mocked. "The first time Saylor Burkhardt's ever felt what it's like to be on the outside."

I checked my phone. "I have to get to class. Wilder, we still on for tonight?"

"No," he gruffed. "I told you, I will not meet at an unknown location in the middle of the night for an undisclosed reason."

I giggled. "Otherwise known as a surprise date where I pick the place. I told you I'm not giving anything away. You'll just have to trust me."

"No."

"And wear the blindfold."

"Fuck no."

I smooched his cheek. "Oh, you'll be there. I have ways of making you do what I want, O'Rourke."

His brows climbed his forehead. "Challenge accepted."

I went around and kissed all my guys goodbye, then left for English class. The closer I got, the heavier my steps fell. I was excited to see Adonis and nervous to see Victor. I hadn't spoken to Adonis since we got each other off on his desk—again. And I hadn't spoken to Victor since I manhandled him in the café.

Things were up in the air with both of them and Thor help me if I knew why. Adonis wanted me, and Victor wanted to marry me. It should be as simple as that, but the Wilson brothers didn't do simple.

I arrived at the door, pausing to take a deep breath. Whatever they threw at me, I wasn't taking any shit. This was the new Luna who didn't play games and took what she wanted.

Stepping inside, both brothers looked up and latched on to me immediately. Adonis broke off quick, returning to straightening the papers on his desk.

Victor smirked.

The insufferable jackhole.

I flipped him off and got a howling laugh in return. Steaming, I stomped past him and went to my regular seat in the back. It was like Victor knew I went the weekend twisting myself in knots, and he loved that I was getting mixed up over him for a change.

Didn't make sense that I was. Victor and I didn't have good memories to share. We didn't have good sex to miss. He was just the guy I let put a ring on my finger in exchange for tuition.

So why did my heart fall out of my chest when I read that note and thought it was over?

"Good morning, class. If you haven't handed in your essay, bring it up now."

That was for me. I climbed down with my paper, hanging back until the other students walked away. Adonis didn't look up from his laptop when I approached. "Set it on the pile. Thank you."

"Yes, Professor Anthony." The vein in his jaw jumped. "I wanted to say that I really connected with this week's prompt. Write about the person you believe you are at your core. My true self," I said. "It got me thinking."

"Glad to hear it." His gaze didn't venture a centimeter in my direction.

"I didn't phone this one in, sir. I know you'll like it. It's a pass for sure."

"Wonderful, Luna. I'm excited to read it." He turned his back, facing the whiteboard. Flashing his hard, round ass was hardly a stinging dismissal. "Take your seat. We're about to begin."

I went back, flashing Victor another middle finger on the way. He winked and blew me a kiss in return.

Professor Anthony began the lesson on the tenets of a proper literary technique. It was all prep to help us with our papers since they were worth twenty-five percent of our grade.

"All right, class. I hope this won't be another painful lesson on doing the supplemental reading," Adonis announced. "Books and binders away. Quiz time."

This got a few groans, but only a few. After weeks of this, we were used to it.

"Rose, do you mind?"

Rose handed out the quiz sheets and the room fell quiet. I snuck glances at Adonis while I worked.

Like I said, we'd been doing this for weeks. I knew he liked to use class downtime to read our papers. Mine was near the top, so it was only a matter of time before—

Adonis's brows bolted to his hairline. He snapped to me and saw nothing close to remorse in my eyes. The opening line of my paper read:

Who I am at my core is a dirty, cum-hungry slut who will do whatever you ask, whenever you ask, and in whichever position you like.

It did not get more school-appropriate from there.

Just so there wasn't any confusion, I shared in great details many of the things I wanted him to do to me. He must've gotten to the part where I suck his cock under his desk while he's teaching, because he glanced down as if measuring if I could fit.

Suddenly, my paper was shoved to the bottom of the pile and a harsh look was shoved my way. I knew what I was doing to him. I didn't feel bad for a second. There was something between us. Something real. It was only right that we explore it since I was likely going to kill his brother anyway.

Class finished thirty minutes later. Adonis was up and off with the first wave of students that left the room. He wasn't risking me cornering him and climbing on his desk again. Smart thinking because I was absolutely going to.

With one brother out of my reach, I went after the other one.

"Victor, wait."

He didn't stop or turn around. "Unless you're down on one knee, I've got a class to get to."

"Dammit, Victor. What does that even mean that you want me to propose to you? I want to marry you. I torpedoed my relationship with my mother to marry you. So yeah, I sabotaged a relationship, but it wasn't ours."

Victor halted at the entrance, but didn't face me.

"I said I wanted us to start over. We went on that date and had a good time before our clothes came off. Things were going well before that ridiculous fight," I said. "I don't know what else you want from me."

"You really don't, do you." That odd note was back in his voice, quieting me. "If you really don't get this, Luna, then there's nothing more you want from me either.

"I've got class." He took off.

I stood there, feeling more mixed up than ever.

***

I Dare You To Leave Wesley A Little Surprise.
  Dare: Accepted
  Dare: Accepted
  Dare: Accepted

That night, I waited at the fountain for Wilder, overdressed for the autumn weather. Slinky black boots; tight jeans; lace panties; sheer tank top; soft blouse; cashmere vest, trand a faux leather jacket.

Honestly, I wasn't sure Wilder would come. I had him at the part where we met out in the open and arrived separately. I lost him at the part where I took him blindfolded to our date spot, fed him food he didn't make himself, and didn't allow him control over one single aspect of our night.

I wouldn't be surprised if instead of meeting me, he was holed up in his room, doing another deep background check on me to prove I was a North Korean spy, finally making my move to take him out.

"Luna."

Wilder climbed the slope, perfect in a pair of dark jeans and a white tee. I tried to keep the smile off my face and failed.

"Go ahead. Be smug." He held out his hand. "You said you had ways of making me do what you wanted. Challenge lost."

"We'll call this a draw," I said, laughing. "No one could've resisted."

"Where are we going?"

"I'll let you walk as far as the arboretum, then you've got to put on the blindfold."

"Once again, no."

I wiggled my hips, molding to his side. "If you do, I'll make you a video."

"Where is it? You got one, or do I need to buy a dozen right now?"

I cracked up. "I'm not any sexier in video."

"But you are replayable in video." Wilder took his chance, wrapping his arm around me. "You spend far too much of your day in clothes."

"Oooh, well, that's something you can help me with."

We set off, our flirting getting more outrageous along the way.

My chemistry with Wilder was a mystery—much like him. He did things I couldn't believe, and said things I didn't want to. Everything from his anti-government rants to the stockpile of weapons said insane doomsday prepper who's already put the faces on the volleyballs that'll keep him company those long years underground. What about that was my type?

Let's see, the fact that he handles each of those weapons like they're an extension of his cock. Watching Wilder take apart and reassemble a Glock in fifteen seconds was a kink I didn't know I had. And the rants. Those should scare me off, but when he spoke, all I heard was his passion for the truth.

Then, because it had to be said, there was the big issue of his overwhelming, smirking hotness. You could crack a walnut on his chiseled jawline, and don't get me started on his body. The man kept it tight.

I pulled out the blindfold within steps of the arboretum. Wilder looked askance at it despite his promise.

"You're not a fan of giving up control."

"Not to anyone." Wilder gently took my hands, bringing the blindfold up to him. "Except you."

Bubbles grew and popped in my chest. What did you do with guys who said things like that to you?

You never let them go.

His blindfold on, I led Wilder down a stone path.

It was a quiet night—broken only by singing cicadas. A cooling breeze caressed my barrier of clothes, seeking to slip beneath and chill my heated skin. This close to Wilder, nothing could do that.

"Careful." I came around him and laced his fingers through mine. "There are steps. We'll go slow." I took him up one step at a time, marveling that I asked him to trust me, and he did.

Coming out onto the deck, I scurried behind him and tugged off the blindfold. "Surprise." I cheesed as he swept the space. "What do you think?"

"A man tells you to win him over and you go all out."

That I did. Regalia University, being the overpriced private university that it was, had state-of-the-art facilities for all the subjects taught there—including an observation tower for the natural sciences. Surrounding us were three-sixty views of the night sky and all of Regalia. It was so beautiful; you could almost believe this town was a wonderful place to live.

But I didn't want to think about Regalia. Right then, I was high above the world and all its problems... with Wilder.

The glow of fairy lights shrouded us, illuminating the flecks of gray in Wilder's eyes. Laid out on the wooden slats was a picnic blanket, pillows, and a basket full of Wilder's favorite food—sesame noodles, honey chicken wings, spring rolls, and mugs of sweet, warm tea. In the middle of it all was my laptop and a small wrapped box.

"Dinner and a movie?" he asked.

"Yes, actually." I checked the time. "Let's get comfy. It's about to start."

Wilder reclined on the pillows, gaze sweeping the sky. "Not bad. Not bad at all, Sinclair. I couldn't have topped this for our first date. I'll have to step it up for our second."

It made me ten kinds of intensely happy that he knew there'd be a second.

"You know that virus, or app, or hacker spy-craft thing you put on the guys' computers that time we locked them in their rooms?" I turned on my laptop. "CrankDance17 was kind enough to accept a little dare from me. They will see that we get our show."

I pulled up the video app. There was nothing to see but darkness. It was nearing midnight. He was still asleep.

"Do I get to find out what's in here?" Wilder shook the box. "I'm sorry, I didn't know we were doing presents. I would've gotten you something."

"Wilder, you've given me so much. My revenge wouldn't be possible without you. Each of you. You've gotten me this far and..." I shared his pillow, draping my arm over his waist while I rested my head on his chin. "...now I want to go farther with you.

"Under that wrapping paper is a box. In that box is your present," I said. "To get to your present, you have to unlock the box with a four-digit keycode that is somewhere on my body."

My grin turned wicked. "You can get to that code if you entice me into taking off my clothes, and there's only one thing that'll work."

"I'm listening."

"One fact about you in exchange for one item of clothes. Tell me everything I don't know about you, Wilder Last Name Unknown." I pressed a kiss to the corner of his mouth. "Unlock your secrets, and I'll unlock mine."

Wilder raked me up and down, war raging on his face. "This is cruel."

I laughed. "Your girlfriend getting to know you is cruel? Just wait until we start baring our souls to each other. You'll beg for mercy."

"One fact for a piece of clothing?" he dragged out. "And pairs are treated as one?"

"Yes, but you have to make it good. I'm not a cheap date." I plopped back on my elbows, letting my legs sway and dip, open and shut. "You won't get my clothes off for your favorite color or Powerpuff girl."

"Blossom," he dropped. "Okay, Sinclair. I respect your game. We'll play by your rules. For now."

Wilder drew closer, laying me on my back with the linger of his presence alone. Pulling me in, his hand was warm on my thigh. The other gentle and tracing circles on my scalp. My pulse quickened under his touch.

I ached for him fully clothed. Was I ready for what would happen when there wasn't a barrier between us? Not the physical ones, or the ones he built between us to keep me at arm's length.

"O'Rourke is my mother's maiden name," he said. "My parents never married, but she did name me Wilder Weston after my father. Then she changed her name, and I changed mine to O'Rourke. My family has a long history of changing our identities. People who dig up dirt on the kind of people we do, can't be easy to find."

"Wilder Weston," I tried, rolling it on my tongue. "I like it. Makes me think of outlaws and mercenaries. It fits you."

I reached for my boots. Wilder grasped my hand, slowly returning it to my side. Holding my gaze, he slid my jacket off my shoulders.

"I taught myself how to hack. My parents both knew how, but in the Weston-O'Rourke clan, nothing is given to you. Not even a computer. I stole my first one."

"Wow. That's a lot of pressure."

"No," he said, undoing the buttons of my blouse. "It taught me something most people learn too late or not at all. We're all on our own. We can either make the best of it and come out on top, or we can watch all the people who do pass us by."

I cupped his cheek. "You can also learn a lesson too soon."

"Speaking of lessons, I know how to play the tuba. I learned in middle school and got quite good."

"Were you in—?"

"Band." He grinned. "Hell yeah."

I burst out laughing. "You, Wilder O'Rourke-Weston, used to be a band geek. Basically what you're saying is I should never think I have you figured out."

"I plan to keep surprising you for a very, very long time."

Biting my lip, I whispered, "Looking forward to it."

Again, I reached for my boots. Again, Wilder stopped me. He ignored my shoes—fingers skating over my belt. How cute was I thinking I could tease him into handing over control? My body was his. I was his. Wilder would unwrap me as he saw fit.

"My mother lives in Ireland. My father lives in New York. I was emancipated at fifteen and stayed in Regalia after they left."

"Why stay?" I was working hard to be calm and chill as he slid my pants over my thighs. I don't care how much experience I racked up. The first time with the guy I've been lusting over since we met, would always be nerve-wracking.

"New York. L.A. Austin. Miami. D.C. To the rest of the world, it looks like those places are the seats of power. But they're wrong. It's right here in Regalia where one decision, one business deal, one marriage can turn the tide for the whole country. I dig out corruption where it hides, and we're standing on a mountain-size pile of it right now."

Wilder finally took off my boots, but only to tug my jeans all the way off. The wind skated over me like an eager lover, but I wasn't cold. Up there with Wilder, we were caught in our own world.

"I've written two sci-fi novels."

Vest gone.

"I'm fluent in three languages: English, Spanish, and Korean."

Blouse tossed over his shoulder.

"I met you before that night we found you with Owen."

"We did? I don't remember."

"It was over summer," he said. "You were sitting on the beach, staring at the waves while people laughed and ran and had a good time all around you. That's what drew me to you. You were apart from it all, looking so sad that I couldn't walk away from you.

"I wanted someone to run up and join you, so I'd know you weren't alone."

The day he spoke of came to me sharp and clear. There was only one day that summer that I left the beach house, and went out to watch the waves.

"But no one came," he said. "I saw a woman with a small stand selling—"

"Roses," I whispered. "You bought me a rose and dropped it at my feet. Then you took off too fast for me to say anything. Wilder, I can't believe that was you. Why didn't you say anything before?"

"Wasn't sure if it was a good or bad memory."

"It's a good one now." I kissed him slow and sweet. "It's my favorite."

His hands were warm on my hips, tugging my panties down. He grinned at the numbers scribbled above my entrance. "One, two, three, four. Nice."

"Open your present."

Wilder looked me up and down with such a naked, hungry look in his eyes, my knees clenched together. "Which one?"

Giggling, I placed his present on my stomach. "Please. You'll like it."

It was a tiny black box tied with a purple ribbon. Wilder opened and tipped it over, letting the flash drive drop onto his palm.

"That video I promised you..." A smirk stretched my lips. "I already recorded it."

His eyes popped. I knew right then that he thought I was teasing him. He never expected to be holding that in his hands. "What's on this?"

"You know," I said. "It's me... in my room."

Wilder brushed the sensitive skin under my belly button. "Doing what?"

My cheeks heated. "You know what."

"Tell me."

The command in his voice—both subtle and unyielding—loosened my tongue. "I take off my clothes and get on my bed. Then, I play with myself—"

"Where do you start?"

"Wilder," I cried, covering my face. "Don't make me say. You'll see it when you watch it later."

"Yeah, I'll see it later, but right now." Wilder drew back, stretching out across the blanket. "I want to see you."

My goodness. What was happening? "You want me to... masturbate for you?"

By way of answering, Wilder unzipped his pants, freeing his straining cock. Ah, so that is what's happening.

"What did you do first, baby?"

"I..." My skin tingled under a thousand sparks lighting up my nerve endings. "I teased my nipples. Tasting them for you."

"Tease them for me again."

I settled in the glow of the candles, hoping against hope that they weren't lighting up my red face. I teased myself to tempt Adonis, but that was different. Adonis was playing hard to get, and Wilder's playing hard to get me. The pillows cradled my body, warming me though my pebbled nipples said I was anything but.

I rolled my fingers over the sensitive flesh, sensing my core ignite faster than usual. Doing this for Wilder was a lot different than a camera.

"Oh," I breathed, head falling forward. I sucked my nipple in my mouth and released it with a "pop."

Wilder grunted sharply—jerking hard on his cock. He watched me taste, tease, pinch, and lick them, his strokes near strangling by the time my hands moved lower.

"Did you scream my name?"

"Over and over again. Wilder." I plunged my fingers deep, imagining it was him like I did that morning. "Uh, Wilder. Yes, baby, stretch my pussy."

I scissored my fingers open inside my dark cavern. Wilder's sharp hiss of breath spurred me on. "I love what you do to me. Make me come."

"Don't come," he growled. Wilder roughly stripped off the rest of his clothes. "Not until I say."

My goodness, I was with the worst bunch of dominating fuckable pricks, and I loved it too much.

"Yes, Wilder."

"Show me how you strum yourself."

I was very much into this now. I stopped my teasing, dipped in another finger, and started moving hard and fast—moans echoing off the tower.

"Ah, ah, Wilder, yes."

"Give yourself more."

I obeyed without question, adding a third finger. Wilder was stroking his dick so hard, the tension was a living thing inside his body.

"Did you use a dildo?"

I nodded, peering at him through my lashes. "Biggest one I got. But I don't carry it around with me."

"Why would you need to?" Wilder caught his leaking precum and swirled it around his uncut tip. "You've got the real thing right here."

I arched my back, enjoying the delicious grunts and sounds coming from him as he watched me. This was not how I saw our first date going, but that's what happens when you fall for a Rogue.

You end up on your knees, slapping your clit on the deck of an observation tower. No way around it. It's inevitable.

"Show me what you do with those plastic cocks that you should be doing with me."

My body spasmed involuntarily, rocked by a concussive wave that clenched me around my fingers. Using this man as my personal dildo was literally my sex dream.

I crawled over to him, moan escaping me at the sight of him. His body was unreal. Not an ounce of body fat disturbed the hard, corded muscles climbing down his abs to molded, tree-trunk thighs.

No, the tree trunk was the stalk at the apex of his Thor's V. Way bigger than any rubber friend I've fooled around with, I looked at it and genuinely asked how I'd make it fit.

Wilder stroked my knee—his touch gliding up my thigh, caressing my side, and traveling to my chin where he grasped and tugged me down. Our lips met. Not a wild, crazy fare, but a sweet, gentle meeting of two mouths, two bodies, and one heart.

Wilder told me he liked Winter because she never called him crazy. I knew my sister. Knew she wouldn't have believed half of his theories on sleeper cells infiltrating grocery store chains, or spy organizations recruiting out of boarding schools. But she didn't need to believe the words to respect the passion behind them.

Because that's who my Wilder was.

He was passion, intensity, protectiveness, and authority. When he believed something, he believed with everything he had. When he wanted something, he went after it with everything he knew. And when he loved someone, he loved them with every corner of his heart.

In one kiss, he overtook me—sweeping me under the tide of emotions he held back. The whole time, he wasn't waiting for me to win him over. He wasn't cool and unbothered while Rafael, Cato, Lucien, and Victor got closer to me.

Wilder was waiting for me to come to the one and simple truth—to be loved by him was forever and unyielding. There was no turning back or slowing down. He had me stripped and laid bare, my only hope was that he'd showed mercy to the heart I tore from my chest. There was nothing I could do to stop what we'd become now.

I was hacked.

"I love you," we whispered—perfectly in sync. Like the goofy, beaming grin that dimpled our cheeks.

I stole one more kiss—loving it. Needing it. "I believe I was about to show you how I fuck myself." Sliding down his chest, I gripped the base of his cock. "How I angle my dildo on the sheets just like this..."

I turned my back and pressed Wilder to my entrance. "How I get on my knees like this... and bounce on my toes like that." Moving slow, I impaled myself on him—taking him in as far and deep as he'd go. "Ah, yes. But that is much better than a dildo."

"Fuck, you're so damn beautiful," Wilder traced down my spine. "Faster, Luna. I know you're not shy when you're alone in your room, giving that pussy what it needs, exactly the way it wants."

I wasn't shy then or now. I picked up the pace—holding him just where I wanted him, and pogoing on that secret, yummy spot. Sweat beaded on our bodies that glowed in the candlelight. It was incredible how perfectly we fit. My cheeks molded to his lap. My breasts were gloves to his hands. Why did I wait so long to claim a guy who was meant to be mine?

"Just so you know," I said, "my dildo rubs my clit."

A deep, husky chuckle rolled from his chest. "Oh yeah?"

"Uh-huh. It pinches my nipples and kisses just under my ear too."

"Quite a multitasking toy you've got, but I did tell you to do all the things you do with it for me." Wilder rose up, pressing his warmth to me. I melted as he cupped my breast, rolling the sensitive nub under his callouses. "What else does it do?" he gruffed, nipping the shell of my ear.

"It's amazing actually. Right about now it just starts fucking me all on its own. No hands needed. Hard, fast, and deep. It makes me forget my own name."

"Hmm. Like this?"

Wilder dipped between my legs and slapped my clit. I jumped, crying out at the sharp, sudden spike of pleasure tearing my resolve to shreds. I hoped he gave me permission to come soon, 'cause I would not last long.

"And does it put you on your knees like this?" He pressed my cheek into a pillow and raised my ass up. "Or taste you like this?"

My toes curled as his tongue tangoed with my slit. "Yes and yes."

"And does it—" Wilder thrust inside.

I gasped, strangling a cry from my throat. Flattening his palm between my shoulder blades, Wilder held me down while he started pumping.

"Yes," I cried. "It definitely does that. It does it harder!" My eyes rolled up in my head and moans rolled loud and free. No one was out to hear us, but

I wouldn't care if they did. Katie was right. Receiving the best sex of my life was nothing to hide.

Our bodies moved in time, making sinful music. Slaps, grunts, moans, whispered promises, and over and over again *I love you.*

Pressure built in my middle—rising to a fever pitch with each hard, targeted slam inside me. Wilder had me stretched and fucked to the limit. I straight begged for my orgasm.

"Please, baby. Let me come for you."

"Come with me," he strained. "Same... time."

"Whoa," I shrieked, suddenly finding myself upright.

Wilder held me under the knees, lifting me wide-eyed onto his dick. This was a new position. Very, very new.

I didn't get a word out before he bounced me on his lap, lifting and impaling my pussy like it was hammering a nail.

White dotted out my mind. I knew nothing. Felt nothing. Was nothing but a creature of pure sex and pleasure.

"Come, you beautiful, dangerous, perfect woman," he growled. "Come for me."

Wilder had me at the first consonant. I came hard, belting out a hoarse scream as my body jerked and spasmed under explosion after explosion—orgasm after orgasm.

"Fuck," he roared. Wilder spilled inside me, filling my pussy with—

"Ahhhh!"

We jumped. A sudden scream ripped through our perfect world, throwing Wilder off-balance. We went down in a shrieking tangle of limbs.

"What the fuck is that?" Wilder shouted.

I scrambled up, clutching my pounding chest. "*That* is my second surprise of the night. Someone in the club carried out another dare against Wesley, and he's finally seen it."

"Wesley?" Wilder rolled up, chest heaving. "Never had the shit scared out of me mid-ejaculation before. Wesley Hill ain't worth the first time."

I kissed his cheek in apology. "We will definitely pick up where we left off. Trust me on that. But I knew you'd want to see this." I angled the screen for us to see. "Multiple times you reported Wesley for animal abuse, and no one did anything against the pampered rich boy. Let's see how he likes this."

The lights were on in his dorm, allowing the webcam I secretly turned on to capture the entire scene.

Wesley flailed on the bed, hopelessly tangled in the sheets he was fighting to escape. It was a crime scene.

Blood streaked the sheets and covered half his torso, soaked his hair, and got everywhere as he tumbled off the bed. Lying on the pillow next to him, sharing his bed as he slept, was a pig's severed head.

"No! No! Ahhh!"

Wesley shouted his head off, throwing everything he got his hands on at the thing as if it would come alive and attack. When he read the message I dared KiwiGirl3 to leave over his head, his bellows got louder.

You're Next

I gasped. "Oh my goodness, is he...?" My eyes widened at the growing dark patch on his boxers.

"Yes, Sinclair. Hill just pissed himself in fright."

Clapping my hand over my mouth, I burst out laughing. "Oh, that is good. It's better than good. How could tonight be more perfect?"

"I'll tell you—" Wilder snapped the laptop shut. "I get that bastard and his piss-soaked shorts out of my head, and return to a certain thing he interrupted."

"That is the correct answer."

Wilder pounced on me.

That night ranked top among the best dates anyone ever had. Up on that observation tower, high above the world, we made love in every position there was, and a few we made up. In between, we talked and laughed and fed each other spring rolls.

Every now and then we checked on Wesley, who passed out after Wilder shut the laptop, and spent three hours splayed out on the carpet.

I lay safe in his arms—warm and content as the sunrise bathed us in golds, reds, and tangerines—a gift just for us.

"He's on the edge." Wilder dropped kisses on the sensitive spot under my ear. I practically purred. "Passing out in his own piss? One more push and it's over. He'll tell you anything you want to know to make it stop."

"I know just what I want that push to be. But first..." Flipping over, I popped a kiss on his lips. "There's a little something that's going to hit everyone's student emails in about an hour. I timed it just right. Want to be there with me when it goes down?"

"Does it involve us getting dressed and leaving this spot?"

"Yes," I said, peppering him with kisses. "But afterward, we'll go home and you can watch me and my dildo in action for real this time."

He groaned. "Tempting. So very tempting." Wilder kissed me hard. "But no."

It took a lot of coaxing and promising an obscene number of sexual favors before we finally dragged ourselves away.

Wilder held my hand across campus. His thumb tickled my knuckles and his lips found his way to mine at least every thirty seconds. It surprised and delighted me how affectionate he was. After weeks of frisking, tossing away anything I cooked for him, accusing me of being a spy, and disinfecting me before letting me touch him, this Wilder who had his hands all over me and told me he loved me without hesitation... this guy could put a ring on my finger while I was sleeping too. I'd marry him in a heartbeat.

A needle pricked my happy balloon, setting it on a slow leak. Thinking of marriage made me think of Victor. I kept messing up with him lately and I didn't know why. What was I saying that was wrong? What did he want me to do that I wasn't?

What if I just propose? He wants a sign that I'm committed to this marriage, then I'll give him one. Whatever it takes to remove the question mark hanging over our heads lately.

My phone buzzed, pulling me from silly thoughts of if I had to buy him a ring.

I opened my email and my smile returned. "Just in time. Hope she doesn't make it to the café before us."

"What did you do, Sinclair?" Wilder checked the link that showed up in his inbox. True shock blew up his handsome face. "Okay, *how* did you do this? You didn't get this from me or the HapApp messages? I didn't know shit about this."

"I know," I sang, beaming away. "T.O.D. helped me with this one. You could rule the world with an army of amoral, empty-headed followers behind you, but then every dictator knows that."

"Did you just call yourself a dictator? And did it just make my dick hard?"

I snuggled into his side, hand slipping under his and stroking the skin above his belt. "Yes and yes."

Wilder and I set foot in the café, and a wall of sound smacked us over the head.

"Oh, shit. Did you see this?"

"I can't believe it."

"It's not her. It can't really be her."

Wilder and I stepped up to the buffet, watching from the sidelines. "Hungry?" I asked. "We could split one of those strawberry scones."

"We'll split the ambulance ride to the hospital when we overdose on the mood-stabilizers and antipsychotic meds they've been pumping in this food. It's how they control the student population, keep everyone calm, and prevent fights that'll have lasting effects on the country."

I kissed him, then plopped the scone on my plate.

Naturally, Wilder put it back and said he wasn't having another sex marathon with me while I was under the influence.

That was too sweet and responsible for me to get mad at, so I smiled indulgently while he loaded me up with food that came prepackaged.

"It's not in the water yet, but give them time. I told you no one is normal around here. Just look at the way they're reacting."

We turned from the tea station, watching the pandemonium unfold. Everyone was on their phones, showing their friends, texting more people, and shouting it across the café just in case there was anyone in the room who didn't already know.

I glanced at the clock. We couldn't have missed her. She didn't have class until nine, and she didn't cook for herself any more than any other Royal. That left her walking in here around eight o'clock to grab breakfast and take it to—

Katie strolled in, walking right past us and the drinks station. "She swears it wasn't her. Maybe we should hear Saylor out. We both know that list isn't her style anyway. If she wanted to get back at Piper sh-she..." Katie paused, suddenly noticing all the attention coming her way. She shook her head, dismissing it. "Anyway, if she wanted to hurt Piper, she would've come at her direct."

"That's true," Everleigh said. "Still, it's uncomfortable finding out how many secrets there were between us. Piper in love with me. Gabriella dating the son of her rival family and pushing his girlfriend off cliffs. Is there something I should know about you—"

"Hey, Everleigh. Looking good, mami." A sophomore guy encircled them, coming in so close Everleigh smacked his grasping hand away. "Don't be like that."

"Fuck off, Dreg," she snapped. "Who gave you permission to talk to me?"

"Oooh. Sorry." He waved his hands all wild and exaggerated. "I should've paid for the privilege."

Raucous laughter went up around us—more than that comeback deserved.

Everleigh's eyes narrowed to slits. She backed away. "What's going on?"

Alice climbed up on her table. "What's going on is the Book Lady is going to give us a show."

Everleigh froze.

"This enough to cover it, right?" Alice threw a handful of twenties at her.

"What are you talking about?" Everleigh cried. "How do you know that name!"

I eyed the clock, ticking down the seconds. "And three, two, one—"

The lights winked out. Over our heads, shining on the faces of former deans, a projector turned on.

Everleigh's scream echoed through the building.

I hissed, wincing. "Wow. I only told them to show the website. Didn't think they'd go for the preview."

A riot of limbs, flesh, and sweat joined the hallowed educators on the wall. Dean Villeneuve was treated to a pale backside on his face, and the dick that was plowing it. A masked woman moaned and carried on—wrapped around the guy in a position I now knew was called the Queen of Heaven.

Despite the intricate green-and-blue mask covering half her face, it did nothing to hide that tawny fringe or her dreamy hazel eyes. There was no mistaking it. We were looking at Everleigh Starling.

"Turn it off! Take that down!" Everleigh ran at the projector, then doubled back. Her ankle bent, tipping her off her high heels. "Ahh!" She crashed hard on the floor—dazed in the wake of her classmates' howling laughter. Forcing herself up, she raced to the broom closet. The projector was high up on a window ledge, without a ladder, it wasn't coming down anytime soon.

Everleigh emerged with a broom. Eyes wild and bruise already beginning to color her chin, she went at the projector—shrieking her head off as she tried and failed to knock it down.

Katie might've helped her if she wasn't standing in dumbfounded shock at the talents of the Book Lady.

"Everleigh did not mention this to any of her friends in HapApp of course," I said. "She's a lot smarter than the rest of them. She didn't reveal any secrets that could sink her, and I read through hours of old texts. Turns out she has a reason to be cautious. That's how it goes when you lead a second life."

"But the Book Lady," he murmured, neck twisting to follow a position she was tangled up in. "She's not just selling sex, but she's selling it in all the positions of the *Kama Sutra*? No one could possibly do all sixty-four. Some of those you've got to do a lot of stretching beforehand, and you still end up popping your back out."

I narrowed on him amid the chaos. "How would you know that exactly?"

Grinning, he winked at me—seriously risking injury. "You can't get jealous when you spent all last night benefiting from my experience."

"Everything you've done with those girls, you're doing with me. *I* will be who you think of when you remember the *Vadavaka* position."

Face grave, he held a hand over his chest. "Harsh punishment, Sinclair, but I bravely accept it."

I laughed, bumping hips with him. Wilder bent down to kiss me.

"Who did this!"

Katie popped the bubble we tried to close ourselves up in. I refocused and landed on her dragging the ladder out of the janitor's closet. One of the Handmaidens was thinking clearly—too bad for me.

Everleigh ran to help her and tripped again. Alice's pudding cup exploded on her head, dripping vanilla crème on that fringe. Within seconds, the entire cafeteria was pelting her with food. Everleigh lay there on the floor and straight bawled.

Wilder cringed. "This is almost hard to watch."

"Is it?" I cocked my head, searching for an ounce of sympathy. "I didn't find secrets in her old messages, but I did find the conversations Everleigh, Piper, Gabriella, and Saylor had about my sister when the school was torturing her. Everleigh in particular thought Owen's website and the video of her getting sexually assaulted was hilarious. She made a bet on how long before Winter left school. Or blew her brains out. None of them thought she'd last the first semester."

Alice threw a whole tray at her head. I didn't know what the beef was between those two, but Everleigh must've served it up big.

"Hmm," I said while Everleigh cried harder. "You ask me, I went too easy on them."

"Stop it!" Katie screeched. She fell on Everleigh, shielding her. "You monsters! What is wrong with you?" She found me through the crowd. "Luna? Luna! Help us!"

I bit off a groan. Helping Everleigh Starling was the last thing I wanted to do, but I couldn't blow Katie off. She delivered Levi a punishment worse than I could ever come up with by taking away everything a Royal cares about. And she did that for my sister. I couldn't walk away when she asked me for help.

I made to go.

"Don't," Wilder said, holding his arm out. "They're throwing everything they can get their hands on. I won't have you in the line of fire. I've got it."

Wilder pushed through the crowd. Calm and imposing, he shrugged off his jacket and draped it over Katie and Everleigh. The shouting, laughing, and food-throwing slowed as he hefted the ladder and climbed up to get the projector. Like I said, a guy that could hack your bank accounts, put you on the sex offender registry, and expose all your secrets, wasn't a guy to make your enemy.

I took my chance to run across and help them up. I shouted *shame on you* and other bullshit as I helped Katie and Everleigh escape. Everleigh got outside and kept running, her wails leaving a trail that followed her out into the parking lot. I doubted anyone would see her for the rest of the day. Or the week.

"Holy shit," Katie cried. "I can't believe— Who is doing these things!"

"Maybe you should go after her. Make sure she's okay."

"You're right," she said, taking off. "Thanks, Luna. We'll talk later."

I waved her off, dropping the sympathetic moon eyes the minute she was out of sight. "I'm hungry." I skipped inside. "I think I will have that scone."

Chapter Nine

I weaved through the desks, making for mine near the back of my psychology class. What happened to Everleigh that morning was on everyone's lips.

"Can you believe it?"

"I heard so many people flooded the site that it crashed. Sucks because I never got a chance to book an appointment with the Book Lady."

That set off a round of laughs in the huddled group of girls behind me.

"Another Royal princess taken down. Someone really has a hard-on for them lately."

"Good. How many times have those girls called us sluts, bitches, or trash because we stood there existing? That's if they acknowledged our existence at all. It's about time they got a taste of their own medicine."

"But who do you think is doing it?" Bethany asked. "Could it be that club I heard about? The truth or dare club? Or something like that?"

My ears perked up.

"Oooh, I heard about that too," said Debra. "*I dare you to make those stuck-up bitches cry*. If that's what they're about, I'm in."

I drew away from their conversation to answer my phone. It vibrated with a message from Wilder.

Wilder: ThreesTease sent this to you for a prompt payment of two thousand dollars.

I quickly tapped the screen, letting the video play. Wesley came on the screen in all his hideous glory. Yes, by society's definition, he was a mess of classic good looks and a body most guys would die for. But when I looked at him, I gagged.

Wesley scurried across the quad, twitching and looking over his shoulder every two steps. Puffy, bloodshot eyes told the story of how he slept the night before. I was pretty sure the pig was still there, rotting away on his pillow. Wesley for sure didn't get rid of it when he woke up on the floor, grabbed a pair of pants, and bolted.

He wore said pants in the video. They hung low on his waist, revealing he ditched the piss-stained boxers between his dorm and the quad, but didn't find a shirt or comb on the way.

He's done with dorm life. I bet he's running home to Mommy.

Wesley threw open his car door. His shout blared through my speakers, startling everyone around me. He flew back and hit the opposite car, setting off the alarm. Turning tail, Wesley ran.

He ran and ran through the parking lot, tearing for the main road. The video ended there but I didn't need to see more. I dared another member to put another severed head on Wesley's front seat. The final head would be exactly where Wesley was going—on his pillow-top bed in Hill Manor.

Wesley would learn there was nowhere he could go to hide from me.

Me: Pay the man. He does excellent work.

Of course I didn't tell anybody to kill an innocent animal. I wasn't that far gone. I sent them to the butcher shop on Crest Avenue. The creatures were already gone. There was no saving them. But they could be used to force an evil little shit into doing the right thing, and telling me who hired him to drive my sister to suicide.

I leaned back, letting the cackles over Everleigh and the whispers about secret clubs wash over me.

It felt good being the one with the power.

I'm coming for you, Phantom. Go ahead and watch your back, because I'm coming from the front.

***

That night, I rested in Lucien's coffin—scrunched and comfortable by his side.

"This is surprisingly cozy."

"There's a reason it's used for eternal rest."

I dropped my head on his shoulder, sighing. "I'm sorry our date got cut short. I'm even more sorry we haven't had time to pick up where we left off."

"We couldn't go now either way. I have to take you during a full moon. We missed our chance this time. We'll get another one."

I gazed up at the ceiling. "Is it weird to say that I've never been happier than I am right now, but I've also never been unhappier?" My voice was barely a whisper. "My sister's gone. My mom isn't speaking to me. Victor has my head in knots. I'm doing things I never in a million years thought I would. It's like my whole life went off-track and left some of the most important people behind.

"But even with all that going on... I'm here with you guys. You, Rafael, Wilder, and Cato found me on this new path, and I can't stop myself from being happy that I get to walk it with you."

"Nothing weird about that, Luna." Lucien lazily stroked the sensitive skin above my thigh. "It's just human."

"This club though. It frightens me, Lucien. Everything I've asked these members to do, they've done. No outraged replies that they'd never do such a thing. No threatening to call the cops. Nothing. They've just been doing the dares without question and taking the money. I have to wonder how many awful things that happened around here were because of the club. How will we ever know?"

Lucien didn't answer, because he knew I wouldn't like it.

"I just wish I could figure out what Winter knew and how. So many secrets stayed buried in Regalia. How did she dig that one up?"

"There's only one person who can answer that now. And they're another secret."

I tossed my head. "Enough. I will get Levi or Wesley to tell me the truth, until then, I'm driving myself crazy with this. Distract me."

"What did you have in mind?"

I traced his lips, and the canine slightly poking out. "What do vampires always have in mind?"

His eyes darkened. "Are you sure?"

"I'm sure."

Lucien tipped my chin, exposing my soft, pale throat. "No, Luna. Are you *sure*? Are you sure you want to feel the ecstasy of my bite? To feel the tingle beneath your skin?" His voice was low and hypnotic, wrapping me in calm. "Are you sure you're ready for the heady rush of guilty pleasure as my fangs pierce your flesh and fill me with everything that's you?"

"I'm ready."

We undressed slowly for each other—granting the gift of watching the one we want lay themself bare. As Lucien peeled off layer after layer, I got pissed. Why was this body always hidden from me?

Long coats, baggy pantaloons, and thick vests were tossed to the floor where they belonged, and the perfect body hiding underneath offered itself up for my devouring. Looking at him then, I finally understood why he wore those clothes instead of joining everyone in the modern world.

Lucien was pale.

Ivory skin untouched by the sun drew me in. My finger skimmed his unblemished chest, skating along the fine hairs that had the pleasure of clinging to his hard pecs all day and night.

Maybe I should've been put off, but that was nothing close to how I felt. I had the wrong nickname. It was Lucien who was gorgeous.

He was Heathcliff running through the moor—dark, brooding, and timeless. The sun dare not kiss his skin without permission, which it did not have. But I did.

I pressed my lips to him, gifting barely there kisses under his collarbone. Lucien tangled in my hair, pulling me closer. Pulling me up.

Our mouths connected like puzzle pieces. Two people meant to be together that were broken up, scattered, and waiting through time to find each other again.

Lucien kissed me hungrily, his canines scraping as we battled for dominance.

I pushed him back, laying him on the cushioned velvet of the coffin. Straddling him, I removed the last barrier between us—flinging my bra somewhere it wouldn't be missed.

"I've lived a hundred years and I'll live a hundred more. In all that time, I'll never lay eyes on a creature more beautiful than you."

I bit my lip, sensing a blush coming on and feeling silly for it. I could no longer call myself inexperienced. I've said dirty things and done filthier things than I'd ever dreamed of, and I loved every minute of it. It shouldn't make me duck my head and blush just to receive a compliment, but I couldn't help it.

Before I met the Rogues, no one spoke to me, looked at me, touched me, or made me feel the way they did. It's an amazing thing to be precious to someone. And the most incredible miracle to be precious to four.

"I want to say something really sweet and poetic right now," I told him. "Something that says everything about how I feel for you. But my brain went offline the minute your clothes came off. If you existed during the time of Michelangelo, it's a sculpture of you that'd stand where David stands. You're the representation of male beauty. Period."

Lucien grinned, bringing me down for a kiss. "And you said you couldn't think of anything." He caressed my lips, then skated up—nipping my ear. "Ever sat on a vampire's face before?"

My brows blew up. My fortune did say that a vampire would fuck me hot and dirty. All the same, it was a delicious surprise to hear Lucien talk this way. We could be a lady and vampire gentleman out there. But safe in his bedroom… I really wanted to sit on his face.

"Can't say that I have, but it's something I've wanted to try since Peter Facinelli walked on screen playing Carlisle Cullen."

"Wait. Am I the definition of male beauty, or is your *Twilight* crush?"

"It's still you," I teased, placing my knees on either side of his head. "But if you happened to be absent the day Michelangelo got to work, Carlisle could step in."

"Could he?" Lucien licked a slow, languid strip between my lower lips. "Could he step in and do that too?"

"I mean… if he offered—"

A firm swat landed on my backside, pulling a giggling squeal out of me. What was it about me? I just loved getting myself spanked.

"Just kidding, baby." I lowered myself, sigh escaping me as I started rocking on his tongue. "You're the only vampire for me."

I gripped the edges of the coffin, my grinding getting more insistent as Lucien slipped his tongue somewhere interesting. Shudders rippled up my body, curving my back and hardening my nipples to points.

Those long months in my French boarding school without any guys my age around did not turn me into the Pussy Muncher, but it did turn me into the Dick Fantasizer. I imagined what my first time would be like, all the time and in all the ways. I could say absolutely and one hundred percent that nothing in my fantasies came close to the real thing with Rafael, Cato, Wilder, Adonis, and Lucien.

Just Lucien's hands on me undid me like twine. I felt like the beautiful creature he saw when I was with him. Beautiful and sexy and mature like this was more than a college romance destined to simmer down by graduation.

We were like his *descendants*, Sam and Nina. We saw each other and we just knew.

"Stop holding back," Lucien demanded. "You can't hurt me."

The tide broke.

I bounced on the balls of my feet, driving his tongue deeper and deeper within me as my cries ratcheted up to wanton. Lucien locked around my thighs and held me down, smothering himself in my folds. He attacked my pussy like a wild animal—licking, tasting, and punishing the lucky thing. Tiny pinpricks of pain followed his fangs. Each one almost made me come on the spot.

"Ah," I cried, eyes rolling up. "Yes, Lucien. Right there, baby."

"Tell me when you're close."

"I'm close. I'm so cl— Ah!"

Lucien popped me off him without so much as a spanking for warning. He sat up, drawing a surprised, and peeved, me onto his lap.

"You're going to come, but not yet. You said you were ready."

It took me a second to understand what he meant, and where this was going. "I am ready," I whispered, tracing his cheekbone. "Don't hold back. You can't hurt me."

"I can, and I will." His lips peeled back, revealing glinting, dangerously sharp implements of my pain and pleasure. "Because you want me to."

Lucien dipped my head back. I shivered under his tongue's exploration of the pulsing flesh covering my artery. He teased me—dropping nipping kisses under my chin and down to my collarbone. I'd be covered in love bites the next morning, and I'd make no attempt to hide them. He slid two fingers inside me and I knew what was coming.

Pain traveled through my neck, enticing a gasp. Lucien made a noise deep in his throat—long, rolling, and getting louder. Was that a moan?

Lucien moaned wild and loud, licking the blood pulsing free from me. I couldn't get caught up in the shock at what we were doing, because he wasn't giving me a chance to string a thought together.

He moved inside me—finding that spot with no trouble or help from me. I tossed my head back, letting loose as his fingers scrambled my inhibitions in a blender, then threw them out the window.

Deliciousness competed with discomfort. I felt my strength leave me and feed him. I was limp and helpless in his hold, draped over his body while his hand worked me like a puppet and blood flowed free from my neck.

Lucien, on the other hand, came alive in my arms. He picked up the pace—furiously finger-fucking me like he wanted to play a tune with my hoarse screams. He rutted against me—rubbing his erection against my thigh. Bouncing me on his lap. Spreading my ass and—

"Oh."

I jumped at the finger that found its way between my cheeks. It teased my puckered entrance, begging to delight me with another first. In all my fantasizing, I hadn't imagined this.

"Yes, Lucien. I want this. All of it."

He didn't need me to say another word. Lucien plunged inside, working me from both holes. He warned me that he tended to lose control, and that was the understatement of the century. I didn't recognize this man pumping me like a butter churn. His moans vibrated up my throat, telling a truth I accepted long ago.

"You're mine, Luna. In this life and the one after."

I broke under his blurring pace—two fingers in one hole and one in the other. They brought my orgasm back quick and merciless. Sunspots burst before my eyes, bringing me into the fantasy world that Lucien inhabited.

We were the only two people in the world, sharing our deepest and darkest fantasies there in that coffin. I was weak in his arms, but I also never felt stronger. So what that Lucien wouldn't admit he wasn't a vampire? With him, there was nothing I could say or do that would be judged. Lucien accepted me completely. Wanted me absolutely. And trusted me totally.

I got to live in this dreamworld with him, and in the morning when I woke in reality, he'd still be by my side.

A shudder rocked me, arching my back and pressing me harder against his erection. Heat rose to a fever pitch, then spilled over, taking me down and driving me to my knees before my climax. I couldn't think—couldn't breathe as it demanded my surrender. Tearing through my senses, I came hard, bouncing on the fingers dominating my holes.

"Uh," I cried, melting in a limp heap.

Lucien tensed and I quickly reached between us. Grasping his cock, I whispered sweet, dirty things in his ear, jerking him as furiously as he fingered me.

Hot wetness exploded on my thigh, painting us both in the perfect memory of what we just did together.

We flopped back in the coffin, chests heaving and covered in all the juices you can be covered in. Lucien held his ascot to my neck, stemming the bleeding.

"How was that for a distraction?"

"Fucking fantastic," I gasped, then a wicked smile tugged my lips. "But I wonder if Carlisle could've done it any better."

"I wonder if you planned to get any sleep tonight. Because that just went out the window."

"I bravely accept my punishment."

****

The next morning, I watched Wesley's bodyguard scan the area before opening the door for him.

I wasn't surprised Wesley hired a bodyguard. I was surprised it took him so long.

Mr. Sunglasses and Muscles changes nothing. Today Wesley gets broken. Today he tells me the name of the Phantom. Or tomorrow the next shot doesn't miss.

I was done playing games. I always thought truth or dare was for little kids anyway.

"Do you think he's there already?" Impatience climbed as Wesley crossed the quad. "We're running out of time. It has to be now."

"Rafael said you'd know when," Wilder replied.

Lucien agreed. "The sign will be unmistakable—"

Loud, baying barks broke the morning calm. A handsome black blur streaked across the grass, heading straight for Mr. Sunglasses and Muscles. Cato was only too happy to help me with Wesley's final taste of revenge... because he didn't have to wear the muzzle.

The bodyguard turned toward the sound, then scrambled for his weapon. He lifted the stun gun an inch when Cato leaped, tackling him to the ground. I winced before it happened.

"Aggh!"

Cato sank his teeth in the man's neck, tearing through flesh and veins. Inhuman screams ripped through the peaceful morning.

"Hey, what are you doing?" Wesley whirled around and ran at Cato. "Stop! Get off him!"

Cato finished him off with a brutal punch to the face. The guard lay there—out cold.

My muzzled love took off as quickly as he came, scaring off the onlookers who lingered too long. None of them were going to interfere. You don't get between Cato and anything.

"You, get up!" Wesley kicked the man none too gently in the side. "Get up, you idiot. You're supposed to be—"

"Protecting you from a girl half your size?" I finished, spinning Wesley around. "He can't do that. No one can. So leave the poor man alone."

"What do you want, you crazy bitch! Leave me alone."

I whistled. "Whew. You are not striking the proper tone, Hill. Is that any way to speak to the person who has your balls in a vise? I might get angry… and squeeze."

"Get it through your head," he hissed. Wesley got in my face. "I don't know anything. You can keep coming at me, but there's nothing I have to say."

"We both know that's not true. Someone dared you to make my sister's life a misery. You've been blackmailing them ever since. All you have to do is tell me who it is, and Levi will be the one waking up in a puddle of his own piss."

Wesley reeled back, eyes huge. "How did you—?"

"Or you can refuse me again," I plowed on, "and I move on to Levi either way. I've been as patient with you as I'm going to be, Hill. Tell me who dared you guys to drive Winter to the edge." My gaze flicked down. "This is your last chance."

Frowning, Wesley followed my line of sight. He froze.

Holding steady over his heart was a single red, glowing dot.

"I know what you're thinking," I stage-whispered. "Maybe I could run. Maybe I could wake that useless lump of a bodyguard up and he'll protect me. Trust me when I say you'll be dropped a millisecond after you twitch. There's no more running, Wesley. You have ten seconds to give me a name."

"Wait—"

I held up a hand. "Ten, nine, eight—"

"Wait! You don't understand what they'll do to me. I can't betray— I just can't!"

"You don't have to be afraid of them anymore," I said, "because you'll be dead. Six, five, four—"

Pale and shaking, a sheen of sweat soaked the pits of his arms faster than I counted down. Wesley tossed his head, throwing desperation at everyone walking by, and making them veer farther away from him. "Can't— I c-can't—" he stuttered, eyes rolling up in his head.

"Give me a name, Wesley. Three. It doesn't have to end this way. Two. You can still make this right," I said, holding up my final finger. "Who killed Winter?"

"Nooo!"

My teeth clenched. "Levi was the smart one after all. He outlived both of you." I dropped my finger. "One—"

Wesley blurred. Roaring, he seized my neck—hauling me forward and in the path of that red beam. Bulging, crimson eyes stabbed through mine as he strangled me.

"I'll never tell you, bitch. Your sister is rotting in hell—tough shit. You're not dragging me down there with her."

"Let her go!"

"Luna!"

"Do your worst," Wesley hissed. He squeezed harder. He pulled me in tighter, blocking the path of any bullet with my body. "Your little pranks don't come close to what they'll do to me. Neither does death."

Malice and hatred seeped into his voice, banishing the whimpering weakling who fainted and ran around screaming. I wasn't talking to that Wesley anymore.

I was talking to the murderer.

"Luna!"

Thundering footfalls bore down on us, racing ahead of the black spots dancing in my vision. I gasped—slapping and clawing at his hands.

"For as long as I live—one hundred seconds or one hundred years—I'll never tell you their name."

I miscalculated. I pushed too far. Wesley didn't break.

He snapped.

Lucien and Wilder rushed us—Lucien's cane raised to strike. Wesley threw me at them. I fell into their arms, their first instinct to catch me, and the three of us went down. Wesley tore across the quad.

I untangled from them, jumping up and running to... where?

Wesley was gone.

***

"Are you sure you're okay?"

I lay across Wilder's lap while Lucien stroked my cheek, Rafael massaged my legs, and Cato massaged my clit. He thought orgasms would make me feel better. I certainly wasn't about to say no to them.

"I'm okay," I replied, or more like moaned. All of us were in my room, resting on my bed. "You don't have to fuss over me. Wesley is a noodle-armed bitch. I barely felt his weak attempt to strangle me." I said that, but the angry red marks on my neck told a different story.

"That noodle-armed bitch should never have gotten his hands on you," Rafael growled. "I should've had a real gun on him, instead of some over-priced laser pointer."

"We talked about that—oh."

Cato slipped inside and scissored me open, stretching me as he moved. It was difficult having a serious conversation while getting finger-fucked, but when I tried to wiggle away, he bit me. I was getting an orgasm—no argument about it. Like Wilder said, some consequences just have to be endured.

"Everyone... is hanging on by a thread," I got out. "Ashton dead. Giovanni dead. Owen dead. Royals under attack. If there was a school shooting on top of it, the dean would close campus and all of my targets would disappear behind the gates of their mega-mansions. Plus, there were too many students on the quad. A shooting would've caused a stampede. A lot of people would've gotten hurt."

"We didn't play this smart, Luna," Wilder said. His voice was rough but his touch gentle. "*You* could've gotten hurt."

"I'm the one who didn't play this smart. I underestimated Wesley. Thought he was the weak one. I looked into his eyes and he meant every word he said. He won't tell me who the Phantom is no matter what I do."

"He will tell you," Lucien corrected. "Just because we pushed the wrong pressure point, doesn't mean there isn't one. There's something Wesley wants more than he wants to protect the Phantom. If that's not his life, we find out what it is."

"Your life is usually good enough," I muttered. "He's afraid of this guy. He knows the Phantom can send an army of anonymous members after his friends and family if he doesn't stay in l-line." Cato picked up the pace, arching my back off the bed. "Oh, shit yes."

"Wesley may care about his friends and family. That psychopath Levi doesn't," Rafael added. "We should've focused the pressure on him because he's all about self-preservation. The Thompkinses have lost their Royal status and everyone knows he abuses women and sides with rapists. Whatever the Phantom promised, they can't get his reputation or his place back. They won't get back his life. He's got no reason to be loyal to them anymore."

"Levi will talk, Luna. Let's kill Wesley and be done with it," he dropped without a tinge of conscience. "Then we'll put all the pressure on Levi until he cracks."

"Ahh!" I came hard, twisting off Wilder's lap and ending up flopping face-first on a pillow.

Cato climbed on me, his growl arousing in my ear as he punishingly pumped me as I came down. Between Wilder's comfort, Lucien's steady presence, Rafael's words of reason, and Cato's pussy domination, I did feel twenty times better.

"Okay," I said when words returned to me. "You're right, Rafael. Everyone hates Levi right now, so the members will jump at the dares I have planned for him. I—"

My phone went off.

I pushed up and went nowhere. Cato lay on me, nose buried in my hair, and fingers teasing me for another round. Seemed he was content where he was.

"Hand me that, please." Lucien passed it over.

Number Blocked

"Hello? Who is this?"

"Hello, Sinclair."

I grasped Cato's wrist and shook my head. Frowning, he withdrew and let me sit up. I had a feeling I'd need a clear head for this conversation.

"Saylor," I said, snatching the guys' attention. "I didn't know you had my number."

"Got it from Katie."

"For what possible reason? You and I have nothing to talk about."

A light chuckle floated through the speaker. "We both know that isn't true, Luna. I got to say, you're a more worthy adversary than I gave you credit for. It's time we talked."

"We are talking."

"No, in person." I couldn't read her tone. Saylor was light and breezy as if speaking about the weather. "Just you. Leave your boyfriends behind."

"You have to be kidding. You can't possibly think I'd meet you anywhere alone."

"Who said anything about alone? Tomorrow morning. Eight o'clock. The music hall. There'll be plenty of people around."

"Plenty of *Royals*."

She laughed. "What? Don't tell me you're afraid to be surrounded by Royals? Look at the town you're in, sweetie. That's your every day."

"I'm not afraid of you or anyone. Tomorrow at eight. See you then."

"Good."

Click.

"Sinclair, what did you just do?"

I gave Wilder a look. "How many times do I have to suck your dick before we're on a first-name basis?"

"I'll let you know," he rebounded. "Now what did you agree to that you'll be taking back?"

"Saylor wants to meet for a chat tomorrow morning. No Rogues allowed."

I got four rounds of *fuck no* in response.

"We're not meeting alone. She told me to come to the music hall."

"Why would you go?" Lucien asked. "What could you possibly have to say to her?"

"I'm going because she's got something to say to me." A smile tugged at my lips. "And I've been waiting a long time to hear it."

***

I got up early the next morning and tried on six different outfits. It's what you do when you go into battle. Settling on the last one, I walked out of my room wearing a gorgeous cutout dress held together with buckles.

This was the dress Katie forced on me that popped my stepdad's blood vessel and got me put on a budget. I could finally say the two thousand dollars were worth it. Something about the right clothes made a person feel unstoppable.

It's about time my outside matched my inner resolve. After that day, no one would look at me and see a helpless little Sinclair-Bowden who was beaten down by the Royals. Those shits would look at me... and know their time is up.

Rafael and the guys were all in the kitchen when I came down—dressed and ready to leave.

"Seriously? Guys, I'll be fine. Why don't you believe me?"

"Because Saylor didn't call you out to discuss her end-of-semester party," Wilder said. "The last Royal you pissed off strangled you."

"Thanks for throwing that in my face," I muttered.

"If Saylor figured out what you did to her and her friends..." Wilder trailed off, knowing I'd fill the blanks in just fine.

"Yeah, I'm not expecting to be greeted with hugs and kisses, but she won't hurt me physically. With that off the table, what can she do to me?"

Rafael lifted a brow. "Saylor literally punched you in the face."

"Because I punched *her*. I've sized her up from all sides by now. Violence isn't her style because she never needed it. She's had everyone around here cowed since birth. She's got no reason to think she can't cow me too, but she'll realize her mistake by the end of our chat."

"Even so, Lady Luna." Lucien came around and took my hand. "She'll have the Royals backing her up. You should have us backing you up."

I shook my head. "This is war, guys, and I admit, Saylor has been playing longer than I have. Every move matters. Every word is important. She told me not to bring you, then she taunted me asking if I was afraid of Royals.

"If I show up with you guys behind me, I'm not only proving that I'm afraid of her, but I'm also proving that you guys were really the ones who went after the Royal Wenches while I cowered in the corner. The boss doesn't need to hide behind her boyfriends."

The guys traded looks. I could hear the silent communication between them and the reminder of their promise not to get in the way of my revenge. I was here for my sister. They wouldn't interfere. But they also weren't here to watch me stumble home bleeding and bruised because a bunch of Royal girls beat the crap out of me and ran over my hand.

Yep, I knew my guys very well. I also knew the minute they made up their minds.

"We watch from our spot," Rafael said. "Under the tree where they can't see us. But we'll stay out of the way and won't interfere unless she pulls something."

"You're going to do that whether I say yes or no, right?"

"Yep."

"Absolutely."

"Obviously."

Cato just got up from the table and walked out, expecting us to follow.

I accepted my fate, grabbed a granola bar, and left the Gallery. The guys hung farther and farther back the closer I got to the music hall. But I felt their presence nearby. Watching over me. Protecting me.

Voices filtered over the balcony, telling of the healthy crowd of Royals enjoying their breakfast in the only Dreg-free zone. Squaring my shoulders, I climbed the steps and brought silence to the group with my presence alone.

Dozens of pairs of eyes latched on me, then drifted to the right. I followed their gaze, landing on a lovely figure in blue.

Why not call her lovely? Saylor was beautiful in an Oscar de la Renta belted blue lace dress and matching ankle-high boots. That was a fact. She truly looked like a queen, delicately sipping her tea and smiling up at the clouds—as if the day was destined to go her way.

I slowly closed the distance, nearing her table and the other women sharing it. Gabriella, Piper, and Katie watched me approach with varying expressions.

"Morning, ladies."

Saylor turned her smile on me. "Sinclair. Nice of you to join us. A few of us thought you wouldn't."

"Don't know why." I claimed the single lone chair at the table. "I'm happy to chat with you, Saylor. If you remember a certain engagement party, I'm not the one who turned this relationship sour."

Her smile didn't waver. "Is that why you've done all this? One little argument on a balcony and you think you're justified in everything that's happened since?"

"What exactly have I done?"

"Don't take her shit, Saylor."

I stiffened. Twisting around, I saw Levi emerge from behind a group of guys. He fell in beside Saylor with a shit-eating grin so obscene, I realized I lied to my guys. Violence would be done on this balcony.

"What are you doing here, Thompkins?" I strained to keep my voice calm.

"What do you think? I told Saylor everything," he replied. "All about your vendetta against the Royals for what happened to your sister. Saylor was there the day you showed up here unwanted—crowding me, Wesley, and Owen when we were trying to eat our breakfast.

"What she didn't hear was you going on an unhinged rant about taking every single one of us down by any means necessary. Lies, tricks, fakes, pranks—doesn't matter. You'd make our lives hell, then kill us like you did Owen and Giovanni.

"She's a fucking psycho, Saylor," he said, turning on her. "Making up lies about Ashton being a rapist and me protecting him? Why the hell would I? I never even spoke to the guy. And yet, your friend, Katie here, gave her exactly what she wanted by kicking my family out and further dividing the Royals."

I laughed out loud. "Oh, so that's your play, Levi? You went running to Mommy Saylor, bawling your innocence, so she'll override Katie and reinstate the Thompkins family into the Royal cesspool. Pathetic."

Levi bared his teeth. "Watch your mouth, b—"

Saylor held up a single finger, quieting him. "I do override Katie, Sinclair. Her intentions were good, but nothing is done around here without my permission. This is my town," she said without a trace of irony. "The fact is that someone has been on a crusade against the Royals since Owen woke up on the ceiling.

"I know all about the website he made of your sister, so if it had stopped with him, I wouldn't have given a shit." Her face changed. "But it didn't stop with him. You came after me and my friends, and don't deny it."

I said nothing. My face held blank while she searched me for a hint of the truth.

"You were the one who showed me the creepshots of Gabriella and Giovanni that you were hoarding on your phone," she continued. "I wasn't surprised when I saw you lurking in our class, masturbating to her getting arrested. You were the one who sent those pics and videos to Annika."

"Hmm," I hummed, looking to Gabriella. "Getting arrested doesn't seem to have slowed you down."

"I'm out on bail," she snapped. "And eager for revenge."

"Don't let your parole officer hear that."

Gabriella leaped over the table and had to be shoved back into her seat by Saylor.

"Not yet, Gabby," she said. "She has a lot more crimes to confess to."

"Such as?"

"Piper. I knew you were behind Gabriella, but I couldn't figure out how you found out Piper had feelings for Everleigh. Then I remembered Rhys. Piper and I never spoke about Rhys or Everleigh out loud, but we did in an old text chain from a million years ago. You hacked our phones." Her lips twisted. "Or you fucked the guy who did.

"The rest of the stuff you put on Piper's list were lies," Saylor announced. "I give you credit for knowing enough to put one true thing so that everything else looked real. But that fake website of Everleigh and the *Book Lady*?"

She laughed. "You didn't even try with that one. Those videos were so obviously edited and photoshopped, no one bought it. Right, guys?"

"Right."

"Obviously it was fake."

"What did Everleigh ever do to you?"

The lemmings chimed in right on cue, but I couldn't blame them. Saylor said it like a question, but it was a demand.

"And for me, you drove a wedge between me and my friends," Saylor said. "You made us doubt each other, fight each other, and nearly ruin nineteen years of friendship, and for what? Some stupid revenge crusade that was always doomed to fail. We know it was you, Sinclair. Don't bother denying it!"

"I wasn't going to," I said, shrugging. "Yeah, it was me who released Piper's list, sent those pictures to Annika, revealed the Book Lady to the world. Oh, and got you punched in the face. *Again.* I never said it wasn't."

Saylor's lips parted, surprise flashing across her face. She clearly wasn't ready for the part where I admitted to everything without a trace of shame or remorse.

"See?" Levi said. "Told you she was a lying piece of trash."

"You really did this?" Katie cried. "Luna, I know why you'd hate the bastards who protected your sister's attacker, but why would you go after my friends? You humiliated Piper, and now she and Everleigh can barely look at each other. Gabriella's getting fitted for an ankle monitor, and Everleigh is refusing to come to school. Why?"

"Why?" I repeated the word, rolling it around on my tongue. "Why did I do it? I could tell you it's because your precious friends dressed like drowning victims to retraumatize me. I could say that after that day, I've had nightmares so bad that I have to keep a bucket beside the bed for vomit. I could tell you about the messages on their phones, and how in the many, *many* group chats without you in it, they mocked and belittled Winter while she was going through the worst time of her life."

My eyes narrowed on Saylor. "I could say it was about all or any of that, but the truth is I did it because they hurt me. They hurt me and my sister, and I wanted them to feel half the pain that I do every day."

A rough scoff gritted my teeth. "What did I tell you?" Levi crowed. "She's a psycho. Nothing she said is true."

"You'd like everyone to believe that, but no. I didn't have to lie about any of it because the truth was right there for everyone to see. Your ex confessed to Iris that you attacked her." I flicked to the crowd. "He really wants you to forget that part."

"That was another photoshopped pic. You got to Sadie," Levi announced, raising his voice. "Told her she could get revenge against her cheating ex. All she had to do was back up your lies." He fished his phone out of his pocket. "Go ahead and call her. Anyone. Sadie's finally telling the truth now. I never touched the chick and you can hear it straight from her."

My chest tightened. "You got to Sadie. What did you do to her? You put her through enough."

You had to be looking closely to see it.

The gleeful malice in his eyes.

"The only thing I did is expose that you're a liar. You made up that stuff with Sadie, and you lied about me and Ashton. Saylor knows the truth now."

"Saylor knows you're full of bullshit because she is. She's never going to reinstate your family, because she knows nothing I said about her crew was a lie. So why would I have lied about you?"

"It is lies and no one believes them," Saylor snapped. "That Book Lady site was faked. So was that stuff about Piper and the pills."

Saylor rested her hand on Piper's arm. "I told you it wasn't me. This all happened because Katie let this psycho near us." She swung to her. "I'm hoping we don't have to tell you *again* to stay away from her, Katie. Do you finally get that she's crazy?"

"I..." Hesitating, Katie looked from me to Saylor. It shocked me that there even was a hesitation. It was hard to be sure amid her daily insults... but Katie really did see me as a friend. "She..."

"I'm not crazy, Saylor, and I'm not a liar," I said calmly. "But that's what you and Thompkins were hoping. That I'd go off on some teary rant—shouting and losing my mind on you Royals. Maybe even give a speech on how you'd all rue the day you set eyes on Winter?" I chuckled. "Then I'd lose all credibility. Sorry, no. That's not how it's going down today."

Saylor rose from her seat. "No, I'll tell you how it's going down. You came into our house and fucked with us. I don't care what happened to your sad, pathetic sister. She shouldn't have started a fight she couldn't win, and neither should you.

"You trapped one of our own in an engagement. You assaulted me and destroyed my property. You manipulated one of my friends," she said, squeezing Katie's shoulder like she cared about her. "And you tried to ruin the reputations of the others. One of those was enough to end you, but all of them?"

She shook her head, appearing almost disappointed. "You left me no choice, Sinclair. I won't have you sneaking around my town, taking your vendetta out on innocent Royals because you don't know what suicide is. No one killed your sister. She jumped off that bridge all on her own. For all we know, it's because she wanted to get away from your sick, twisted self."

"Saylor, easy," Katie hissed.

"You're out." Saylor towered over me—ever the imposing queen. "Jack Bowden is removed from the Royal line. His land will be repossessed. His business ties dissolved. Since the dean knows what's good for him, you can consider this your expulsion letter. You don't go to Regalia University anymore."

You could see it clear as day now—the gleeful malice in Levi's eyes.

"Victor Wilson can still marry who he wants, but since a Wilson can't and will never override a Burkhardt, I doubt he's interested in moving to be with you, because you, the housekeeper, and the tire salesman have one week to pack your shit and leave. None of you are allowed to set foot in my town again."

"Wow," I said, tone even. "I didn't know until now that you had this power, Saylor, but I see how effective it is for keeping people in line. You really are the queen of Regalia—handing down sentences to everyone who crosses you."

"That's correct. Too bad you didn't figure out you shouldn't be one of those people."

I kept going like she hadn't spoken. "But like any queen, you can't resist handing down those punishments in front of an audience. You have to so that everyone knows to stay afraid." My grin widened. "I was counting on that."

"Excuse me? What are you talking about?"

"I knew you'd find out that I was the one behind it all, and that you and your friends would deny everything and call me a liar in front of the other Royals. But answer this for me, Saylor..." I got to my feet, squaring her off. "You also just told everyone that I only know what I know because I hacked you.

"Why would anyone believe I got the truth about Piper and Everleigh from your messages, but the rest I pulled out of thin air? Pretty sure they figured out I got the pill addiction, the cousin-loving, and everything else from those messages too."

Saylor didn't waver. "They believe me because they know me. And because you're insane."

"They do know you, don't they? They know you get what you want by any means necessary. Like, for example, telling Ahmed that Piper cheated on him while she was in Aspen." Piper's jaw slackened in sync with Saylor stiffening. "I don't know why you texted him that or if it's true, but I'm guessing that's why he ran to Katie and said they were broken up. He thought they were, and he wanted payback by hooking up with her best friend."

"That's not true!"

"She did what!"

Piper and Katie sounded off at the same time.

"Saylor would never," Piper carried on. "Fuck's sake, you can't quit lying for a—"

"I've got the screenshots ready to show you at any time, but who says you have to believe me? Just ask Ahmed."

Katie whirled on her. "Saylor, is it true? Did Ahmed say they were broken up because *you* told him they were? Piper and I were fighting over a problem you created in the first place?"

Saylor was very still—her gaze darting between them.

"I bet she got a kick out of it," I said. "You both being oblivious, then her getting to whip it out and use your sex secret against you when you pissed her off, Katie. From what I read, it's kind of her thing—"

"Shut up."

"She's the puppet master behind the scenes—pulling strings, ruining lives, messing up relationships—and no one knowing she's behind it."

"I said shut up!"

"Lizzie Duke," I announced.

A girl to the left of Levi jerked, surprised to hear her name come out of my mouth.

"Did you ever wonder why your parents' seemingly happy marriage suddenly ended with screaming, lawyers, and you forced to move out of Regalia with your mom in your junior year?" I shone a beaming smile on Saylor. "Look no further than her. She sent your mom photos of your dad with hookers—plural—when it looked like you were going to beat her out for the highest GPA that year.

"I bet she thought the stress would tank your grades. Worked out even better for Saylor because you left school, and she became valedictorian."

"What?" Lizzie breathed. "That can't be true. My mom cried herself to sleep for months. She stopped going to work and the board replaced her as CEO of her own company. Her whole life fell apart!"

I threw up my hands. "Well, that's what happens when someone's in Saylor's way—"

"Shut the fuck up, Sinclair," Saylor screeched. "I never sent a thing to her mother. It's just more of your lies. More of your fakes! Whatever screenshots you think you have, you pulled out of your ass."

"That's your answer to everything. Tell that to Shane Montgomery. After he got a girlfriend and stopped being your go-to secret hookup, you paid a girl to scare her off by saying Shane left her with an STD, and a kid."

"Are you kidding me?" cried a gruff voice. "I searched for months, tracking down every hookup and one-night stand. You made me think I had a son out there!"

"Didn't happen," Saylor said. "Why are you idiots listening to her? I never—"

"Ava Bell," I sliced in. I fixed on a girl with big green eyes and a polka-dot dress. "Saylor was the only one who knew what happened to you at the cabin you guys all rented over winter break. You thanked her over and over again for *being there for you* and *listening to you* while you processed the trauma, but what you didn't know is—"

"That's enough!"

"—she invited you on the trip and arranged the whole thing so that she could be your shoulder to cry on. Her dad needed your dad's support for his campaign. Saylor used you as an in, and if that didn't work, she would've blackmailed you both. Saylor and her friends actually laughed about what an easy mark you were."

Ava gaped at Saylor. I wasn't messed up enough to reveal Ava's story to the entire crowd, but it was clear that if it benefited her in the slightest sense, Saylor would without blinking. She certainly felt no remorse over tracking down Ava's birth mother and paying her to show up unannounced at the cabin.

A terrible surprise for Ava because she didn't know that she was adopted, or that her mother was her dad's sister—the aunt/mom who gave birth then ran away to escape her older brother's repeated rape and domination.

"That's not... Who would do such a...?" Ava's face crumpled. "You... You... You bitch!"

Tearing across the deck, Ava launched at her, popping Saylor off her feet with a truly impressive tackle. I ignored the screaming, wailing tangle of limbs and turned on my audience.

"That's not all, my friends. That's not even the worst of it. I've got years' worth of lies, tricks, secrets, and manipulations that was all tucked away on HapApp's server." I held up my phone. "If you want it, it's yours."

"Don't you dare!" Saylor lurched to her feet—freed from Ava by Gabriella and Katie. The two struggled to keep a hold on her. "I swear, Sinclair, if you do this, I'll—"

Dozens of chimes, beeps, and buzzes went off at once.

"Oops," I sang. "Too late. Everyone, you just received the 'behind the scenes' into the real Saylor Burkhardt, and everything she's done over the years to control and destroy any Royal who steps the slightest bit out of line.

"It's all yours for the low, low price of two hundred and ninety-nine dollars and ninety-nine cents." I snapped my fingers. "Come on, people. Revenge isn't cheap. As you'll find out when you take yours against Saylor, because trust me, you'll want to spring for elaborate and over the top."

I'd never seen trust-fund babies whip their daddy's plastic out faster.

"Stop it! No!" Saylor ran at Iris and tried to snatch her phone away. "Those texts are private. You have no right to read them— Stop or you're out! You're all out of the Royal line!" She flew at another group of girls who ran to get away from her—fingers speed-typing their card numbers all the way. "Sinclair!"

Saylor grabbed my collar, hauling me up to her bulging, red eyes. "Shut this down! Do it now or I'll—"

"Shut up, Saylor," I barked. "I'm giving the ultimatums now. I kept back the worst of the texts. The truly horrific things you've said and done to people—including your best friends for nineteen years." Saylor paled. "Yeah, those.

"If you don't want it to get out, you'll back off my family. Jack isn't out of the line, and he never will be. He's going to live happily in his home, with my mom, running his business until the end of time. Repeat that, Saylor. I want to hear you say it."

"I'm going to end you, bitch. No matter what it takes. No matter how long," she hissed. "I'm going to put you right next to your sister."

I believed her. I knew true hatred when I saw it. It reflected in the mirror whenever I thought of the Phantom.

"Wrong answer." I shoved her off me. "But you're heated, so I'll give you a chance to cool off before we talk again. I have a lot more demands."

I walked off.

"Did you hear me!?"

Katie and Gabriella had to restrain her, then they had to pull—tugging her to the opposite staircase as credit payments went through and people started to read.

"You'll regret this, Sinclair! Do you know who I am?! No one stands against me!"

I flapped a hand over my shoulder. "Yeah, yeah."

"You're dead! You and every freak who helped you! Dead!"

I strolled off the balcony, laughing my head off.

Something pressed to my side.

"Don't scream."

My lips parted and a hand slapped over them, snapping me to their chest. My muffled shout swallowed in their palm.

"You just don't quit, do you, Sinclair?" Levi's rank breath blew on my ear. "All I needed Saylor to do was get my family back in, but you had to fuck that up too. Let's go!"

"Hphm!"

Levi hauled me off. The rough handling jerked my body and rocked me back on the object pressed above my hip. It split my seams, then my skin.

Stumbling over my feet, I shouted into his hand—calling for my guys on the other side of the concrete and cinderblocks. Levi dragged me farther away from them. From the Royals. From campus.

And through the trees.

"Pick up your fucking feet!"

We stumbled over tree limbs and ant hills, going in so deep my shouts wouldn't be heard if he did remove his disgusting hand.

"Not like I asked for any of this." Levi kicked the back of my leg to keep me moving. "I didn't give two shits about your sister until they private-messaged me. They offered me two million and a place at the top tier! What was I supposed to do? Say no?

"Four generations of Thompkinses have tried to elevate our status, but I was the one who was going to do it. *I* would rise higher than my father or grandfather ever did. All I had to do was mess with some Dreg." He laughed. "I didn't even have to think about it."

"Hmm! Hph!"

"What was that?" Levi roughly shook my head. "You're sorry for being a poisonous bitch who blew in and ruined everything? Too late!"

I went flying.

A hard shove flung me at a tree. Feet tangling, I fell against the bark—losing the skin off my arm as an offering.

"The chick was dead," Levi shouted, spittle flying. "It was all over, then *you* had to show up and stir the shit again. Who the fuck do you think you are anyway? Getting in my face and threatening to kill me? I should've put you down right then and went on eating my pancakes."

I was barely listening to him. I saw nothing but the knife in his whitening grip—its tip coated with my blood.

"I was so close. Now my family is out of the Royal line. Business partners are canceling contracts with the company out of nowhere. Mom's friends have stopped answering her calls. And my dad... My dad is going to kill me," he rasped.

"Everything they promised me is gone. I can't be on top of the Royal line if I'm not fucking in it!" Levi scrabbled at his pocket. Snatching out his phone, he opened an app and shoved it at my face. "That's why you're going to take it back."

I inched to the side, hugging the bark. "What are you talking about?"

His hand flashed. I stilled as the blade kissed my throat.

"Don't move."

"Okay, relax," I screamed, chest heaving. "Fuck you, Thompkins. You call me the psycho."

He grinned. "I know, right? In another life, we'd be soulmates. But in this one, you're a piece-of-shit Dreg who doesn't get to ruin my life and walk off laughing." He practically slapped me with the phone. "You're going to take back everything. Ashton didn't rape anyone and I didn't help him cover it up. You convinced Sadie to lie about me carving up her skull, and... you murdered Owen." Levi pressed the knife deeper. "Say it."

My throat bobbed against the knife's edge. "You really think this will work? Some recording on your phone? What good will it do you? Saylor isn't in a position to help anyone at the moment."

"Saylor isn't the only Burkhardt, dumbass. When her father hears that you're a liar and Katie Langford's pet, he'll take back what she did. Now, say it."

Here were more hate-filled eyes I could read clear as day. Levi wasn't bluffing. He would happily hurt me if I didn't do what he said. Part of him wanted me to give him a reason.

Taking a deep breath, I let it out slow, and said, "Fuck you, you sadistic piece of shit."

Levi's face hardened.

"I spent months planning the perfect revenge against you, then Katie served it up on a silver platter all on her own. She took away the only thing you care about just like you bastards did to me." I spat in his face. "I'll die if it means ruining your worthless life. No contest."

"You're a stupid fool." Levi said it like it was a fact of life. "I can kill you, but no one said I'd do it quick. How much pain—?"

I kicked him in the crotch.

"Agh!" Levi doubled over—the knife falling away.

I seized my chance and ran.

"Get back here!" He grabbed me around the waist.

"Help! Someone help! He's got a knife!"

Levi threw me at the tree. "Take it back! Admit it was all a lie." He snatched up the phone he dropped. "Do it now or—"

"Nooo!" I ripped the cell and smashed it against the bark. Over, over, and over again, I screeched my rage and pain as it became nothing but glass, plastic, and silicone. "I'll never do what you want! You're a murderer and a beast. And you'll die as what you hate—" My gaze pierced him through. "A Dreg."

His face went blank—leached of all emotion, even hatred.

I bolted to get past him, and he struck. The knife sailed in a graceful arc, leading straight to me.

My hands flew up. To block. To grab. I didn't know under the white-hot terror that flooded my senses, blocking out the flashback of my life.

In that final moment, I didn't get to see my mom's smile or hear Winter's snorty laugh. I didn't bask in the summer we went apple-picking. Or the single sweet moment with Jack when he presented me and Winter with rings the night of his engagement party, saying his ring to Mom made him a husband, but his rings to us made us a family.

I wasn't gifted any of those treasured moments in the final seconds of the knife's path. All I saw was the sunlight reflecting off the blade in Levi's dead eyes.

Fierce, hot pain ripped my stomach. The knife struck, sheathing itself in my skin.

It was okay that Winter didn't come to me at the end.

Because I was finally going to her.

Chapter Ten

"Argh!"

Levi shoved me back, straining to drive the knife deeper.

Limbs trembling, sweat soaking my back, I gaped at the weapon, and the little metal buckle that stopped it going further.

My ears popped. Sight, sound, smell, and rage all flooded in.

Rearing back, I backhanded him across the face. Levi snapped around and fell, sending the knife flying. I dove for it. A hand closed on my ankle, yanking me off my feet. I dropped flat on my front—rocking pain through my wound.

"Ahh," I sobbed hoarsely, my mind bleeding white in agony.

Levi scrambled over the dirt and leaves, crawling for the knife inches from my fingertips.

Move, Luna.

He closed on the hilt.

Move!

I shot forward. Grabbing his wrist, I slammed it on the ground, releasing his grip. The knife fell half a foot from my nose. I snatched it up, twisted, and—

Levi stilled. His face screwed up, grimacing almost in confusion. Slowly, we both drifted down to the knife sticking out of his chest.

A breath passed.

Two.

Three.

Levi flopped back, eyes staring unseeingly at the cloudless sky.

I ran.

Racing, tripping, crying, screaming—I dashed through the trees, running as fast as I could, and too slow to put enough distance between me and what I'd done.

"Luna?"

Wilder, Rafael, Cato, and Lucien circled the music hall—calling for me and roughly stopping Royals on their way out. "Luna!"

"Rafael!"

He twisted around, letting go of some poor freshman. Rafael took one look and ran to me. "Luna!"

I gasped, my breaths coming too quick and shallow for my lungs to fill. Shock leadened my feet—slowing me down just yards away. I lifted my hand, bloodstained fingers reaching for him.

"Rafael..."

Darkness bled into my vision. The last thing I saw before the ground rushed up to meet me.

***

I lay under Lucien's black silk sheets, safe and warm under his attention. But I was not sleeping.

And I was not relaxed.

"I can't believe I did that," I croaked. "I killed him. I wasn't thinking, Lucien. I just stabbed him."

"It's one thing to sit back and watch others dole out your final revenge against them. It's another to carry it out yourself. Killing takes its toll on a person. You never really get used to it."

"No, it's not that." I pushed up and immediately regretted it. My stab wound wasn't deep, though it bled a frightening amount. The guys brought me home, bathed me, bandaged the cut, and put me to rest in Lucien's bed. I woke up an hour earlier from a nap and saw the bleeding had stopped, and the pain somehow tripled.

Lucien eased me back onto the pillows.

"I can't believe that I killed him because I ruined my chance." My eyes swam. "He knew who the Phantom is. I had to get away from him, but after I did, I could've used his desperation as leverage to force him into giving me a name. Now he's gone and he'll never be able to tell. One split-second decision and I failed Winter. Again."

"Luna, you can't do this to yourself." He grasped my chin between two fingers, gently raising me to drown in his eyes. "He was trying to kill you. You did what you had to do to defend yourself. Winter would've wanted you to walk away from that monster alive.

"Besides, we haven't lost the Phantom yet. There's still Wesley," he said, stroking my cheek. He caught my tears on his pinky and licked them away. "We'll make him talk. Doesn't matter what it takes. He'll give up the Phantom."

I nodded, sniffling. I had to believe him. The alternative was impossible to consider.

"I need a new plan for Wesley. It's not enough to scare him. He's already scared and it's not of me. He's more afraid of the Phantom. How do I change that? He doesn't care if he dies."

"How do *we* change his mind, Lady Luna? You're not doing this alone. I've had over a hundred years of learning every way to make prey beg for mercy. In the end, they all fear death. And they all beg, plead, and offer up their very souls to be spared."

Wilder and Rafael walked in. They dropped the tarp and shovel on Lucien's damask carpet.

The guys decided the last thing we needed right after Levi went around shouting that I killed Owen and planned to kill him too, was for him to show up dead. They went to take care of the body, and I was too exhausted to stop them.

I frowned. "I don't understand." I took in the spotlessly clean tarp and shovel. "Did you change your mind?"

"We didn't have to," Wilder said. "We went to the area where you said you guys were. Found blood on the ground and everything, but there was no body."

Rafael leveled me a grave look. "Levi's gone."

I stared at him. I couldn't have heard that right. "What do you mean he's gone? How can he be gone?"

"The how is easy. Either he survived and crawled away, or someone else got to his body before we did. Are you sure he was dead?"

"I didn't check his pulse or anything, but I stabbed him in the chest." I tried again to sit up and cried out. "Stabbed him deeper than this! He couldn't have walked away with a wound like that."

"If someone took his body, who was it?" Lucien asked. "And what are they doing with it because it's been hours and police haven't swarmed the campus."

Looks passed between us. I didn't like what I read on any of their faces. There were two options and they were both too terrible to contemplate. If Levi was alive, I now had a violent, homicidal psychopath lurking in the shadows, waiting for his chance to get back at me. If his body was taken by someone, it wasn't for a good reason. That was easy to tell because an innocent person didn't go around secretly hauling off corpses. They would've left Levi where he was and called the cops.

"You don't think that his body was taken by the Phantom, do you?" My voice rose barely above a croak. "Why would they do that?"

"Everything they've done so far has been to hide and protect themselves," Wilder said. "Maybe it doesn't help them either for his body to be discovered. You've been vocal about the awful things Owen, Wesley, Ashton, and Levi have done. If another one of them turns up dead so close together, the police will be forced to look into what connects them.

"They'll look through their phones and computers. They'll interview all their friends and family."

"They might find evidence of the club," I finished, "and of an unknown Phantom that bribed them to attack Winter."

Rafael stretched out next to me, pulling me close. "We can't prove that's what happened, but it makes sense. It's what I'd do if I was the Phantom and I got to that body before anyone else."

A thought came to me. "Maybe we can prove it. Not if the Phantom took the body, but if there was a body. If Levi got up and walked away, then he dragged himself to a hospital or home to Mommy. It's scary how good these club members are at tracking people down. For the right reward, they'll find him if he's somewhere to be found."

"The right price won't be difficult," Wilder said, taking out his phone. "That's the other thing we have to tell you. You offered up Saylor's secrets less than twelve hours ago. Look how much you've made since." Wilder showed me the screen.

My eyes about popped out of my head. "Did you accidentally add a zero to this! Wilder, this says thirty-six thousand dollars."

"And there'll be more by morning," Rafael said. "This goes beyond the sophomores. I bet the first thing they did was call their mom, dad, sisters, cousins, and the kid down the street who used to feel them up in their treehouse. Getting their hands on something like this is big. You should've asked for triple, baby. They would've paid without blinking."

I tossed my head, brows blown. "No doubt there're some juicy things in there, but all I thought this would do is take the shine off her. People stop bowing and scraping real quick when they find out you caused their parents' divorce, or arranged for you to be blindsided by your birth mother. Why is this big? Will it drag the Burkhardts down the line?"

"It's not that big," Rafael admitted. "You saw the chart. The Burkhardts own a piece of every Royal family. That doesn't go away because Saylor used it to make their lives hell. But there is a reason she went out of her way to hide what she was doing. A boss may have power over her employees, but there's zero benefit in treating them so badly, they all quit.

"The Burkhardts need the other Royals to run their empire. They're the ones who donate big money to Senator Burkhardt's campaigns. They choose his company to contract with over others. They're his friends.

"Finding out his daughter fucked with them to her black heart's content? Those campaign funds are about to dry up. CEOs are about to take their business elsewhere. And his friends..." He whistled. "They're going to have some shit to say, and they won't be nice about it. The Burkhardts had power, but they also had trust. That's gone now."

I was quiet taking that in. "But how angry can they get? How much could they strike back? If they piss the Burkhardts off, won't they just kick them out of the Royal line?"

"Can't," Wilder said, chiming in. "You have to commit an act that nobody can come back from. Carving your initials on a girl's forehead and protecting a rapist? That's downright fucking scary. No one wants to be around or do business with a person like that. Even the Royals want his ass in jail.

"But it's got to be on that level, because they need the other Royals to back them up. Right now, the Royals aren't backing them up on anything."

"Wow. So Saylor really is hurting from this." I couldn't see my smile. I couldn't see my eyes. But the gleeful malice... it was fucking dripping from them. "Good."

I sunk into the pillows and draped Lucien's arm over me while Rafael found his way to my buttons. I very much liked that the Dumont brothers believed the best way to cheer me up was orgasms.

"We'll get as many club members that we can on tracking down Levi. If he's alive, he's desperate and hanging on by a thread. He can't get anything the Phantom promised him and now he knows I am willing to kill. He'll tell me who it is because I'll give him something that he now wants more than anything."

"What?" Wilder asked.

"To bring down every Royal that turned their back on him. And he's in luck," I said, smiling wide. "That was on my bucket list."

***

I Dare You To Find Out Where Levi Thompkins Is Hiding
  Dare: Completed, Awaiting Reward
  Dare: Completed, Awaiting Reward
  Dare: Completed, Awaiting Reward
  Dare: Completed, Awaiting Reward
  Dare: Completed, Awaiting Reward

Five photos of proof on my screen, all saying the same thing in different ways, and I still refused to believe it.

"He's gone?" I cried. "Levi survived and the first thing his coward ass did was run away? This can't be true."

But it was true. Stark on my screen was a photo of a pale guy in a wheelchair who could only be Levi Thompkins. My strike didn't kill him, but it injured him enough that he had to be carried onto his private plane. CounterCurse12 said the flight plan was filed for a one-way trip to the Maldives.

"I'm not surprised." Wilder rocked in his desk chair, monitoring three screens at once. One was the site selling Saylor's text messages. It crashed three times because the servers couldn't handle the traffic. "Levi knows he's never getting near you again, because I'll rip his fucking throat out if he tries," Wilder growled. "Since he can't get you to take back the truth, his family has no hope of getting back into the Royal line. There's nothing left for them here except cold shoulders and hostility."

"So he just gets to fly off and spend the rest of his days sunning it up beachside?! Everything aside, he still mutilated a girl and was an accessory to rape. He belongs in prison!"

Wilder just took my hand, kissing my knuckles.

"No, no," I said, tossing my head. "This can't happen. It doesn't get to end like this. We have to bring him back."

"Not even the United States government can do that, Sinclair. Non-extradition country."

My mind rebelled. Winter's killer did not get away free with nothing but a little boo-boo to show for it. He just couldn't!

"It's not over. The members found him, maybe they can bring him back."

"There're limits even to what they can do."

"Then we do it ourselves. Lucien has a private plane, we can—"

"Luna," he said softly, cutting me off better than a raised or harsh word. "I'm sorry."

My legs gave out. Collapsing onto his lap, Wilder held me while I broke down.

He got away with it. Levi Thompkins, the worst of all of them, got away with torturing my sister. Who cares that he got kicked out of his little Royal club? He was still rich, connected, and privileged, and that got you far no matter where you go. His suffering was over.

He'd spend the rest of his life exactly how he always lived it—fawned over, catered to, and indulged. He'll have learned nothing and make no changes to how he treats people.

Levi was out of my reach, and so was everything he knew about the Phantom.

"What do we do now?" I had a stranglehold on him, needing his warmth and comfort more than ever. "Levi's gone and Wesley's surrounded by an army of bodyguards. After Cato ripped out the guy's throat, his bodyguards hired bodyguards! We'll never get near him."

Wilder stroked my hair. "We will. We just have to get creative about it. This is what we do, baby. Your Rogues have never failed a job. We won't start now."

"Severed heads and seeing his friend killed right in front of him didn't work. The worst that he's done, we've already put on his truth list. We can't blackmail him with some deep, dark secret. And Saylor isn't about to remove him from the Royal line for me. Where does that leave us?"

Wilder looked at me steadily. "It leaves us picking him up for a little chat."

I opened my mouth, and slowly closed it. That was the option we had left. If Wesley wouldn't give it up willingly, then he left us no choice.

We had to beat it out of him.

"It didn't have to come to this. If he'd just do the right thing and give up the person who ordered the torture of an innocent person, this would all be over. He chose this. He chose it when he accepted that dare."

Wilder waited me out.

"Let's do it." I braced for a twinge of conscience and felt none. "How do we get to him? He's not sleeping in the dorm anymore, and he has his guards with him on campus."

"We'll never get near him," Wilder confessed. "That's why it can't be us. We use the club. His guards don't know to look out for dozens of anonymous screen names. Once they separate him from the guards, we'll take care of the rest."

I nodded along, latching on to his thought process easily. "We can't ask them to do something that'd make him suspicious though. Or that'd get his parents to call out the National Guard. Wesley needs to *choose* to send his guards away." I grinned. "Like he would on a date.

"If he's about to get lucky with some girl, his guards aren't coming into the room to watch. We just need her to lead him back to a room where we're standing on the other side of the door." I climbed off and pulled up another chair, sitting down in front of the club site. "I hope Wesley's type is 'anyone willing to be in the same room with me' because we don't know who they are or what they look like."

"I'll grab us something to drink," Wilder said, leaving me to it.

I followed him to the door. "It can't really be over with Levi. I won't accept that he gets away with it after what he's done."

Wilder pushed my hair back, kissing my forehead. "I won't let up on him. If he's ever stupid enough to get homesick, we'll be on the tarmac waiting for him."

He left, leaving me standing there, listing all the ways I messed up with Levi.

This is my last chance to get it right and find out who the Phantom is. I won't mess this up. I—

I turned around and stopped dead.

"Hello." Smiling, the face on the screen tipped his head. "You must be Luna."

Long, black hair framed the angular face taking up the entire screen. He smirked, and it crookedly pulled on full lips and a pointed nose.

"Who are you? A friend of Wilder's?"

"I'm the guy who's been looking for you, my little club crasher. You didn't think you'd get to run free—fucking with the club and its members—and no one would have shit to say about it, did you?"

I didn't move or speak. My mind went blank in the space of two breaths.

He beamed. "Call me the IT guy. I secured the site and made it unhackable, but it's always the simplest trick that you never see coming. Stealing a dead guy's computer and using his recruiter access to make your own profile?" Shaking his head, he whistled. "Impressive.

"I won't ask why you did it, because I have access to every dare and truth on this site, Luna Sinclair. I know what they did to your older sister."

My body went rigid.

"If you had stopped with fucking over Levi Thompkins and Wesley Hill, I might've been tempted to leave you alone. I like a good revenge story as much as the next guy. But alas," he said, sigh whooshing through the speakers. "You took it too far by trying to expose the club."

"Who are you?" I croaked. "How are you doing this? These are Wilder's computers. No one accesses them but him."

Smiling, he shrugged like *who knows?* "Guess I'm just that good."

"What do you want from me?"

"I want you to accept praise," he replied. "You're not the first person whose hatred of the club drove them to expose it. But you are the first who came damn close to doing it. Or maybe you have done it. Using Natale's recruiter account to message every Dreg in the club and tell them they'll receive five hundred dollars for each new member they bring in? Genius.

"The club got fifty new members in a day. And none of them have the long list of threats/reasons to keep quiet. You had to know someone would notice, but by then, what would it matter? Word would spread too far and wide for anyone to contain the secret."

"It has spread too far. People are already talking about the mysterious Truth or Dare Club. I hear whispers about it all over campus."

"An issue the founders are paying me good money to take care of." He tipped his head to me. "Naturally, you're out. I'm shutting down your account, Natale's account, and every new account you've created."

"No," I cried, running to the screen. "You can't. Not yet!"

He continued like I hadn't spoken. "I've got the IP addresses of every computer in your place now, so if you come near the site again, I'll know."

"No! Don't do this." I shook the monitor. "Please, just give me another ten minutes. You said you appreciated a good revenge story. I'm so close. I almost have mine. I just need to send out one more dare."

"Sorry," he sang—his handsome face lit up like destroying my hopes was better than Christmas. "Can't be done."

Crash!

Wilder stood in the doorway—the mugs of tea he made shattered ceramic at his feet. "Wolf?"

"Hello, little brother." The now named Wolf smiled a different kind of smile at Wilder. One that made me step back. "You know better than to play in my sandbox. That never worked out for you when we were kids."

"Luna, move!" Wilder shot past me, diving under the desk. He yanked out the power cord and Wolf winked out—replaced by blackness.

"You know, if you want my attention so badly—"

We whipped around. Wolf smirked at us from the monitor on the far end.

"—you only had to ask."

Wilder ran to shut him off. Wolf was on the screen beside me before he touched the plug.

"I've been thinking. It has been a while since I've been home."

Wilder went mad—yanking, pulling, ripping every plug in his room from the wall. I could only stare dumbfounded as Wolf hopped from computer to computer, making one of the most secure systems in the world look like it was guarded by a gate made of tissue paper.

"We're overdue for a brotherly reunion."

Wilder grasped the last plug.

"See you soon."

Wolf winked out, leaving behind the faint sound of his laughter.

"Wilder, what just happened?" I breathed. "You have a brother? Why didn't you tell me?"

"He's everywhere," Wilder muttered, head twisting. "In the computers. In the system. It all has to go."

"Wilder—"

He picked up a computer and threw it at the cage. It popped apart like puzzle pieces over my screaming. Wilder fished out the hard drive, got a hammer, and reduced that to pieces too. I stood unheard and unseen as he destroyed his most prized possessions.

"Wilder, talk to me. Why are you so freaked?"

"Can't talk right now, Luna." Wilder retrieved a bat from his closet. "He's coming. He might already be here."

I watched helplessly as Wilder moved through the house, destroying everything with internet access. He was deaf to my pleas as he beat the security system keypad off the wall. When he was done, Wilder left me behind and went upstairs to the room that was always locked.

Wilder closed himself in with his stockpile of lethal weapons, and didn't come out.

***

"Wilder has a brother?"

"You didn't know?"

Rafael shook his head over a pan of creamy garlic shrimp. "It's Wilder."

"Fair point." My gaze drifted to the ceiling. "What do we do? He's been in there for hours. He destroyed every electronic in the house. Should we be worried about this Wolf guy? Because Wilder clearly is."

"He ripped out the security system," Rafael said, handsome even when he was grave. "The unhackable, top-of-the-line best system in existence. He wouldn't do that for an imagined threat. Yes, gorgeous. We should be real fucking worried."

My stomach twisted. "What do we do? I can't stress about some long-lost brother right now. Wolf kicked me out of the T.O.D. Club. I tried but I can't even get on the site. The tab has disappeared from my student account. I get an error message when I pull up the page. I just needed one more dare. One more to get to Wesley. Now what! I'll never get near him with all those bodyguards."

"Luna." He shut off the stove. "This is what we do. We completed jobs before the club. This is the most important job we'll ever do, but we still have to look at it that way. Lift the pressure and work the problem from every angle. We do that and Wesley doesn't stand a chance."

"But how? They were packing stun guns before. After Cato put that man in the hospital, they switched to real guns. I won't let you get shot over a piece of trash like Wesley."

"We won't. A guy needs alone time for reasons other than sex. We'll get him away from them. I already have an idea."

I pushed back from the table, moving to him. "Tell me."

"No, you tell me. What's something you couldn't stand to have an audience watch you do?"

"I... I don't know..." I searched my mind. "Have sex. Shower. Use the bathroom—"

He winked.

"The bathroom? Baby, that's good, but I saw. They wait outside while he uses it. We still can't get past them."

"We can if they're clutching a toilet bowl too, praying for death."

"Hmm." I backed up, reclaiming my seat, then my lunch when Rafael passed me my plate. He sat down to eat—grinning at me while I arrived at the same place.

"We put something in their food. Knock all the pins down at once, then snatch the one we need. Where will we bring him when we got him?"

"We won't have a lot of time. Once the guards realize what happened, they'll call for backup. Probably call the cops too. We'll bring him back here, get what we need out of him, then dump the body."

Yes, it still struck me that a year ago I was a sweet little Catholic school girl who wouldn't dream of hurting anyone. But a year ago, my sister was alive.

"How do we do it?" I asked. "When?"

"Wesley stays on campus all day Mondays, Wednesdays, and Fridays. Some of his guards bring lunch. Some buy on campus. But *all* of them get their coffee in the café."

"The coffee." I laughed. "It's always the addictions that get you in the end. Thank Thor for caffeine."

"We do a dry run tomorrow," Rafael continued. He reached across and held my hand. The affection from my guys so automatic and constant, they lifted my mood without even trying. "We slip something harmless in the carafe just to prove that we can. Then we track when they come to fill up and how much time that gives us once the emetic starts working."

I nodded along. It was arousing watching Rafael's brain work in action. He was a grinning devil ninety-nine percent of the time, but when there was a job to be done, he was all focus and drive. The same energy he devoted to giving me countless orgasms in bed.

"Wednesday we do it for real. You ready for this?"

"Absolutely," I said before he finished the question. "The Phantom has kicked back in the shadows long enough. He can do that in hell." Rising up on the stool, I kissed him. "I want to do it. Spike the carafe. Get the truth out of Wesley. Lucien said it's different when you're giving the orders, and someone is carrying out the punishment for you. He was right.

"It's way less satisfying. I don't need the club to destroy the Phantom or bring down T.O.D. The minute I set foot on campus, they already lost."

"Once again, you are so fucking sexy right now. We're not going to make it upstairs."

We didn't make it upstairs.

Rafael plowed me right there on the kitchen table. At some point, Cato wandered in, grabbed a plate, and started eating without a care to what we were doing next to him. After he finished, he bent my head back and stuck his dick in my mouth without so much as a growl.

The Dumont brothers spit-roasted me for most of the afternoon and into the evening. Eventually we took it upstairs and explored every position a threesome could twist themselves into until we passed out in a pile on Rafael's bed.

Sunlight streamed through the blinds the next morning, painting light on two sleeping forms and one figure writing, erasing, and writing on a scrap of paper. I said I wanted to be the one who ultimately brought down Wesley. That left me to work out the plan.

The staff were pretty invisible. They set out the food for the buffet, then stayed on the other side of the counter—only interacting with us when they cooked something to order. They'll set the carafes out and walk away without a problem.

Getting to the carafe is the easy part. It's spiking it in a room full of people that's tricky. Lots of students grab food early because of sport practice. Even more of them hang out in the café late when they're fueling up for a long night. From opening to closing, the place is never empty. I had to spike the coffee in plain view of everyone.

I went back and forth, jotting down ideas for distractions. I had to get people to look one way, while I carried out business in the other. If only the Book Lady had made her debut that morning.

I filled the guys in when they woke up.

"The best time is early morning when only the jocks are up. What we'll do is..." I walked them through where to go, what to do, and where to stand. Rafael accepted all of it. If my plan wasn't good, he would've said so. This was it. I was getting one step closer to the Phantom.

"About Wilder," I said, drifting up to the ceiling again. "Do you think he's still in there? I've called him dozens of times and he's not answering."

"He could be in there. He's got a stash of food and water that'll last him for weeks," Rafael confessed. "Either way, we should count him out for this one. If he thinks his brother is a threat, the best thing he can do is prepare for it."

"What kind of threat could he be though? And why didn't Wilder mention him when we talked about his family?"

Rafael shrugged. It was Wilder. He didn't know any more about his deep secrets than I did.

"Let's go," I said, checking the time. "I don't want to wait another minute. Let's do this now."

Now was forty minutes later.

Rafael, Cato, Lucien, and I were a silent group, strolling up the stairs at six o'clock on the dot. As early as we were, a group of guys from the basketball team loitered in front of the entrance—rushing in the second one of the staff opened the door.

The guys and I exchanged looks, then split apart at the threshold. Cato, Rafael, and I went in while Lucien stayed outside.

I went up to the buffet, taking my time choosing between waffles or French toast.

"Morning," Rafael greeted, leaning over the counter. "I've got a big order, ladies. Hope you got your whisks warmed up."

Giggles and flirty replies floated out of the kitchen. I didn't blame them. Rafael charmed everyone he met.

"I'll have the bacon, cheddar, and potato hash. Strawberry pain au chocolat. German apple pancake. Avocado waffle sandwich. Maple and blueberry crepes."

"Coming right up."

The staff went scurrying around the kitchen, all of them needed to fulfill his orders on time. Good thing the stoves all faced the opposite direction of the drinks station. That done, I turned to Cato.

My phone beeped me.

Lucien: They're coming. Five minutes.

Me: What? Already?

Lucien: Hurry

Wesley's first class of the day was at seven thirty, which meant he usually strolled into the café at seven. What the hell was he doing here at six thirty?

I threw a desperate look at Cato—who stopped everything to flick his lighter on and off, mesmerized by the flames. Closer I moved to the drinks station, my hand tight on my plate, and the little bottle concealed in my palm. Wasn't even the real emetic and sweat was beading on my back. I could have the best plan and everything still goes wrong. Levi and Wesley taught me that lesson the hard way.

Cato was still playing with the lighter.

"Cato, baby, please," I whispered. "Please."

Flicking it on, Cato picked up a paper towel holder and set it on fire. He tossed it at the table of jocks.

"Hey!"

"What the fuck!"

"Psycho!"

They fell out of their seats—running, scattering, bellowing at Cato. Their focus was entirely on him and the open flame in the middle of the café. Not me.

Moving fast, I forced the lid off the top and dumped the drops of liquid vitamin D—our test poison.

"—not going to happen, Mom." Wesley's voice pierced my panic. I fumbled and dropped the lid.

Clang! Clang! Clang!

Each strike on the floor was an arrow through my chest. Choking on a gasp, I dove for the lid, snatched it, and slammed it on.

"Because Saylor won't let her." Wesley broke the entrance the millisecond I spun around. "Langford can't—" He saw me and the rest of the sentence clogged in his throat. His brows crumpled. "I'll call you back."

Wesley fell back into the circle of his bodyguards. He drilled a hole in my head all the way to his seat.

"Put that back on!"

"You're not allowed to do that!"

Cato's muzzle went flying. He tore after the basketballers—barking and snarling like they'd committed a crime worse than being in the wrong place at the wrong time.

The guards snapped to their guns as Cato and the jocks blew past them. One of them didn't lower it until Cato was out the door and chasing them clear across campus.

I left my love to his fun and joined Rafael. Everything he ordered sounded delicious, and I earned a treat.

"Smooth, baby."

"Shut up," I said, laughing. "I think I shit my pants."

"Sexy."

"I see why we practice. Wednesday will go much smoother," I said. "Although, we'll have to think of another distraction because I'm pretty sure Cato just got a lifetime ban from the café."

Soon, we got our food and found a table at the back. The opposite corner of Wesley, and still I felt his eyes on the back of my head. Lucien joined us. Naturally, he didn't glance at our feast. While we ate, the guards got up and poured coffee one after the other.

"We need another distraction on Wednesday," he said, echoing my thoughts. "Wilder would come in handy for that. He could mess with the lights or rig up another projector."

"Have you talked to him? I haven't seen him at all since Wolf shut me down."

Lucien shook his head. "No, but this isn't good. Destroying his computers? Dropping off the planet when you need him the most? Wilder has gone up against some fierce opponents, but he's never reacted like this. Whoever Wolf O'Rourke is... I don't believe he's someone we want to know."

"I need to see him." I pushed back from the table. "If he is in his prepper bunker, I'm not going away until he opens the door and talks to me." The guys got up too. "No, stay. You have class in twenty minutes. You'll be late if you walk me all the way back."

"So?" Rafael said. "I'm on my career path. I only came to college to find clients."

"Wilder would be more likely to talk if it's just me and him. Besides, I'm the safest I've ever been walking around campus now. Ever since Saylor's texts went wide, she, Gabriella, Piper, and Everleigh haven't been at school. Dregs and Royals are falling at my feet for yanking her off her shining throne. She has zero friends left after those messages were read."

"Are you certain?" Lucien asked.

"Yes." I kissed him and Rafael. "See you after English."

I left for the Gallery, reworking the plan on the way. I didn't have the club members for the same reason I might not have Wilder's help. Wolf O'Rourke.

I looked him up and found nothing—not even a porn star with the same stage name. That wasn't surprising of course, but there had to be a way to reach him if the club founders hired him as the *IT guy*.

Once I started tricking members into inviting new people into the club, I knew it was a matter of time before I was found out. I just didn't think it'd happen so quickly, or that Wolf would get a look at me and be able to tell the founders exactly who's been fucking with their club.

The T.O.D. Club was too dangerous. People were so afraid of the consequences of denying a dare that they'd do *anything* they're asked. My final payback was shutting them down, taking away the Royals' entertainment, and the Dregs' easy money. The problem was I didn't know if I'd done enough. People were talking about the mysterious dare club, but were enough whispers going around to make the founders nervous?

I couldn't answer that but there was one thing I did know. The Phantom didn't want me dead.

It was horrifyingly clear to me how easy it would've been for the Phantom to use the club to get rid of me if that's what they wanted. What did it mean that they didn't want to kill me? I could only guess. They attacked Winter because she knew something, and they're leaving me alone because they know I'm clueless? Just how close were they to me that they were certain I didn't know them, or know what drove them to destroy my sister's life?

Were they someone who looked in my eyes every day, secretly laughing at me?

I reached the steps of the Gallery and took out my key. I let thoughts of the club and the Phantom go, and returned to Wilder.

What could he be doing in there and what did I say to get him to come out and talk to me?

Pushing open the door, I shrugged off my jacket. "Wild—"

Pain exploded in the back of my head.

I dropped and my arms tangled—caught up in the half-on, half-off jacket. I couldn't get them up fast enough to break my fall.

"Ahh," I cried, skull bouncing off the hardwood. "Wilder? Wilder!"

"Shut up!"

Hands grabbed and flipped me over. I gazed up into the glittering eyes of Wesley Hill.

"What are you doing!" I kicked at the blurry figure overhead. I was seeing two of him. "Get off me!"

"You left me no choice," Wesley said, fumbling to pin down my arms. "You shot your mouth off about me, Levi, and Owen giving Ashton an alibi.

Everyone was focused on Levi, but he disappeared. Now they're looking at me and asking why I haven't been removed from the line— Hold still!"

Wesley got the zip tie around my wrists. "Saylor stopped Katie before she could do the same to me, but then you released those texts. The Royals hate Burkhardt, Alvar, Starling, and Montana right now. They won't do a thing they say, but of course, you protected your friend.

"Katie still has the power to fuck with my family, and I can't have that. My mom is terrified of what's going to happen, so I'm getting rid of the problem—you."

"What... do you think you're going to... do to me?" Agony spiked through my skull with every breath.

"Easy. You're going to meet with an accident." His nasty grin spun. "Fatal."

Wilder, where are you? Please, come. Help me, please!

"You just couldn't back off and leave it alone. I didn't want any of this," he burst out. Wesley moved down to my flailing legs. "They dared me. You can turn down a truth or dare one time each. Only once. Go for a second and they spill every dirty little secret they'd got on you—"

"Wilder! Wilder, help!"

Wesley jumped up to cover my mouth. "I said shut—"

His head snapped to the side. Going limp, Wesley flopped on top of me. Cato threw him off like a sack of trash.

"Luna." He knelt and heaved me gasping and shaking into his arms. "I'm sorry. I'm here."

Five words, and they were everything. I buried my face in his chest—just breathing him in as my terror leached away. I was afraid. For all that I've done, and for all that I convinced myself I was an untouchable badass. With those ties around my wrists and hatred burning in his eyes, I knew what was coming, and I was afraid.

Cato lifted me up and carried me to my room. I was helpless to stop him wrapping me in blankets and laying me on the bed.

"Ten minutes."

Ten minutes and he'd come back to me. After he took care of Wesley.

I knew we couldn't leave him sprawled half out the door when armed guards would come looking for him at any minute, but practicality be fucked. I wanted Cato to leave me right then like I wanted a hole in the head. I almost cried when the door shut.

Relax, Luna. I breathed slow—in and out. *Wesley came for me because he thought the guys were all in class. He was wrong.*

That's what mattered. Cato stopped him. Cato was coming back. I was safe.

I repeated that to myself while listening for his footsteps on the landing. He returned in ten minutes exactly.

"Cato." I held my arms out to him. "Are you okay?"

"We're ready."

"Ready? Ready for what?" I snaked around his shoulders and found myself lifted out of the bed and carried out. "Cato?"

Cato said nothing as he brought me into the living room. I took one look at what he had done, and quieted so deep and through to my soul, speech left me—possibly for good.

Wesley sat on the carpet—zip ties around his wrists and ankles. Blood dripped from his ruined nose and mouth, garbling what he started shouting at me when I came into the room.

His distress was understandable. Spread out next to him was a rollout case filled with matches, lighters, flammable chemicals, and a blowtorch.

Cato grabbed his chin and snatched his head back. Bursting into tears, flames glinted in the wetness staining his cheek as Cato led the lighter close, closer, and millimeters away from his eyes.

"Ready."

My swallow echoed in my ears. *Torture. Cato expected me to torture this guy here and now.*

Who says I have to? another voice answered. *Wesley is perfectly free to save himself the pain and give me the name of the Phantom. If he chooses to continue protecting that murderer and monster, he chooses what he gets.*

Lifting my chin, I steadied myself. "Let's not waste time. Who dared you to go after Winter?"

Wesley's eyes rolled in his head. Sweat mixed with tears, soaking his face in a thin sheen. He was quickly realizing there was no way out. I had a feeling there was about to be another accident on the carpet.

"O-okay," he rasped. "Let's just calm down. You don't—"

Cato flashed, pressing the fire to his cheek.

"Arrrggghh!" Wesley screamed, curdling my insides.

"I believe that's Cato's way of saying that if you give an answer other than what I'm asking for, you'll get your... face burned off." My nose wrinkled.

A dark growing patch stained Wesley's pants and the carpet. He pissed himself.

"Don't make this harder," I said. "Give me their name."

"Fuck you!" Wesley half shouted, half sobbed. "I know things about you too, Sinclair. Shit you don't want anyone to know. Let me go or everyone finds out— Arrggggh! No, no! Stop!"

I forced myself to look, still my trembling veins, and close the distance. I asked for this. I didn't get to flutter and blush and look away now. This is who I'd become.

I owned it.

"Who sent the T.O.D. Club after Winter?"

"I can't say! You have no idea what th-they'll do to my family. So do your worst," he said with tears and snot running down the blistering welts on his face. "I'll never tell you."

I looked to Cato, and nodded. His scream punctured my eardrums.

"We will do our worst, Wesley, and eventually you will tell me everything I want to know. Save yourself the pain and stop protecting them. Get it through your head that the Phantom isn't going to hurt your family." The look in my eyes pinned him to the floor. "They won't get the chance."

Something flashed across his face. The first crack in his armor.

"Who killed my sister?"

His mouth parted.

"Luna? Luna, are you here?"

"Victor?"

Footsteps came down the hall, squeezing panic around my neck. "Hey, I need to talk to you about—"

"Victor, wait! I—"

He stuck his head in the living room. The grin died on his face.

"I can explain," I blurted. *No the hell I can't! Cato is holding a lighter to the face of a tied-up man on our carpet. There was no explanation that would get me out of this.*

"Luna, what the fuck is going on?"

"Victor, thank God!" Wesley strained in Cato's grip. "Help me, man. They're crazy. Look at what he did to me! You've got to help me."

I shot between them. My pale face reflected in Victor's wide eyes. "This looks bad—"

"Bad?! It looks like you're torturing a man in your living room next to the *Hangover Trilogy* DVD collection."

"Because that is what's happening! But I have a good reason, Victor. He left me no choice."

"She's lying. I never—hmh hphf!"

His muffled shouts told me Cato took care of his noise.

"Look, it's hard to explain quickly, but the truth is that my sister didn't just commit suicide. Someone bribed Owen, Giovanni, Ashton, Levi, and this piece of shit to bully her so badly, she lost hope. Her suicide was exactly what they wanted."

His face changed. "Are you serious?"

"They're murderers, Victor. No better than hired hit men. And the worst thing is none of them will give up who rewarded them for beating, manipulating, torturing, and raping my sister. If they had— If *he* would, I wouldn't have to do this."

Victor tossed his head. "You're willing to go this far? Look around you! Your asylum-escaping boyfriend is burning a man's face off!"

"Yes," I said, expression hardening. "I'll go as far as it takes. How far will you go?"

He stepped back. "What is that supposed to mean?"

"It means what are you going to do? Call the police? Try to free him? Are you going to help the guy who ruined my sister's life?"

Victor held very still. He gazed at me for a long time, expression unreadable. "Are you going to stop me if I do?"

"Yes." There was no hesitation.

"Are you going to tie me up and make me kneel on that piss-stained carpet too?"

"Yes."

"Even though you love me?"

My heart thumped too hard, bruising on my rib cage. "I loved Winter first."

There was a thump behind me. "Don't let her scare you, man. She's not going to do anything. She'll let this freak do it for her, and we can take him together."

We locked in our stare. Neither moving. Neither breathing.

"You got no reason to be loyal to her," Wesley burst out. "She's fucking your brother!"

I whirled around, jaw slack. "What did you say?"

"Don't bother denying it." He smirked past Cato as he thrashed on the floor, struggling against him. "You had me stalked, so I stalked you. Friend of mine found the little love letter you wrote your English professor—also known as your fiancé's brother."

No. No, no, no—

"I'm a dirty, little cum-hungry slut who will do whatever you ask, whenever you ask," he mocked in a high-pitched voice, then laughed. "That was my favorite part."

Cato hauled him up onto his knees. He growled a terrible warning as he dropped the lighter and grabbed the blowtorch. But it was far too late.

"Victor, listen to me," I rushed. "It's not what you think—"

"Of course it is! She's a slut, Wilson. We all fuck around on our forced fiancées, but us Royals have the decency not to do it with fifty people at one time. And never with their brother or sister." He strained his neck leaning away from the torch, but Wesley wouldn't be stopped. "The filthy Dreg whore told your brother she'd do things I haven't seen in porn.

"You can do better than her," he spat. "You always could. So call the cops on these freaks and be done with it. Your ring doesn't belong on that piece of trash."

"Shut up!" I ran to Victor. "Let me explain. I didn't mean for it to happen the way it did—"

"Stand aside, Luna." His voice was flat.

"Adonis and I have a real connection. I wanted to tell you so many times, but he asked to do it himself. I... I..." I was speaking to a brick wall for all the emotion I was getting out of him.

Heart sinking, I understood. In that moment as everything small, fragile, and growing between us crumbled into nothing, I finally realized what Victor was asking of me. Months and months of this guy driving me out of my mind, but I kept opening the door when he showed up unannounced at the beach house—filling the empty, silent tomb with passionate bickering. Months of him mixing flirts with insults, but I kept doing it back. Months of me falling for him… and pushing away the guy who'd bring me into the world that ruined my sister.

"Victor," I whispered. "Will you marry me?"

Grasping my shoulders, Victor firmly moved me out of the way. He stepped up to Cato and held his hand out for the torch. Over his shoulder, I nodded at Cato to let it go—tears streaking my cheeks.

"Thanks, man," Wesley said. "I owe you. Let's get away from these fr—"

Victor smashed the canister across his face. Wesley did a complete one-eighty, spinning on his knees and crumpling on the carpet. Mouth gushing blood, he spat out a tooth.

Victor yanked him up by the collar and hit him again. "Don't ever fucking talk about my fiancée like that. You'll have some respect on your tongue, or I'll cut it out."

I stared round-eyed—not knowing what I was seeing. Not knowing what to say if I did.

Victor dug a finger in one of his burns. Wesley's scream was all sob. "Apologize."

"S-sorry. I'm sorry!"

He tossed him back and returned the torch to Cato, who was looking at him in a whole new approving light.

"Victor?"

He flashed a wide grin on me. "The answer's yes. I'll marry you."

The words barely penetrated. "Did you just…?" *Savagely beat a man and then hand a torch back to his torturer so he could finish the job?*

"Why aren't you calling the police? Stopping us?"

"Why would I do that? You ask me, you guys are going too easy on him." Victor straightened, and the sarcastic, playboy, asshole side of him faded away. "I never did finish telling you about the time I drowned. I told you what those guys did to me, but I didn't get to the part about what I did to them."

"You're one of us," I whispered. "You're a Rogue."

"Well, don't spread it around," he said, smirking wolfishly. "I've got a reputation to protect. But let me stick around. If this guy did to Winter what you say he did, I want a piece."

I took a step, then two. Then I was running.

I leaped into his arms, crushing my lips to his. "Holy shit, you're so fucking sexy right now. Why didn't this guy fuck me the other day?" I swallowed his initial grunt of surprise, then Victor got into it. *Hard.*

"This guy can fuck you right now."

"Do it." I was already tearing off his shirt. "Now."

I didn't have to ask him twice.

"Cato?" I called. "Would you stick him in the closet, please? Maybe some quiet time to think, and bleed, will help him change his mind about protecting the Phantom."

Cato carried him off, leaving me and Victor to our business. Our hot, clothes-ripping, moaning, meeting-the-real-us-for-the-first-time business.

Victor flung my clothes all over the place. One minute I was dressed, the next my leggings were torn fabric decorating the television. My bra was only half off when he spun me around, bent me over the arm of the chair, and rammed inside.

"Ah." I lifted off my heels onto the very tips of my toes as he started pumping.

Who was that guy who pulled my hair and elbowed me in the boob? He had nothing to do with this rough, insistent, confident guy who felt no shame blowing past foreplay. He wanted inside me right then—no waiting necessary.

"Yes, Victor." I anchored him to my breasts, cupping me in both of his hands. We formed the most delicious sex formation—each point of contact delivering sizzling pressure to the long smolder that was my need for Victor.

It was so obvious now why things had been such a struggle between us. A struggle we couldn't seem to overcome by simply staying away from each other. We'd both been hiding who we truly were, while continually coming back to the person we deep down knew we needed. I couldn't stay away from Victor, I'd been searching for him all my life.

Smack!

I moaned under the firm swat on my left cheek. I didn't know what was with the Wilson brothers and spanking, but my core contracted so painfully, I drew a strangled grunt from his lips. We were moving too fast for actual words to pass between us.

Spreading my legs, I took each thrust deeper—eyes rolling up in my head as he pulled nearly all the way out and slammed back in. Victor wasn't exaggerating. He was far from crap in bed. If I ever rutted on the couch like a wild animal with a guy again, it would be him. It had to be him. There was no future that didn't have this insufferable jackhole in it.

The *slap, slap, slap* of our bodies filled my ears, providing the most perfect music to the fevered jumping in my chest. I was hot and flushed and shaky—coming alive to the feel of being pounded without mercy. Victor took it just as easy on me as he did when we got into our no-limits, knockdown, drag-out fights.

Victor had never been the guy to hold back or act like I couldn't take all he had to give me.

Smack!

"Oh, yes! Right there." My back bent in half. "Uhh!"

We were out of control. Thrusting, grunting, smacking so hard against the couch, we slid it across the carpet and banged into the opposite wall.

Victor slipped his hand under my chin. My grip held tight for purchase as he lifted me up, tipping my head back on his shoulder, and not slowing his pumping for a second. Victor captured my lips, kissing me hungrily—plundering another moist cavern that was his to explore and conquer.

"Mine," he growled as though he heard my thoughts that I was his to claim, and had to let me know in no uncertain terms. He already had.

I came hard—screaming and shaking in his hold. Victor pumped me all the way down, extracting chain orgasms like his cock was the gun and my pussy the hostage. His body tensed against me and he was gone—spilling inside me while I spread wide, murmuring filthy things to him as he filled me up.

We tipped over the back of the couch and fell on the cushions in a tangled heap.

"That was unexpected," Victor said, chest heaving. "To think I came back here bracing myself for another fight."

I burrowed in his side, inhaling his sweet cedar scent deep into my body. "Why would we fight?"

"Because I was going to pack your shit and move you into the mansion whether you liked it or not. I heard you're selling Saylor's text messages. Everyone heard about it, Luna. You pissed off the most powerful enemy you could have in this town, or any town in the country. You'd be safer if you stayed with us. Mom is insisting on it."

I studied the side of his face. He had a tiny beauty mark under his ear. It's because of how up close and personal I'd gotten with him recently, that I noticed Adonis had one in the same place.

"Are you insisting it even after... what Wesley told you?"

"What? About you fucking Adonis? Oh, I knew about that."

I blinked. "You what?"

"I saw you that day we went to the marina," he said, casual as ever. "You on his desk fingering yourself while he jerked off. Were you two trying to get caught? It was between classes and you didn't even lock the door."

"But— But why didn't you say anything? Aren't you upset? You freaked on us when you found out I kissed him."

"That first split second when I saw you two, I felt it all. Rage, betrayal, rejection. But then I realized what I was looking at. Don wouldn't risk his job or our relationship for anything. He'd jump off a cliff before he fucked me over. And becoming a literature professor? He worked damn hard to make that happen on his own.

"Yet, here he was risking both of those things on a reckless romp with you, and I finally understood. It was your fault."

"Wait, what?"

He turned that smackable grin on me. "It's completely on you, Sinclair. You got in his head and fucked with it until he didn't know which way was up. It's what you do," he breezed. "It's what you've done to me for months, and if anyone should get what Don is going through, it's me. He's got the Lunavirus. It strikes hard and fast, and is nearly always fatal."

My jaw hung open. Did this jerk just call me a virus! "I swear you beg to get your ass kicked. I didn't mess with anyone's head. I like him. He likes me. I like you. You like me. Nothing but a simple boy-girl attraction and three adults exploring that connection." I stroked his cheek. "And I'm glad we can do it out in the open. No more secrets."

"Hmm. While we're telling the truth, you can admit you more than like me. You're love-drunk obsessed with me. You asked me to marry you. Which you'll have to do again, by the way," he added. "Next time, more romance, more nudity, and less piss on the carpet."

I shoved him off the couch.

Howling, Victor snapped up and tugged me squealing down with him. I melted into his kiss.

"You're really okay with me and Adonis?" I whispered.

"Yes, Luna," he said, smiling into my eyes. "I want my brother to be happy, and the only way I know to be happy, is to be with you."

I bit my trembling lip, stopping myself from doing something super embarrassing—like crying. "You can be such a jerk, then you say something like that."

"My personality was warped pretty early on," he teased. "I told you we belong together. I saw this darkness in you from the first day."

"I just found out my sister was bullied into committing suicide. I'm all darkness right now. It's yours that surprises me. All this time you've acted so disapproving of the Rogues."

Victor looked away. "It's not that I disapprove. It's that I have to. There's a lot you still don't know, Luna."

The change in his tone unsettled me. What was going on? What happened to our sweetening mood?

"There's a reason they're called the Rogues. They stand apart from everyone. Royals will always need them, but they'll never marry them to their daughters, invite them to the annual charity ball, or make any deals out in the open. They are three factions in Regalia. I can marry you and nothing will change, but if I marry them too, I'm signaling to all of the Royals that the Wilsons have gone Rogue. That, Luna, is what would change."

Understanding dawned. "You mean that's why you've held back on giving me your answer? Agreeing to be in an open marriage between you, me, and the Rogues will have consequences for your family?"

"I might as well strike my family from the Royal line myself. If it were just you and me, I wouldn't care, but I've got pretty decent folks and a good brother when he isn't hiding that he's screwing my fiancée. I couldn't bring them down with me."

"But why would that bring them down? If I want to share my life with you and the Rogues, why is that anyone's business?"

"Because everyone picks a side in this town, Luna. Us or them. That's the way it's always been. That's how it'll always be."

I was quiet taking that in. As stupid as I thought it all was, I knew he wasn't exaggerating. They clung so tightly to hierarchy and social status in Regalia. Katie had to tell people repeatedly and often that Dreg Dean was not her boyfriend, even though anyone with eyes could see she was crazy about him.

"Just say it to me, then." I pressed a soft kiss to the corner of his mouth. "Give me your answer."

"Yes, Luna. I'd share you with the Rogues, with my brother, with the janitor, or that weird forty-year-old man who sneaks on campus and takes pictures of people's feet."

"Oh, yeah, baby. He's so my type."

We laughed, settling into that sweet mood again.

"I'll share you with anyone who makes you happy because I was first. You met me first. Fell for me first. And out of all of them, you'll marry me first. You'll wear my ring, own my last name, and carry my babies. I can share you, Luna, 'cause no matter what happens, I win."

Smiling, I kissed him. "Just knowing you feel that way is good enough for me... for now. Once I destroy the Royal line and bring the system crumbling at my feet—status won't matter anymore. I'll have all my men where and how I want them."

"Uh, run that by me again? Destroy the Royal line?"

I nuzzled his nose. "Oh, future husband, we have so much to talk about."

***

Rafael paced the length of the carpet. It was just me, him, and Victor in the living room. Lucien and Cato went to get Wesley.

"You're telling me that shit Wesley attacked you, and you called for Wilder and he didn't answer?" Rage lived beneath his skin.

"No, he didn't. And that's how I know he isn't in that room or in the house at all. Wilder would never abandon me when I needed him. Something happened, Rafael. We need to find out what and we need to do it soon."

Lucien and Cato dragged in a bleeding, whimpering mess.

"Right after we finish this."

Rafael scanned Wesley's face. "I see you started the party without us."

"Then we stopped because we weren't getting anywhere. If knocking out his teeth and burning his face won't work, what will?"

"N-nothing will..." Wesley lifted his head, and spat blood at my feet. "I'll never talk."

Rafael kicked him in the chest without a break in expression. "I don't like your tone when addressing my lady. I'd watch that. My next kick will jam the cartilage from that broken nose in your brain."

"Fuck you! Fuck all of you!" he screeched, unraveling before my eyes. "You can't do this to me! I'll ruin you!"

Rafael turned his back, ignoring him. "I know how to end this if you're cool with me taking over, gorgeous."

"Yeah, absolutely. All I care about is finding the Phantom."

"Then we need to move him." Rafael moved to the window and shifted the blackout curtains. "And you need to go, Wilson. Unless you made a change."

Victor and Rafael shared a look I didn't understand.

"I'll go," Victor said. "But you better finish it. For her."

"I will."

I didn't know what we were doing or where we were going. But I trusted Rafael.

Lucien got the biggest suitcase he could find, and stuffed Wesley bound, gagged, and raging inside. I felt all eyes on me while we wheeled him through campus to Rafael's car. It was just him, me, and Cato. Lucien stayed behind to clean up the blood and all traces that Wesley was ever there.

I didn't breathe again until he was safely in the trunk and we were pulling out of campus.

"Where are we going?"

"There's a spot near the Bluffs where no one goes. We'll have privacy to do what we need to do."

I almost asked what we needed to do. Wesley wasn't the only thing we put in the trunk. Rafael also tossed in a backpack, and it wasn't Cato's pack of fire-starters. He had that on his lap.

"If only the bastard waited until we got to him on Wednesday," Rafael said. "I might've been tempted to go easier on him. Too bad he put his hands on you again."

It was too bad for Wesley. I heard Rafael speak in this tone once before when he talked about his father. Whatever the plan was now, it had nothing resembling restraint.

We were a silent crew, driving through the winding, tree-lined streets of Regalia. Twenty minutes in, Cato decided we were going to make out in the back seat. He unbuckled and carried me over, pouncing with his usual confidence. Even so, there was a subduedness to our passionate, nipping kisses. By the end of that day, it would be finished. We'd know who the Phantom is, and a new war would begin.

Rafael suddenly slowed down and pulled off the road. "It's just through there," he said. "Five minutes of walking."

He got out, hefted a kicking suitcase from the trunk, and hitched the backpack up his shoulder. Together, we tromped through the trees until they began to open up.

I didn't recognize the spot in particular, but I placed us about a mile away from Giovanni's beach house where Annika went over. The beach below us was rocky and the trees above grew thick and tall, blocking the sun. Neither made it a good spot for beach-going or sunbathing. No one but us had a reason to come out there.

Rafael brought the suitcase to a clearing near the edge of the Bluffs. The red-faced fury of the guy who came out of that blue Samsonite called me to feel something.

Not a twinge stirred my soul.

I saved my compassion for innocent people, pets who spend all day chained, and those who know what it is to love, and lose it. I had none to spare for animal-abusing, violent ex-boyfriends who fuck with brakes, and protect rapists and murderers.

"Here's how it is, Hill." Rafael set him on the ground and checked his zip ties. "Whoever sent you that dare offered you a prize you've never had before: something you couldn't get for yourself."

Rafael slipped his bag off his shoulder. "Between the chance to catapult to the top tiers of the Royal line, and the penalty if you refused, you probably thought the choice was easy. Whatever made it feel right in your desiccated heart to accept that dare, I don't want to know.

"What I do know is that you made the wrong choice then, and you're making the wrong one now. Understand something, Wesley, your family isn't moving up the Royal line." I watched Rafael—transfixed by the deadly serious man before me as he took out a bomb.

"Hmmphf!"

"It's a new era, Hill. We believe women. You gave Winter's attacker a fake alibi, and no one is hearing your bleats that Luna is lying. Which clarifies your options considerably. You won't collect on the grand reward the Phantom promised, so if you walk out of here, your life is ruined anyway.

"But you know this," he said. "At this point, it's not about their reward, it's about their punishment if you reveal who they are. You've been using the power of knowing their identity to blackmail and keep them at arm's length. That power goes away if you tell anyone, and everything they had done to Winter, they'll do to you."

Wesley wasn't tossing, kicking, or shouting anymore. He was still and sweating, fixed on the bomb.

"That's why you think it's better to let us kill you now than let them kill you later, and again you're wrong. We're going to kill them, Wesley. We'll make them pay for every horrible thing they had done to Winter. They'll die screaming while you—as Luna promised—will be spared your life. A life outside the Royal line, but you'll still be a rich, able-bodied white boy, so you'll do just fine. Consider that option A.

"Now for option B…" Rafael set the bomb down next to him. "You die now."

Wesley burst into tears.

"You want to be the martyr, you'll get your wish. This bomb will count down from five minutes. If you've shouted out the name of Winter's killer by then, I'll shut off the timer and everyone goes home. If not, then at least you'll get the pointless death you were looking for, because we will find them—no matter what it takes. What's it going to be?"

I bent and removed his gag.

"You won't do it," he gasped, chest heaving. "That's not a real b-bomb. You're trying to trick me."

Rafael just smiled. "I guess we'll find out in five minutes."

Taking my hand in one, and removing the remote from his pocket with the other, he pressed the button.

"No!"

Five minutes flashed on the small digital screen three times, then the countdown began.

"Nooo! Don't do this. Turn it off!"

"You know how to do that."

Rafael led me and Cato away—outside the blast radius.

"Rafael," I said softly. "Is that a real bomb?"

The look in his eyes told me before he spoke. "He shouldn't have touched you."

I chose my words carefully. "But what if he still thinks it's a bluff and doesn't talk?"

"Then, he dies."

That was the obvious conclusion, wasn't it.

We ducked past the tree line. We could hear and see the figure trying desperately to roll away and getting nowhere.

"All right, that's enough. Turn it off," Wesley called. "We all know you're not going to blow me up, so just turn it off."

One minute passed.

"You're sick, Dumont! A twisted, psychopath freak! You're dead when I get out of here. Dead!"

Two minutes passed.

"I know it's a fake. You're not fooling me." Wesley tried and failed again to get his feet under him. He fell flat on his front and nearly dropped on the bomb. "Turn it off. Stop fucking around and turn it off!"

I'd never seen men more relaxed than Rafael and Cato Dumont. They both leaned against a tree, watching a nesting mother feed her baby birds—Rafael. Or taking a blowtorch to the bark—Cato.

Three minutes passed.

"I don't know their name, okay?" Wesley shouted. "I never knew their name. Giovanni told Levi, and Levi lorded it over us. Said if we wanted something from them, we had to go through him. If you want a name, you need Levi."

I looked to Rafael. That did sound like something Levi would do.

"Hey! Are you listening? I don't know their name!"

"I think you're a liar," Rafael sang, "and I'll find out in two minutes."

"Bastard! I can't tell you what I don't know."

Four minutes passed.

"Joke's over, turn it off. Turn it off, Dumont."

Fifty seconds left.

"Okay, you win." Panic crept in. "I'll talk. Just get this thing away from me."

Thirty seconds left.

"I won't tell you until you turn it off. You think you can find them on your own? Good fucking luck. You need me!"

Twenty seconds left.

"Turn it off, Dumont, please! Don't do this," he wailed. "I can't tell you! They won't just stop at killing me. They'll kill my family. My friends. It's not my fault. I wish I never accepted that dare!"

I squeezed my eyes shut as the timer hit ten seconds. I wanted my revenge, but I didn't need to see a man blow up to get it. Rafael would not touch that button. Wesley sealed his fate.

"I'll tell you. I will." Wesley sobbed fit to make other grown men cry. "Please, turn it off. I'll tell you anything you want to know."

Five.

Four.

"Please!"

Rafael was unmoved.

Three

Two.

"Noooo! Their name is—"

I dove for the remote—snatching it from him and hitting pause at the last possible second. I fell against him, adrenaline leaving me just as fast as it came.

"Mercy, gorgeous?"

"No," I said. "I don't give two shits about his life, but you're the one who said we can't be emotional about this. Giovanni and Owen are dead. Levi is out of reach. We can't kill the only person left who can get us to the Phantom."

"Once he knows that, he'll have all the leverage. He'll be blackmailing *us.*"

"No, he won't. Hope you don't mind, baby, but I'm taking over again." I kissed him. "You need to cool off."

"And I hope you know," he said, shadows dancing on his face. "That either way this ends with him dying. No one hurts you and lives."

I forced myself to walk away. Dropping down and sucking his dick for being so freaking hot and protective would not send the right message. I wanted us to protect each other like this, but I didn't want us to blow up our only chance at finding the Phantom.

I approached Wesley.

"Sin... Sinclair..."

"This is your last chance. The next time I hit this button, there won't be time to stop it even if I wanted to. Tell us—"

Wesley shot up, gasping. Angry red splotches covered his face and neck, blistering before my eyes. "Sin... clair..."

"Rafael!" I screamed. "Cato!"

My guys raced toward us. I dropped to the ground, grabbing and holding him upright.

"What's wrong with you? What is this!"

"...name... is..."

Rafael skidded across the dirt, falling down next to me. "Shit. He's in anaphylactic shock."

"What? How?" I cried. "I thought he was only allergic to peanuts."

"Ech... ech... ech..." Wesley rasped, straining to breathe. His lips turned blue.

Rafael slapped at his clothes. "He doesn't have his EpiPen on him. We have to open an airway. Cato, the car. There's a knife in the glove box. Get it!"

Cato didn't move. "Why?" he asked, genuinely curious.

"He hasn't told us the name yet," I said. "We still need him, Cato. Please."

"All right. For you."

Cato left and Rafael set Wesley down. He grasped his neck to tilt his chin back and stopped.

He raised his hand. Resting on his palm was a tiny tranquilizer dart.

"Luna, there's someone else here."

In spite of the warm day, those words chilled me to my core.

"They could be in the woods right—"

Loud, raucous barking rebounded off the trees.

"Cato!"

We ran—stumbling over the same roots, tripping on fallen branches.

Cato lay slumped against the car, rubbing the back of his head. His hand came away tacky with blood. Someone took their chance and hit him when he bent to get the knife.

"Stay with him," Rafael ordered. "Anyone comes near you, show them these." He dropped the bag of explosives near my lap. "They'll be one hundred feet away in ten seconds," he said, taking the knife.

I wanted to be one hundred feet away in ten seconds. What was going on? Someone followed us from campus? Who? They lurked in the trees, watching us play bomb roulette with Wesley? Why?

Are they watching us now?

Rafael returned as quickly as he left.

"Rafael, no," I whispered. "Wesley. Is he—?"

"He's dead, Luna. I was too late."

I clutched my twisting stomach as I scanned the trees. "You were supposed to be."

Chapter Eleven

I sat on the front steps that night, gazing up at the sky. My guys would have something to say about me being out alone after midnight. I'd hear it when they caught me. Until then, the ocean of glittering sky jewels calmed me. After an ugly, hateful day, I needed to bask in beauty.

I sighed, slumping against the door. The stars were beautiful. My blanket was cozy. The mug of tea in my hands banished the chill. But it all changed nothing. Wesley was still dead.

My last chance to find the Phantom gone in the time it takes peanut oil to spread through the system.

The truth of that would hit me soon. I would rage and cry and mourn having let down my sister. I wanted it to come, because I hated what I felt right then.

Numb.

"What now?" I whispered to my namesake. "How do I find one rotten, evil Royal in a sea of spoiled garbage?

"How did you find them, Winter? I know you minded your business, were kind to everyone you came across, and didn't get sucked into drama. Still, you found out something that scared the Phantom. What could it have been? Regalia is full of secrets that people would kill to keep. How do I find the one that took you?"

My phone vibrated against my hip. I sighed in irritation. I'd been getting calls from a blocked number nonstop for hours. Ever since it went wide that I was selling Saylor's texts, people have been stopping me and asking how I did it and if there were more. These requests came with an obscene price tag.

For those who couldn't roam around campus searching for me, they tracked down my number instead. It was disturbing how many middle-aged men begged me to get them access to a college girl's text messages.

My phone went off again.

"Ugh. Give it a rest."

If only Wilder was here. He'd know how to stop—

I bolted up. Wilder? What if it was him calling? Blocking his number is exactly what he'd do.

I scrambled to pick it up. "Hello? Wilder, is that you?"

"No, I'm afraid not."

My hopeful smile melted off my face. "Who is this?"

"Can't you guess? Who else would call you using a digitally altered voice?" said the machine I was speaking to.

Male or female—I couldn't tell. The noise coming from my speaker sounded like words run through a garbage disposal.

"Levi."

"Hmm. That is a fair guess, but no. I'm much closer to home," they said. "I heard you call me the Phantom."

My limbs turned to lead.

"Cute."

"Who is this?" I rasped. "If you have the nerve to call me, then you have it to use your real voice. Who is this!"

"Relax. We'll get to that." I couldn't be certain, but they sounded... amused.

My nails pierced half-moons into my palm. When I found this bastard, I'd show them something funny.

"First, I wanted to thank you for taking care of Scott, Thasher, and Thompkins for me. I had to take care of Natale and Hill myself in the end, but even so, we made a good team."

"What are you talking about?"

"I wanted them dead as much as you did. You're supposed to do the dare, accept your reward, and move on. Instead, those bastards tracked me down and have been blackmailing me ever since. You arriving on campus with all that hate in your heart was the best thing that could've happened."

"Oh my— That's why you didn't come after me too. You wanted me around to clean up your loose ends. Then why the hell did you try to frame me for Giovanni's murder?"

"No choice. No one told him to go shooting his coke-dusted mouth off. I had to act fast. The next thing I knew, I was standing beside two unconscious people. Taking the stun gun with me would've proved a third person was there, so I had to put it in your hand. The cops figured it out anyway but they're clueless and so are you. No harm done."

"No harm, huh?" My voice scraped from my throat. "There's been plenty of harm, you fucking monster. Why did you d-do it? Why did you kill my sister!"

"That's another topic we'll get to," they replied. "You want to know who I am. Find out what started all this. The truth is you never had to try this hard, Sinclair. I'm more than happy to tell you. Honestly, I was getting impatient waiting for you to finish all those shits off, so we could finally talk. There's just one more thing you have to do for me first."

Fury strangled me. "Do for you? I haven't done anything for you, and I'm not starting now! Fuck's sake, you're sick. Even with that fake voice I can hear you're enjoying this."

"Of course I am. That's what happens when you're so close to getting everything you want. I bet Owen, Levi, Wesley, and the others thought you were sick too when you stood over them, smirking away over their last good-bye."

My lips peeled back from my teeth. "Don't ever compare me to you."

"Why not? We're more alike than you think. I'm willing to do whatever it takes for revenge, and so are you. There's only one more thing you have to do to be in the same room as the person who took your precious sister from you. Are you really going to turn me down?"

"You're going to ask me to do something I can't. Cross a line that not even in my darkest moment I would cross," I said. "I might as well tell you fuck no now."

"Depends on if you think hanging a flag off the pole on the quad is a line you couldn't cross in your darkest moment."

I opened my mouth to snap back and nothing came out. What did they say? Hang a what?

"Excuse me?"

"Get a flag—any kind will work—and paint it purple. Hang it up on the quad before the sun comes up, and that's it," they said. "I'll come to you and tell you everything you want to know."

I frowned, searching their request for the trick. "Why are you asking me to do this? You can hang a damn flag yourself."

"That's another thing I'll tell you—after."

"Tell me? Do you really believe that once I'm in the same room with you, we're going to sit down and chat?"

An odd, clicky, mechanical laugh buzzed out of the phone. "You can do your worst, Sinclair. I'm not afraid of you. Never was, never will be. You Sinclair-Bowdens like to act tough, but in the end, you turn out to be weak-ass little bitches who can't swim.

"Buh-bye."

Click.

I gripped my phone so hard the screen cracked. Furious tears dripped in the mug I forgot I was holding.

Bastard. Monster! All this time, you were watching and waiting—dangling me like this was just another game.

But what should I do? They asked me to hang a flag. It sounded harmless, but there had to be more to it. Why would doing something so pointless get them to reveal themselves to me?

There's only one way to find out.

And didn't I already know I was going to do it. It wasn't a question. If this was all it took to get in the same room with Winter's killer, I had to do it. Obviously, it was a trap, but some traps were worth springing.

I clambered off the steps, racing inside to—

I ground to a halt in the front hall. I knew exactly how the conversation between me, Lucien, Rafael, and Cato would go. They'd say it was a trap, and I shouldn't go anywhere near that flagpole until I found out the real reason the Phantom wanted me to go around painting flags. Someone who drove a person to suicide to protect a secret wouldn't suddenly decide to give it up over a meaningless chore.

They'd say all of those things, and they'd be absolutely right. *That's why I'll tell them after it's done.*

I couldn't have them in my ear, listing all the reasons this was a huge mistake and all around being sweet and caring over me. This was my revenge to take. It was my choice to make, and I made it.

With six hours left until sunrise, I couldn't spend it arguing with the guys. I needed to find an open paint store and figure out where they sell flags.

Decision made, I went up to my room and dressed quietly in the dark—careful not to disturb Cato.

Rafael's car keys hung on a clip in the kitchen. I took them and left with a heavy feeling in my chest. As I walked through the dark, it grew smaller and smaller, lighter and lighter. By the time I reached the parking lot, I couldn't hold back my smile.

The monster was right. There was no stopping your happiness when you're so close to getting everything you want.

***

Morning rays crept over the horizon, determined to dispel the darkness for those not ready for the light. The soft *cling, cling, cling* of metal on metal broke the silence, ringing a steady chime in my head while I hoisted the flag.

I stared at it after I was done, watching it whip in the breeze. What was meant to happen now? Would the Phantom materialize out of thin air? Would the camera crew pop out with all of them laughing at me for completing a pointless prank?

I don't know how long I stood there, eyes glazed on the possible end of my journey to avenge Winter. It was long enough that the sun won its battle—chasing away the darkness for another day.

Leaving the quad behind, I returned to the Gallery. I had a full day of classes ahead of me. The world didn't stop for ghosts and phantoms.

"Morning, gorgeous." Rafael stood over the stove, cooking something that smelled heavenly. "I'm making cinnamon roll waffles. I know it doesn't make up for losing Wesley, but we're not going to sit around acting like we're mourning that human pile of manure. We will find the Phantom, Luna." He grasped my chin and kissed me soft and sweet, his lips tasting of cinnamon. "I promise."

"I know we will." I tucked my paint-stained hands behind my back. "I'm going to run upstairs and shower. We'll talk, and eat, after I'm done."

"Cool."

I ran upstairs and hopped in the tub. I lingered longer under the spray than I needed to, lost in my thoughts. It wasn't that I was worried the guys would be upset that I acted without them. It's that I knew I walked into something uncertain and dangerous, and now I had to explain why that was okay after telling Rafael less than twenty-four hours ago that he couldn't get emotional.

Time to suck it up, I thought. *They're not going to say a thing that's not true, but afterward, they'll get past being pissed that I acted alone, and we'll make a plan for my meeting with the Phantom.*

A plan that ensures they don't make it out alive.

Lucien and Cato were in the kitchen too when I came down. My chest panged looking at Wilder's empty seat. Where was he? What was so bad that he had to take off the way he did? Your brother coming to visit shouldn't be a reason to squeal out of the driveway with the lights on and the water running.

"Morning." I kissed Lucien and Cato, then Cato again when he tugged me back. "There's something I have to tell you," I said, making each one stop what they were doing. "The Phantom called me last night."

"What?" Rafael dropped the waffle iron. "The Phantom called? And you're just telling us now?"

I took a deep breath. "There's a reason you're finding out now. They asked me to—"

The front door banged open, shotgunning my heart out of my stomach.

"Guys?"

Is that—?

"Lucien? Rafael?" Wilder bellowed. "You here?"

Wilder skidded into the entrance. I ran at him full speed, jumping in his arms.

"Wilder, you're okay." I kissed him all over. "What the hell happened to you? Do you have any idea how worried I was? Why did you just take off?"

"Luna, I'm sorry. We have to talk about this later." He set me firmly on my feet and sidestepped me. "Which one of you did it?"

"Did what?" Lucien asked.

"Which one of you hung the flag? Was it Wolf? Did he do something?"

Rafael went very still. "What are you talking about?"

"A purple flag is waving over the fucking quad. If you're pissed at me for taking off, I get it, but stop fucking playing dumb!"

I blew back at his shout.

"Who hung the flag?"

"Wilder, we don't know what the fuck you're talking about. We didn't hang the flag." Rafael threw looks at Lucien and Cato. "You didn't, right?"

"Of course not."

"No."

"I did it."

The kitchen fell quiet. Four heads slowly twisted to me.

"That's what I had to tell you. The Phantom called me last night and said if I hung a purple flag in the quad, they'd end the cat-and-mouse and reveal themselves... to... me." I flicked between them. "But judging by your faces, doing it was the wrong move?"

It was hard to judge their faces. The big-eyed, slack-jawed expressions were ones they never made before.

"Luna, you— Why didn't you—" Rafael couldn't find the words. He fell back against the kitchen counter, clutching his head. "This is not good."

"Wait. It might not be too late," Lucien said, jumping off the stool. He fell on me, grasping my shoulders. "How long has it been up? We'll take it down before anyone sees it."

"I put it up before sunrise, but we can't take it down!" I quickly added when my reply caused a burst of activity. "The Phantom has to know I followed through. They—"

"Luna," Wilder sliced in. "The Phantom is not who you think they are. Whatever they're about to do next will be terrible for all of us. We need to take that flag down"—he darted for the front door—"now!"

"Wilder, wait! Someone explain to me what's going on?" I chased after Rafael going up the stairs.

The front door opened.

"Hey— Luna, run!"

Thud.

"Wilder?" My heart stopped. "Wilder! What was that sound?" I ran back downstairs, ignoring Rafael's shout for me to come back. "Are you o—?"

I skidded to a stop. Freezing in the kitchen entrance, my eyes crossed staring down the weapon.

"Hello," the masked figure sang. They pressed the stun gun to my forehead. "Remember this?"

"Luna!"

Rafael's voice reverberated through my mind, following me down the path of darkness and pain. My love and myself—I lost both before I hit the floor.

***

Bitterness seeped through my lips, leaving an acrid kiss on my tongue.

I coughed—rough and hacking and dragging my senses back to the surface. Blinking, I came to, straining as my vision cleared.

What happened? Where am I?

I squeezed my eyes shut, forcing tears to fall. My eyes were watering, it was so blurry. And what was that noise?

I opened my eyes again, fighting to adjust in the gloom *Why can't I see? What's wrong with...?*

Twisting my neck, I saw past the couch to the staircase—where the smoke freely billowed down. *Smoke?*

"It's about time you woke up. You're the one who wanted this little chat. You're wasting your own time."

I turned with difficulty, achy bones creaking. It was hard. Tight pressure around my wrists and ankles proved I was bound.

A vision in white stood on the very spot Wesley spat out his bloody tooth. She lowered her face mask and smiled at me. "Hello, Luna."

"Everleigh?" I croaked, then immediately started hacking. My lungs shredded trying to force out smoke that kept flooding in. "W-what's... going on? Where are the guys?"

"Your boyfriends are safe. I sent them away so we could have some privacy. You wanted to meet me. Here I am. What do you think?" Everleigh twirled, spinning the lace edges of her ivory summer dress. "Am I what you expected of the Phantom?"

The words barely penetrated. My head hurt so much, the idea of putting two thoughts together drove a spike through it. Smoke was filling the room, making it even more impossible for my blurry eyes to focus, or my tortured lungs to breathe.

"Hello." Everleigh snapped her fingers in my face. "Focus, Sinclair. We don't have much time. This place is about to burn down with you in it."

The fog blew out of my mind. Sense came back to me, latching on to that statement as the ladder to bring me back. "What did you just say?"

"You going to make me waste time repeating myself, or are you going to ask me what you really want to ask me?" She flicked my nose. "Quickly, bitch. It's getting a little too smoky in here for my taste."

I gaped at her. Everleigh Starling? Saylor's best friend with the model looks, and the dreamy eyes that spent too much time looking at my fiancé—

"You're the Phantom?"

She winked. "That's right. Love the nickname, by the way. Much better than the Book Lady. Now that we're here, did you enjoy my performance?" She laughed. "All that weeping and wailing on the café floor. I keep telling Maman I was meant to be an actress."

She frowned into my wide eyes. "What? You don't get it? Damn, you're stupid," Everleigh muttered. "I'm Jezebel12. I gave you the link to my site for your boring little revenge against me, Saylor, and the others. You weren't going to dig dirt up on me on your own, and I couldn't have you sending the T.O.D.ers after me. I don't need stalkers."

Everleigh shrugged. "I also don't particularly care if people know about the Book Lady. I started doing it to get information from stupid, horny idiots that you can't get when those horny idiots are dressed. That information led to your mother, which led to your sister, which led to you. So yeah, I'm glad everyone knows. The Book Lady is my greatest accomplishment."

"But…" I searched for the words and found only one. "Why?"

"Why did I send those guys after your sister?" She pushed out her lips in mocked sadness. "Ah yes, poor little Winter."

"No," I said. "Why… are you a psychotic bitch?"

Everleigh laughed out loud. "For the same reason you are. Revenge. There's something I needed and your sister got in the way. Thankfully— Well, thankfully for me, you were much more obedient and did what you were told. You hung the flag."

"A flag? That's why you did all this? You had Winter tortured all for a fucking flag!" I tried to shout but wheezed it instead. I went into another coughing fit, jerking and banging my back against the coffee table legs. "Why d-didn't you just hang it yourself!"

"It had to be a Sinclair. When your sister died, I gave up. Those bastards were supposed to drive her to follow my orders, not kill herself. I almost killed them myself... then you showed up." Everleigh looked around. "Time to go. See you in hell, Sinclair."

Everleigh turned and walked off.

"Wait! That's it? You destroyed my family for a flag and that's all you have to say? Why?" I screamed. "Tell me why!"

"I'm actually not into the evil-villain-monologuing. Especially in a burning building." Everleigh snapped her fingers. "Come."

"I can't come." I thrashed against the table legs. "You tied me up."

"Not you."

A tall, silent figure dipped in black stepped out of the hallway. His face so like Rafael's beheld me coldly.

"Shoot her."

Ice dumped down my spine.

"I want to see her die for myself," Everleigh continued, tone light and cool as could be. "Do this and your freak boys are safe. No one touches them. No one even gives them dirty looks. The Dumont brothers won't die of anything except old age."

Leon Dumont drew his gun and leveled it on my chest. The expression on his face was no different from the one he had when we drank tea.

"No, wait!"

Dumont flicked off the safety.

"Tell me why," I screamed. "Just tell me why!"

"Why?" The first crack in her amused, happy mask appeared. "It's simple. I've been waiting almost ten years to make that bastard pay for what he did to my father. For years I've searched for him. For years I couldn't get close. Then, Daddy's little girls enrolled in Regalia University."

Daddy's little girls? Jack?

"I've waited so long," she hissed. "Finally, he's going to come. He can't hide from me anymore." The smile she flashed me turned my stomach. "Don't let it get to you that you'll die without ever meeting your father. I promise, I'm sending him to hell right after you."

She jerked a chin at Rafael's father. "Do it."

"Forgive me, Miss Sinclair-Bowden. I truly wish there was another way."

"Mr. Dumont, don't—"

Bang!

Pain ripped through my chest.

Darkness came for me again, and didn't let go.

***

[*If you'd like to read the next book in the series, Reign By Wrath, click here.*](https://mybook.to/ReignByWrath)[1]

---

1. *https://mybook.to/ReignByWrath*

Keep In Touch

Join Ruby's mailing list for news, teasers, and more: https://www.subscribepage.com/rubyvincentpage
Join Ruby's Facebook Reader Group: https://bit.ly/3bNuCOq

ABOUT THE AUTHOR

Ruby Vincent is a published author with many novels under her belt, but after taking a fun foray into contemporary romance, she found her love of saucy heroines, bold alpha males, and weaving a tale where both get their happy ever after.